Betsy Be Good

Good Girls Book Four

I0667567

Christine Young

ISBN: 978-1-62420-746-4

Editor: Sherry Derr-Wille
Cover Art: Designs by Ms G

Chapter One

Glasgow 1826

Evan Murray stretched then yawned as he woke himself. *He was feeling lazy, definitely lazy.* At least he had every intention of doing as little as possible until his disagreement with his brother as well as the University of Glasgow ended. He'd never been so bored in his entire life. This dean-imposed sabbatical was going to be the death of him if this new and unique assignment didn't beat layoff to the punch. Pulling out his pocket watch, he realized he was a half hour late. He found his hat and pulled it onto his head.

When he was issued the warning from the University of Glasgow to either apologize to the student or not return to his classes until he could do so, he said to hell with them all then walked out the front door. It wasn't as if he needed the groats. Dean Ritter had the scenario all wrong. Didn't take the time to listen to all the facts. His older brother, Duncan, was just as bad, agreeing immediately with the dean.

Evan was an outstanding professor, one of the best.

The devil with them all!

Duncan firmly planted himself on the opposing side also, not bothering to hear him out. Told him in no uncertain terms he couldn't work for him either until the necessary apologies were given. How the hell could it hurt him to apologize?

His unrelenting, stubborn pride would be in agony.

He pushed himself off the hard bench where he'd been dozing. Stretched one more time to ease his tense muscles. He'd been on edge for the past two days mulling over all that happened that afternoon. Once again feeling betrayed as well as used by his brother, he decided there was no need to rush. He didn't owe anyone his time even though it seemed others disagreed.

The lady he was here to escort, his new assignment, could wait until he was good and ready to find her. After a quick perusal of the coach station, he realized she must have gone outside to look for him. The devil, searching for her was on him, finding her before something happened was crucial. If he lost the woman, he'd never get back in his brother's good graces. The woman was a friend of his brother's wife. The only thing that could happen was that she would give up on him then hire a coach herself. If she did, that wouldn't be so bad. He could always find her at the hotel. Well, he'd have to admit he failed. He didn't know what hotel she planned to stay in. That was a little matter his brother neglected to tell him.

He tapped his finger on his chin, thinking. What was her name, Betsy Darling? He hoped she was darling. Amusing himself during the interim might be fun. If he found a stimulating woman, this assignment might not prove too boring. Though, at the moment, he wasn't entirely certain what he was supposed to do with her except deliver her to a hotel. What did Duncan tell him? That the woman would give him the list of duties she required.

The argument that cost him so dearly was over a young woman, a student at the university. In his mind the young pup who he found in a back storage closet with a student's dress hiked to her waist should be doing the apologizing, not him. Of all the possible outcomes, Duncan agreed with the university. That fact surprised him even though Duncan gave him numerous reasons why he did so. One was that he might want his job back. The boy, student, should have chosen the location for his tryst more carefully. While the girl seemed willing enough, a storage closet on the second floor of the biology department was not a place of romance. The boy obviously wasn't romantic, just filled with lust. The other problem was that the lad's father had some title along with a great deal of wealth and power. Evan's family also possessed the same pedigree. So, why was he the scapegoat?

Evan didn't need to work. He only did so to stimulate his mind as well as cultivate new friendships. He enjoyed almost all aspects of teaching. Nonetheless, his older brother was a financial investor, no, a financial wizard. The devil, Duncan made them all rich. Several years running, the last ten to be exact, Duncan doubled and sometimes tripled their holdings. There was enough invested as well as in the bank he'd never be able to spend all the easily-earned groats. If he wished to do so, he could sit back, idle away his time as well as twiddle his thumbs. He could afford to keep several mistresses. His townhouse was in the nicest neighborhood in Glasgow. He'd gone all out in furnishing the place, paying meticulous care in the bathroom, having custom made a tub that would easily hold two perhaps even three people. In the bathing chamber there was a large stove with plenty of room to keep water warmed to add to the tub if he wished to remain there for more than a few minutes. Ah, he could use a good long soak. His muscles were sore from doing nothing.

Damn, he was going to miss the university, the everyday challenges, the learning environment. He sifted in a huge breath of stale air, thinking about everything that happened. There was nothing he would change. The altercation had not been his fault even though he sported a couple bruised ribs because he attempted to reprimand the student. The boy reacted badly when he opened the door.

His annoyance grew ten-fold every time he thought on the experience. In the first place, the boy shouldn't have been tossing the young lady's skirt in a public building. In the second place, if they hadn't been so verbal while making love, he would have never opened the door to the store room to see what was happening. His first thoughts had been that a young woman might be in trouble. In the third place, if he'd taken a moment to think over what he heard, he should have known what was going on having listened to the sweet sounds of ecstasy from numerous women. No, he had to interrupt them right when they climaxed, when the boy emptied himself inside the girl and she screamed out his name.

Even he, a notorious rake, felt the swell of heat rush to his face when he realized what had just happened. Only to himself would he admit embarrassment. The boy turned on him, outraged in his own right. Before the youngun' hit him, the boy didn't even right the woman's corsage or smooth her skirts to cover her lily-white thighs. A protective instinct should have surged through the boy. The interesting part was that he was witness to a pair of beautiful white breasts, topped with rosebud nipples coupled with long shapely legs. Perhaps he understood why the boy couldn't wait to find a more appropriate place to sexually engage the young woman. She was a beauty.

At the time, after the first punch, he didn't intend to hit back. The boy tackled him. That little incident changed everything. The skirmish was on. Evan recognized the fact his temper was hot, the hottest of all his siblings. He was always the first to rush into a fight, especially if that fight was for a good cause. Self-defense seemed to be a good enough reason for him, reason enough. Good God, the boy attacked him after hitting him square in the jaw. In his mind, the boy should have been disciplined then and there for hitting a tenured professor. Now, he was the chastised man.

The woman who was fornicating inside the closet, along with the students gathering around them, cheered the student, encouraging him to continue the altercation. Several other teachers finally came to the scene then pulled him off the boy. Having felt incensed, he was not easily pulled away. He swung a few more good punches just so he'd feel more satisfied, leaving the student with a bloodied nose. Evan imagined that very fact was most likely one of the main reasons he was asked to take a sabbatical from teaching until he cooled off enough to apologize. No way in hell would he lower himself to tell that young man he was in the wrong.

At this point, saying he was sorry just wasn't going to be part of his speech. He could hold out until hell froze over. Working wasn't necessary for him to live splendidly.

Damn, he'd only been away from his students for two weeks. He missed each and every one of them, especially the few young women who were admitted to the school. Admittance for women was a rare event. The ones he taught were amazing, brilliant in every case. He took great pride in the young women when they graduated. Most of them ended their schooling with honors, humbling their male counterparts. More than most anything he respected an intelligent woman. If she was also beautiful, even better.

He enjoyed composing classroom lectures, creating challenging tests. The grading was always interesting, especially when new, creative ideas were put forth by his students in their essays. The only part of his teaching assignment he didn't relish was that part which involved busy work set forth by the administration. Now, his schedule was blank. In the interim, he was left with nothing to do during the day, nowhere he wanted to go. He hoped the woman he was supposed to escort for the next month or months would prove stimulating. He stifled a yawn, examining the room once more. As far as he could tell, he was the only one at the station.

His sister-in-law was into tracing characteristics of humans such as eye color among the many. Caroline wanted a position at Glasgow University until she held her baby in her arms. Eventually, she might pursue her academic dreams. As it stood now, his brother and his wife were so enamored of each other that wouldn't happen too soon. They had one child. Another was on its way in about four months, give or take. Neither could say when the baby had been conceived. Even taking care of a baby they could not keep their hands from wandering. From what he gathered from whispered conversations at the family dinner table, they had sex just about everywhere as well as anywhere. Once he spread a cinnamon-sugar-butter concentration on her breasts so he could lick and suck the sweet confection from her. The devil, he suddenly wondered if Duncan spread the sweetness to other more intimate places on his wife's body.

He groaned. Even thinking about such things concerning his brother was none of his business. He shouldn't even know about what they did in private. It was just that they were so verbal when they lusted for each other.

Stretching again, moving his shoulders to push out the kinks as well as to keep his mind on a different train of thought than sex, he looked around the waiting room realizing he wanted something just as enduring as what his brother found. Possibly, the woman he was supposed to escort could provide an interesting diversion for the short time he was obligated to see to her needs. He grinned. He would see to any needs she wished him to see to. That undoubtedly would not lead to a lasting relationship. What the hell? Right now, any kind of sexual relationship would help him get through each boring day, would ease his body as well as his mind.

His breath stuck in his throat. What if she wasn't someone...well hell, he just assumed she'd be as beautiful as Caroline and Scarlett. She was, after all, their friend. What did Caroline say? That she was a colleague of sorts. That she met her at the university in London? She could be...long in the face, a veritable old maid. She might be well and truly on the shelf sporting a horse-face. Caro said she wasn't a debutante. What the bloody hell did that mean? How old was this woman? If she wasn't a debutante, did that mean she wasn't a virgin? He didn't want a virgin. All he wished for now was a passionate woman, in his arms, beneath him, astride him on her belly in front of him, her delicious backside in the air. Someone who would give as well as take, a willing sexual bedmate. He wasn't looking for a partner in life.

He groaned again, suddenly wondering if the woman was in her forties or even her fifties if she had white hair. He was tied to this woman for the next month or more. His body lost all thoughts of a quick dalliance or even a long one. The woman was a scholar, he assumed. She would not be interested in sex, only book learning. That couldn't be possible. Caroline wanted a child so she seduced his brother. She was a scholar, brilliant in her field. In reflecting back on their journey to marriage, he was certain they seduced each other. His brother had been forced to wed because Caroline conceived. That had been her intention. She plotted their times together. Suddenly, he wished to run in the opposite direction. If he ever wanted his life back, he could do nothing of the sort. In a sense, the most important people in his life hog-tied him to this lady.

Something else he resented. This woman owned his life for the next month or more. The time they spent together was up to her. Where they went was up to her. She would be in control, controlling and directing him to her whim.

A high-pitched child's squeal followed by a cheerful British voice distracted his musings. He turned to search for the source.

"Please do let go of your sister's braid, Reggie. If you don't, I'll be quite cross with you. You wouldn't like me to be angry, I can assure you."

The woman turned her attention to a little girl, shaking her finger at both children. "For you, Victoria, there is no need to carry on so. If you hadn't licked him on his nose, he wouldn't have grabbed your hair. Now apologize to each other then behave yourselves."

Evan jerked before he grinned as he saw the woman barreling through the front door with two young children in tow. The first thing he noticed was her hat, a perky confection with several white feathers sticking out in all directions from the rim. She wore a muslin traveling gown with lace edging along the top of the corsage. The lavender skirt swirled around her. She was moving so quickly he caught several glances of neatly trimmed ankles.

With one hand she hung onto a young boy, along with a bag the size of Scotland. In the other hand, she held a mean-faced little girl, a parasol that matched the color of her gown, lavender along with a deep purple bag bulging with newspapers, books, and another parasol this one was sunshine yellow. He realized she was quite fetching in an unusual sort of way. He found himself intrigued.

Her light honey-kissed hair curled this way and that way from beneath the brim of her deplorable hat. Whatever enhancements to her face she started out with that day were long gone. She blew strands of errant hair that must be tickling away from her face.

From Evan's point this lack of added color on her face was possibly a good thing because even without color she had about the most sensual mouth he'd ever seen. It was wide with a plump bottom lip and top lip that formed into a distinct bow at the center. He was suddenly touched with the notion he wanted to taste that lower lip, tug on the plump flesh with his teeth. Her jaw was firm. Her cheeks were baby doll round, the bones finely sculpted. Her nose was a bit narrow, not thin enough for him to lose interest. To Evan her best part were her eyes. She had the most amazing pair of thick-lashed cornflower blue eyes that peeked out from skin that was alabaster so very creamy he thought of lapping up the cream.

He mentally redressed her in a sheer lavender negligée, one where he could see every glorious curve she possessed. There were times he'd kept a mistress. For some reason after the incident at the university, he let his current lady go. He never went to brothels for sex. Doing so was just too dangerous to a man's physical well-being. As he thought earlier, this woman could keep the boring out of his life until the dean decided he needed him more than he wanted an apology. She might wish for some extra groats in order to take care of the two hellions who tagged along beside her. He would consider setting her up just for him. After that he would employ a nanny to take care of the demons while they played in the big bed he would buy for her apartment.

To his surprise, she looked at him, her eyes bright with what appeared to be instant recognition. "Mr. Murray?" She blinked a few times. Those sooty, long lashes rested on her cheeks for but a moment.

Fantasy intruded on reality. As he gazed at her then the children his stomach turned sour. This couldn't be the woman he was supposed to escort. He was never told about children. They couldn't be hers. Of course, they could. She didn't appear old enough to have two children. The notion she seemed to be expecting him, told him this could only be Betsy Darling, the woman Evan agreed to babysit for the next weeks of his semi-retirement. Duncan never mentioned anything about children. He damn well wasn't about to take these children in tow no matter how much it would mean to his reinstatement. He was suddenly put off so thoroughly he choked.

Evan recognized after the fact that he automatically nodded in response to her question instead of hightailing himself out of the station and straight to his waiting coach with the earl's emblem boldly printed on the side. With a heavy breath of air then just as heavy a sigh, he couldn't pander to his fears. More than anything he needed to get back to work. He had to make the best of this situation. Next semester wasn't that far away. He didn't have time to prevaricate.

"Wonderful," she beamed, her eyes alight with mischief.

The next instant she charged forward, skirts swirling around her tiny ankles, sucking him into more carnal thoughts that he now fought instead of encouraged, dragging the children as well as the parasols while her newspapers and books waved in the bag and her honey painted hair flew around her doll-like face. The lavender feathers sitting atop her hat danced in the wind created from her swift rush toward him.

Looking at her exhausted him. She constantly moved.

She let go of the little girl, grabbed his hand then began to propel it up then down. For a tiny woman she had a lot of energy in that shake. "Enchanted to meet you, Mr. Murray." The feathers swayed and floated around the brim of the hat. "Betsy Darling."

The little boy drew back his foot and, before Evan could dodge out of the line of fire, kicked him hard in the shin. "I don't like you! You have mean eyes!"

Mean eyes?

The wind was suddenly knocked from him. Evan glared at the boy. For this child, his eyes were mean. Well, he didn't like him either. For a moment he thought about smacking the rude-mannered lad or turning him over his knee. After he put that thought behind his teeth, he thought about smacking his sister-in-law along with her friend Letty for setting him in this horrendous situation. They were the perpetrators of this ridiculous adventure with a woman. By God, she had two kids! What was a man like him to do with two kids who didn't like him?

With her brows furrowed together, Miss Darling turned to the boy. Instead of smacking him on his hindside or reprimanding him as he so thoroughly deserved, her golden brows drew together in a miniature scowl. With the softest voice imaginable, she spoke, "Reggie, dear, remove your finger from your nose. Having your appendage there is most unattractive. Now, apologize to Mr. Murray. There's a dear boy."

Finally, someone who was asked to apologize to him.

The hellion wiped his finger on his buff trousers. Now, he had green slime across one thigh. With a sound of disapproval in his voice, he pulled out his handkerchief to wipe the smear off his pants. After that he tossed the handkerchief in the garbage. This was the second time he'd been attacked and no one offered an apology.

Evan was just about getting ready to toss the boy into the same pile of refuse when another lady rushed toward them. She was waving her hand in the air, her skirts raised high so she could move faster. She was pleasantly plump. Her considerable bosom bounced then swayed as she rushed forward. Her dark hair was tied up in a plain bun. She wore a dark brown muslin gown that did nothing for her bland coloring. She was breathless when she spoke. "Thank you for watching the children for me. How were they? Reggie, Victoria, were you good for Miss Darling?"

"Perfect angels," Miss Darling replied while he stood in front of all of them, his mouth gaping open in obvious astonishment.

"You can't be serious?" he bellowed.

Then, when the other lady glared at him, he stepped back. The better to get rid of these two brats before something else happened he wouldn't like. More snot on his clothing would never be appreciated. He found himself quite pleased to see the children leaving, walking with the second lady to some point unknown. A few minutes ago, he had a nightmare about these children accompanying them in the coach. They would have demolished the interior before they could find the hotel. Now, he had other ideas. His mind jetted back to his earlier carnal thoughts with this lady, thoughts before he noticed the children clinging to her.

"Well..." Miss Darling smiled at him, a tiny dimple forming at the corner of her mouth, a very kissable dimple. "Are you ready?"

Was he ready? Ready to make certain the next weeks weren't boring? Hell bells yes. Evan felt dizzy he was so ready. Part of his emotions might have been the shock he was just getting over. The rest of it might be the way her eyes twinkled, drawing him into some type of web she was weaving around him.

"Are you?" she asked again snapping him out of the nightmare turned dream he wallowed in. She was pointing her parasol at him, right at his chest, at his heart. He didn't like that. "We need to pick up my luggage."

The devil, he was eager for anything she could toss his way except for the absurd parasol pointing coupled with the commands she spouted as if she was a general. Unintentionally, he snapped to attention then offered his arm to her. She accepted, her hand resting lightly on his forearm, the parasol tucked beneath her other arm. Her bag swinging from her free hand.

"Yes, where would you like to go?"

He expected her to ramble off a downtown hotel. For the moment he had other ideas. Ideas that were rapidly taking shape in his head.

"Something to eat first would be nice, maybe a cup of hot tea along with a scone or something sweet. I do love sweet things."

She looked at the vendors outside the station as they stepped through the door.

Evan loved sweet things too. She looked pretty darn tasty. Sweeter than sugar. A little bit spicey too.

He supposed food would be in order. "What would you like?"

"Not too much, just something to tide my stomach over until

dinner time. We ate early this morning. Since we were behind schedule, the driver wouldn't stop at the noon hour. I've been tossed around quite handily as were the children. That is why they were grouchy. They truly aren't that bad. A long trip such as the one they endured would put anyone out of sorts."

Evan had other ideas about the devil children she referred to. If he never saw them again, the moment would be too soon. Nonetheless, he wasn't about to get into an argument over their rude behavior. "They aren't going to show up again, are they?"

"No. You don't like children?" she questioned, her scowl once more marring her beautiful forehead.

"Good God, not those children!" As soon as the words were out of his mouth, he understood he should never have uttered them. On a much calmer note he tried to make amends. "I love my nephew. He is two." Evan suspected his nephew could become just like the little boy he just encountered. He decided he loved grown children, children who were nearly twenty or older. By his mind, those hellions needed a good spanking or at least their noses in a corner so they could think about what they did.

"They've had a long journey from London," she told him with the utmost sincerity as well as resounding patience, her words sugar-coated. "A trip like that is hard on little ones. Have you ever ridden in one of those coaches all the way to London?" She perused him from head to toe. "No, I don't suppose you have."

"You like to make excuses for bad-mannered behavior. He smeared his snot on my trousers! The boy kicked me! Hard. I'll have a bruise."

To his ears he sounded ridiculous. A grown man complaining about a child's kick was preposterous. He'd been hurt more by his brothers when they wrestled. He imagined it was the idea that bothered him more than the deed.

"I'm not at all certain this arrangement will work out. Caroline assured me you were most compatible, that you were an esteemed professor with infinite tolerance. I didn't expect to be met by a man with violent tendencies. Vicious tendencies toward mere children."

With that said she stepped back appearing to wait for him to make a statement.

Violent tendencies? Vicious?

By God, she was tapping her toes, her arms crossed beneath her breasts. Well, that wasn't bad. Her arms pushed her delightful globes up higher. He appreciated the view. Taking a moment to evaluate this further, he replied, "I am. We will be compatible. I must be," he mumbled.

Backing out of this would make him ecstatic except for two things. One, he wanted his job back before hell froze over. Two, he wanted to get to know this woman better, a woman who was beginning to fascinate him. Evan realized he wanted her more than he'd ever wanted another woman. The errant thought was uncanny.

"That is not what you've just shown me," she countered appearing to bristle more with each passing second. "You wanted to hurt that little boy, Reggie. Didn't you?" she accused. "Admit it."

He liked the way her bosom heaved when she was angry. Anger could easily turn to passion. Revealing those tender globes would be enjoyable. He would have to fight his way past this issue over the children. He decided ignoring her was this best alternative to an answer.

They stopped in front of a food cart. If he fed her, she would lose her pique. "Would you like to get that food now or later?"

He pointed to benches situated beneath a tree. While the weather wasn't hot, the sun was shining. Shade would be nice. He would calm her concerns with soothing words, perhaps a glass of wine instead of a cup of tea would do the trick.

"Tarts are fine," she told him, her British inflection giving him reason to smile at her. She marched up to the cart looking the food over.

Was she implying he was a tart? Men couldn't be tarts. He imagined he could be a bit sour though. He ordered two lemon tarts, wine for them. His stomach grumbled. Possibly a bit of food coupled with a good Chianti would soothe his temper. Though with each passing second away from the demon children, he found himself much more amiable. He was beginning to relax.

They sat down on the bench. He watched her for several seconds. She ate daintily, sipped the wine. He decided he would try out his big tub with her as soon as possible, as soon as he could convince her he was harmless. He imagined her rosy-tipped breasts bobbing on the surface. She couldn't possibly be a virgin. She was too old to still have that barrier inside her. As beautiful as she was, she must have had a lover at some time. He didn't believe he dared ask her age. If he did, he wouldn't be surprised if he caught her wine in his face. Two could play at any game she created. He wouldn't mind licking, or drinking the red drops off her lips or any other part of her. The tips of her breasts would be incredible to suck on.

"Why are you here in Glasgow? Caroline told me you are a scholar."

That line of questioning was much blander than asking her age or if she was still a virgin. If she wasn't, he needed to know who her lovers had been.

Miss Darling nodded. "I assure you, Mr. Murray, that fact is true. I'm researching for a book I intend to write. I've only just begun the exploration."

"Evan."

She looked up from her half-eaten lemon tart, a startled expression on her angelic, baby-doll face. The cornflower blue eyes pointed his way darkened. "What?" She blinked a few times as if she didn't understand.

"Please call me Evan."

His voice was rough around the edges. He imagined how dark those eyes might be when she reached her pleasure. He supposed his brother would not be pleased with his train of thought. What the devil could Duncan expect when he placed an older, experienced woman on his doorstep? He handed her to him on a silver platter. If Duncan wasn't married, he would have thought the same way.

He watched her bosom rise then fall, still enticing, still intriguing. Discovering the treasures beneath her dress became a priority. Would she be a willing bed partner? He would have to discover the truth soon; else he might just explode. The sweet-talking could commence when he drove her to his townhouse. He wasn't about to take her to some squalid hotel in town. She would stay with him. At her age, she wouldn't care about her reputation.

"Evan." She nodded seeming to accept his first name as the way she would address him.

He wanted to call her Betsy. So far, she didn't give him permission. Powdered sugar dusted her plump lips. He wished he dared lick the sweet confection until there was nothing left. His body was a tight hard knot of lust, his sex hard as a boulder.

He wasn't about to wait for permission. Placing her hand in his he lightly kissed the back thinking he'd rather kiss the powdered sugar off her mouth. "Betsy."

He turned the palm up then kissed her there making sure he brushed his tongue across the sensitive flesh.

The rose color blush rising to her cheeks was delightful as was the way her pulse thundered at the base of her neck. He imagined how fast her blood would race when he stroked her, caressed, and kissed every part of her especially the soft moist folds between her creamy, white thighs. She was proving to be every bit the woman he imagined her to be.

Her lashes lowered softly against her baby doll cheeks, shielding her eyes from him, keeping him from reading her emotions. His finger beneath her chin, he lifted her face. She ran her tiny pink tongue across her chubby bottom lip whisking away the sugar. The devil, he had more thoughts about that curvy, swelled bottom lip than he should have.

After he set her hand on the table, she sipped her wine, watching him over the rim. She was skittish, nervous. The sudden shivering of her shoulders mesmerized all his male parts. He made her that way. In this case, she wasn't telling him to stop, to cease his blatant perusal of her. His gaze wandered from her eyes, to the slight swell of her breasts he could barely see above the fabric of her gown. Her waist was trim, her hips curving nicely, rounded beautifully for a man's hands. She might even now be hot and wet, her nectar sweet as honey in the most secret parts of her.

He shook himself back to the reality of this moment. His sexual thoughts were for a different place and time. At the moment, he needed to make certain she wanted him to drive her to the destinations she had in mind. If she changed her mind and didn't want him for her driver, she would have to approach her from a different angle. He wasn't willing to let this woman go quite so soon. If she was agreeable, he had big plans for them.

Thinking this was way too fast, too soon. Wooing a woman, one wanted always worked better in the long run versus the short term.

"Why are you staring at me?" Her words were feather soft, enticing him to more blatant thoughts.

Her hands fluttered in front of her curvaceous bosom.

"Was I?"

He tilted her a rakish grin. One he knew could turn hearts. "Didn't realize I was." Once more his gaze swept her length.

She waved her hand in the air as if to blow away his question then shifted her position. "You were. It is very rude of you. You should have a few manners. I've met your brother. He's quite the gentleman. Were you raised by the same parents?"

Evan sucked in air. If her words got back to Duncan, his brother would never forgive him. What he wanted from this relationship he would have with Betsy was forgiveness from Duncan so he could go back to work. If she spoke to his brother about his behavior...he didn't want to think of the consequences.

Though, he didn't intend to apologize for his wayward thoughts or sight-seeing the most tempting parts of her luscious body. Leaning back against the bench, he crossed his arms over his chest as he began to explain the reasons for his bad behavior, "I'm the second son. Our parents ignored me completely since I wasn't intended to be the earl. You see, I'm the spare. Hence...the problem with manners. I was never taught." His parents would have a fit of apoplexy if his words got back to them.

Her plump bottom lip met the sweet bow of the top one in a scornful thin line. He was happily amused. "I don't believe a word you are saying."

"Suit yourself." He stared at her plate. It appeared she was finished. He rose, extended his hand to help her to her feet. "Shall we leave?"

~ * ~

This was her time to take a good long look at the man who intrigued as well as fascinated her. She meant to assess his attributes just as he did hers. When he stared at her with those golden-brown eyes of his, she grew hot all over. Her body seemed to hum to life when his golden eyed stare rested on her bosom. Crisp, dark brown hair curled rakishly from beneath the top hat he wore that looked so at home on his head the fashionable prop might have been permanently attached. His navy frock coat covered a broad chest, one that she would like to discover more intimately. The buff trousers fit his long legs as if they were a second skin. They molded to narrow hips. Going back to his legs they were both lean as well as muscular. She noted the shiny black boots reaching nearly to his knees. His face featured a well-constructed nose, strong cheekbones, a well-formed mouth, and most assuredly strong white teeth. His eyes were the color of golden honey surrounding a deeper brown interior. At times when he starred at her they grew so dark they appeared black. His lashes were long and dark, curling just a bit at the tips. Outrageous for a man to have eyes like that along with lashes so long. They made him strangely vulnerable. Evan would never be defenseless.

Her cursory inspection told her all she needed to know about this man. While she wasn't experienced in *amore*, she'd dealt with men like him on a daily basis. They just weren't so blatantly gorgeous as this fine male specimen. When she closed her eyes, she tried to imagine what he would look like if he wasn't wearing anything. After she opened her eyes, she saw indolence, in his slouching posture, arrogance in the angle of his chin, along with the flicker of something unmistakably carnal in those sultry half-lidded eyes, golden eyes. All in all, she knew she wanted to know him better. She was thrilled he was going to be her driver, her escort around Glasgow.

She repressed a small shiver of what she thought could be desire. He certainly aroused passionate emotions in her, sensations she wasn't quite certain she understood. They were both standing by the bench. He held her hand in his. She thought the moment had come to move on to something else before she started drooling. While she knew he baited her, she tried to keep her thoughts to herself.

"Let's be off then, Mr....Evan. You are, after all, a bit late to begin with. Whatever kept you? I've been waiting for you to show up. I do hope no one has taken my luggage."

She extended her bag for him to take. Instead, she hit him in the chest. The Glasgow Herald fell out along with a few of the lemon drops she'd been bribing the children with. The paper was open to the section she'd been reading while she waited, the advice column on love written by her friend, Caroline, his sister-in-law if she understood correctly. Her bribes didn't have the desired outcome with the children. Maybe she could bribe this man. Back to the countess, amazingly Caroline became a countess when she wed Evan's older brother.

Betsy bent to pick everything up just as he took a step forward. The brim of her wide hat bumped his thigh. Her hat flew off to join the pile of items on the floor. She hadn't noticed the ribbons loosening as she'd been so caught up in her perusal of the big handsome man who was going to escort her around town. After that she'd been so disconcerted when she caught him staring at her bosom, she lost all train of thought. Caroline told her he had extensive knowledge of the best libraries as well as museums in Glasgow. He was well read, intelligent as well as funny. At this moment, he appeared more disagreeable than intelligent. So far, he hadn't been funny at all. Despite those facts, he held her spellbound.

She set the hat back on her unruly curls. To her dismay, or was the feeling delight, he tied the ribbons, his knuckles brushing gently beneath her chin. Her gut tightened. Butterflies danced inside her belly. After that dragons breathed fire. "There, you won't lose the darn thing if it's properly attached. Though, I do like to look at you better without the confection on your head."

"Sorry, of course, you're right. I do forget to fix the ribbons when they loosen. I was thinking about other things."

She wasn't normally clumsy. In this instant, she was so distracted by her troubles lately that her best friend in London told her she was in imminent danger of turning into one of those ladies all males put on the shelf then don't take another look at. The crux of the matter was that her best friend was right. She always had her nose in a book. Never took the time to pay attention to the male species. It wasn't as if she wasn't interested. She was. She just didn't have time for them. After her one and only debacle with one of the male species, she was quite terrified of a repeat performance.

She didn't like the idea of being labeled as a spinster or on the shelf when she was barely twenty-five. Though she knew women younger than herself bore the nametags. The thought depressed her unbearably, so she didn't allow herself to mull over the thought more than when the horrible notion popped into her head as it had today. Besides, if everything went according to her plans, that worry would disappear. Despite Caroline's assurances that Evan was a rational man, after his behavior with the children she wasn't at all certain she believed her. Nonetheless, she was desperately hoping he would see something in her he couldn't ignore. In this situation, she would have time to get to know the man.

Evan didn't help her collect her possessions nor did he offer to take her bag, which gave more credit to the notion his parents left him on his own because he wasn't to become the next Earl of Downberry. How much initiative could be expected from a man who had been born so physically blessed? She could drum it up to the fact he was ignorant, but he wasn't. No, he as well as all his brothers were quite brilliant.

"Let's be off then."

She pointed the exact direction with her closed parasol. Betsy understood she was repeating herself. With this man, she needed to make certain he understood all her desires.

She nearly reached the long walkway to where she assumed the carriage waited before she realized he wasn't following her. She turned to see what exactly was keeping the darn man.

He was staring at her parasol as if he wanted to break it into two pieces. It was a perfectly ordinary parasol, one that all women used to keep the sun from ruining their complexion. She couldn't imagine for the life of her why he seemed so mesmerized, or perhaps it was anger she saw in his expression. Maybe he wasn't as brilliant as she'd been told. Possibly, his brothers caught the bulk of the intelligence while he positively got the amazing male body. She couldn't be happier. In this case she didn't so much care about brain power. His perfect masculine body would delight her.

"You...uh...always point the direction you intend to walk like that?" he asked, his voice seeming now to be coated with sugary sarcasm. "I don't need you to direct me with that thing of yours." His voice held a wealth of mockery.

Betsy glanced down at her lavender parasol then back at him, confused by the question. She didn't understand what he seemed to be implying. She continued as if he didn't say anything negative to her. She jabbed the air with the parasol. "We need to get my trunk. I was just..."

Finally, she began to understand of what he spoke. She lowered the parasol before sticking it into the bag she was carrying, suddenly embarrassed by his pointed question. The words he uttered stung. The tone of voice far from flattering. She got the distinct impression he didn't like her.

"I know that," he spoke softly before he took an angrier tone. "I'm not going to be led around by my nose or by your damn rain napper!"

Or by you. She heard the distinct words even though he didn't utter them.

"Well then."

She couldn't help but use her hand in lieu of the parasol, wishing she hadn't put the thing into her bag. She wasn't about to be dictated to by an arrogant male even though his body appealed so very much to her.

He developed a slightly dazed look before motioning to her with his hand. "Never mind. Doesn't truly matter."

Twenty minutes later the driver had her trunk loaded onto the carriage. She found herself sitting across from him. The coach was well-sprung, comfortable, more than comfortable. She'd never ridden in anything this...comfortable or with such an appealing looking man sitting across from her.

Betsy bounced on the seat, feeling like a child. She almost clapped her hands together before she thought better. One of his dark, brown eyebrows rose in speculation. They hardly said a single word to each other over the last twenty minutes. She was growing increasingly wary that her plan that he seduce her was not going to come to fruition. It seemed he looked disdainfully at her from almost the moment he first saw her. She did want to lose her virginity...and to this man. Caroline explained to her that she held the utmost confidence in Evan Murray's ability to do so gently, tenderly. First, the man would have to like her.

"You aren't going to take me everywhere in this. I can't afford the rent it would cost me." Her dismay must have been evident to him when she heard him laugh slightly.

"Rent? I've no intention of renting this one. My brother owes me. He will allow me to have the use free. It's not as if this coach is the only vehicle at his disposal."

"Oh," she mouthed softly. "Never thought of that."

Betsy did an excellent job tutoring children in London. She was always able to receive amazing recommendations from her employers when she was forced to move on because the children were too old for her talents. Since there was always time between employment there could be weeks even months when she had no income. She would have to use her meager savings to support herself in those cases. As a result, she was operating here with limited funds. The use of a coach free of charge would certainly help.

"Free," he told her again.

She couldn't quite hide her embarrassment. "I'm afraid there has been a misunderstanding, Mr. Murray. I'm operating on a limited budget. I can't afford the upkeep for this vehicle or the feeding of the cattle. You say it's free. Well, sir, nothing is free. We must use something different. I told Caroline I could only afford to pay my escort ten pounds a day; that would include the maintenance of the vehicle. She told me ten pounds would easily cover your services. It can't possibly be enough to cover the cost of the earl's carriage. He would want more. I'm certain of that fact. The driver would cost me. No, you must find some other vehicle to use when you escort me."

"Ten pounds a day?"

He appeared stunned.

Betsy wanted to believe her head was pounding from the long ride in the bouncing, swaying coach she took to reach Glasgow, but she'd always been a good traveler. The ride never bothered her before. Now, she was deathly afraid this headache had more to do with her escort along with the costs that seemed to be looming in front of her. Costs she could ill afford. She didn't come from money as the Murray's did. She couldn't afford their lifestyle. He would have to understand.

"Free," he reiterated as if she wasn't cognizant of all the other factors.

"I will not take advantage of your brother."

Communication from this gorgeous man was more difficult than dealing with her slowest students. She'd heard that brilliant men were hard to talk to, that they somehow went through life on a different level than normal people. Even after the earlier incident with the children then the food, it had taken her forever to get him to the location of her trunks. After that he didn't lift a hand to help put them on the coach. No, he allowed the elderly, frail driver to do everything.

"This is way too embarrassing." She would have to explain in no uncertain terms what she could manage to pay him only if they were conservative. "I believed Caroline would have discussed all this with you. You're expecting more than ten pounds, aren't you?"

She found herself tapping her foot, a habit she absolutely detested in herself. Despite her every effort to stop, when she grew frustrated or angry, she always found herself with a tapping foot. She supposed the act was similar to the pointing of her parasol.

Once again, the man appeared to be ignoring her. She wished she could read his mind. Doing so would certainly help her figure out how to proceed. He moved so slow. A tortoise could move more quickly. Her eyes strayed one more time to the well-developed muscles his clothing couldn't completely conceal. Wouldn't a person actually have to expend energy to build muscles like that?

"Well," he paused, smiling at her, "I guess that depends on what besides escorting you to libraries and museums the groats are supposed to cover." He took her bag with the two parasols protruding and set the item aside. "I'll have to give this grave consideration before I decide what to charge."

She sucked in a breath of air, wondering what in tarnation he was speaking about. "We need to return to the posting station so we can come to an agreement as to the cost of your services. I need to know exactly what you will be expecting from me, money to cover...your services." She was babbling. If she knew it, Evan must know it too. "We'll have to draw up a contract."

"Too far away. Don't want to walk more than necessary. We're not turning around. We can discuss this further in the carriage on the way to your lodgings."

He crossed his arms then leaned against the soft leather cushion. Before she could mention anything else, he tapped on the roof. The coach began to move, slowly at first then the vehicle picked up speed.

She panicked for a moment. Her destination had never been explained to him. Where the devil was he sending the vehicle? "No! You must stop this! Where are we going. I never told you the address of my hotel."

"I'm taking you to a very nice but cheap place where you can stay free of charge. Since you are so concerned about finances, I'm merely helping you out. You've no need to worry." He closed his eyes seemingly unknowledgeable of her distress.

For a second, she thought he might fall asleep. She held the distinct feeling he was late picking her up because he was sleeping. "You can't just take me somewhere without my permission. That's...that's kidnapping!"

After opening his eyes, he lifted a dark brown eyebrow before slanting her an amused half-grin. "That's exactly what I'm doing. So, for now, just settle back and relax. You look a little haggard around the edges. A nap might be in order. Promise you will like the place. If you don't, you can always leave."

"I don't have a say in this?"

Her hands were shaking. She was always the person in control. He ripped that from her, the overbearing lout

"No."

"All right." She didn't understand why she conceded so easily. She imagined she couldn't change his mind. The frustration she felt now kept rational thoughts from her muddled brain.

Stubborn man. Domineering. Conceited.

"If you don't wish to take a nap, then tell me some of what we will be doing while I play the escort, or you could tell me about yourself."

While she debated how much to explain to him, she gazed at the cheery August sunshine she saw out the window as the earl's coach, the expensive earl's coach, trundled its way out onto the streets of Glasgow. The thought of the sunshine outside did nothing to change the dismal thoughts rushing around in her scrambled head. She just didn't know how to combat his bossy commands. Since it was her groats paying the man, why, then she should have the last say or the only say.

"Very well." She placed her shaking hands in her lap, entwining her fingers to keep them still. "So, you want to know something about me," she began. "I've tutored a great number of children, and..."

Truly she didn't understand where she was going with this. Though she did. She needed for him to understand why she couldn't afford certain amenities. Why extra services would not be needed.

"Tutored? A great number?" A supercilious eyebrow arched upward. "How many is a great number?"

"Yes, and..."

Obviously, he didn't believe her. She stopped short of saying what was on her mind while her breath caught in the back of her throat.

"That's commendable. I lecture university students."

As if that would put her in her place. A professor at a university would look down his nose at a woman who only taught younger children. She could manage tit for tat as well as anyone. "I hear you get in fights with them too," she blurted realizing after the fact that was not the way to get on his good side, if he had a good side.

She did need his services. Attempting to calm her rattled nerves, she inhaled slowly then let go the air just as slowly out of her lungs before she replied. "I tutor children. Presently, I'm between jobs. Caroline and Letty encouraged me to come here to follow a passion of mine. I've already begun the research."

To Betsy, he looked vastly amused. His grin was lazy, slanted half way on his mouth. If he smiled using all his lips and showing his teeth, the sight would knock her stockings off. "For proper English aristocrats, I assume." His blandly sarcastic tone piqued her temper.

If any other Scotsman teased her about how she made a living, she might have laughed. This man, this thick-headed, self-centered, fascinating man caused her to set her back straight then tilt her chin defiantly. Truly, she didn't understand how she would survive the months until all the research was completed. Lands, what if it took her more than a month?

"Be that as it may..." She paused as the stuffy words resounded between her ears causing her to heat. "I've spent the last six months working on a paper about Mary of Guise, sometimes known as Mary of Lorraine. She was the regent of Scotland in the mid fifteen hundreds. The research is just beginning. There is so much more I need to discover about this woman before I can even begin to write. This seemed like a good time for a trip as I'm between students. Caroline recommended you as my guide. She indicated that ten pounds a day would pay for your services. Perhaps she was wrong. Was she?"

Indignant, she felt irate, outraged that she needed to explain all this to him. He should have been apprised of all this before he volunteered for the job. The man should have understood what to expect for his pay.

"Services?"

One of his infuriating eyebrows lifted skyward again.

"As my guide," she repeated. "As my driver."

If stamping her foot would garner more respect, she would certainly try it. Instead, she was tap, tap, tapping her foot.

He stared at her foot for a moment then back to her eyes. "Uh-huh. Well, I'm pleased that is all you've got in that pretty little feminine head of yours, because when you mentioned *services*, I thought you might be implying something else entirely different, in which case ten pounds wouldn't be nearly enough to cover the suggested duties."

He still appeared as if he was about to break out in a gale of laughter. She certainly didn't understand the amusement she saw in his eyes. Although she understood the laughter behind his teeth was at her expense. She braced herself against the back of the soft leather seat as the vehicle hit a deep rut in the road. Stiffly, she began again, "There will be quite a bit of driving. In addition, possibly to Edinburgh if I can't find all the information here in Glasgow. Most of my time will be spent at the Glasgow University. I would suppose you could put me in contact with some history professors who could help."

"Driving, that's all you want? I don't usually drive the earl's coach. He sent me with this one specifically for your comfort. Caroline asked if I could use it to pick you up. Nonetheless, I can use a smaller vehicle if you'd like."

"Whatever is easiest for you. What other services do you offer? I might be interested if it will enable my research to go smoothly."

His grin widened to the point where his entire mouth was involved. "Tell you what. I'll start out with the basics of any escort. After that we can speak of additional things to be added. I'm certainly open to added...duties."

With her limited amount of money, she wasn't pleased with the conversation. She wanted specifics, needed to know exactly what he'd be charging for. By the way he skirted around the topic, he wasn't going to expand on what he seemed to be thinking. "It is my belief that when dealing with another person, all facts should be made clear from the start of the relationship. Don't you agree?"

"We're clear enough for now. Let's allow this to play out the way we would like. Take the situations we encounter from one minute to the next. We are, after all, both adults who can make decisions. Planning for the future sometimes just doesn't work out unless we leave decisions open ended." The carriage swayed a bit when it went around a sharp corner. "Just to be specific, at this second, you will pay me ten pounds a day to drive you around Glasgow or possibly other places for a month or more."

"Possibly more. I have a list."

She fumbled in her bag in order to find the parchment to show him.

"I'll just bet you do. Suppose it's buried somewhere inside those newspapers. Possibly it's inside one of those parasols of yours. Do you put your lists between your breasts? I could look there for you."

He paused as if he was waiting for her to react. She wasn't going to give him the satisfaction. He went on, "You could save money, you know, by renting a horse. We could move more quickly through the city."

"I can't ride."

"We could change that fact. However, I'd have to charge you if I were to teach you how to ride. Imagine there might not be savings in that case. Nonetheless, you would learn a valuable lesson. Riding can be quite enjoyable. I do enjoy a wild, untamed ride."

He crossed his long legs, stretching them out. His calves touched hers. She moved back. His lopsided grin widened. His amusement at her expense irked her to no end.

"There are other ways to save money."

He sat forward, his forearms on his thighs, appearing to look into her bag. He would do what he wanted.

Pulling out the newspaper she'd been reading on the last leg of her journey here, he tapped the article. "My sister-in-law's work. Did you know my brother helps her with the articles? Caroline was an innocent, but giving out advise to love starved women. Is that what you are, Betsy? Love starved. I could give you advice on how to change that situation. Give you pointers. Show you the way." He tapped a finger beneath his chin. "Ah, but then I would have to charge you. Wouldn't I? I could give you the first piece of advice free. What would you like to ask me?"

Quickly, she turned away, heat flooding her at his insinuation. She didn't want him to see the strangled expression on her face. He was too audacious. Ask him questions about love? Never!

"Nothing. I don't want advice from you."

"I'm well-versed in love. What about you, Betsy. How many lovers have you had? Ten? Twenty? Maybe more?"

She heard the amusement back in his voice. Telling him none was not going to happen. She meant to turn his question back on him. "How many have you had?"

"Ah, you put me on the defensive. Imagine I've had more than my fair share of lovers. Never counted the number. Never felt the need to keep track. So, how about you?"

Before she could utter another word, he tugged her across the seat. She landed on his lap, her hand winding around the back of his neck to keep from falling off. He blindsided her. She was shaking, completely taken off guard, surprised. "N...nine."

"Only nine? That's not nearly enough. Oh, well, I could possibly find some young swain at the university who could teach you about love.

I don't dally with virgins. Is that what you are, Betsy, a virgin? No, with nine lovers under your belt, you're not a virgin. Too old and too beautiful to still be untouched by a man. What do you think? Would that be something you would enjoy? A bit of sexual play between two experienced adults?"

No, she wouldn't enjoy anyone except him. Evan didn't seem to be offering. Or was he? Was all this play coupled with innuendos she didn't understand leading toward a relationship of sorts? All she wished for was a short-term lover. A dalliance, as she didn't want to go to her grave a virgin. When she spoke to Caroline, she felt certain Evan would do just fine. Letty came to the same conclusion. Although Caroline tried to convince her she might just want something more than a short-term relationship with him.

"No, I'm not looking for a lover." She lied outrageously. "I'm here for research not pleasure."

"I could change your mind." One of his long-bronzed fingers swept down her throat then back to her chin. He kept moving, touching, stroking. She gulped air. Squirmed. The devil, she remembered staring at his hands. His nails were clipped neatly, his fingers long, bronzed from time in the sun. She'd thought about him doing something like this. His fingers traveled lightly across her collarbone.

"Evan..."

"What?"

She turned to look at him. Saw the moistness of his parted lips. She pushed on his shoulders. "I shouldn't be sitting here."

"Instead of advice, thought I could give you a free lesson. Won't charge a groat."

Now, his fingernail traveled the length of one arm then the other. "A lesson in what?"

"Whatever you like? Would you like a kiss? Has a man ever kissed you, Betsy? Of course, I forgot. At least nine men must have kissed you," he asked as his roaming fingers dipped a little lower, travelled across the tops of her breasts.

"Kissed me?"

Once. She recalled the young man, a neighbor who grabbed her behind the carriage house. She was only sixteen. His lips on hers was not something she wanted to repeat. Somehow, now, staring at Evan's mouth, she didn't believe a kiss from this man would feel as disgusting as the first and only time she'd been kissed.

"Yes. Who has kissed you, Betsy?"

~ * ~

Where she was concerned, he had mixed emotions. At times, he didn't think anyone ever kissed this gorgeous woman. After that, when he thought more thoroughly about her, because of her age, she couldn't possibly be innocent. By now she must have had multiple lovers. Nine, as she told him. Maybe that was an exaggeration.

Back to her innocent act, if they had, the kiss happened a long time ago. Even now she was pushing herself away from him. She'd been so worried about money; he knew he needed to change the topic. He'd wanted to laugh when she puzzled over the idea of learning how to ride. She understood in the end, he wasn't talking about riding a horse. Her problem was that she didn't comprehend of what he spoke. Perhaps she'd never sat astride one of her lovers. That was a possibility.

He dipped one finger in the valley between her breasts, caught the gasp of air she almost choked on along with the shiver of her small frame. She certainly wasn't immune to him.

When she was telling him what to do or pointing her parasol in the direction she wanted him to walk, in her own way she was an absolute delight. Nothing would cost her, her hard-earned groats teaching spoiled brats. Nonetheless, she seemed to delight in the job. Betsy even liked Reggie and Victoria.

She moved to get off his lap. He held her still, enjoying her lush curves pushed against him. His hands pressed against the trimness of her waist. He wondered about the weight and texture of her breasts. If he could keep her from telling him how to explore her sweet body, he might enjoy the adventure. His hands rose up the ladder of her ribs.

She wriggled on his lap. Seemed to always be wiggling. "About your extra services. I won't be needing any of them. I won't be paying for kisses or love advice. I know you were speaking of something different than riding a horse. Whatever that was, I won't be paying for that either."

No, she wouldn't be.

When she started speaking about the services, a small crease formed in her forehead. She began to chew on her bottom lip. He wished she wouldn't do that. It was the damndest thing. She annoyed the hell out of him from the moment she'd first opened her mouth. He swore to God the next time she pointed at something with her rain napper, he was going to break it over his knee. Now, seeing that moist wonderful mouth working away made him wonder how he was going to survive these next weeks, let alone months if it came to that. He thoroughly hoped to be reinstated before that time.

In bed.

In bed, that's how he would survive. The notion popped into his head then had the audacity to stick there, play with his senses. He'd enjoyed teasing her. Never once, until now, had the intention of bedding her popped so thoroughly into his head. True, he skirted around the thought. If his instincts were right, she wasn't a damn virgin; an over the hill, long in the tooth, maiden. If that was true, all her lovers had been old men. He bedded experienced women. Her experiences weren't what he expected. Usually, he liked his women a tiny bit younger as well as knowledgeable. A woman who would have no expectations other than giving as well as receiving pleasure. This was exactly the kind of thinking that could get a man into a hell of a lot of trouble. The best way to avoid strangling her with his bare hands was to get her naked as soon as possible. Preferably in the next couple of days.

Moving in on this starchy woman who he was lusting after the moment he saw her would be a definite challenge. In any case, Evan didn't have anything better to do with his time. So, he figured he was up to the task. He thought of the ten pounds a day she was supposed to be paying him. After that, he recalled the two thousand pounds he earned in compounded interest each month. This was the first time he smiled about money in a very long time. Then he remembered just exactly why he was on escort duty, the student who attacked him. Bloody hell, there was no way he would just stand in front of that young pup and let him wail on him. Apologizing was also out of the question. If this went on very long, he might never get his job back.

His wavering grin turned to a frown as he imagined Caroline's amused reaction when Betsy offered him ten pounds a day and her even greater amusement when she decided not to pass that particular piece of information on to him. It never ceased to amaze him that his brother snared one of the most beautiful women he'd ever seen. When they were together fires blazed. The ball, when his sister-in-law won a not so coveted award. The moment Duncan saw her there he whisked her away to his bedroom. There wasn't anything he or his brothers could do to get him to go back to the charity ball. The scandal was huge.

After that incident, the ensuing humiliation, Caroline's pregnancy, only grew larger over time. He decided he would never allow a woman the upper hand. If he did, that would be utter folly.

He glanced at Betsy's softly parted mouth with her sun kissed curls, baby-doll cheeks, feathers that every time she bent her head tickled his nose. He'd been maneuvering women all his adult life. He'd never yet let one of them forget the place where he could adore them.

Right beneath him. Everyone had been eager for the position.

~ * ~

Caroline sat with Duncan's arms around her, her back pressed against his chest. His hand caressed her slightly swollen belly. Their two-year-old played with a ball in front of them. The sky was clear blue. Sunrays hit the earth softly. Green grass shimmered waving slightly while a breeze caressed the tips in undulating rhythms.

"Hmm..." She did enjoy the sweet stroking of his fingers. The potent heat they spawned. "What do you think will happen when Betsy offers Evan ten pounds a day for his services?" Caro sighed softly as his lips brushed tenderly on her nape.

His hands rose to cup her breasts, his thumb moving lazily across the tight hard tips. Heat rose swift and pure. She wanted to melt into him. Duncan spent most of the afternoon seducing. With their toddler in front of them, he couldn't act on the seduction until the nanny arrived. Caro closed her eyes enjoying the peace of the moment, the sweet surrender.

"Hard to tell where my brother is concerned. He won't like the fact you implied he was an escort. Nonetheless, if he appreciates your friend, she might get what she wants. At least something close to your intentions."

He let his head fall against the tree trunk behind him, his hands slowly inching her skirt upward.

She pushed his hands down. "Behave yourself. Do you think he will do what Betsy wants? She doesn't wish to get with child though. All she wishes for is to learn about pleasure. She doesn't want to go to her grave a virgin. Evan has to see the sweet beauty she possesses."

Nervously she was folding her gown between her fingers wondering if this scheme wouldn't backfire. In the process have atrocious repercussions.

What they planned could turn out horribly.

"Maybe. She is a beautiful woman. One a man might have difficulty resisting. Isn't this something like what you did to me? I was furious when I discovered how blatantly you lied to me. You were going to take my child from me," he said letting his thumbs glide across nipples that were covered by too much fabric. "You should unfasten some of those damn buttons keeping me from my goal."

"Not until the nanny gets here." She held onto his hands, laughing as she heard his groan of discontent. "No, she doesn't want a baby. If you recall, you stole all my assets. You left me with nothing, no place to live, not even a penny to my name. I had no choice except to follow along behind you as if I was your well-trained puppy dog."

His raspy chuckle sent shiver down her spine. He wasn't about to stop the exploration of his hands. "All Betsy wants is to lose her virginity. In that case, I'm more than certain Evan will oblige her. He's going to be bored these next few weeks. Caro, I've apologized more than any man should have to about stealing your wealth. Haven't I made it up to you? I've given all that I could back."

"She's a beautiful woman."

"One who can be damn annoying," Duncan said. "Seems I recall a certain parasol she wields as if it's an extension of her arm."

"There is that."

Chapter Two

Evan leapt from the coach as soon as the lumbering vehicle slowed to a stop. He pulled out the steps then gave her his hand. Clutching the warmth he offered, she stepped down, swayed slightly as she got used to the ground. She never did like riding in carriages. Would much prefer a good fast walk. Once settled on the street, she looked around her. A path led to a three-story building. The grass on either side was green, tended lovingly along with the plants in front of the townhouse. A beautiful tulip tree was the focal point of one side of the yard. Colorful flowers bordered the home.

Betsy didn't know where she was. Wherever he took her, this wasn't a hotel. Her breath caught while all coherent thoughts left her speechless. What was he planning to do with her? She was still trembling from the way he touched her, stroked her arms, her neck, her shoulders. Now, she felt certain he had more plans. She just hoped they coincided with hers.

Trying to get her emotions under control, she turned to him, scowling at the smile creasing his strong features. With a quick breath of air, she blurted, "This isn't a hotel. Where am I? You should have asked me where I wanted you to take me."

She wanted to poke him in the chest with her parasol. When he started the trip without asking her for directions, she held the decided opinion, he didn't intend to take her to the hotel. Now her guesses were proved true. This had to be owned by his family, perhaps the earl.

"Since you expressly told me you needed to save money, I decided to lend a helping hand. Thought you could stay here with me instead. It's free. Won't cost you a single coin. Just as the coach is free. All that will cost you is for services rendered, by me if you need any. I'm beginning to think there will a great deal of added amenities. I have skills you might ask for. Skills you might be needin'."

"This looks like a private residence." Betsy was swamped by misgivings.

While she didn't care about her reputation, she might not want to sully his any farther than he'd accomplished by fighting with a student. *Why should I care?* Still, there were certain proprieties that needed to be adhered to.

"I can't stay here. My staying wouldn't be appropriate. Who owns the place?"

She would be surprised if this wasn't his place. She knew from what Caro told her about Evan Murray, he did have funds though she implied he spent more than he made. That was why he needed the extra coins.

"Very astute, Miss Darling."

Her blood pulsed, he was laughing at her again. One more time, she was the subject of his amusement. "You're not funny."

She clenched her teeth together wishing she could see into his mind. Knowing what he wanted would make dealing with him so much easier. Unfortunately, she could read his mind all too well. Too many times to count, she didn't even understand what he was telling her. Over, then over again she replayed the strange conversation they had in the carriage, most of which went beyond her meager abilities to understand his play on words. Even though he was an exceptionally handsome man, he could be infuriating most of the time, bossy as all get out, arrogant in the extreme. When he spoke, he expected to be obeyed.

"I'm quite serious. There is plenty of room in the townhouse. The place is much more comfortable than any hotel you could afford. There are no bed bugs in the mattresses, no fleas in the carpets. The servants keep the rooms immaculate, free from dust. I've a competent cook who will be delighted to create wonderful dishes for your culinary pleasure. When he is around that is."

"This is your townhouse."

Betsy felt the blood rush from her cheeks. She grasped the side of the carriage to steady herself as the world around her seemed to turn, "I can't possibly stay here with you. What would people think? They would say..." *That I was his lover...*

"Why not?" His wicked grin did nothing to bolster her confidence. "It's your choice, Miss Darling. Don't let it be said I forced you in any way."

"You're a man," she shot back at him the most obvious of her objections, the only objection.

Her gaze raked over his splendid form. He was everything a woman's dreams were made from. This was what she wanted, she had to remind herself. He was the next thing to a God. The need to pinch herself to make certain she wasn't dreaming swept through her.

"Here I thought you hadn't noticed. I was beginning to feel as if you didn't appreciate my manly good looks." Gallantly, he offered her his arm. "Shall we take a look. I'll give you a guided tour of my city home. You can have the room next to mine. That will be most convenient since we will need to discuss everything you want."

"Next to yours?" she queried softly, her voice wavering.

No matter her intentions this was happening faster than she expected. She'd thought it would take most of her time with him for her to get what she wanted. True, she wanted this man to take her virginity. It was just that...just that...the devil she didn't know. This was too soon for comfort.

"Didn't I just say so?"

"But..."

"You don't want free lodging, fine by me." He stepped back to the carriage and looked up to the driver struggling with her trunk. Began to tell the driver to stop. "The trunks..."

He looked to her again as if anticipating her acceptance or to just make sure he was doing what she wished. His masculine gaze seemed to shout out that she truly had no choice but to except his invitation.

She hugged her bag carrying her parasols, books, along with the newspapers to her chest. "No wait. I..." She swept her tongue across her dry lips, tried to swallow. Found the gesture useless. "I don't know. I'm not sure. Evan..." The sound of her voice echoed in the humid air as a thin undecided wail.

Never before in her life had she been indecisive, especially when she didn't understand the reason she protested. It made no difference if this was his townhouse or his brothers. She felt certain he had more than one place to live. This was close to the university. She could see some of the buildings from here. In some cases, she would be able to walk to the library. A brisk walk in the morning always stimulated her senses so she could think better. She wouldn't need him to accompany her everywhere. She sifted in a huge breath of flower-scented air feeling as if she was in over her head where this man was concerned. She could never guess what he was going to do or say next. The man was outrageous.

Hadn't she come on this trip for the precise purposes of losing her good name? If she didn't make herself unsuitable, Oliver Tindell would continue to ask her to be his wife. At first, she believed he wanted her for his mistress. For some reason that evaded her, the man changed his mind. The man was loathsome. Thinking about him caused her to shudder violently. She would do all in her power to disgust the man, including losing her virgin status.

Why was she fighting this man who was handsome as sin? Her stomach turned over a couple of times at the thought of lying with Evan. The churning was nerves. She'd made her decision. She wouldn't let herself down. Evan was the man she would give herself to. He just was making the doing so easy it frightened her. Was he? She felt as if he read her mind, understood what she was praying for.

This was what she wanted. If she slept in the room next to his, wouldn't it be easier to let him seduce her. He could come to her in the middle of the night...or the other way around. The devil, he charmed her quite thoroughly in the carriage on their way to his townhouse, a stroke of his long neatly clipped nails here then there. He touched her places. When he did, she desired more from him. Oh, she wasn't positive what more entailed but what she did know was that she wanted to find out. She'd never felt so breathless in her life. Her heart never beat so incredibly fast. Parts of her throbbed with an ache she never felt before. At one point she even leaned into him. His chest was hard, just as she thought when she first set her eyes upon him.

"Make up your mind. I don't have all day." His hands rested on his lean narrow hips, his words impatient, his eyes hard. He was staring at her as if she lost her mind.

Perhaps she had.

Evan didn't have all day? What else did the infuriating man have to do? Why was he acting this way? Well, she never understood men. She certainly didn't understand this man. He was an enigma to her parched brain, "Yes," she said sounding out of breath. "I'm sure this place will do just fine."

With a smirk, she also didn't understand, he waved to his driver to continue with her trunk. "There's a real nice tub up in the master bathroom adjoining my room. It's large. Lots of hot water heating close by so the bathtub can be filled then refilled when needed. Takes the kinks out of a hard day's work. I call it my hot tub. Eases all the strain. You will enjoy bathing there. It's refreshing."

"Tub? Hot tub?" She felt her eyes growing wide. Why on earth... "Hard day's work?" Did this man ever lift a hand to work? Let alone hard work? "I would enjoy bathing there? I'm sure." Her stomach turned over again. Did he mean...did he think they would enjoy bathing in the water together? He astounded her.

What if...

...could she?

"Don't they have them in London?" he asked, the sound of laughter clearly resounding in his voice. "All the tub needs is some bubbles to further soothe strained muscles. Ah, do you like a bubble bath? Not quite what I was thinking." He made a gesture with his hand. "If we are in the tub together, there will be no bubble bath. Sorry I brought that up. Don't want to smell of a brothel."

"Don't have what?" She blinked a few times wondering if she'd suddenly gone insane. Betsy wasn't at all positive she was following this conversation. "Bathe together?"

Betsy was lost. Bathe with a man? At the same time? In the same water? That was impossible.

"Bath tubs, of course. What did you think I was talking about?"

She didn't know. He baffled her. The driver left the trunk on the ground before leaping up to the seat. He saluted then pulled away. Without looking back, Evan started up the drive to the front porch.

"Mr. Murray?"

He turned.

"My trunk?"

From his lips came a weary put-upon sigh. He moved to the trunk, opened it, looked inside. After righting himself, he shut the lid. "You do know, hauling around heavy things is not good for a man with a bad back."

She was astounded as well as startled by the declaration. "Do you have a bad back?" He positively did not move like a man who had back trouble.

"No, but if I lift heavy objects, I could. Not at all good for the male disposition. In my future years I don't want to walk around bent over at the hips."

She thought she might teach him a lesson. With a great deal of effort, she lifted the trunk, grunted, then heaved in a huge lungful of air. She wasn't going to be able to get the trunk to the porch let alone up the steps. Teaching this man a lesson through his stubbornly hard head would never happen.

"I'll get the door for you," he said as he bounded up the front porch two steps at a time.

When he reached the door, he did exactly as he said.

Unable to stand this a moment longer, she sat down on top the trunk, pushing her bag to the grass below. He didn't stop to see if she was following. A moment later, he disappeared into the house. At least at the hotel she would have had help.

From the initial effort of lifting the huge trunk, sweat beaded then dripped in the valley between her breasts.

He poked his head out the door. "What is taking so long?"

Unable to help herself, she picked up the parasol jabbing it in his direction. "I can barely lift the thing let alone carry it."

"Why didn't you say so? I would have asked my butler to bring the trunk to your room."

He disappeared again.

She heard him calling out to someone in the house. Only a few seconds passed before a very large, well-dressed man hurried down the steps. He looked much like a man who could lift anything. Tall, muscles in all the right places. Long sandy hair was tied in a que at the back of his neck. Betsy thought he might have scooped her up with the trunk if she didn't stand up quickly. Easily, the butler lifted the trunk to his shoulder then walked to the door.

Betsy followed the man. Once inside, Evan waited for her. She smiled at him ready to start giving him the benefit of all her doubts. "This is lovely. You're right. This is much nicer than staying at a hotel in the city."

"Much less expensive too. I'll show you to your rooms."

He tossed his top hat on the coatrack. He ignored her when the tall man who carried her trunk up the steps walked into the room then bent to speak to him. For a while Evan and the butler talked to each other in hushed tones. After the conversation seemed to finish, he bowed, turned crisply on a heel to exit.

"That was my butler. His name is Alexander. He will get you anything you wish. All you need do is pull the bell chord. There is also one in your bedroom. Before he does anything else, he is going to heat water for our bath."

His gaze roamed the length of her. Settled on her bosom as if he meant to memorize the slight swell above her traveling gown.

He turned to her then yawned. She stared at the elegant clock on the mantel. The time was three o'clock. She wished she knew what he was thinking.

Betsy couldn't help the next questions even though he just sent his butler to heat water. Nerves caused her mind to scramble. "What do we do now?"

"You're buying my services. What would you like to do? For me, I thought I would relax in the tub, soothe my strained muscles. This trip to pick you up was exhausting. If you don't want to take a bath...no, of course you want to join me."

The not-so-subtle innuendo in his voice sent a pulsing vibration through Betsy. Vividly, she was brought back to the last part of the carriage ride when he held her on his lap, stroked her arms, her collarbone, lower to touch almost intimately. She swallowed hoping to bring moisture into her parched mouth.

"What are those?" Trying to take her mind off Evan's outlandish suggestion, she found herself staring at a bag sequestered in the corner.

"Clubs for golf," he said almost reverently. "Do you play? I happen to love the game. We could go a few holes. That is if you have the time. It would be fun. We could wager something. Perhaps a riding lesson."

There it was again. She thought her eyes would cross. "I thought that is what they might be. Is that how you exercise. I do like to walk and I'm a great believer in exercise. I've never played golf, so there will be no wagers."

"I believe in a good round of exercise too."

Once again, he stared at her blatantly. When he lifted a dark eyebrow, the gesture looked suggestive to her.

What the devil was he advocating?

Betsy didn't think they were speaking of the same type of exercise. One more time this conversation flew beyond her reach or her muddled brain. She was growing angry with the man. "Would you teach me or is that a lesson I would have to pay you for?"

"Yes, to both," his voice softened to a slow husky sound his golden eyes seeming to be touched by sunlight. "Very definitely, yes, to both."

"Several of my employers play golf," she said adding to the conversation that seemed to take on a decidedly stilted tone.

"You don't say."

His doubting tone disturbed her. Unable to think of what else to say she blurted, "I walk for exercise."

"Uh-huh."

She was repeating herself. Didn't like that fact too much. She tilted her chin as if that would make her point. "Exercise is good for a woman."

"A good glass of Bordeaux is important for a man. You want a glass?" He stopped for a moment, tapping his chin. "Certain types of exercise are very good for a man."

"No, thank you, I..." She stopped herself. The hour was early for wine. Nonetheless, she found that a little fortitude might get her through the hours until the time for bed. "Yes, as a matter of fact. I'd adore a glass of wine."

"Good, wise choice. You can have the bedroom at the end of the hall upstairs. I'll meet you in the bathtub in the master bathroom with a couple of glasses as soon as you take your clothes off."

Take my clothes off?

Her body went numb with his words. The room swayed slightly. He was always doing that to her. Before she could tell him what she thought of his proposition, he vanished. She scowled. For a man who moved slowly, he seemed to cover a great deal of territory in a remarkably short amount of time.

What was she to do now?

Take off her clothes? What then? She drank in a huge breath of air that didn't seem to go where she wanted.

The question for her now was what was she going to do? If that invitation wasn't blatant as well as bossy and arrogant, she didn't know what was. She walked the distance to her bedroom. The door connecting their rooms was open. Quickly, she shut that door understanding the wood wasn't much of a barricade. If he wanted to walk inside, that was exactly what he would do. There was no lock on the door.

After that she reminded herself she didn't want a barricade from him. Wasn't he playing into her hands quite admirably? Before she could blink, she might be well used, not at all what Oliver Tindell wanted. The disgusting man wanted a wife. That woman wasn't going to be her. What she did know now was that she wasn't going to take all her clothes off for Evan Murray.

Was she?

How else was her virtue to be compromised?

While she wouldn't mind sharing the tub of hot water if indeed it was as large as he told her, she would never get in that water naked. She sifted through the clothing in her huge trunk pulling out a chemise that would cover her to her knees. The top was laced together with blue ribbons. The cotton was sheer, would be sheerer when soaked in the water. The covering would never amount to much of an obstacle. While she pulled out a small hat she adored, she reminded herself she didn't want an impediment between them. This one didn't have feathers decorating the brim. There was an assortment of colorful ribbons that held tiny silk roses. On to the bathing room.

Her body quivered wondering what he would do in the tub.

Bathe, you ninny. What does everyone do in a bath?

For some reason she didn't believe that was all the arrogant, self-assured man wished to do. Oh my, when she closed her eyes, she too easily recalled the path his fingers took when they were exploring her. She would like him to do that again. Sightsee. Charm. Seduce. Wanted a kiss too. Never truly been kissed.

In the carriage, he didn't appear to want to kiss her. All he did was investigate those parts of her body that were left uncovered. He told her to take all her clothes off. Did that mean he wanted to scrutinize all of her. She would certainly appreciate inspecting all of him. She wanted to see if he was as hard as he appeared.

Heat sprinted upward to spread over all of her. Her hands flew to her hot face with the idea to cool the skin. With a heavy sigh, she stripped all the dusty traveling clothes from her body. Getting naked with him would just be utterly impossible. She shivered as the cooler air flowing into the room from the open window caressed her flesh.

Her nipples tightened.

Swiftly, she dressed in the shift. After that she grabbed a robe and put that on too, added the hat. Belted the robe. Removed the hat. Thought again. Donned the hat. The clothing just was not enough protection. The man didn't wish for her to wear anything, no armor.

Betsy knew this scenario with Evan was happening way too quickly. She thought perhaps after they got to know each other a bit better she would feel more comfortable with a dalliance. Now, she knew almost nothing about the arrogant beast.

All she liked about him was what little she'd been able to see of his body as well as how he felt when she sat on his hard thighs. For her purposes, his intellect had little to no bearing. She would take whatever he would give her if it kept Oliver from her. As a desperate woman, she couldn't be too picky.

Would he be naked?

That thought was almost too much to bear. Her knees wanted to buckle. Instead, they knocked together. She clutched the back of the chair to steady herself. Once again, the room around her seemed to whirl and spin with alarming speed. To gain equilibrium she closed her eyes.

Heavens, she wasn't at all certain she could walk to the bathroom. Perhaps she should get down on her hands and knees then attempt to crawl.

"You coming this year?"

Oh Lord, he was calling to her. Impatient, he might not wait for her to figure out how to go about gaining the courage to put one foot in front of the other so she could get to the tub. What would he do about that?

"Y—yes," she murmured softly.

A lump began to grow in her throat. By the time she finally reached the bathing area, the lump would be gigantic.

"What was that? I'm going to have to put more hot water in the tub if you wait any longer. Don't like extra work."

Oh, yes...he would have to do that. When he stood, he would be naked. She would see all of him. Convincing herself now that she wanted to see all of him was difficult. All her nerves seemed to be stripped thin. Her stomach fluttered. Heat pooled in parts of her she never understood would feel that way.

She should tell him that she didn't want a bath. If she did, what would he do? He seemed to always get what he wanted. He would most likely come after her. The wine, ah, yes, the wine would do wonders

Remember your motives. Don't forget the end game.

Betsy reminded herself one more time she was not typically indecisive. Around Evan Murray, she couldn't make up her mind about anything. He was so suave, confident. That was because all the decisions he was forcing her to make were outrageous, challenging her. What other man would expect a woman he met that very day to get naked into a bath tub with him?

She could tell him no.

Saying no to something she wanted would be foolish.

Lifting her chin, she walked to the door she closed earlier, found that he opened it sometime when she debated with herself. The devil he might have watched her disrobe. Might have already seen her without a stitch.

Hesitantly, she stepped inside. His bedroom was decorated in blues, all different colors of blue; navy blue, light blue, turquois and more. Her feet sunk into the plush carpet that must have cost a few pounds. A clock chimed four times. At the sound, she jumped. For a moment her heart stopped. Had it truly been an hour since she first arrived?

"Are you coming?" his words were spoken slowly, slightly husky yet smooth too. He sounded impatient.

"I'm here."

She stepped into the decadent bathing room breathless from her spiking nerves.

He was right. The tub was huge. Would seat at least three fully grown people. The water lapped at his shoulders. He grinned at her then lifted his glass of wine in salute. "You made it."

Behind him there was a table. Resting on it was another glass along with a freshly opened bottle. A huge mirror was hung on the wall in front of Evan. When she did get in, he would see her in the reflection of the glass.

Betsy looked at the nearly full bottle. She never drank more than one glass.

"What are you waiting for?"

~ * ~

Evan leaned back in the tub, relishing the feel of the hot water swirling around him. The grin on his face he knew was self-satisfied, keen on what was going to happen between him and Betsy as soon as he could work his sweet-talking vocabulary on her sensual side. Now as to this wonderful bathtub, he marveled on what a bit of money coupled with a creative idea would buy. He always wanted a huge tub he could share with the woman he was seeing. At this time though, he couldn't help the thoughts that kept revolving around Betsy Darling and what was hidden beneath her hat as well as her clothing.

Ah, the woman was everything that annoyed him. That damn rain napper was not to his liking. Her hats were hideously unflattering. She would have to leave the blasted parasol home when they traveled to the museums and libraries. He would insist. Even at all that, he was almost shocked she agreed to accommodations in his home putting her in a very precarious situation for a female especially when he decided to put her in the adjoining bedroom to the master chamber.

What the devil was he supposed to do when she had her nose in a book? Rock on his heels with his hands behind his back while he watched her? At the first opportunity he meant to ask Caroline or his brother or Letty. Ah, but Letty, with Bobby by her side, fled back to their country estate. Perhaps they could visit. No, he was thinking at least for the time being he needed to keep Betsy close to him. He didn't want distractions getting in the way of their relationship. Privacy with her was just the way to get what he wanted. Two days or possibly three, he would have to make certain he increased his efforts to get her into his bed.

Alexander poked his head into the room to check on the necessities. Everything was perfect. Water heated. His butler and valet left an extra bottle of wine on a counter near the tub. A tray of delicacies was nearby in case either grew hungry. Seduction, in his mind, would just be a matter of time. If not tonight, then soon. He could almost taste her.

The door leading into the bathing chamber was opened. Betsy walked through, her chin in the air. That was another thing that annoyed him, that damn little chin always tilted to the sky. She was armored. He noticed that first thing. Next, he noted the hat. Good God, she was going to step into a bath tub wearing a hat! What she wore beneath the heavy brocaded robe was anyone's guess. Anything except the shield would have been out of character. There were a few things he learned about her on the way here. One, that Betsy had an instantaneous temper. What would she do if he provoked that flare of anger into fiery passion? Two, he understood she liked to be in charge of the moment. When they got around to lovemaking, he wouldn't allow anything but her passion to surface. He would control the moments; when she climaxed would be at his whim not hers.

Nostalgically, he sipped his wine then tilted the lip of the crystal her way before motioning her inside. Evan intended to make certain she understood exactly how this would play out. Women didn't get in this tub with him wearing clothes. Ah, there weren't many women he invited into this male sanctuary. "You naked underneath all that fabric? In a bathtub you don't need to wear your breastplate. Naked?" he queried, his voice soft, enticing her he hoped.

Exciting. Generating a wealth of excitement. He wanted to know if her sweet nectar was raining down.

Those cornflower blue eyes of hers flashed too many kinds of surprise for him to count. With his question, her shoulders stiffened. The devil, her entire body stiffened. If she carried any of her parasols, she would have pointed the fabric covered stick his way. "You didn't think I'd come here naked, did you? Of all the absurd notions."

Well, he did but he didn't. Lifting his shoulders in a masculine shrug he continued with his dictates, "Can't get in the tub with your clothes on. That's not how a body takes a bath. Naked. It's a house rule. If you want to share water with me, you have to abide by my rules."

True amusement flickered in her eyes. Instead of her parasol, she pointed a finger at him. "Your rules don't mean anything to me. If you close your eyes, you won't know what I do or I don't have on. What a person doesn't know won't make a bit of difference in the long run. Now, will it?" Her fingers stalled at the fabric belting her waist. She peered into the water. "Are you naked?" she shot back at him before biting her lip as if she regretted the question.

He took another sip of wine then regarded her innocently. "Now, that's one of those things a true born Scottish lady would have the answer to without asking. Leave the question to the British."

She hesitated. Something shimmered in her eyes. Temper? Anger? Embarrassment? He wanted to understand every facet of Miss Betsy Darling. She unbelted her robe then let it drop to the floor. Wide eyed he stared. She was an amazing bit of fluff. He never dreamed...not in his wildest imagination.

After his first bout of astonishment, Evan choked. Wine sputtered into the heat of his liquid paradise. Right there in the hot water, his penis shot to full attention. Miss Betsy Darling wasn't at all what he expected. The devil, what had he expected? Not this!

It wasn't the fact he could partially see her sensuous form through her chemise. The cloth was soft cotton that molded to the sweetest curves he ever witnessed. No, it was the entirety of the body beneath the fabric. This was one lady who didn't believe she had to be reed thin to be in the height of fashion, not that she was overweight. He'd bet his last dollar that she finished her meals with gusto as well as passion. Betsy Darling had herself a true woman's body, with nice curvy hips and real curvy breasts, pink tight nipples that seemed to be begging for kisses. He was just the man to accept and relish their plea to be sucked into his mouth. When a man was in bed with her, he wouldn't have to do a sight check to make sure he was touching the right things.

Her skin was milky white, flawless, nothing marred any part he could see. Soon he would welcome all of her to his gaze. If he had his way, the chemise would not cover her silken flesh for much longer. Her legs were long, endlessly long, nicely shaped as well. She possessed delicate little toes. Despite Betsy's abundant curves, he also noticed all of her was trim including a narrow hand-span waist. Although she didn't possess a hard, muscled body the only parts that wiggled were the parts that were supposed to do so.

Must be all that walking.

Interesting, she must have pinched her cheeks before walking into the bathroom. She also put some lip tint on those amazing full lips turning them a nice rose shade. He was happy that the shade wasn't darker or redder because that mouth, red, courtesan red, would have proved to be more than he could handle, gazing at that plump bottom lip of hers. Betsy Darling was turning out to be one of life's great jokes. Putting that face coupled with her delectable body parts on a woman with a domineering, commanding, order shouting general's voice had to have given the Almighty more than one round of laughing.

He picked up the wine he had waiting for her—not that he believed for an instant she would drink the liquid—then held the glass her direction. She strode toward him. His aggravation returned. She appeared as if she was on the fringe to liberate Napoleon, not relax in the heated tub. Her chin pointed up, her shoulders stiff, her spine even stiffer. This woman didn't know the first thing about taking life less seriously. During the next month or so, he could certainly teach her a few new techniques.

He found himself both looking forward to that as well as intrigued.

She settled into the water as far away from him as she could maneuver. It wasn't long before only her shoulders and a pair of thin white straps could be seen above the level of the water. What was under the water was an entirely different story. For a few seconds he feasted his eyes. Despite her covering, he could see her breasts, rosy-tipped, bobbing on top of the water.

"We're inside the house. No sun shines down on you to create freckles. You might consider taking your hat off—that is if you're not self-conscious about your—you know. Promise I won't judge you."

"What?" Her eyes widened in what appeared to be alarm. If it was possible for her chin to point higher, he felt certain it did.

Inside he was grinning at Betsy. He lowered his voice to a husky soft level. "You know. Your bald spots."

She flashed him a look that might have melted stone, could have set paper to flame. Her amazing body shifted beneath the liquid heat, sending water lapping against him. "I don't have a bald spot!" She was furious, her passion raging.

Temper, temper, saucy lady. Let's see what happens when it detonates.

That was the emotion he was interested in igniting. Women with blazing tempers were always passionate in bed. He manufactured a look of compassion. In a soothing voice, he began, "Lack of hair on one's head isn't something to be discomfited about, Betsy Darling. I'll have to say, the condition is more acceptable among men than women. Needless to say, a bald woman might have some endearing qualities. I can imagine how soft the top of your head might be. Kinda like a baby."

"I'm not bald! Whatever put such an outrageous notion into your feeble brain?" Underneath the water he watched her small hands clench then unclench several times.

"Admittedly, I don't have a great deal to go on. However, every time I've seen you, you have a hat glued to your head. What kind of a person wears a hat to take a bath? You've got to agree, my assumption was reasonable. How do you go about washing your hair with a hat atop your honey-kissed curls? Now, that is a reasonable question. If you ask me, that is."

"I adore hats... I'm not asking you. Of course, I remove the hat if I intend to wash my hair. What would you think? That I would ruin one of my favorite hats?"

Her temper was clearly growing.

"I suppose that if I had your particular problem, the loss of hair, I would find soothing comfort in wearing one."

"I don't have..." She rolled her eyes, looked at the ceiling then without a blink she tossed her hat aside. "You have an unearthly sense of amusement, Mr. Murray. Are you happy now?"

When he taunted her about the hat, he did himself in. His gaze rested on a wealth of golden curls touched by fire, kissed by honey more pronounced when the shifting sunlight filtered through the window across the top of her head. The streaming locks appeared so soft, so pretty, the fact she was such a pain in the butt left his head. If he sifted his fingers though all that silken glory, he could more than tolerate her sass. The best thing about the loss of the hat, he only had one more garment to get rid of. He supposed her anger again might do the trick.

He was mesmerized. Enthralled by all that golden hair.

That amazing second passed him by the moment more words left the confines of her mouth. Reality bit him in the butt again.

"About tomorrow, we need to discuss our agenda. I've several necessities I need to take care of, Mr. Murray."

She was back to business, all starch and vinegar. "No, we don't. Are you going to drink your wine or just hold the glass. Your arm will get tired. My name is Evan. Anything else makes me sound like a school teacher."

"You are a school teacher, Mr. Murray," she blurted out as if he didn't have a brain in head.

"Evan. No, I'm a highly sought out professor of biology. That's far different from a school teacher."

"What do your student's call you?" she asked him sweetly, her voice turning to syrup it was so sugary.

"Why are you really here, Miss Darling?"

For a moment Betsy looked stunned as if with that simple question he uncovered some dark secret she wanted to stay locked in her head.

She smiled. "I've told you. Research. A paper to be written."

He sipped thoughtfully, before topping off both glasses. To add to her wine, he had to move closer to her. The glimpse of all her soft curves displayed so tenderly beneath her clinging chemise didn't help the throbbing pulsing part of him that needed relief.

After he moved back to his section of the tub, he began. "I think you've other reasons for coming here. I think you are running from someone or something."

Her reaction fascinated him, telling him he hit the nail on the head.

Downing a goodly portion of the wine, she scowled at him, then stuck her bottom lip beneath her teeth. "Running? Whatever did I say to give you such an absurd notion?"

"Yes, I might be able to help if you let me in on your secret. Has some man threatened you."

The look on her face changed as she paled to the color of freshly fallen January snow. Ah, there is a man involved. His guess was right. For some reason the thought didn't please him. She should never be made afraid. A myriad of possibilities raced through his head. None of them he liked.

"No," her voice was tight.

She finished off her wine setting the glass behind her.

Evan wasn't going to let her get away from the question he wanted an answer to. "A man wants to marry you but you don't love him."

That was one possible scenario.

She shook her head, seemingly unable to utter a word. He wondered if she needed more wine. Wasn't going to ask. Once more, he moved to her side, filled her glass. He stayed right where he was, shoulder touching shoulder, male hip to feminine curve. When he looked down, he saw the long expanse of her white thighs, the tawny dark hair covering her woman's mound. He somewhat kept his reaction back. If she looked beneath the surface of the water, she would see his stiff arousal, something he couldn't hide.

"A mistress...this man you've come to Scotland under the pretense of research wants you for his mistress. I would run too. I can protect you." If she became any man's mistress, she would be his.

Her head jerked up. Her face turned the color of a death mask; smoke and ashes. His thoughts hit on the truth or very nearly the truth. He didn't intend to torment her with the fact. If she didn't want to be some man's mistress, that was her business not his.

"I..." He watched her swallow hard. "I loathe the man."

"Why not just tell this detestable fellow, no?"

"I have numerous times. He thinks if he forces me, I'll have no choice but to except him. I had to leave. Caroline invited me as did Letty. The research though is not a lie. I am working on a book, perhaps it will be an article. Depends on what facts I uncover. Remember, that's why I need you. You're my escort."

Ah, but she needed him for more than escorting. "Tomorrow then?"

He actually did not want to discuss tomorrow when there was so much of today left to speak about. Betsy needed to relax. Her nerves were stretched to a snapping point. In this home, the man she loathed was nowhere close. She was still about as stiff as a poker.

"First things first," she began. "I want to go to the university's library just to scope out the lay of the land, so to speak. Could we do some sightseeing too?" She looked hopefully at him. "Before that I need to buy some new clothes. I left a lot behind because what I had wouldn't fit in the trunk. Also, would you happen to know of someone who could give me a tattoo?"

This was the second time since she waltzed into the bathing chamber he spewed wine. This time half of the stuff went up his nose and was now dripping out. A few momentous seconds passed him by before he could speak. "What did you say?"

She couldn't possibly have said what he thought she said. *Tattoo?*

She pushed some of her unruly damp curls from her face then regarded him earnestly. The devil but he'd give good money to know what was whirling around in that pretty head of hers. "My first choice would be a Celtic cross. I'm afraid that might be too hard to draw or the color might be all wrong. The thing might look like a bruise. That wouldn't do at all. There are so many possibilities. What do you think? Any ideas? Normally, I don't have trouble making decisions. Since I came to Scotland my head has not been attached completely."

For the first time in his life the power of speech deserted his agile mind. The experience of Miss Betsy Darling was so disconcerting he slid beneath the water and stayed there. He had to have some time to think before he could confront this woman again. Not long enough. There wasn't enough time. Before he ran out of breath, she started tugging on his armpits trying to bring him up for air. Her breasts nearly touched his cheeks as she straddled him. If he wasn't careful here, he would drink in a gulp of water or one of her beguiling breasts. That just wouldn't do. Her tugging coupled with his need to escape for a few more seconds annoyed the hell out of him. His scowl was plastered to his face when he emerged for air.

After several drinks of air, he was finally able to say without a hint of the censure he felt. Women weren't supposed to get tattoos. "You want to get a tattoo?" Her nerve to smile at him annoyed him more.

Lifting delicately creamy shoulders into the air, she spoke softly. "I didn't realize there would be such a language barrier in Scotland." She pointed one lovely long finger at him. "The next time you decide to dunk your head underwater, please have the courtesy to tell me before you do it. I thought you were drowning."

Unfortunately for him, the moment he emerged from the liquid, she returned to her seat as far away from him as possible. His blood pumped harder and faster than he thought possible. He felt the vein in his neck pulse a damning speed. On top of his thighs his fingers clenched into tight fists while he tamped down the annoyance with this woman that now turned to anger. "My question has nothing to do with a language barrier. Women don't get tattoos!"

Her body stilled as she seemed to assimilate his quick-tempered fiery words. Good, she should think about all he said. Out of the blue, she pushed hair from her face once more. Her rounded breasts bobbed on the surface. This time she wound the long shimmering strands into coils before she fastened her hair into a tight neat bun on top of her head. If the woman had any idea how much he saw of her when she did that, she would undoubtedly faint. After that, as the seconds ticked by, she stared at him with her cornflower blue eyes.

"What exactly do you mean? Women don't get tattoos. You cannot dictate to me. Where you are concerned, you've no rights. No say in my life."

He sure as the devil could dictate anything he wanted. She wasn't going to mar that lovely flesh with an inked pointed needle. "Only sailors get tattoos." Bloody hell, it was clear she was riled. For the life of him, he didn't understand the anger. "Women are respectable, conservative. Does this have anything to do with that man who wants you for his mistress?"

She blanched. With his question he hit the mark. To his surprise, she rose from the water. Without the parasol, she directed a finger toward his chest. The expression on her lovely features told him she wasn't about to back down or give into his command. "I'll have you know, Mr. Murray, if it's what I want, I'll damn well get one with or without your help! It's a wife he wants. Not a mistress. I refuse to be either."

Evan started to laugh but found himself distracted by the way her chemise was stuck to her breasts, her hips, her legs. How he could see the coral tipped buds pushing against the fabric then lower the honey flaming hair covering her mound. Arguing at this point would be a waste of time as well as energy. "You don't say," he got out trying to keep his tone bland but failing.

"I am—I am...entirely dishonorable! I have no morals to speak of," she murmured the last. "I'm in a bathtub with a man I only met a few hours ago. I'm ruined."

As he looked at her appreciatively, his grin widened. She couldn't possibly know how much her flimsy cotton chemise uncovered. Though he certainly did. "You aren't naked. Can't be too ruined. You've been avoiding the rules. A woman can only be ruined if she follows the rules and wears nothing at all."

This was a fact he couldn't stop from pointing out to her, a fact he was on tenterhooks waiting to witness her reaction.

Her face turned a beautiful shade of rose then as she stood with her hands pressed to her hips, the color heightened to a wonderful red. Even her mouth turned fiery red, theatrical red. He drank into his lungs a secret breath. The plumpness of her scorching red bottom lip enticed, dared him to kiss to taste as well as suckle until her tiny shrieks of pleasure could fill him. She wasn't ready for kissing. Before he could blink or inhale from the pure pleasure of watching her bountiful curves sway and dance beneath her chemise, the minimal covering left her body. She tossed the fabric on the floor a goodly distance from the tub. The chemise landed with a soft plop. His nerves splintered to a scattering point.

"There! Don't ever tell me I'm respectable again. Obviously, I'm not! Now I'm ruined!"

Standing in front of him bare-ass naked, she was the most delightful site he'd encountered for a long time. When she placed her hands on her hips that part of her that was supposed to move oscillated invitingly, begging for the strokes of ecstasy he longed to impart.

Unable to help himself, his amusement cracked from his mouth. This was like taking candy from a baby. In all his wildest dreams, he never expected anything like this. In this rare instance, there was no seduction necessary. As if she suddenly realized exactly how vulnerable she was, her hands flew to her breasts then lower as she tried to cover all her feminine assets. Those womanly charms were so bountiful two hands would never shelter them. Suddenly, she sat down, looking from her chemise to him before doing the same again.

With her back to him, she grabbed her glass of wine. Took a long, deep swallow. Seeming to think better of hiding from his perusal, she turned back. Her lips thinned into as much of a line as possible given just exactly how ripe the bottom lip was.

"Should we talk business or pleasure?"

Evan couldn't stop himself from asking, excited to see her next passionate reaction. Watching her closely, he understood her sudden regret. Her remorse was his God send. This was exactly what he wanted and it was happening so much sooner than he anticipated or even hoped for.

As she fumbled around, first with her obvious bravado then with her shaking hand on the stem of the glass, he knew she was having a bit of trouble coming to terms with her temper as well as the finality of what she just accomplished with her pique. Her temper seemed to constantly work in his favor.

What the devil would she do next? He imagined it was just a matter of time before she waged war on herself again. All he had to do was prod her the tiniest bit to get a sensual reaction from her. Give her a reason for her temper to do battle with her common sense, he'd reap the rewards.

"You never answered my question."

"Business."

"Believe I don't want to give you a choice. We'll talk more business tomorrow over breakfast. That will be soon enough for me."

Miss Betsy Darling was turning out to be deliciously unexpected. He stared at her heaving bosom while she seemed to be attempting to rein in her seething temper. When she moved in any way, the hard ripe berries tipping her breasts would show themselves above the water. The fact she was stark naked in a bathtub with a naked male made the task difficult for her. If his guess was correct, she'd never even come close to disrobing in front of a male. Probably made love with the old stodges that were her lovers fully clothed.

"That suits me just fine."

He chuckled softly. She was staring at him as if she wanted him to leave the tub. Fortunately for him, Alexander showed up just then to add hot water to their bath giving them another ten minutes of heated bliss along with whatever sensual conversation he could inspire.

After tucking in a few more gulps of wine she began to speak with bravado he understood she didn't feel. "Now that we have that settled."

He didn't think anything was settled between them. He could wait until she unwound herself again. "Go on."

"I want to know where I can have my tattoo done. By tomorrow afternoon would be more than nice."

Regarding her with a bland expression, he suffered all her demands making a mental note she wasn't going to have her way in this particular scheme. There would be no tattoo for Miss Betsy Darling. He would figure out something. Didn't have the slightest idea as of this second. Helpfully to him, there was nowhere around the university one could get a tattoo. She would have to go to the waterfront. That was too damn dangerous for a single woman. At least she couldn't walk there. She could always hire someone else to take her to the waterfront. He'd be damned if he would allow that.

Bit by bit, he was beginning to put her story together. At the root of her problems was a loathsome man, one she detested quite thoroughly. But then...he was also becoming one of her problems. For some reason he didn't understand, she wanted to do things to make this man dislike her. From his experience, her reasoning was faulty. If the man wanted a mistress, well, hell, all she had to do was say no. Wait, she just amended that to wife. She could still say no. Refuse to say the vows. Why would she have to get a tattoo to keep the lord away from her? Something that would be permanent. Once again, he reaffirmed his viewpoint on this issue, on his watch she wasn't going to do so.

"Search services are extra," he murmured sporting a wry grin of enjoyment as he watched her eyes darken a sure sign her temper was rising. "If this is what you want, I'll do all in my power to see that you have it."

"Even if you disagree?"

"Yes."

He thought she was going to stand again.

~ * ~

"How much extra?" she gritted out through tightly clenched teeth.

"That ten pounds a day doesn't even come close to covering the demands that will be made on me if I must look for someone who will give you a tattoo. I would have to go to a dangerous part of the city, putting my life at risk."

"You consider finding a person to give me a tattoo as extra service? It could not be so very difficult."

"Yes, Miss Darling, I do. Sailors get tattoos. You understand what that means?"

She didn't.

It didn't take a clairvoyant to know his fee was too good to be true. He was going to charge for anything and everything he could. To Betsy it seemed he arranged things specifically for his benefit. Plain speaking was needed now. Evan would have to be upfront with her. "Exactly what does my ten pounds a day cover?"

With a bland grin, he proceeded to tell her. "Driving, making certain you're not accosted by the riff-raff, waiting for you at these libraries you want to see as well as the museums. Finding a place that will give you a tattoo is extra. I also don't do hair, or manicures, or helping you to dress though assisting in undressing would never cost extra. If I must waste my time at a modiste, that would be extra. If my opinion is needed on a fashion plate or fabric, that would cost you more."

Unable to help herself, she hissed a breath of air. "I didn't ask for those extras. I don't need help dressing."

Lifting an arrogant eyebrow upward, with a grin that spread broadly against this face, "Undressing?"

"No!"

"Massage as well as assistance taking your clothing off before bed or a bath is included. Of course, you know that."

"Massage..."

Her mind whirled. That would involve him touching, stroking...

"Suitcase hauling is not included as you discovered earlier. However, if you insist or are unable, the amenity will cost you an extra fifty pounds. My back, you understand. Taking you sightseeing is included in the basic fee. If I need to do any translation, some of the residents of Glasgow still like to speak in the old gaelic, sometimes the nuances of their dialect are difficult to understand, I'll need to charge you by the hour. As for sex, that's an additional thirty pounds. Does that seem fair to you?"

Even though she knew her mouth was gaping open, she couldn't find the wherewithal to shut it. She wondered if she'd somehow gotten water in her ears. She didn't think so. He'd been rambling for what seemed an eternity. She was positive he most likely left something important out.

He shook his head. "You do have a point. Well, your open mouth does. Please don't drool in the water."

"I don't drool!" She jerked upright furious he would imply something so ludicrous. When she noticed the rosy tips of her breasts swaying on the surface, she slunk down.

Continuing, "I need to be more generous with my fees. Perhaps a discount if you promise to keep your parasol at the townhouse. Let's make it fifteen for sex and that will cover the entire night, not just one time, you understand. A woman on a limited budget would have to agree you won't find a better rate than that. You could always ask Letty what her women charge for an entire night. I assure you, they charge more."

With a great deal of effort her tongue came unglued from the roof of her mouth. "Sex?"

"You look as if you've never heard the word before. Yes, the entire night for fifteen pounds." He popped a chocolate delicacy Alexander left on a plate near him into his mouth. "Lately, I've been thinking about Letty as well as her girls. Just how unfair this double role is to male escorts. Her girls charge much more for just one time, never the entire night. The devil, it's discrimination, that's what it is."

Betsy couldn't stop her heart from thundering, nor could she take her gaze from his mouth, a mouth that was shocking her to the tips of her toes with his outlandish words. She found she was both disgusted as well as strangely captivated by his services. She'd never imagined anything like this went on. "Women pay to have sex with you? I didn't think it was done that way. You being the son of an earl and all. Why would you need money?"

With lazy eyes, coupled with a secret expression, he regarded her as if she was slow witted. "Don't get me wrong here. You were the one who hired an escort. Because I am the second son, the spare, I don't own the privileges of my older brother. Don't have the resources he does. I along with my younger brothers have been quite overlooked. We need to find our groats wherever we can."

"Caroline assured me I hired a driver."

"A guide, an escort, a driver; didn't Letty explain to you what you are paying for? They are all the same."

"Evidently not."

He bit into a pastry, chewed thoughtfully casting his gaze toward the mirror. "You've quite a lovely back. Your little butt, what I saw of it, is nicely rounded."

"My what?" Her eyes widened.

"I'm going to have to talk to her about this. Don't like it when my clients don't understand what their hard-earned groats are going for. There shouldn't be any deception. She should have taken into consideration the Sassenach often misjudge their neighbors to the north. Because of this miscommunication, I find myself in an awkward situation. Don't like uncomfortable. What I mainly like to talk about is pleasure as well as the talons of ecstasy that will race through a woman while I see to her needs."

Talons of ecstasy?

Betsy thought she'd never been put in such a difficult situation as he claimed he was in. Nonetheless, as her mind began to digest what he was saying, she understood her deflowering might happen sooner than she expected. With little trouble, she could deal with that. One night with him and she would no longer need to worry about Oliver taking something she didn't want to give to him.

Sex for hire? The thought roughed around in her head.

Had she just been given the answer to all her troubles? If she didn't have the necessary maidenhead that Oliver coveted, he would no longer want her for his wife. Would he take her word? No, but he might if she could induce Evan to sign a document claiming he'd received that pleasure. Her stomach clenched at the thought of what she was about to commit to doing. No, this was unconceivable. Unreasonable.

She could. She couldn't. She wanted it. She didn't want it.

Why not? She only had until she returned to London to escape the net the despicable Oliver Tindell had woven so tightly around her. Sleeping with the second son of an earl would be ever more scandalous than a tattoo.

She considered the possibility that Caro along with Letty had chosen Evan for just this reason. The man was absolutely perfect. Neither Caro or Letty knew about Lord Tindell's plans. However, both knew something else—how much Betsy's regretted her limited experience with men. They both understood she wanted to return to London without her maidenhead.

Chapter Three

When Betsy heard of Caro's behavior with the older brother, she'd thought of the possibility of becoming part of Letty's household. Caro was purchased by the younger brothers as a birthday present. What no one knew was that Caro wanted to get pregnant. She calculated the very best time to do so. Not one person involved expected the oldest Murray sibling to take umbrage at the fact the woman he'd come to adore vanished. When he discovered she was also increasing, he put all his vast knowledge at work to make certain she had to rely on him. Unfortunately for Caro, no one would disregard the feeling that Caro gave the house a bad reputation. The ladies who worked their walked a fine line. More scandal would never be tolerated. It was, however, Letty's idea to hire Evan who created the scandal himself.

They were both between jobs.

She had no experience with men. Even when she ventured out on her own as a tutor for the children of aristocratic families, she was never allowed enough freedom to see men. Since she usually lived on the third floor of their homes, suitors, if she'd had any, would have never been allowed access to the third floor.

Even if that wasn't the case, she never had the time to meet people. She did love her research as well as the children she taught to read and cipher. Had spent time in the libraries in London along with all the museums. Once she did meet a man, Scott. That's all she wanted to recall of his name. She didn't want to think of him as the situation became more than uncomfortable. Until she met this man, she began to resign herself to a single, childless existences. Within a few months of meeting Scott, she fell head-over-heels in love with him.

When she met him on her days off in the library, they usually strolled through the park. They would stop for tea as well as a bite of something to eat. They would speak of the country's history, enumerate on various philosophers. Maybe it was wishful thinking on her part. She thought he felt the same about her. Scott was kind, good-humored, and attractive in the scholarly, rumpled fashion that had always appealed to her. They shared so many interests a friendship ensued.

She allowed herself to be satisfied with their comfortable companionship until a drizzly day last February when she spent several hours with one of her charges. The gloomy weather combined with her upcoming twenty-fifth birthday and the sight of the little girl sick with the flu overcame her common sense. She went to Scott's rooms that evening then as subtly as possible, indicated that her feelings for him went beyond friendship.

With the first sight of the stricken expression on his face, she understood she made a terrible mistake in judgement. He was suffocatingly kind as he let her down gently telling her they could only be friends and that he wasn't attracted to her in that way. "You're, well, you're just so commanding, determined. A general in female clothing. I could never... I need a docile woman. One who will dote on my every word."

When he looked pointedly at her parasol, she began to understand. Seemed the parasol also annoyed Evan. She certainly didn't understand why. All she did was point with the darn thing.

Nothing he said sounded as if it was a compliment. A bit later she'd been forced to smile during his wedding to a pretty, twenty-year-old shop girl who didn't know where America was. At that instant she supposed he didn't want a woman who was possibly more intelligent than he was.

Betsy remembered both Caro's as well as Letty's expression of sympathy when she told them about Scott. She understood Caro was just as naïve when she met Duncan. He taught her everything about the ways of men as well as the intricacies of sex. Just as Bobby taught Letty. They were two of a kind. Letty too, even though she owned an escort service, didn't have any idea about the ways of gentle, sweet men.

"So, you're still a virgin," Caro said seeming to understand her problems more thoroughly than she did. "What do you want to do about that little fact?"

"Well, I did have one relationship. It ended quite badly. Other than that, I know nothing about men. Don't want to return to London the way I am now."

Still, hiring a man for the sole purpose of sex seemed nothing less than outrageous. She gave up the pretense as there was nothing for her to explain. Yes, quite embarrassing. Of course, she didn't know that was what Evan was when she hired him to drive her around the city. Damn and blast, there was so much she didn't know, she didn't have one clue where to begin to learn.

"You should never be embarrassed about lack of knowledge where men are concerned. You are simply, discriminating. For you, only the right man will do," Caro told her one time over a cup of tea and chocolate cookies. Caro did love her chocolate.

At his moment those words rattled around in her head. She was about to propose sex with a man she barely knew. Was about to pay for the sex, that could hardly be described as discriminating.

Hiring a man for sex would never occur to her if it weren't for Oliver hovering over her, waiting to get her where he wanted her, naked in his bed. She wasn't actually aware of just how different this would be. Nonetheless, the biggest difference was that Evan fascinated her while she loathed Oliver. Evan possessed abundant masculine power as well as grace. Oliver's stomach hung over his belt. She felt heated tremors when Evan touched her, when he looked at her with his glorious eyes. Oliver made her skin crawl with revulsion. After agonizing for so long as how to rid herself of the pesky lord that haunted her, could the solution be so simple?

So different?

Needing to understand more of Evan's proposition, she began by moistening her parched lips. This was so much more than she expected. Her heart lodged in her throat as she began, "Um... Your sexual services..." Hoping for more courage, she cleared her throat. "What exactly do they involve?"

His wine glass stalled have way to his lips, his eyes darkened to warm honey. The smile that had hinted at amusement vanished while he tapped one finger on the crystal. The dinging set her nerves on edge. For several seconds, he stared at her. Opened his mouth to speak. Shut it. Opened his lips again. Downed the rest of his wine.

"Well..."

"Yes?" Frantic, eager...she waited.

The muscles in his throat convulsed as he swallowed the wine. His surprise, no, his shock was obvious by the stunned expression on his gloriously handsome features. He positively would not be difficult to kiss. She wasn't at all certain as to what came after the kiss. That was something else about him that made him more appealing than Lord Tindell. As she thought earlier, Tindell wasn't at all handsome with his sagging jowls coupled with beady pale eyes. Imagining kissing that man was an impossible feat.

At this second, Betsy felt certain she could read Evan's mind. Shuddered at the thought he might reject her as Scott did. She didn't think she could take that type of rejection from a man who expected to be paid for that very service. Her next thought was to change her mind before he turned her down. Just his wide eyed honeyed-gaze seemed to burn her to cinders. What his hands on her body would do? His kiss? She couldn't begin to imagine.

Evan would believe she was too conservative to hire him for sex. She was certain he regretted reducing his price so quickly. She would have paid just about any amount he demanded for one time with his gorgeous body. The devil, she didn't know what to think. Before this was over and done with, he would probably raise the price to something she couldn't afford.

Somehow, she would manage.

He set his glass on the table behind him. When he turned, the expression he slanted her was something entirely different. "Uh...anything the customer wants...within reason. I decide what that is."

Her mind whirled with the possibilities as she tucked her bottom lip between her teeth, worried the flesh as she thought. She had to force her mind on the practical. Considering this emotionally was all wrong for her. This relationship was not about love, just about sex. Continuing on a rational vein was imperative. There were, after all, practicalities to consider. There would be nothing demonstrative about this relationship. What they did would be impersonal.

"What about syphilis? You know, disease, sexual diseases? Do you take precautions." Making eye contact with the man was impossible so she pretended to study the floor of the tub, focused on her toenails. She saw her knees, then her toes before swirling the water to make it more difficult for anyone to see her. When she looked toward him, she witnessed more of him than she thought possible.

He was indeed naked underneath the liquid heat. The dark hair on his chest swirling lower to his...groin, was quite obvious. Betsy swallowed air. She burped. Shocked, she covered her mouth. He grinned.

For a short time, she didn't think he was going to answer her. She didn't understand why she didn't look earlier. His face was contorted as if in pain. She thought then some of that last gulp of wine he drank must have slithered down his throat to the wrong place. "I don't have any diseases. I've always been careful with my clients. You don't have to worry about contracting something from me."

"How can you be certain?" Before she slipped into bed with this man, she needed to be positive he wouldn't give her something she'd come to regret.

"Ninety-nine percent. I don't visit brothels or seek encounters from the street. Don't need to find women that way." He paused for a few seconds while it seemed he studied the mirror behind her. He lifted his masculine shoulders in a heavy shrug. "It's like Letty says, sex always holds some factor of risk. However, I'm positive I've no disease." It was then he turned his vivid honeyed gaze in her direction. "What about you?"

The question startled her. Her face along with her hands turned cold. Obviously, he didn't realize her status as a virgin. If he did, he wouldn't ask such an irrelevant question. "Me?" She shifted her head a bit sideways to look into his eyes. "A disease?"

"Yes, you. If I didn't want to know, I wouldn't have asked. If you are...well...with disease...I do have condoms we can use. Just allow me to know the truth. I'll take care of everything else."

"Are you daft?" was her first question then realized once again, he might not understand he dealt with a virgin.

He deserved to know the truth. She also discovered she didn't want him to hold that fact in his head. If he didn't know, she wasn't about to explain things to him nor was she about to take a chance that he would refuse to dally with an innocent. Once she dropped her gaze to what was underneath the water, she wondered how much of her he could see. She could certainly see a lot of him. After that, she wondered if he would find her lacking. She kept her gaze down while she spoke again.

"This is purely commerce? Handled professionally? You don't kiss and tell? We don't talk to anyone about what goes on in the bedroom."

"I would never..."

He ran one of his big hands across his chest. He grinned, "I, uh, offer a money back guarantee if you are not satisfied, no, more than satisfied."

She thought she was going to stutter. Somehow, she hung on to clear concise words. "The customer would dictate how the...encounter would go?" She didn't want that last to sound like a question Didn't want him to hear the absolute terror in her voice. Yet somehow the words came out in a question.

Thoughts seemed to be scattering in his brain as she watched the play of expression across his features. He nodded then began to speak in a voice that wouldn't allow argument. Evident, that he set the rules. "The client dictates the boundaries. I dictate the specifics. For example, if the lady has any particular fetishes..."

Her eyes crossed as he sent her off balance. *Fetishes?* She actually didn't know of what he spoke. Waving her hand in the air, a lump in her throat grew to gigantic proportions. She understood she was once more in way over her head. "No, oh, no, none. No fetishes."

She wasn't at all certain about sexual fetishes. In actuality, her only conceivable fetish was to make love with a man who loved her. Since this wasn't going to happen any time soon, she could say she had none. All she was going to make of this time with him would be only about sex.

Just sex.

No love.

Clearing his throat, he began once more to speak of the encounter they would have if she wished. "...if for example, the customer might say something to me like, 'Evan, love, I want you to tie my wrists to the bed posts...'"

Her head shot up. Her pulse fired into flames that couldn't get the blood past the huge lump hovering in her neck.

"Tie! As in slavery or captivity?"

Two rows of even white teeth shot to her attention behind his firm lips. He nodded. "If that was the case, I'd go along with her wishes because it's a boundary, her choice. However, the order of events after those wrists were tied is pretty much up to me. I would then make the decisions when everything else would happen. When she would beg for more. When she would reach her delightful climax. I like my women to plead before I grant them their pleasure."

"I...I see."

She didn't see anything at all. Bright red patches seemed to burn her cheeks. How could she actually be considering doing this? For her purposes, allowing Evan Murray to take her virginity would certainly be more effective in dissuading Oliver than getting a tattoo. Although both would be part of her for the rest of her life. One would show. The other would not. In her mind, Evan was still the perfect man for the job—physically irresistible. Handsome as sin. On the other hand, he was foreign to her as a soul mate. If she was going to be honest with herself, she wasn't likely to find her soul mate, the perfect match for her. A woman on the shelf rarely did. She didn't know of any cases where it happened.

"I should tell you I won't stand for any histrionics. Drama is out of the question. Once you've committed to something, then that's that. Are we in agreement?" He paused again as if thinking about his other jobs. "I also won't use a whip even if you plead. Well, if you just like to have the whip run across your naked flesh in order to increase your pleasure, I imagine I could do something like that. Some women like the feel of leather slowly sliding across their nipples as well as more dark, secret places. I would never hurt a woman."

Thank God.

"Many of my ladies do enjoy a little light bondage, of course there is no problem with that. At least not in my mind. Chains are also out of the question. Don't like the idea of chaining a woman to the bed or a wall.

Chains?

"Although, I'd be pretty much out of business without the scarlet scarves I use to tie wrists to bedposts. Women seem to love the scarlet scarves. In any case, suppression is your decision. I'd be more than happy to oblige if that is what you would choose."

She bent forward, knowing her eyes were wide as she tried to assimilate all he told her. Just as her blood stalled in her throat so did her breath. "You tie women to bedposts? With...with scarves? Scarlet scarves? I've never heard of such a thing."

This conversation seemed to be getting out of hand. All she wanted was to lose her maidenhead. Experimenting with whips as well as silk scarves boggled her already rattled mind. She began by shaking her head. Unable to help herself, she pointed her finger at him, wishing she had her parasol to emphasize her point more thoroughly. "Oh, I don't think so..."

He raised his hands in the air, water sluicing down his arms to plop into the bathtub. "Now, don't go all judgmental on me. I never thought I'd enjoy scarves at first. Not until I tied those tiny wrists above her head...that first time. Well, I'm not saying any more on the subject. If that's not to your particular tastes, then we'll try something else you might enjoy more. You just think about scarves though. I'd most likely be more than happy to oblige. Women do enjoy having warm brandy dripped onto their nipples. I suck the liquid off. Makes them squeal with delight. I find that to be quite delicious also. Would you prefer brandy or sherry?"

Sucking warm brandy off my...my, nipples? Sherry? Squeal? I've never squealed in my entire life.

With tremendous effort she sipped in as much air as she could devour in such a short amount of time. She didn't need any more convincing this might well be the answer to her prayers. What she needed assurance of, was if she would survive the encounter. One time and she would have no more need of his sexual services. So, why did she feel tears stinging behind her eyes. She realized then to her surprise she needed more than one night with him. Just listening to this man rattle off what he intended had butterflies dancing as well as fire burning her in places she didn't ever think of before he began speaking of fetishes. Waving a hand in front of her face, she tried to cool herself. She needed to duck her head into the water.

Courage hovered just behind her teeth. She willed herself to give him the approval he seemed to be waiting for. That agreement seemed to be stuck in her throat along with her pulsing blood and desperate pleas for breath. When she began this trip, she knew her life would never be the same again. She tried to weigh the different options using both her hands. Sex with Evan Murray in one hand, a tattoo in the other, there was nothing more to consider. Sex with Evan won out. Though a tattoo would make a definitive statement. A tattoo would repulse Oliver. She needed both.

Without giving herself any more time to change her mind, she nodded, almost stood, caught herself before she found herself naked in front of him again. That would happen soon enough. "Very well then...all right. Yes, that sounds satisfactory. How do I pay you?"

His other customers must be more worldly than she because her inquiry made him lift an eyebrow. She regarded him coolly until he grinned using both corners of his mouth. This one was not a lopsided smile.

Raising his head, he looked startled. "It does?" He stared at her, looking at bit dumbstruck. "Cash is fine, I'll also take vowels as long as you can prove that you will pay them."

"Tonight would be fine for me. What about you?"

Best to get this over with before she had the inclination to say no. Second as well as third thoughts still assailed her, maybe even fourth. Fire danced in her body when she thought about his earlier words.

"Tonight?"

She finally managed to say something that didn't need more courage than she possessed. Indignation in her tone. "Do you have another client? If so, we could put it off until tomorrow. Though I don't think when I'm paying you the exorbitant fees you are requesting that you should escort someone else."

"Oh, well, no, tonight is just dandy for me."

All conversation seemed to come to a standstill. The water was growing chilly. She shivered but she didn't think the shudder that went through her had anything to do with the coolness of the liquid surrounding her. No, Betsy was certain the cold she felt had more to do with what she just bought. More than anything, she wanted to get out of the cooling water then hide away in her room. She couldn't because she was stark naked and trapped. Her stomach felt queasy. Her mouth was parched. She closed her eyes as she sank farther down into the water.

She bought sex.

Never in her wildest dreams did she ever hold the belief she would do something so different from her basic nature. Despite the attempt to convince Evan she wasn't conservative, she was.

She still couldn't believe what she did. Caro would never believe her. Perhaps she would. Caro didn't buy sex. What she did was lie to a man. Pretended to be a prostitute. When all that was accomplished, she tried to steal his baby. After a lifetime of propriety, she turned her back on everything she believed in.

She bought sex from the sexiest man she ever encountered. May the good Lord save her.

What to do now except to go through with the plan. Her body heated anew. Whenever she thought what was said in the bathtub, her cheeks felt hotter. Talons of flame swept through all of her.

"You can look now," he said, his voice raspy, sounding whiskey smooth to her.

A few minutes ago, he didn't sound that way. A few minutes ago, he sounded amused. Now, he sounded as if he was in pain. If she looked, what would she see?

Now, she declared her stupidity like a bumbling fool. Well, where sex was concerned, that was what she was. As soon as he began lifting himself out of the tub, she dipped her head like a skittish old maid. Okay, that was indeed what she was. So, perhaps her actions were true to character. As much as she didn't want to be on the shelf, she was. Why couldn't she be nonchalant as well as urbane about his nakedness.

Because she'd never seen a man wearing nothing.

Evan certainly wasn't self-conscious about his body. It was only natural for her to want to see him. Quite badly.

Now that she did, her mouth went dry. If she tried to swallow, she wouldn't be able to do so. Even with a towel wrapped around his slim hips, he created such extreme dancing of butterflies in her she could barely fight the sensation. The towel fell low, inches below his navel. Trickles of water slithered like tiny fingers down his chest and along the flat plane of his abdomen through the dark hair adorning his chest.

He possessed a beautiful body.

She hired that body for the night.

"Like what you see?"

Her head jerked up to see into the warmth of his eyes. "Excuse me?"

"Your eyes crossed."

"Oh, well, I was thinking. Believe I'm getting a bit chilly. Would you mind fetching my towel?"

She tried not to stare at his chest or his face, or his knees that poked out beneath the bottom of his towel or his long feet. There was hair on his toes. *Oh my!* "That is, if there's no extra charge."

What a ninny. You'd pay for the delivery because you don't want to spend any more time naked in front of him than will be required tonight. If he brought her the towel, he would see all of her through the crystal water. Undoubtedly, he would wait for her to step from the tub so he could wrap the towel around her.

Slanting her the overwhelming grin he'd undoubtably been using to demolish women since he was born, he nodded. This man was unprincipled. Decadent. Immoral. Along with a wealth more adjectives she could articulate now. That very fact made him perfect for what she needed. His self-indulgence also made him perfect for his job, an escort.

The moment he vanished through the bathroom door, she hurried from the bathtub and pulled on her robe of armor. He ignored her question. Why did that surprise her?

"Never mind," she called out to him as soon as she fetched her chemise. "I got it." She rushed through the adjoining door to her bedroom then closed the tiny barrier between them tight. Shaking her head, unable to stop thinking about tonight, she leaned against the solid wood, breaths straining her lungs.

This evening she would take a giant irreversible step toward the fulfilment of all her dreams. She would be free of the loathsome man who coveted her. As soon as dinner was over, she would lose her virginity. It was why she came here.

~ * ~

Evan rested in his office thinking about the woman, Betsy Darling. When he sat across from her in his bathtub, he watched her shoulders disappearing into the tub. The small gesture did little to conceal her. He could see all her generous curves quite nicely through the crystal-clear water. Even when she wore her chemise most of her was visible. When she moved, tantalizing parts of her showed while other parts disappeared until she moved again. He'd never been with a more appealing woman.

Each time she nervously licked her lips as he watched the tiny pink tip of her tongue sweep along the crease of her mouth, he felt as if was going to explode. The dewy moisture left behind, he needed to taste and savor as he tugged on that same lip. He couldn't believe the things she'd said to him. When he began talking about fees as well as fetishes, he'd just been amusing himself, having a bit of fun at her expense. Betsy was so adorable when her eyes crossed. If he didn't know better, he might believe she was virgin, a very long-in-the-tooth virgin. Not for a moment had he thought she'd believe his outrageous statements or be drawn so quickly to his machinations. He discovered she was one serious woman. When he told her he accepted vowels, he'd thought she would understand he was bluffing. Baffled by the ease with which he lied to her. He actually had her believing he escorted women for extra money. Evan was certain that one notion would eventually do him in. Eventually the woman would call him on his lies. He imagined he would deal with that when it came to pass.

His chuckle rattled around in his brain for a few seconds while he sorted through the mountain of paperwork on his desk. Daily, the reams were growing. Damn, he didn't have one urge to take care of this. Even so they would be removed from his desk. He never liked leaving work for another day or even an hour. Today, he couldn't concentrate on work. All he could focus on were the sweetly generous curves of Betsy Darling. Oh, she was most definitely a darling woman.

He gave himself a couple of days to seduce her. The deed didn't take more than about twenty minutes in the bathtub. He'd always been good with women. This was a record. He should pat himself on his back. Well, even though she agreed to the rendezvous, she wasn't as of this moment in his bed. He shouldn't assume all would proceed as planned. Anything could go awry.

Ah, memories were always so good. He didn't even have to close his eyes to vividly recall that twenty minutes of heated bliss. As he'd gazed at the liquid heat swirling around the base of her neck, he felt a moment's hesitation. After that he recalled how bossy as well as controlling she was, his least favorite kind of woman. Recalling the brief moment of semi-remorse, his hesitation disappeared. Betsy wasn't any dewy-eyed virgin. The woman was experienced to the tips of her lovely delicate toes. This lady understood exactly what she was about.

She wanted sex.

He was willing to give it to her.

She was willing to pay.

However, she would get sex his way not hers. He could just imagine what her lovers were like, probably a bunch of old guys with names like Leopold or Ichabod, perhaps Osgood. They would allow her to dictate all that they did together. Wouldn't give her any thrills, either. At this point in time, she was on an extended vacation, between jobs as she so neatly described her present situation. For her, there was no one around to tattle the secrets of her nightly escapades. He certainly wouldn't kiss and tell. Seemed she had a hankering to get laid by a man who still owned his teeth. Who possessed a body worth exploring.

He was more than pleased to oblige most of her whims as long as she left the damn parasol tucked neatly away in her trunk. Her personality didn't draw him. It was her curvaceously feminine body that did the trick along with the gorgeous smile she flashed him when she wasn't trying to decipher his outlandish suggestions. He would make sure those scarlet silk scarves were nearby just in case she asked for them.

The devil, recalling the conversation when she told him, she wanted to keep the lights on. Well, that suited him just fine. He loved seeing the body he was going to get himself into. Hers might be very different. He was pleased she wasn't shy.

When she began to dictate the terms of their lovemaking, he tried to hide his surging irritation. She told him no cigars or cigarettes, no tobacco of any kind. Next thing she'd be telling him when to kiss or stroke her.

"I don't smoke," he told her blandly.

"Would you provide brandy or perhaps sherry?" she'd asked.

"Uh-huh," he'd supplied with a flat tone.

Whatever spirits she wanted he would make certain they were on hand. Didn't he tell her some women like to have brandy sucked off their tightly swollen nipples, other places too. He didn't mention that other place. Perhaps that was exactly what she was thinking. In any case, he wasn't about to give away all his professional secrets.

"Music, I do like music. Classical would be the most soothing. Mozart, I believe."

When she said this, she'd placed one of her long slender fingertips on her bottom lip pulling it slightly forward. Fire shot with lightning speed through him. If such a tiny gesture did this to his body, he was going to be in for a night he would never forget. Did she expect him to stop in the middle of lovemaking to play the pianoforte?

Retreating to the basics. Another list. Why didn't that surprise him? It didn't. She seemed full of herself now that she bought his services, she meant to control what they did. Didn't she listen to him? No, apparently not. No woman would direct or dictate his lovemaking. The very thought was downright offensive.

Evan steepled his fingers beneath his chin. He'd known he had to put a stop to this surge of control before she got right down to the color of the sheets. He cleared his throat taking in the taut lift of her chin.

"No music." He'd told her with enough force she'd jerked her face up to look at him. The cornflower blue of her eyes darkening with what emotion, he was unsure of. He went on to tell her, "Keeps me from concentrating on the job at hand. Need to focus on all your delicate erogenous places that beg to be kissed." To give emphasis, he was shaking his head. "Absolutely no music. There is no way if you take a moment to think about it. I won't hire a musician to play for us while we have sex."

"Oh," she swallowed, he'd noticed the motion in her neck.

A moment later, she sipped on the wine left in her glass. She must be feeling a bit muzzled by now. She hadn't eaten a morsel. Now she'd downed three good sized glasses of the sweet Bordeaux he offered her so she'd relax.

"If that's one of your dictates. No music. I can deal with that. I don't suppose you would want to stop what we were doing to play. I don't play." As she seemed to be fascinated with what was beneath the water, she was looking their again. Suddenly, she looked up. "Imagine then I should tell you I'm terribly ticklish."

"Forewarned is forearmed."

Ticklish, was she? That thought spurred on others. He loved ticklish women. Tickling was such a delight. Naked body meeting, rubbing over more naked body.

"Claustrophobic." She moistened her lips again. He could hardly wait until he tasted that tender pink tongue along with the liquid heat left behind with each slow swipe. "So, the position might be important to dis—"

He had to quash that notion, nip it in the bud. "Pardon me for interrupting here. Let me point out that I am trained in the art of sex. I will dictate the positions, not my client. I do know best. However, you can make suggestions. I will regard each one carefully."

Those words about positions gave him even more reasons to believe she was far from innocent. What virgin would speak of different positions during sex? Tonight might be even more fun than he imagined. It wouldn't be beyond the notion she might teach him a thing or two.

"Oh...yes." This time she actually bit on her plump lip, worried it as his gaze fastened there and his arousal spiked harder than before. He realized she was seducing him with what appeared to be practiced ease. "One more thing, after we are finished, Mr. Murray, we won't discuss what happened."

With a sigh of satisfaction, he sank into the tepid water. "Miss Darling, you just turned into every man's fantasy."

She cocked her head as if she didn't understand. "Thank you."

"By the way, you are cooking this evening. For privacy, I gave my chef the night off. You do know how to cook, don't you?"

His was a question he shouldn't have to ask. All women knew how to cook. He reminded himself that Caro wasn't that great a cook though she could bake anything that contained chocolate. Hmm...he'd also heard about the cinnamon rolls she baked one afternoon. That might be fun to try.

"I don't know how to do anything in the kitchen except boil water."

"The devil!"

He would have to rummage around the pantry and see if there was anything he could put together quickly for a light dinner. Something else he might have to teach her. Cooking had never been one of his greatest's skills. Nonetheless, he would never starve.

Good Lord, he would remember that conversation in his bathtub for the remainder of his life. Restlessly, he rose to pour himself a brandy. After that, he once again made himself comfortable in the plush chair behind his at-home-desk.

Returning to the present, he pulled out a stack of scientific papers that needed to be rehashed before he wrote his next lecture. His next lecture had no date associated with it. After several minutes of blank staring, he cursed softly beneath his breath. All he could see when he looked at the reams of biology research he was supposed to read was Betsy's bubbies.

Ah...Betsy's bubbies...beautiful...delightful.

The problem now as he saw it was that he wasn't going to get any work accomplished until he made love with this woman. Once that happened, he could put her out of his mind. Rarely, did he ever want a woman more than once or twice. Boredom would set in. When that happened, he would say his goodbyes. The fact occurred to him; he couldn't say *au revoir* to Betsy until she was ready to return home. That could be months away.

Evan wasn't at all positive why she attracted him so intensely. While she possessed a body he needed to explore, there were other women with forms as well made as hers. Well, he did have to admit even though he didn't want to do so, the instant attraction came from her amazing body. Her personality still managed to exasperate him to no end. Somehow when he got her beneath him, he didn't think she would rile him.

The devil, she wanted to talk about positions. What could she know about positions when all she had as lovers had been old men with no teeth. Maybe she found a book when she was about her research. What was she researching? Ah, he sat back in the chair, stuck his feet on his desk and smiled. With his hands behind his head, he drank in several long breaths of air. Spurs of fire flamed from his groin. He burned just thinking about this evening's adventures with delectable Miss Betsy Darling. Desire for a woman with a baby doll face and cornflower blue eyes and a bottom lip that begged for attention held him in an enticing vise.

Tonight. All night.

He could hardly wait and he wasn't going to settle for anything less than the entire evening, even if for some reason she tried to renege on what she purchased. Sitting back, he sipped the fiery brandy, enjoyed the warmth slipping down his throat. Wondered if she would burn beneath his touch. From what little he knew of her, he sensed she was passionate. He needed to feel her passion explode.

Back to the present. Bloody hell, he understood there were a wealth of papers he needed to go through before dinner. She couldn't cook. He couldn't concentrate. The clock on the mantel read five-twenty-five. He'd mentioned six as time for dinner. He could get started on the meal if only to see what was in the pantry. Maybe his chef left something for him to concoct. In that case, dinner preparations might not be too hard.

Even before his suspension, he'd begun to worry about himself, stress about the course of the rest of his life. He was restless. Though he loved the students, adored the job, he began to doubt this was how he wanted to spend his future. He didn't have any great research projects or ideas that he could pursue. There were no grants with his name on them waiting for him. More and more, he'd become interested in the financial and business affairs that swept through his brother's office. The few times his brother sent him in his place to negotiate deals that could change a person's fortunes, he'd found he was more than up to the challenge, the encounters exciting.

He'd always had an active sex life, but he hadn't felt the need to look for another woman since his last paramour left him. When he attended a ball, the women were all the same; colorless, disingenuous. They wanted him for his wealth, nothing more. He wanted a woman who would want him as much as he did her, needed one whose passion raged. A woman who might climax just looking as his jutting hard arousal. For Evan that woman didn't exist. Instead, he was plagued with the feeling that a man who had more money than he could spend in a lifetime should be happier with his life. Ah, now that Miss Betsy Darling appeared seemingly out of nowhere, his body as well as his agile mind miraculously returned to life.

Despite that bloody parasol, her order-giving, the lady was exactly the distraction he needed. In addition, he didn't have to worry about Betsy stirring up another scandal—the last thing his career could stand—when he dumped her. There was no way a conservative soul like Miss Betsy Darling would let on that she'd used her vacation time to satisfy her hankering for sex to hop in bed with a stranger.

Besides, she amused the hell out of him, which was strange, since he generally couldn't abide domineering women. Betsy was so clueless that being around her was pretty much like standing in the exact middle of a flawless joke. She never knew what to think of his eccentric suggestions. At times neither did he. They seemed to just pop into his head.

Now, he intended to use her to keep himself from thinking about the young pup who attacked him, the one he was supposed to apologize to in order to regain the life that he was growing bored with. Yes, indeed, Miss Betsy Darling was just what he needed to perk up the next month or so while he waited for the Dean of Student's temper to cool. If it never cooled, Duncan's eventually would.

Betsy dropped the potato peeler he'd handed her for the third time.

For some perverse reason, he thought he would teach her a few things in the kitchen. A woman should know how to cook at least something. She said she could boil water. He'd assumed that was for tea.

She caught her lip beneath her teeth, did that crazy thing with her teeth while she drove him to the point where he wanted to put her on the table, lift up her skirts then bury himself deep inside her. That was not what she was paying him for. Though he could mention the scenario to her when the time was ripe. When she returned her attention to the carrots, he held back a howl of laughter. Her nervousness was written all over her face, her body, the tension of her shoulders.

"How are the potatoes doing?" he asked, remembering since she could boil water how hard would it be to drop potatoes into that hot liquid. Grinning, he sauntered to her. A little kitchen foreplay might be in order. Fondling her beautiful jewels might be fun. She was so nervous; she wouldn't be any good in bed if he didn't ease some of her apparent anxiety beforehand. Foreplay might make the nerves more apparent. A few sexual games before hand might ease the way.

She dropped the peeler again then spun around.

He took in the daffodil yellow day dress she had changed into after the bath while he'd been trying to sort through his paperwork, failing miserably. The dress caught the golden fire of her hair. The lace around the corsage was just low enough to reveal the rounded tops of her breasts. She wore no corset. That was good he supposed. One less piece of clothing to remove before he could thoroughly seduce her. Her cornflower blue eyes stared at him as if they couldn't look away.

He lifted the lid on the pot of boiling water and potatoes, picked up a paring knife then poked at the potatoes. "These are about done. You got those steaks ready?" He understood all she'd done was peel vegetables.

"Steaks?" Her eyes widened in question.

"You forgot about the beef?" He straightened then nodded to the pile of carrots she was peeling. "If you're expecting rabbits, they will be more than pleased. Put the peeler away."

She blinked and looked down. Instead of peeling just a few, she'd peeled all that was in storage. Enough for a dozen people or more. Her expression was endearing, confusion written in her eyes.

He gave her a knowing grin, combined a couple of lazy stretches while retrieving a bowl and pan from separate cupboards. Somehow a cannister of flour appeared along with a stick of butter. With a slow flick of his hand, he dredged the meat then set it sizzling in the pan. Would she sizzle as hot? He groaned.

"You watch those while I get us some wine."

His chuckle he felt certain could be heard when he walked away. Her stomach was most likely doing flip-flops. She looked so nervous he almost felt sorry for her. The pulse at the base of her neck surged. For another second he watched her with tender concern he never felt for another woman. What was it about this demanding woman that both intrigued and fascinated then managed to annoy and exasperate? Other men might fantasize about a woman with cornflower blue eyes and honey hair, but he didn't believe in fantasies or dreams. He knew exactly why he was so jaded. Her name was Savanah McNeal. Once he thought he'd been in love with her.

Evan left for the wine cellar, a wealth of conflicting emotions in his head. He didn't want to remember his past. Tonight, was all about his present enjoyment of a woman with baby doll cheeks and cornflower blue eyes. When he got back to the kitchen, he lowered the heat on the steaks before pouring them each a glass of the red Bordeaux he brought with him.

Holding the glass out to her, he began with a flourish, "Miss Betsy, you've got to try and relax or you're going to expire before we even reach the bedroom. I wouldn't want that to happen." He felt a hoot coming as her eyes crossed again. Maybe that was a precursor to her temper. It seemed to him that happened when she tore off her chemise. It also happened before she asked about his services. That was when she stripped. He'd remember that bath fondly for the rest of his life.

"I am relaxed!" she spit the words out, her cheeks a blazing glory of red. Her bosom heaved upward as she inhaled a deep breath of air. "Alright," she murmured. "I'm as tight as that cork you just took out of the bottle of wine. While I don't want to admit anything, you're right. How do I relax?"

"Glad to see you understand what's going on inside you. Admitting to emotions is always a good start." He handed her the wine. "Drink as much as you like. I'll finish the dinner."

"You just don't want the meal burned." She looked peeved at him as if she now wanted to volunteer for the duty.

He choked back a bark of laughter not wanting to irritate her further. Well, what she said was very true. He was hungry for both the food as well as the tempestuous woman he was spending time with. "I need my stamina for the entire night. You will too. I promise." He winked at her then howled when her eyes crossed again. The devil if he got her temper blazing here, she might just disrobe in the kitchen as he recalled the erotic scene in his bathing room. He reminded himself she had the most exquisite pair of hands, other parts in addition. Thoughts of those long, slender fingers traveling over his body descended to his groin. He had to stop thinking about her until after they ate. Until she was naked and in bed with him, he needed to keep all the fantasies rambling around his head in check. That was when he should give her his full concertation.

"I'll try not to be too jumpy," she murmured softly.

To his delight she drank in a few more deep breaths of air then she sipped more wine. "Let's put you to the test." Negligently, he leaned against the counter, slowly tasting his wine, watching, studying. After a short pause, he began. "Here's what I'm going to do. Just to make a point, mind you. I'm going to touch one of your sweet body parts. While I'm doing it, you've got to remain perfectly motionless. If you jump, or squeal then you lose and I win."

"I agreed with you about my nervousness. You don't need to test me. I'll be just fine when I finish my wine. I don't squeal!"

"Now where is the fun in that? If I just gave in, I'd never have the proof. You will squeal when I have you beneath me."

"I don't want you to touch me!" She seemed to think better of what she blustered then quickly spat out. "Not until tonight."

The humor he saw in this was vivid as well as potent. He wasn't about to listen to her so he kept going with his original plan. "The body part of my choice. Let me see." His gaze ran from the top of her head to the tips of her toes then back to settle on the most potent part of her.

"Oh, my, that's not a good idea. Not a good idea at all. I'll decide the body part." Her voice was shaky, erotic, tantalizing.

"No, absolutely not. Here's where we disagree again. A small bit of sexual stimulation will help to get you ready for the bedroom, for my big bed. This idea of mine is a very good notion indeed." He took the glass of wine from her to set it on the counter. When their fingers touched, she jumped.

"You lose." He wanted the game to last a bit longer even though he understood he'd win with the first encounter. He should have stroked a different place. She had so many parts, he longed to fondle he had the devil's own time making up his mind.

"You cheated!"

"Why do you say that?"

She played into his hands. Obviously, she wanted the game to continue too. Continuing the game would be no problem for him.

"Because...when you said body part...well, naturally I thought...should we try another one?"

"Would you win if I touched the tip of your breast?"

"If I knew the game started, I would not flinch."

She would drown herself in words if she kept that up. He found he was enjoying each word. "You thought what, Miss Betsy? You could resist me? I don't think so."

"Just Betsy! I thought... Oh, never mind!" She snatched up a cucumber. "You're right as I told you before, I'm nervous. That's only natural. I've never...never done anything like this in my past." Her gaze was now focused on the cucumber she meant to peel. Her fingers were tightly wrapped around the thing. Clutching the vegetable as if it was her lifeline.

He was glad she only held one cucumber. Who knew how high the pile would reach if he'd bought more? Dang if she kept squeezing the cucumber, he might just have to show her something else to wrap her slender fingers around then hang on to as if she never wanted to let it go.

His voice cracked as his mind wandered over territory he should leave alone until further notice, "You've never bought a man for the night? Is that what you're telling me? What about the old men you've entertained?"

He was stretching her thin, challenging all she'd ever known about herself along with her preconceived ideas about men.

"Dear Lord, do you have to say it like that? What old men...?" Her voice squeaked on a high note. Her face which a second ago appeared normal, turned red again.

Damn, he liked watching her blush. Getting tired of that beautiful shade would never happen. "Simply put, I was trying my utmost to put the situation the way a gentleman might. Though I've never claimed to be one, I do try sometimes." He flipped the meat, listening to them sizzle just as Betsy would when the opportunity presented itself. "Now, why don't you finish with the vegetables so we can eat. Once we end the meal, we can proceed to more pleasant endeavors upstairs."

"Upstairs?"

"Unless you want our first encounter to be on the kitchen table, or the dining room table or..."

"No, no...this is fine. We need to eat. You're right again." She sounded as if she didn't want him to always have the last say.

To Evan, she seemed to be forcing herself to concentrate on everything except what they would be doing upstairs in his big bed. Occasionally, her gaze would roam to a point above her. He didn't think she was going to be able to eat a bite of this mouthwatering food. After a few more missteps, they were seated at the kitchen table. The dining table, he felt, was too large for just two people. If they sat opposite with such a great distance looming between them, she would inevitably be a bundle of seething, splintering nerves by the time they found his bed. He wanted everything to be perfect for her. This way he could keep an eye on her, refill her glass each time it was emptied. He would have to make sure he didn't give her too much of the potent liquid. He wanted her aware of every body part his nimble fingers caressed. If she fell asleep during their lovemaking, he would be devastated. Nonetheless, he would find a means to wake her.

Her face paled, turned a bit green around the edges. Perhaps eating first had not been the best notion. Obviously, she was feeling a bit nauseated. The thought that sleeping with him made her sick to her stomach didn't sit too well with him. None of the women he bedded before this got sick. To his relief, she sipped the wine. Dinner could always wait until a more convenient time.

Discounting her nerves for a moment, he began to fill his stomach with the delicious food. Her scowl told him she knew he wasn't the least bit nervous. He felt certain when he smiled, she knew he was amused. At every turn, Betsy did seem to entertain him.

"Your townhouse is very nice."

It seemed she was making idle conversation.

So, she thought a bit of small talk would ease her mind. Perhaps it would. "Thank you."

What more could a man say to a compliment? She nibbled a small bite of potato. Her gaze focused on the plate.

She set her fork down, was now wringing her hands. Once they seemed to stop shaking, she held out the glass. "More wine?"

He poured about two fingers high in her glass. "That's enough for now."

Startled, frowning again, she looked aggravated with him. "Have you ever had second thoughts about the way you add to your income?"

What more could he do or say? He shrugged, enjoying this conversation. "Not really." He dug into his steak. When he finished chewing. "Whenever the university bores me. You know how conservative the professors who work there are. Well, the escort service suits my needs. There is nothing about my outside activities that isn't...stimulating while the day and day out same-o-same-o at the university leaves a man wishing for something more exciting. Every charming woman I offer my services too is unique."

Obviously, she didn't bring her parasol so she used one of her long slender fingers to point at him. "Doesn't it ever present a problem for you when someone asks what you do to add to your income and you have to tell them you're an escort?"

"Problem? What kind of problem?" He set both forearms on the table, his gaze was what she thought was filled with humor

"People must know that you're just having sex with random women. Wouldn't that hurt your other career? Your reputation as a valued member of the university staff? Wouldn't they frown whenever a new rumor circulated. Did you ever stop to think that very reason might be the cause of your dismissal?"

"My other career?" He lifted an eyebrow speculating until she shot him another glare. "The two professions don't have anything to do with each other. What I do during my off hours has nothing to do with my status as a professor at the university. They don't own my free time. There are no rumors. I'm discreet."

That way she worried her bottom lip...the devil...as soon as possible he was going to do the same thing. He needed to taste, to savor, to drink in her flavor along with the scent of her. She looked forlorn, as if she meant to apologize. That would be something. She was going to apologize for setting up a situation between them, one that she totally misconstrued. Of course, he'd been the one to set her on the wrong path. He never denied any of her assumptions. Instead, he egged her on with more innuendos. When Caro sent her to him, she didn't think his brother's wife meant for him to bed her.

"Perhaps in London where you live what I do would be frowned upon. Here in Scotland people have respect for a man who's willing to use his free time, his time off work to make his life's work to service lonely ladies, to initiate them to pleasures they might not have received before. There are many women who leave me grateful that I showed them how a woman should feel after a man has made love to her."

Suddenly, she stood, palms flat on the table, her eyes darkening. "I am not lonely!"

Another eyebrow lifted as he focused on her flattened palms then along her arms upward to end looking into her flashing eyes. Ah, but she was a lady who doth protested too much. He amended then, "Ones who are sexually frustrated? Is that your issue, Miss Betsy. Are you sexually frustrated. I'll change that little difficulty for you."

Her eyes crossed as he understood he hit her problem dead center. She would never tell him so. She opened her mouth as if to deny his observation. Only she shut it again. She was sexually frustrated. He was the man to transform her life. Perhaps the sexual frustration was her motive in letting him finagle sex from her. They would both be pleased at the outcome.

~ * ~

Sitting down, she watched him. Everything he did seemed to spark from an easy grace as well as little motion as possible. The lazy persona he first showed her had to be false. So, why did he present an unflattering image?

Too often in her life she set her wishes aside out of deference to others. Tonight, she wasn't going to do that. She steeled herself for some pertinent facts that needed to be settled between them. She began cautiously. Too often what came out of her mouth seemed to amuse him. This was just all too new to her.

"This evening..." Nervously, she licked her lips before catching her bottom lip between her teeth. Quickly, she let it go sensing all too well that little gesture was one source of his amusement with her. "During our...what we are doing... this meaningless interaction...You must agree to stopping if I ask you to do so. If I say no..." She grew bolder until she saw the flicker of his honey-brown eyes.

"That's *no a* problem *lass*. If you say stop, I will. Sweet, Betsy darlin' you won't. I promise you that you'll beg as well as plead for more...and this interaction between us will be neither little or meaningless."

She was shaking at his words, her head her shoulders, her bosom. When she caught the direction of his focus, she tried to cover her breasts with a hand. The gesture did no good and served to entertain him further. "I won't?"

No, of course not, you ninny. You don't want him to stop. At least she didn't think she would.

To her chagrin, he'd finished eating and was now sitting back, his arms crossed over his chest. He'd pushed his sleeves up showing the taunt muscles of his forearms. With little emotion, he declared, "You won't. Simply because I guarantee you're not going to want to call a halt to anything we are doing. Unless, it's to ask for me to untie the silken scarves around your wrists. Although even then...well I'm not at all positive I would believe you."

"I don't want the scarves in the first place."

Her breath heaved with raw hunger. Desire flared whenever she looked in his eyes, at his mouth, the crisp dark hair poking from the opening of his white lawn shirt.

He had the gall to look disappointed. For a few seconds, she thought he might have something else to say about the scarves. If he insisted, she would give in to the intriguing possibility of the vulnerability the scarves would create. She wasn't at all certain she wanted to become more vulnerable than she already felt.

After a moment's introspection, she continued to blurt out her feelings. "I just believe there should be some ground rules established before we begin."

His brows swiftly drew together. He didn't appear to want anything to do with rules or lists. Evan always had this way of drawing his eyebrows together when a list or rules was mentioned.

She heard the long-broken breath of air he let loose.

"You realize I am the one paying for your service. I should have a modicum of say about what will happen." She let go of the cloth napkin that was wound around her fingers, letting the cloth fall to the table.

"You going to eat that potato or just poke it to death?"

Irritation grew. While she was looking at the potato, her eyes crossed. Suddenly, she was hot as blazes. His eyes seemed to rake over her. "As your customer, I was merely pointing out a few specific points. You know it's important to please me."

"Upstairs." With his head he motioned to the long winding staircase beyond the rooms where they sat. "That's where I will do more than please you."

"What?"

"Go on to my bed chamber." He pushed back from the table extending his hand in her direction. "You're a bundle of seething nerves. It's quite obvious that until we get this first encounter over with, you're not going to eat anything. If you can't eat, I won't be able to enjoy my meal. Secondly, you won't have the energy to enjoy the entire night. That is what you are paying for. Right?"

She looked at his empty plate then to the shimmer in his eyes.

He gestured toward her wine glass. "You can take that with you." He grabbed the bottle then the crystal housing her wine. "Here, let me carry it for you. I recall from this morning how much you dislike carrying things. I would oblige you in this strange fetish of yours. Glasses won't hurt my back."

"Fetish! I can carry my own wine glass. It's trunks that outweigh me I take issue with."

Before she could continue her tirade, she was somehow out of her chair finding herself steered by her elbow toward the stairs leading upward to the second floor. Her insides heated. This was it. After tonight, she would no longer be considered a virgin. Oliver would no longer want anything to do with her.

His hand settled low and warm against the small of her back. "Believe we'll use my room. The bed is larger. Don't like having my feet hang over the end. Besides the width give us more room to maneuver." They reached the top of the stairs. "Dang, I forgot to bring along the chains. I left them in the pantry. Had Alexander go out and purchase some just for this occasion. Thought you might like them."

Her fingers nearly snapped the stem of the wine glass. "Chains?"

Staring pointedly at her, he rolled his eyes. "Just kidding. You're so easy to get everything past as you believe all I say."

She bristled. Remained silent, as she had nothing more to say to his comment. If she replied now, she felt certain she would bury herself in the words she would bluster. He'd have more ammunition to taunt her with.

He steered her through the door, lit three candles and turned on one of the gas lights near the bed. "You said you wanted light."

"Yes."

Like everything else in Evan's townhouse this room was furnished elegantly. Her gaze settled on the clock on the counter above the fireplace, which was ticking. He was right. His bed was large, at least as long as he was. Appeared to have been fashioned just for him. Egg shell white walls set off dark blue draperies. The quilt was a deep royal blue.

Betsy gazed at the bed, her nerves trembling with fear as well as anticipation. She was on the precipice of losing her virginity. This was a momentous occasion in a lady's life. *That's where it's going to happen.* There beneath a large headboard that was embossed with intricate patterns with a man she was paying to do the job. She would finally lose her innocence. This was what she wanted. There would be no complaints. Thinking of lost love, this deed she was about to participate in suddenly seemed to be the saddest thing that ever happened to her.

"I..." She passed her tongue between her lips before speaking again. "I...need to use..."

He motioned in the direction of the bathroom. "You know where it is. Go right ahead. This afternoon I also had Alexander purchase a negligée for you. It's hanging on the door. Why don't you slip out of your clothes and put on that little piece of confection before you come back out."

I can't do this.
You have to do this.

"I could undress you. For me that would be more fun. Don't care if I see you anyway save naked." His hand reached toward the small pearl buttons that fastened her gown.

With a startled gasp, she fled to the bathroom.

~ * ~

As the door slammed shut, Evan smiled to himself. She was such a flightily little thing. Adorable. He was going to enjoy this encounter along with the ones to follow. Miss Betsy Darling might be all tied up in knots but he was having one heck of a good time. She was entertainment to his soul. "That negligée feels real good next to naked skin," he called out while standing so close to the door he knew she would hear him.

Silence surrounded him, seemed to reverberate. From behind the closed door, he could hear nothing. Taking a few seconds to think about how next he would proceed with his skittish lady, he walked around the room humming to himself. During their sojourn in the bathtub this afternoon, he knew she liked looking at his chest. He pulled the shirttails out of his trousers then slipped the shirt over his head tossing the cloth aside. After, he sat on his bed. He kicked out of his shoes then socks, leaving them scattered haphazardly wherever they fell. Thought better of stripping off his pants. Instead, he left them partially unfastened for easy removal as well as provocation. If he built the anticipation, he would have her drooling, her beautiful eyes darkening. As he watched the candle light flickering against the bed, he decided the best part of this sexual encounter with her would be the fact that she couldn't give orders when he was kissing her. Keeping her mouth occupied would serve his purposes.

Thinking about the full curve of that mouth against his sent waves of hunger shooting straight to his groin. It was interesting that Miss Betsy didn't have a clue what kind of ammunition the good Lord armed her with. Her lovers either didn't notice or they weren't about to tell her just how amazing her body was. Every curvaceous part. He reminded himself the men she was used to were too old to notice or even comment if they did have some perception of their good fortune. Maybe they couldn't see what was right in front of their faces.

He sank back into a large wing chair that faced the fireplace. A fire would add ambiance. The night was too warm for a crackling fire but he still liked looking at the picture above the mantle. It was a water color he was particularly fond of. He bought it at a street market from an upcoming artist. He finished her wine. The burgundy was from the Bordeaux region in France. It was one he particularly enjoyed. He focused his gaze on the door wondering just how long it was going to take her to change into the delicate confection he purchased with her in his mind. He thought if he stared at the door long enough, it would open.

It didn't.

Finally, he realized if he didn't go in and get her, he might not see her until morning light. He also realized that waiting was having a dangerous effect on his man parts. Instead of calming him down, he was hotter than when he added fresh boiling water to his bath. Hotter still than the last time he negotiated a winning deal that increased his investments to a startling degree. If he didn't get himself under control, he wouldn't be worth the penny he found on the streets last week let alone the fifteen pounds she was paying for his sexual services. The whole reason for the escalating heat flaming through him was that mouth of hers. Sumptuous. Full. Plump. Inviting. Not to mention that voluptuous lush body of hers that he hadn't been able to see nearly enough of.

He set her empty glass on the end table then made his way to the bathroom door, which he rapped once with his knuckles then eased open.

"Betsy?" He looked inside the room, expecting to still find her fully dressed.

She stood frozen just in front of his huge bathtub, her hands clasped tightly in front of her. The sight of her would have knocked his socks off if he'd been wearing any. Surprising to him, she was dressed in the sheer blue negligée that he set aside for her with her clothes folded in a neat pile on a table near the door.

The devil. He thought his eyes would pop the sockets.

Her diaphanous gown clung to every silken curve as if the silk had been drenched in water before she put it on. As he gazed at her, two tart buds appeared caressing the fabric, disturbing the smooth flow of silk over her breasts. At that very moment, he nearly lost any semblance of control he thought he possessed. If he discarded his britches, he'd be at full attention.

When he looked again, he saw that her hands tightly clutched the fabric at her sides which told him how truly nervous she was. He would have to change that. Tonight, the only problem standing between seeing to their pleasure was her anxiety. The last thing he wanted to experience was her fear. As he looked at her long curling hair and those terrified cornflower blue eyes, what was left of his honor reared its ugly head. Suddenly, he was ashamed of himself for teasing her to this point. What he was doing went against everything that had been drilled into his head since the day he was born.

"You do understand, Miss Betsy, you don't have to do this if you don't want to. I have no intention of forcing you. After all, utilizing my services was your idea."

The devil take her, she was the one who pursued the idea of his escort service. All he did was encourage the notion with his outlandish comments.

Her little chin shot up in just the manner he was coming to appreciate. Those full lips of hers were set in a determined yet stubborn line.

"Whatever would give you that idea? Did you change your mind?"

He supposed he poked the dragon in her. While he stood open mouthed, she pushed past him moving quickly into the bedroom to be brought up short seemingly when she set her eyes on the big bed. Suddenly, his empathy changed to irritation. She did know how to deliver different dispositions to him with her sudden and ever-changing mood swings. One second, she blatantly wanted him, the next she appeared to be a child-woman who didn't know what she was doing.

He followed her. Her fingers clenched the slender belt that tied at her waist. When she turned the soft gown whirled above her trim ankles. With her chin still tilted in defiance, she told him, "You may continue."

Bloody, bloody hell, he'd continue all right. He'd continue to drive her right out of her bossy little mind. He unfastened his pants another notch. Her eyes locked on the skin above the opening. He thought he heard her gulp air then a slight catch in the back of her throat as if she attempted to breathe. This was exactly where he wanted her now, under his control. He would remain in charge. Damned if he'd allow her an upper hand ever again. "Before we go any farther, I need to get the shape of you in my mind."

He tucked his thumb in the waist band of his trousers that brought his britches lower on his hips as he strolled lazily in her direction, stopping only when he could feel her breath against his chest. He made a big show of closing his eyes then setting his hands on her shoulders.

Just as he expected, she jerked at his first touch. He was reminded of the test earlier this evening in the kitchen. The brush of his fingers against her generated the same startled reaction. He kept his hands on her shoulders until he felt the barest easing of her muscles. He wasn't about to allow her reaction to stop his exploration. Instead, he simply allowed his hands to wander down the bare flesh of her arms. After he reached her wrists, he picked up a hand then bringing it to his lips caressed the palm of her hand with his tongue, slid his tongue between each finger. He did the same to her other hand. Enjoyed the swift intake of air, the slight fragmented sound. When he was finished, he skimmed his hands along the sweetly delicious curves of her hips. Continuing his investigation, he moved higher until the heavy roundness of her breasts rested plumply in his hands.

She stood very still as he stroked her through the silken fabric of her negligée. So brave, so determined and stubborn. At his hands, she would learn pleasures of the flesh tonight. His hands rested beneath her breasts. There was so much more fire to discover. She responded so swiftly. He cupped them. They were warm and full and round. He heard another tiny cracked sound, the catching of her breath as he caressed her sensitive jewels. Made a soft breathy exhalation of air. Her arms rose, settled on his naked chest, her fingers dancing through the hair she found there. It was all he could do to keep breathing.

Finally, curiosity driving him, he opened his eyes, gazing down to see that her lids dropped, dark lashes fanning across white flesh. A faint pucker of concentration formed on the bridge of her nose. Smiling, understanding she was falling under the spell he was weaving around her, he brushed his thumbs lightly across the hard pinnacles. She gasped. Her lips parted. Her lashes flew open.

The covetable lips blurred before his eyes as he dipped his head to sample them, claim them as his, at least for the night.

The experience was like kissing warm rose petals. Her scent was roses. The notion swept through his mind that this domineering woman had the softest, silkiest skin of any woman he'd ever kissed. Softer than the rose petals she smelled like.

Not that it surprised him. She kept her lips firmly pressed together as if she'd never been kissed by a man. The devil, the *lass* probably hadn't truly been kissed. Perhaps the men she'd been with never pushed their tongues inside her mouth. In hopes of changing the situation, he slid the tip of his tongue over her bottom lip after that along the crease. His sweet *lassie* didn't have any stubbornness left. She opened for him letting him inside the hot, dark interior he sought.

He liked his kisses slow and very hot. Liked them to set an inferno in his blood as well as his woman's. If she didn't flame with hunger with this first kiss, he tried harder. Lots of his ladies never realized what exactly he wanted. Betsy did. She didn't have any trouble giving back to him everything he wished for in return. His body hummed to life as if a firestorm touched upon him. She allowed him to take all the time he wanted while her tongue moved gently against his. Hot blood roared through his body.

She leaned into him. Her breasts settled deeper into his hands. He realized he'd been so involved with her mouth that he'd forgotten her breasts also needed his ardent attention. That never happened to him. Between her breasts and her mouth, he didn't know what he liked best.

Gently, he squeezed the perfect tips. She twisted against him, arched, curved closer. Her mouth opened wider. For the first time but not the last, he rubbed her nipples with his thumbs. They grew tighter, larger, seemed to swell, flowering, blossoming more with each passing second. He wanted so badly to slide his tongue over them but he still hadn't gotten enough of her mouth.

Perhaps she hadn't either because now he felt the tip of her tiny pink tongue glide hesitantly into his mouth as if this was a foreign treat to her. Despite his reputation with the ladies, his ability to prolong the act of making love until the woman begged, this time he was about to detonate.

With a growl of hunger for this body he coveted, he pulled her back on the bed. The change of location didn't provide nearly the distraction he hoped for. He had to see more. As they sank into the mattress, he eased back a bit looking his fill of this beguiling woman.

Betsy was breathing hard. Her breath stirred his hair. He caught the scent of mint. Her sweet tongue passed across her swollen lips leaving them slick with moisture. "Would you...could you...take your clothes off now?"

The soft feminine entreaty was as whisper thin as a soft breeze on a spring day. She didn't command. His hand moved to the remaining fasteners on his trousers. He opened them but he was so hard he ended up fumbling with the last two. About that time, he got distracted by the rapid rise and fall of her chest. Holding back a second longer was impossible.

With his teeth and fingers, he untied the small straps holding the negligée in place. He pushed the fabric to her hips. The material caught momentarily on one of her nipples before sliding downward leaving both rounded globes open for his ardent inspection. Round, pale, blue-veined marble-tipped with puckered peach buds, all open to his gaze.

Chapter Four

Betsy didn't understand what was happening to her. She was caught up in a sea of sensations so exquisitely beautiful she couldn't breathe. She felt his mouth touch her nipple, his tongue flick, his teeth graze. All breath left her body in a rushing, sweeping sigh of ecstasy. His lips closed warmly around her. The tip of his tongue brushed back and forth. She felt as if her body would fly away unless she found an anchor to keep her sane. Her fingers closed over his shoulder, nails biting into naked flesh. Moisture spiked on her lashes. The devil, she wanted him to do this forever and ever.

He began to suckle, pulling her breast deep then deeper still into the hot confines of his mouth.

Her body shivered with the claws of fire he generated deep in her most private places. She would die if he stopped. He was no longer the handsome wastrel who hired himself out for the night to a sexually frustrated woman. Instead, he was her first and possibly her only lover. She meant to cherish every second, every minute, every startling sensation she never knew existed.

Slow and tender.

Fast and hot.

Infinitely priceless.

Her fifteen pounds for the night seemed cheap by the standards he was setting. So very stimulated, her body arched to get closer. All of her melted into the bed turning to liquid sunshine. She felt the slightest scrape of his thumbnail over the taut hard bud he coaxed to swell under his attentiveness. Her body flamed to life, heated higher and hotter than a few seconds ago. She never thought a blaze could burn so sweet or carry her to such wanting all she could do was hang on to the source of the inferno.

"Please...please...do something...I can't." She choked out the words while she writhed with need beneath him, her body undulating to some strange rhythm he put in motion.

In response his hands slid under her bottom, pulling her closer while he suckled her deeper then deeper still into the blaze of his mouth. His fingers squeezed. She arched higher thrusting her breast against him, pushing, pulling, pleading for him to take her even deeper.

What he created was the sweetest pain she'd ever known. Tears of joy spilled over her lids to drip down her cheek then land on the pillow. On the brink of something she didn't understand she opened her legs, willing him to go there, to fulfil that aching pulsing need that hovered just beyond her reach. Just a brush. The merest stroke. That's all she thought she needed to find something incredible. She was so close, to what she didn't know.

He suckled harder. She gave a small sob, a broken sound, a plea for something more.

His head rose. He frowned down at her as he saw the moisture traveling from her eyes to the pillow. "Am I hurting you, sweet *lassie*?"

Speech at this point was impossible. All she could do was emit a low keening sound of pleasure-pain. Deep inside she throbbed, pulsed, vibrated. Cataclysmic sensations rocked her. She was about to explode. While he looked down on her, she lay beneath him, wanton-like, her breasts exposed, his hands caressing, stroking places no other person had even seen. The nipple he'd been suckling was damp and puckered to a throbbing point. Her legs were splayed under the rumpled silk of her gown. She saw that his trousers were unfastened. He was fully erect, in need. She wanted to touch, to savor his hardness, stroke the steel he presented to her. She tried to gather enough air so she could plead with him not to stop, beseech him to caress her again, implore with him to strip off the remainder of his clothes. She needed him naked. Needed to feel his heated flesh against her own.

Seeming different, he moved to the edge of the large bed, shifting his hand through his hair. "What do you say we slow things down here a little?" His voice sounded hoarse, throaty even whisky smooth.

She never heard him sound quite like that. Her instant response "No! Bloody hell, no."

97

Frantic, she shot up to a sitting position. Stop? Slow? The devil take him if he quit now.

With slightly glazed eyes, he stared at her as if she was daft. He was the daft one. Why would he want to stop now? Suddenly afraid of what she'd done. She paled beneath his scrutiny. "Did I do something wrong?"

"No, it's just loving should be slow, lazy, leaving both relaxed, sated. Savoring the moment with you is what I hoped for. This is happening too damn fast."

She swept her tongue over her lip, once then twice trying to understand what he seemed to be trying to tell her. Wiped her tears on the back of her arm. Sniffed once. Gulped in air. Left the negligée where he pulled it.

"No." She tucked her legs beneath her, staring at him, at the strained look on his face. "It's...it's quite all right if we don't go at this slowly. I just..."

"You were so, wanton... I got carried away. I've never been with a woman so responsive and sensual I forget to breathe."

"Actually, you didn't. Well, maybe you did. I...I liked everything you did. Everything...felt...so..." She didn't know how to convince the stupid man he was making her feel...so...she didn't have words to explain.

Bloody hell, she was babbling. Babbling was something she never did. She looked away from the long line of his back in an attempt to collect her thoughts and realized moonlight floated into the room caressing his broad shoulders. A money clip sat on the dresser next to a few lose pieces of paper. Socks lay on the floor, boots too. His shirt had been tossed near the large dresser.

She drank in another deep breath of air to soothe all the aching parts of her, places he brought to life. She caught the scent of him. Moaned. Throbbed.

There were several books on the bedside table including a history of Scotland and a biography of a man she'd never heard of. The Glasgow Harold sat open to a page that wasn't Caro's advice column.

The headline sported a name she recognized. Odd.

She looked more closely. Felt all the blood drain from her head.

Betsy didn't remember picking up the newspaper, but it was in her trembling hands, so, she must have. As she stared down at the bold print, the words in the headline blurred in front of her eyes.

University of Glasgow's Bad Boy, Evan Murray, takes after his older brother. Scandal follows both bad boys as they garner more pounds than anyone can spend in a lifetime.

"Uh...Betsy?"

She dragged her legs over the side of the bed farthest from him. Smoothed down the fabric of her gown so it covered her legs. Her body shook with sudden disgrace. He used her. Her heart faltered. He wasn't an escort. He didn't do this for a few extra pounds he could use for spending money. Swallowing down her shame and humiliation, she brought the straps of her gown back to her shoulders, swiftly tying the knots.

One more look at the caption. Once more humiliation rushed to every place he touched, realization that she'd been duped by the man. She was such a fool there weren't enough words to describe how stupid she'd been.

Buying the man's sexual services.

Claws of fury uncurled inside her, threatening to explode if she didn't get away from the man, get out of the source of her despair. The things she begged and beseeched him to do to her. She hadn't thought anything could be more painful than when she shared her feelings with Oliver Tindell. This was a million times worse.

So, stupid.

So very reckless. Did she never learn?

Men were horrible creatures!

He lied!

She had to be the stupidest, the most naïve person on this earth. He wasn't escorting women on the side for extra groats. No, he was worth thousands and thousands of pounds, perhaps even millions. He was a millionaire professor who seduced her, brought her groveling to her back. In the morning he would laugh at his conquest.

She was a blind fool.

Never! Never again!

Flinging down the newspaper article, she vaulted from the side of the bed, blindly making her way to the bathroom to reclaim her clothing.

She felt him, the heat of his big body, felt the flames collide with her mortification as he followed her. He didn't intend to give her a moment of respite.

"Don't you think we should talk about this?" he said, his hands resting on her trembling shoulders, massaging, attempting to sweet-talk his way back into her bed into her good graces.

Shaking her head, she rushed past him, clothing stuffed in her arms, headed for her bedroom.

"Miss Betsy?" His ferocious voice thundered behind her.

He sounded angry, furiously so. He had no right to his fury. Curse him. The lying sod.

To avoid him, she shot inside the room, slammed the door in his face then twisted the lock before he could push the door open. Talking was not something she could do at this moment. She didn't think she had one word she could say to him without crying. To the tips of her toes, she felt abused, used, a bauble for a man's pleasure. She wasn't any man's plaything.

Lightly, he tapped at the bedroom door. When she didn't answer, his knuckles rapped forcibly. "I know that newspaper article must be piquing your curiosity, so why don't we finish our bottle of wine while I answer all your questions? You can finish your dinner. I'll have Alexander bring it upstairs. You must be hungry."

The seeming remorse in the tone of his voice didn't fool her.

There were no questions she needed answered. Ignoring his attempt to draw her back to his bedroom and most likely his bed, she dressed as quickly as she could manage. Throwing her clothes into the trunk, she snapped the latches. When she tried to pick it up, she understood she could not take the blasted thing with her. She needed help that she wasn't about to ask for as she was positive Alexander would be loyal to the man who paid his salary. Now, she pulled everything out of her bag. After unlatching the blasted trunk, she pulled out enough clothing to last her two days, stuffing the articles into the bag until the contents overflowed, her parasol pointing upward. She marched, her back stiff, through the door.

He was standing on the other side. Having read her mind, he was leaning on a wall near the door to the hallway. Although his trousers were fastened, he didn't bother to pull on a shirt. Loathing spurned on by self-disgust raced through her. Both sentiments revolved around her stupidly foolish notions. She pushed past him then hurried down the stairs as fast as she could go. Tripping over a sleeve that hung from the bag, she grabbed the banister to stop her fall.

"Foolish woman!" His roar echoed down the long staircase.

In her mind she agreed with him. There was no one more ridiculous than her. Her thoughts were all unwise, reckless. She would never again give herself to a man when charming a woman was on his mind.

"Betsy!"

A terrible drumming echoed in her head. She reached the front door, fumbled for the knob. Alexander appeared from nowhere, helping her. Behind her Evan cursed. She ignored him, hoping to put everything the man was in the background of her thoughts.

"Betsy, it's dark and dangerous. You can't go out there by yourself! What the devil do you think you are doing?"

He came up behind her before grasping her arm holding her back, his fingers biting into her arm.

She found she was quickly whirled around to face him, knocking her off balance. He steadied her with both hands on her arms. Much to her dismay, flames pooled between her legs. The memory of his touch ignited her again. She closed her eyes, pushing the feelings aside. Seeing his handsome face served only to remind her of how horribly naïve she was.

Desperate, with more strength than she knew she possessed; she tore her arm away. She slammed the pointed end of her parasol into his crotch. Heard the explicative. Saw that she hit his thigh, not her target. Nonetheless, she made her point. He let out an *oof* of pain along with an explicative as he staggered backward, rubbing his thigh so close to that part of him he would have used to play further with her emotions.

Before he could recover, she dashed outside. Darkness enveloped her. He was right. She shouldn't be here. Couldn't be anywhere else. Bloody, bloody hell, he didn't force her. Willingly she gave herself to him. She had no one to blame save herself.

The humid night air surrounded her, causing shivers to seep into her. She had no idea where she was or in what direction to walk. When they first rode down the drive, she'd seen a few of the university buildings towering above a forest of trees, at least she thought she had. Now, with darkness surrounding her, all she understood was that she was in one of the better neighborhoods in the city of Glasgow. She supposed that was one thing she could thank the millionaire ladies' man for. All the things he taunted her with when she was in that huge tub of his creeped into her mind to embarrass further. Oh, how he must be laughing at her. He'd been so amused. She entertained him with her naiveite.

She had to get away to soothe the wounds he inflicted.

Nursing her anger until the fury drove out her need to weep, she defiantly put one foot in front of the other as she staggered down the long drive. He wasn't dense or dull-witted or any of those things she thought about him. He didn't need his income from the university. He was one of the richest men in Glasgow, nay possibly all of Scotland or beyond. He was using her, toying with her emotions.

Playing.

Once again humiliation rushed through her, tore into her self-confidence, ripping her apart one slender nerve at a time. Tears hovered on the brink of falling. She pushed them back refusing to cry because a cad, a reprobate seduced her into believing he cared refusing to feel sorry for herself. The fact that she wanted him to make love to her no longer mattered nor did the fact she engineered this so she could lose her virginity. To Betsy it didn't matter that this outcome was all her fault.

He manipulated her for a night's amusement. She fell for the ruse. He was most likely still laughing at her. So damn naïve she cursed herself, deciding to find some means of revenge before she returned to London.

She moved along quite nicely until the rim of the bag she carried tripped her up. More than once she pushed the parasol in the opposite direction so the blasted contraption wouldn't bang against her legs. Sluggishly, yet purposefully she made her way to the end of the lengthy road that ended on the street in front of the townhouse. When she reached the end of the long drive, she didn't know which direction to turn. The darkness was complete every way she looked. Not one street light gave evidence that anyone would want to be about this evening.

What if she hadn't seen the newspaper article?

What if she'd gone through with the sex before she discovered who he was? The horrific thought didn't bear contemplating, so she distracted herself by gazing down the street that to her knowledge went nowhere she wanted to go. Right or left? The course to take was a guess.

Too bad the neighborhood was so wealthy there were no cabs she could wave down. No one was walking about to give help. Other than the sounds of night animals playing in the trees and calling out to each other there wasn't a noise to be heard. She was alone.

She listened harder, thought she detected the faint hint of carriage traffic far in the distance. The bag banged against her legs, the parasol catching between them, tripping her again. She sprawled face down on the ground. Picking herself up, dusting the hint of dirt from her gown and hands, determined, she started forward. She kept walking until she was out of breath. That was when she heard the steady clip of hooves behind her. "No...he wouldn't come after her," she whispered softly into the nothingness confronting her. He wouldn't dare. From what she'd seen of Evan Murray, he was a man who would dare anything. Why would he want to further humiliate her? Why didn't he leave her alone now that he had his fun?

Snatching up the bag, holding it close to her chest so the blasted parasol wouldn't wind up between her legs, she hustled forward. From the corner of her eye, she saw a phaeton approaching. Her heart caught in her throat. Without seeing the driver, she knew the man behind the reins had to be Evan. He pulled up alongside her, matching her speed as he slowed the horse.

Leaning over he began to speak softly, "Don't you think you might be overreacting? It's the middle of the night. Women aren't supposed to be traipsing around by themselves when they can't see the ground they are walking on." The pause ate at her. "Besides, we need to talk. It's not what you're thinking. I can explain everything if you'll let me."

Of course, it was exactly what she was thinking. She didn't want to talk about anything concerning Evan Murray.

Her cheeks burned, heated. Once more she felt the humiliation he inflicted to the tips of her toes. Unable to speak to him, she looked straight ahead. She didn't slow her pace even though her breath was rasping into then out of her lungs painfully. She staggered. Caught herself. Kept walking.

When she didn't answer, he continued talking. "There isn't a place for you to stay within ten miles of here. We're so far out of town we're almost in the country. Have you noticed any taxis passing by here, ready to pick up new fare? Besides in your haste you forgot your purse. You don't have any groats."

She kept putting one foot in front of the other, humming to herself in a feeble attempt to drown out his voice.

Dear God, she couldn't walk ten miles. Didn't think she could walk one more. The day had been trying. She was exhausted.

"The devil, I abhor bad-tempered women."

She whirled on him, bringing the phaeton to a quick stop. Enough was certainly enough. She pointed the parasol at him, jerking it to help make her point, "I'm not bad-tempered! Just...just...leave me alone or haven't you had enough fun playing with me for tonight, mortifying me, humiliating me. If you abhor women you think I'm like, what are you doing here?"

He pulled the phaeton ahead of her, angled the vehicle so that it blocked the street then stopped and got out, leaving the reins dangling on the ground and the horse grazing on a patch of grass. With his shirt hanging open and his feet stuffed into moccasins, he approached her. He didn't look any too pleased. In fact, he appeared absolutely furious. The muscle in his jaw ticked.

A moment leapt past her when she felt a flicker of satisfaction then a moment of remorse which she quickly brushed off. He wasn't standing entirely straight. After that a shiver of panic swept through her. No wonder he looked as if he could spit nails. A brief second of sympathy joined the broiling emotions. She might have hurt him. He deserved the pain. Although she didn't physically fear him, she had only the most fragile hold on her composure. She had to get away from a man who could stir so much passion in her she couldn't think straight.

Waddling slightly from the cumbersome bag, she hurried to the far side of the drive, heading now in the opposite direction than her intention. Easily, he closed the distance between him then manhandled the bag away from her.

"Give those back!"

Ignoring her he tossed the bag into the back of the phaeton. With a low growl, he grabbed her parasol before tossing it onto the street.

"You owe me fifty pounds for the rescue!"

Recue? Fifty pounds? The man was insane.

She worried her lip while she looked longingly down the street. After that, she stiffened her back as she started walking. What did she need her clothes for anyway? She could buy more. On her way down the street, she grabbed her parasol using it as a walking cane. Of course, she would have to come back to retrieve her money.

Unable to see him, she could imagine what he was doing. Undoubtedly, his hands would be on his narrow hips. His words were lazy nonetheless intimidating even from this distance. "Tell me, how far you think you're going to get without your money as well as your clothes? See you retrieved the cursed parasol though. You couldn't be the drill sergeant without the rain napper."

He wronged her. Instead of apologizing, he was making everything worse. Trying to review her options, she was left with a mind that was devoid of thoughts. She had no options. Stopping then turning to confront the blasted man. "Drive me to a hotel at once," she finally managed to make a decision.

"Gladly."

Hesitating, she finally managed to walk the distance to the phaeton. His hands on her waist, he helped her into the vehicle. Without looking at him she allowed his help, felt the instantaneous heat his hands generated. Butterflies danced in her belly. They felt more like fire, breathing dragons. *No...*

Now she attempted to make herself invisible as she pushed herself as far away from him as possible. Her lips felt swollen. She recalled the feel of those deep insincere kisses. When his hand touched her thigh, she gasped.

~ * ~

"Go ahead and give me the best of your temper. Know you want to blast me out of the water. I understand you're dying to tell me what an oaf I am."

He was in his mind too. Earlier he drove like a demon out of hell to catch up with her, terrified for her safety. Now, he didn't want to get her to that hotel any sooner than possible. He needed time with her, minutes to explain what happened as well as why. The momentary bout of guilt he felt earlier lashed through him again. He was a cad. Hadn't intended to be but she was so sweet and pliant in his arms. He never rose so quickly, heated to such an inferno. Miss Betsy was an enigma to him.

When he glanced her way, her mouth remained in a thin straight line. She was passionate in her anger too.

At least to a small degree, he needed to give in to her tender sensibilities. "You're right. I was having a bit of fun at your expense, pretending I was an escort. In my defense, I didn't expect you to take me seriously. No other woman I know would have taken the things I said to heart. When you started to question me about my services all wide-eyed an innocent, I couldn't help myself. Needed to figure out what you understood as well as the notions you didn't. Turns out you didn't understand much of anything." He shrugged as if that gave him all the excuse he needed for his bad boy behavior. "I'm only a man. Before you condemn me for being male as well as human, I suggest you take a long hard look at yourself in a mirror. After you've done so, imagine what you would have done if you were me and you were faced with somebody who looked like you."

At his words of condescension, all of her bristled. "How cruel of you to mock me, taunt how I look. I know I'm not ugly but I'm no beauty either. You are still using me, toying with me even under the guise of an explanation which is a far cry from an apology. She sifted in a long, deep breath of air. "I wouldn't have lied! I would never have humiliated another human being as you did. Just because I'm not up to the standards of your other women."

He caught the blast of her anger square behind his eyes. "Humiliated? What the devil are you talking about, *lass*?" Evan sounded genuinely insulted.

"Of all things you do well, it's act." He pulled out through a set of gates onto another street meandering toward the university. He went on to say, further stiffening her back, "Humiliation played no part in my actions or words. What I was about had to do with opportunity...I'll admit to that...however, mainly what happened between us had to do with lust. I wanted you."

"Oh, please, Mr. Murray. I wasn't born yesterday. I'm not a naïve school girl still wet behind her ears. You're a rich, good-looking millionaire who has no need to lie to unsuspecting women to get what you want. You don't have to settle for a long-in-the-tooth lady for your pleasure or your amusement."

"Guess I know lust when I feel it! When you take the time to think, guess you made what happened pretty darn easy for me. Though, why it even crossed your pretty little head that you would have to pay a man for sex is beyond me. You're so damn alluring, men will lie down at your feet."

"Alluring?" She coughed as if trying to process.

Lie down at my feet?

"Truthfully, you're right. I made everything remarkably easy for you. Achingly easy." She was going over his words in her head again then again. He was taunting her still.

Unexpectedly, he stopped, turned to look at her. She sipped in a breath of air, scowling at the focused scrutiny. "Look, Betsy. I didn't mean to hurt your feelings. It's true. I got carried away. Once more in my defense, you were hell bent on having a fling with a stranger. You wanted me as much as I did you." He lifted his shoulders, his unfastened shirt parting, giving her a fine look at his muscular chest. She turned away as if she didn't want to look at him.. "I guess I couldn't see the harm since you're no simpering debutante."

"No, I'm not a simpering debutante. That fact doesn't give you an excuse." Her bosom heaved, small panting breaths that were more arousing than soothing sifted past her lips. To his chagrin, she caught her plump rose-colored lips with her teeth. Letting it go. Indignantly, she bit out, "You lied to me about everything. You're rich as Midas. You don't need to earn extra money on the side. To think...to think...I fell for your lies..." Realizations seemed to strike her. If she stopped to think even a moment, she didn't want sex from him because he needed the money. Even in the darkness, she would see the tell-tale signs in the tilt of his mouth. "That isn't your family's or your brother's townhouse. It's yours." She waved her hands in the air, startling the horse until he could get the beast under control. "You lied about everything."

She looked as if she wanted to bury her head in the sand...or beneath a blanket. He didn't know the first thing about changing her opinion of him which suffered irreversible damage at his own hands. Thinking back on all he would do differently he would have been smart to dispose of the damn newspaper.

He was still on the defensive. Didn't like the position at all. Was used to having complete control. Somehow control was slowly slipping though his fingers. "You provoked me." He brought the horse to a grinding halt. Thinking if he could convince her to return with him, they could begin anew, talk out the problems facing them. A fresh start with her would be nice. He still wanted to feel her amazing body beneath him, on top of him, behind... The devil!

"Me! Provoke! I didn't do anything except succumb to your blatant lies. I believed every word you spoke."

"Be damned, that's a blitherin' lie, *lass*. You started bossing me around the second you laid eyes on me, making lists, giving orders, and poking me with that damn parasol of yours. What did you expect me to do when you offered yourself to me."

"I never poked you with my para..." She stopped short as she knew she just about unmanned him with her sunshade.

"You nearly did me in with that thing. He was pointing at it. I'd like to toss it into the Firth of Clyde."

"I apologize," she told him, ice in her words.

Evan knew she didn't mean the confession, not one tiny bit.

"Good. I apologize too, so now we're even." He wasn't at all certain what it was he was apologizing for.

Her eyes seeming to blaze where moonlight slashed across them. She retorted with no remorse. "Not even close."

The devil, but he wanted to swing the phaeton around, in order to take her back to his townhouse. Once he got her there, he wanted to carry her up to his bedroom in order to finish what they started on his big bed. The thought was a good one as far as it went. She would complain. Perhaps not if he kissed her. When her lips first met his, she flamed to life. Desire along with savage hunger blazed.

For the first time, he thought of taking her to Letty's home. She could have an education, a real education about the escort business. Or...instead of that place of business to a hotel. He could take her to Caro's home across from the escort service. They would have the cottage entirely to themselves. He reined in on his thoughts about Letty's home. The hour was just too damn late. He wasn't about to impose.

He would take her to Caro's then send Alexander with a message to his oldest brother as to what was happening. Her trunks were still at his townhouse. So, she would still be dependent on his good nature. He did understand Betsy's finances were limited. In this case, the comfort of Caro's home would cost her nothing. He turned down a lane then another. Giving the horse his lead, he continued in a spanking pace eager now to get her to a place where she would no longer feel threatened. She clung to the seat as if desperate to remain balanced. At least there was no other traffic to hinder his progress.

He couldn't remember either Caro or Letty telling her he was a professional escort. Somehow, she'd come to believe that to be the truth. If his recollection held any bearing on the conversations, he'd thought he'd been described as a friend or perhaps a guide who would help her negotiate the city. When he thought back on all that was said and done, his need to tease her was the sole reason she thought of him as a professional escort. He never for one second thought she would pay him to drive her around town. That notion had been solely Caro's idea. He was doing penance for misbehaving so badly he was asked to stay away from the university until he told them he was sorry for his actions. There wasn't one ounce of repentance in his entire body. Duncan was also angry with him. Hence the assignment to keep him busy as well as scandal free. The heir apparent didn't like scandal even though with Caro, he created one of the worst scandals the city had ever seen.

Evan cursed. The devil, there was no way in hell.

The softness in her voice caught his attention. Betsy seemed to be talking to herself. "I do remember telling Caro I could pay him ten pounds a day. Bloody hell...my joke... Caro lied to me too."

"Suppose that joke backfired on both of us."

He couldn't help rubbing salt into her wounds as he needed to point out this fiasco wasn't entirely his fault. He'd been just as big a victim as she had.

"You know something, Evan, I don't have the energy for this. I'm exhausted. The trip from London seemed to take forever. We never ate dinner. So, I'm also famished. When I'm hungry, I'm never good company."

"That wasn't entirely my fault either," he murmured clearly annoyed. "Dinner was hot and waiting. You were the one who didn't want to eat."

As if she sensed his irritation, she looked up from her tirade, "Where is this hotel? You understand the arrangement we had originally isn't going to work for either of us. I can't stay with you. It's blatantly clear you don't like me. I certainly don't like you."

"That's not exactly true. When you aren't pointing your parasol or an appendage of some sort at me telling me what to do, I like you just fine."

He remembered how his kisses melted her to liquid fire. How her body enflamed him to the point he couldn't think straight, could only feel the vibrating heat springing from the female curves he needed to possess. "At least you're not boring which is more than I can say for most the women I meet."

She flashed him an insipid smile. "How very flattering. A woman likes to be described as not boring. The fact is we can't recover from the bad start we already made. First thing in the morning, I'll send a messenger to Caro..."

"How? She's in the country with Duncan. There won't be any messages. I certainly won't send anything."

Not for one second did he like this idea of hers. He needed anonymity for the next month or two. She was to provide him with the ability to escape the scandal. Backtracking on him just wasn't acceptable. "Who would you send with a message? Certainly not any of my servants. Do you have enough groats to pay out of pocket?"

That was, he *kenned*, an underhanded question. If he continued, he'd be bludgeoning the point.

The sudden slump of her usually stiff shoulders told him she understood what he was telling her. She was indeed caught by a lack of funds. He shook his head to tell her no when she stared at him as if she wanted to ask for a few pounds. Hell, she could probably afford to pay a messenger. What she couldn't do without his help was get into the city. Caro's cottage was farther away than his townhouse. He needed to put her some place to his advantage.

"I...uh..." she began, seemingly uncertain how to proceed.

"We need to leave both Caro as well as Letty out of this arrangement as well as our bickering."

He couldn't afford to have his life changed again. He needed to see through with his promise to Duncan. This assignment would be just the thing to keep his name clean for the time it would take to get back in his brother's as well as the universities good graces.

"I can't do that. She insisted I send a letter to Letty's house to tell her about my trip. How it went. If there were problems. You are a definite risk. I think Caro understood your basic personality. Womanizer," she slandered his integrity.

"I'll just bet she did," he muttered then glanced at her. He was about to step into deep water. Nonetheless, he had to risk it. "I'll tell you what. I'll pay you fifty pounds a day if you'll let me stay on as your guide. I will do the driving, take you wherever you want, pander to your every whim." Perhaps that was going a bit too far. He would never pander. "All you have to do is enjoy the scenery and keep telling Letty and Caro loud and clear that everything's fine between us."

He could do this. He could even tolerate that damn parasol as well as the orders he knew would be on the tip of her tongue all day long. By her changing expression, she seemed to understand his easy groveling. He was not the type of person to kowtow or crawl. In this instance he found himself left with no other choice. By the suspicious gleam in her eyes, Betsy understood something was afoot. That didn't bode well.

"Caro..." she was reaching, "...or is it your brother. They've got some hold over you, don't they?" She was tapping her finger on her bottom lip as if in thought. "I wonder what it is. It's not the scandal from the university. From how you've spoken, I doubt if you care about what happened. It's your brother's firm, isn't it? That's why you agreed to this ridiculous arrangement in the first place. I'm not quite sure what the exact nature of the blackmail is. Needless to say, Duncan is blackmailing you, perhaps even with Caro's insistence. You don't have the choice as you feel you have to be my esco...guide."

"Maybe." He didn't want her understanding any more than was absolutely necessary. Already she had a strong hold on his ballocks. That fact seemed to be true in more ways than one. He pulled off the road to stop in front of a small cottage. A walkway led to the front door. Scents of roses in bloom captured the warm evening air. The home was dark. He grimaced. He would have to search for the key. It was more than likely above the front door. At least a light was on across the street at Miss Scarlet's place. Torra would probably be up or Miss May if he couldn't locate the key. Someone would lend a hand.

"What kind of hold?"

"I think we've both had too much drama for one night."

The devil, he didn't want her knowing any more than she guessed. She wasn't going to get the information from him.

"Tell me." Betsy didn't seem to be willing to give anything up. She was after him. It didn't appear she wanted to let go.

"One hundred pounds a day. Do you agree? No more questions asked."

Never had he ever felt quite so desperate. He was fast losing his footing in this game he was forced to play. One hundred pounds a day was outrageous.

"I had no idea. You understand your entire countenance has changed. You're used to getting everything you want. Aren't you? Now, you're begging me. No, I believe you are bribing me. What's happened?"

So angry, he could wring her beautiful little neck with his bare hands. He understood now, he underestimated the woman. She might be naïve about sexuality but the rest of the world be damned if she got a hankerin' to double cross a body. Now, she was like a dog with a bone. He understood she would never let up now that she could ask for anything she wanted. Evan didn't think she would ever stop asking questions until he told her his entire life story. He didn't wish to tell her anything. Underestimating this little she-devil was a mistake he wasn't going to make a second time. Until that point where he gained control again, he'd have to sidestep very quietly.

"Two hundred," she blurted out having the nerve to act surprised after the fact. "Plus expenses. Extras are another fifty each. Take my offer or leave it."

If he agreed, which there was no choice except to do just that, he would be handing her the power she needed to control him for however many months she intended staying in Glasgow. He never handed over control. The man was supposed to be in charge. From this moment on Betsy owned him, Evan Murray. What a travesty. His head was muddled with the thoughts catapulting around inside. After the humiliation she thought he set down upon her, she would do her best to bring him to his knees. By looking at her smiling countenance, she wouldn't have any qualms about using him to get what she needed. Even the blasted tattoo she asked for.

The pleased set of her features as they stepped inside the door to Caro's little bungalow told him it hadn't taken her long to figure out that the balance of power just switched hands. Shifted. Tension clipped away the soft edges of his Scottish accent. In fact, his next words were closer to a Scottish burr, something he rarely used only when he was irritated beyond the rational. He fell into the soft sounds when he was so angry he wanted to smash his knuckles through a wall.

"I'll check out the kitchen along with the upstairs guest bedroom. They keep the pantry stocked. If they are not in town for a while, the women across the street will replace the old with the new. You should have more than enough to eat as well as clean linens on the beds. The only thing you're missing is the cook Caro hired when she lived here. Since you can't even boil water, your choices might be limited."

He left, muttering to himself as he watched her through slitted eyes. While he was in the kitchen, she poured herself a glass of sherry. By the time he returned to the drawing room, she was nearly finished. His anger buried deep inside hoping the fury wouldn't show, he bowed to her.

"Everything in order?" she queried softly appearing pleased with herself. She set the empty glass on a nearby table.

Well, hell, the little *lassie* should be ecstatic. Before he knew it, she'd be asking for that tattoo again. Was she never satisfied? He wasn't going to go that far. "I want your word that you'll be waiting for me at nine o'clock sharp tomorrow morning. Right here!"

His voice was harsher than he meant. Nonetheless, he was pleased to see the surprise in her eyes. He hadn't paid her anything yet. She had few choices.

"Oh, I'll be waiting."

Her new confidence was reflected in every feature on what he once thought was a baby doll face. There was nothing babyish or dollish about her tonight. He choked on the fact he once felt a moment's guilt about what he was about when he teased her so far that she was momentarily willing to give herself to him.

Betsy was out for blood.

His.

All he did was bring her pleasure. He could have given her more than she'd ever experienced from her old lovers.

Lie to her too.

That lie was the crux of his troubles. Problem was it was actually a lie of omission. Eventually, he would have gotten himself around to telling her about his financial status.

~ * ~

The next morning the incessant banging on her door brought her abruptly from a deep lazy sleep. She went to bed with the amazing knowledge she held Evan Murray in the palms of her hands. That couldn't be Evan pounding on her door. A quick look to the clock sitting on the mantle in her bedroom told her it was way too early for him to be at her door. She felt a moment's apprehension.

Oliver couldn't have found her this soon.

Quickly, throwing on a wrapper, she raced down the steps to the door. Before throwing it open as was her inclination, she looked through the small peephole. Air hissed from her lips. No! it couldn't be. How the bloody hell did the man find her? He must have had her followed. It wasn't like him to get up this early. Damnation! Of course, it wasn't him, it was his servant standing on her porch. In the scope of her life, that fact didn't matter much. To ease the building tension, she rubbed the sides of her head.

The man was not Lord Tindell but his man, the man who was always a few days ahead of him. Oliver wouldn't be in Glasgow yet. Not too many days would pass before the man would arrive then proceed to take over her life. She needed that tattoo now; either that or the loss of her virginity. She shouldn't have acted so irrationally last night. If she hadn't been such a twit, she would now be deflowered. She would have almost everything she came here to get.

Hesitantly, she opened the door as she hastily examined her options. By her highhandedness last night, she might have done herself in where it concerned Evan along with her attempts to dissuade her most ardent suitor.

"Jasper. Whatever ae you doing here?"

Her innocent voice wouldn't fool a soul. She knew exactly what he was about. He wouldn't leave until he made perfectly clear to her, Lord Tindell's wishes. The man didn't own her. She would never give up her independence. All this did was make her urgent situation more serious. She'd wondered how long it would take him to track her down. Never in her wildest dreams did she expect a visit from his man the very morning after she arrived.

While she waited for the first shoe to drop, she thought about last night. If she hadn't panicked when she read the article, she'd no longer be a blithering virgin. If she lost her maidenhood, Oliver wouldn't want her. Instead, she panicked then ran from the man who was about to take her innocence. Just as she planned. Her bloody temper continually got her into trouble. Well, she would just have to resort to a different plan.

"A message from Lord Tindell." Jasper bowed then handed over a piece of paper she would have to read.

She imagined the missive would have directions as to what she should do while she waited for him to arrive in two or three days.

Betsy, my darling gel.

She groaned reading the beginning since she wasn't his darling at all and she detested being referred to as a 'gel'. The rest of the letter would most likely be more insipid. She recoiled at the direction of his thoughts. Oliver Weldon Tindell, the sixth earl of Holyrod and a man who resembled Henry VIII in more ways than his sagging belly and penchant for over eating. He also happened to hold all her letters of recommendation. Without his approval, she would never get another tutoring job. When she returned, she would have to seek work elsewhere.

For a few blank moments as she shifted from one foot to the other while her eyes blurred looking at the words she didn't want to read, she gulped down raw courage the best she could manage under the circumstances. She imagined sitting across the table from him while he ate, stuffing down crumpets through those fleshy lips. Bloody hell, the thought of him kissing her left her stomach rolling in nauseating waves. Not that Oliver would stuff anything. Even when he ate great quantities of food, his manners were impeccable. He once demolished an entire tray of berry tarts all by himself without dropping even a single crumb. The appearance of appropriateness was as essential to him as his title.

She continued to read.

You were supposed to send a message to me through Jasper as soon as you arrived at the hotel. I expected to hear from you. When I didn't, I was eager to send Jasper with this missive to the residence where you are now residing. If you don't mind my saying so, this little cottage is much more appropriate than the man's townhouse. Whatever possessed you to go with him? We will have to speak of your decorum later. That was not a good choice. I was sorely afraid I might have to break into the house so I could haul you to safety. I was greatly displeased.

Betsy looked to Jasper confused and angry, her breathing rough around the edges. "He's here? You're following me?"

Jasper nodded, his smile beneath his thick mustache barely discernible. "At the hotel. Lord Tindell wants to know why you aren't there where you are supposed to be? Wants to understand why you are residing in this little cottage."

"I'm sorry," she began reluctantly wishing to send both men to hell. This was none of his business. "I was so exhausted it slipped my mind. I didn't expect him to be in Glasgow so I thought I had time. As to why I'm not at the hotel, I met someone who directed me to cheaper yet just as nice lodging."

The man doesn't own me. She wasn't at all certain how to proceed now that Lord Tindell was in the city. Everything changed. She would have to figure out some plan. Realizing at that moment the only plan she could manage would have to involve Evan. Otherwise she would find herself manipulated by Oliver.

"Perfectly understandable. Now, if you've finished reading, you are to come with me. Lord Tindell is eager to see you." Jasper held out his hand as if she would leave the house still dressed in her bedclothes.

"No!" she cried out backing into the room with Jasper following. It didn't appear he meant to give her a choice.

"I have my instructions."

"Your orders can go to the devil! I'm not going with you. I've other plans for the day. If Lord Tindell is inconvenienced and has made this trip for nothing, I'm sorry. I didn't ask him to follow me. He can go back to London. Tell him I won't be staying at the hotel."

This show of force didn't surprise her. Oliver had been against this trip from the first moment he learned about her plans. She already knew the man would do anything to get what he wanted. A shiver of dread leapt up her spine. Just thinking about the horrible person caused her skin to crawl. She wasn't going to become his third wife. Neither was she going to take care of his two daughters even though the two girls were considerably nicer than their father. All he wanted from her was a son to inherit. He would rut on her until he got what he wanted. She wasn't about to allow anything so preposterous.

Evan, yes, he would be so much better than this man. Why did she run last night? This would all be done now and behind her if she hadn't felt the mortification Evan inflicted down to the tips of her toes.

To her absolute surprise as well as relief, Evan along with his phaeton pulled to a stop in front of the little cottage earlier than expected. Her breath of happiness, she was certain Jasper noted. Here she was standing in the doorway with a man dressed in her bedclothes. What would Evan think?

Still, she experienced a small stab of satisfaction as she watched the lazy glide of his footsteps along the pathway leading to the house. He was dressed immaculately. His buff breeches fit his legs as if painted onto his form, showing off his masculine frame. The fine white lawn of his shirt was tucked beneath a dark blue frock coat. His hair was neatly combed with one rakish lock falling across his forehead. His eyes caught her attention, they blazed golden with seeming fury.

"Mr. Murray," she breathed out as she pulled him inside the house with a solid yank on his arm. "You're just in time. I'm so glad you are here."

He looked from Jasper to her then back again, the slow glide of his lips forming a smile he replied. "Just in time for what, Miss Betsy?"

She clung to his arm. Even with the miniscule contact, heat whispered through her. "Jasper, this is Mr. Murray, my driver. He is a little early. So, if you'll excuse me, I need a bath before I dress for the day's research."

Betsy used the time to dash up the stairs. Unfortunately, there was no hot water for a bath. She would have to do with a quick sponge bath from the basin of water she left there last night. Quickly rummaging through her bag, she pulled out a small bar of jasmine scented soap along with clothing for the day. She would have to ask Evan if he would have Alexander bring her trunk to the cottage. No, she imagined it might be best for her purposes if she found a means to finagle her way back to the townhouse. There she would have the protection she needed. Here she was at Lord Tindell's mercy and the man had none. She absolutely could not stay here alone.

At least a half hour later she walked down the stairs to see Evan along with Jasper sitting in chairs that were in front of the fire, cups of what was probably tea in their hands. It appeared that Jasper didn't intend to go anywhere without her. If Evan couldn't get rid of the man, how could she?

She walked up to Jasper, meaning to convince him he was wasting his time. "Jasper, what are you still doing here? I have my driver. We'll leave shortly." Bravado sometimes worked.

"Lord Tindell wanted me to bring you to the hotel. Breakfast, you know. Together with him." The man ran a slender finger between his neckcloth and his neck, clearly uncomfortable with this situation.

"Please tell Oliver..."

She used his given name hoping to placate the man because the next part of what she was going to impart to him would be less to his liking. "Tell him that I cannot afford the time to see him at all. I'm here to work not vacation. I've important research waiting my attention. Tell the man he should go back to London. This is a waste of time for him. I'm not at his disposal."

Jasper stood, seemingly stunned by her revelation. He started to speak, ran the back of his sleeve across the drops of sweat on his forehead. "I...I...can't do that. I do have my orders."

She didn't know how she could possibly convince this man. She wasn't going to be ordered around by Oliver and that she didn't want anything to do with the earl. "You have no choice. I'm not going with you. Tell him whatever you want." She turned to Evan, smiled, extended her hand, "As you can see my driver is here. I'm paying him ten pounds a day for his service. I would never think to deprive him of hard-earned groats he's expecting to receive so he can put food on his plate."

She wanted to laugh when the tea spurted from Evans strong lips. Lips she remembered pressed against hers along with the fire that still burned in very secret places. With determined strides she went to the door to open it. She waited for the man to leave. Finally, and with great reluctance, Jasper walked through the open portal to the waiting carriage.

Chapter Five

When Betsy first saw Evan, she expected to see the hard-edged man from the night before when he pleaded with her. That moment was when everything between them changed. He'd wanted to remain her driver. Was willing to do just about anything to continue as her escort. She still didn't have one clue as to the intricacies of the blackmail. She just understood on a very basic level extortion existed. Nonetheless, he was paying her for his services. How could her situation improve?

Now the affable lazy moving man she recognized from their first meeting assumed his rightful place beside her. He would protect her because protecting her was in his best interest. With Evan she never knew who she was going to get. This time, however, she understood at least two sides of his complex nature. She wasn't going to be fooled by this easy-going millionaire's suave demeanor. Nor was she going to allow him to seduc...maybe she would. She still had her virginity to vanquish. Oliver was still a very real and potent threat.

The sooner the better as far as she was concerned. She didn't know of any other man who was in line to do the deed.

Lost in her thoughts, she walked toward him. At first, she forgot what a reprobate he could be when the mood hit and simply enjoyed the sight of his all-male form along with his mesmerizing golden eyes. He left his top hat behind. His crisp dark hair gleamed in the light filtering through the front door that was standing open after Jasper's reluctant departure. She swallowed in his perfect form, thinking of Oliver as well as the fact the man resembled a past overweight king. A quick sudden intake of air left his grin broader, more appealing than ever. The bounder understood what he was doing. Despite their little talk last night—well, argument—he seemed to be continuing in the same vein. He was charming her with the slow glide of heat down her body. If she could manage somehow, she would kick a modicum of sense into herself.

He bowed slightly acknowledging her. "Good morning, Miss Betsy. Glad to see you got a good night's sleep. Thinking though you should tell me a bit more about this Jasper fellow along with what he wants from you. If I'm going to do my job properly, I believe I need to know what you've pitted me against."

His voice turned harsh when he spoke of Jasper. What would his voice sound like when he learned about Oliver?

She wondered what Oliver's man told him while she dressed. Probably that the Lord was her intended. He wasn't. Never would be. She did mention some of this to him last night, or did she?

"Good morning. What you need to learn about me you already know. I've no secrets. I'm an open book. As to Jasper, there is nothing important to share." She picked up her skirts to start for the door. "Follow me."

"Not so fast. You're hardly an open book. Although I've been able to read between the lines a few times." While he spoke, his hand shot out to grab her wrist. His lazy smile returned as if he didn't have a care in the world. "Glad to see you brought your rain napper. It's sure to rain sometime this year."

She glanced down at the object of his annoyance then to him as if she couldn't imagine how her sunshade got into her hand. She totally forgot what she did to him last evening with this very same parasol. He should realize a woman needed the apparatus for more than keeping the rain off one's head. The parasol was after all useful in preventing freckles. All sense of guilt over last night vanished. Offering him a cheery smile she pointed at him with the offending article. "Let's be off then."

The satisfaction of seeing his eyes narrow while his lips thinned into a harsh line was hers. "Breakfast first then business." His voice echoed through her demanding an answer. His fingers rubbed softly against the fast-beating vein on her wrist.

"I've already eaten." Her stomach growled belying her words.

His grin grew wider. "Little liar. However, the first order of business before we eat is that we will agree to no longer lie to each other. There should only be truth between us if we are to build a successful working relationship. Fair?"

As he waited for her answer, he gazed down at her with those lazy tiger eyes of his then reverted to using his soft Scottish burr to reel her in. He brought her hand to his lips, kissed the back. This kiss of his wasn't a peck, he used his teeth as well as his tongue to send warmth simmering the length of her. "Now, Miss Betsy, don't tell me you've forgotten whose payroll you're on. If you have, I'll take this moment to remind you."

She should have expected him not to forget. She might have assumed the upper hand last night. In the light of day, she was no longer so certain, especially when he was so charming. Now, he believed he was paying her for services rendered. What the devil was he going to ask of her?

He dropped her hand seeming to forget the niceties. "I'm going to have a plate of eggs along with bacon and warm bread," he spoke softly as his hand settled around her upper arm. "How about you?"

Oh, he didn't forget one single thing. He was flirting with her. "I'll eat. You're right. I was so eager to get to my research I thought I could go without food. Eggs and bacon sound fine."

She thought for a second about bringing up the issue of the blackmail. Thought better of proceeding in that manner. The fact would only serve to enrage the man. One could only use ammunition such as that once in a great while. For now, her best course of action would be to lie low and wait to see what transpired.

As they drove through town toward what appeared to be the university, neither said a word. They settled in a small coffee shop near campus. Students milled around him. Several female students told him how very sorry they were for his suspension. Told him also how much they missed his lectures. She snorted as she watched. Couldn't help the feeling he was manipulating everyone. He had this way with females. She didn't like the thought she might be feeling a *wee* bit jealous. Well, he could cock up his toes for all she wanted to care.

While she watched him with practiced ease speak with the women, she wondered what possessed her to act as she did last night. True, she'd been exhausted from the long journey. True, she lost her temper. Flinging her camisole off had to be one of the stupidest acts of her entire life. With too much ease, he caused her temper to flare. The worst of the thoughts was that he manipulated her, purposely made her angry. It was as if he knew what she would do if he pulled the right strings.

What other outcome could she have expected having jumped into Evan Murray's bed after less than ten hours of being in Glasgow? If she meant to sleep with someone, she should have made certain Oliver's watchdogs were aware of what was going to transpire. Otherwise, she would have to sleep with him a second time. Oliver wouldn't just take her word for the fact. He would have to see proof. Well, short of breaking into Evan's home, she realized this was all guesses. She didn't have to actually sleep with this man. What she had to do was convince Oliver she had done so.

How to go about that chain of events, she wasn't at all certain. Wrong word, she recalled when he teased her with chaining her to the bed. Heat rushed through her. Her impulsiveness coupled with her temper these last hours frightened her. All of this was Evan's fault. He pushed and pushed then pushed some more until all she could do was react.

Suddenly, she was no longer hungry. Her body seemed to be rejecting food every time she was close to this man. He made her nauseous. Not in a bad way. Well, it wasn't exactly nausea she was feeling. "Just tea," she spoke out as the waitress approached to take their orders. "I'll have lemon along with honey as well."

Evan beamed his approval at her. "Good choice. However, add some eggs and bacon, also potatoes to her order, along with a loaf of hot bread. I believe I'll have the same. This will last us most of the day. We won't have to take time out to eat again." He reached across the table to take her hand.

She jerked back.

Provoking her deliberately would not get him anything he sought. Instead of retaliating as was her won't, she shot him a smile that was meant to tell him she was on to his devilish bad boy ploys and she wasn't going to allow him to get away with them. "Change the eggs, bacon, and potatoes to a bowl of cantaloup, perhaps some blueberries too if you have them. Whatever fruit is in season here."

The harried waitress added to their tea before rushing away before either of them could manage to complicate their orders further.

They had issues to discuss. Betsy had seen enough of his nonsense. She took only a moment to glance outside the large window in the front of the small restaurant to enjoy the wealth of sunshine pouring into the room. Sunlight always managed to brighten her day. "Will you find me someplace to get my tattoo. I would like to take care of that as soon as I purchase a few new things to wear." Her heart thundered behind her ribs while she asked him for something he disapproved of doing.

"You are not getting a tattoo. As soon as the permanent ink on your white skin dries, you'll have too many regrets to count."

She bristled. His attitude stung if nothing else was humiliating. "I am getting a tattoo. I'm doing it today. This isn't negotiable."

She doubted a tattoo all by itself would put a damper on the upcoming engagement, at least where Oliver was concerned. However, she hoped it would begin to drive a wedge between the two of them that could not be healed. Peering around the small restaurant, she wondered if any of the men hiding behind the Glasgow Herald were employed by Oliver. Every time the little bell at the front door rang out the entrance of a new customer, she thought the same. Paranoid was not a sensation she enjoyed. On the other hand, she wanted him to know where she was going along with what she was doing. As soon as he followed her to the place Evan was taking her for the tattoo, he would begin to have misgivings concerning her character.

Evan peered at her over the rim of his tea cup that looked far too delicate for his large hands. "How are you going to explain the tattoo to your new employer along with his children that you plan on tutoring. We both *ken* tattoos on women are totally unacceptable. Immediately, you would become a bad example, in your world a pariah. We both understand that if you are going to get the tattoo it needs to be somewhere it can be seen. Otherwise, the pretty little picture marring your delicate white skin will be useless."

As her life was unfolding; she wasn't going to have any new charges to tutor. She wasn't about to tell him that. Her future, unless she agreed to the engagement Oliver insisted on, looked very bleak. "I will have the inked design placed somewhere the art cannot be seen." She meant to be contrary, stating the opposite.

"If you want to shock, why don't you do something totally outlandish and get your eyebrow pierced or perhaps your nose? You know like the women who live in Africa? You could die your hair bright red, that would make you stand out in a crowd. Do something outrageous that is not permanent."

At one point in her deliberations, she had thought about all his suggestions. She couldn't bring herself to do any of them accept the tattoo which she could keep hidden most of the time, a very small tattoo. If necessary, she would have to show the tattoo to Oliver. The thought gave her reason to cringe. Oliver needed to believe he misjudged her character. This was all she could think of for now since the loss of her virginity was off the table as far as Evan was named as the despoiler. She didn't know any other man who might come close to suitability. Suffering that kind of mortification with Evan again was unthinkable.

The waitress appeared with more tea then beat a hasty retreat.

"Just where do you plan to get this tattoo?" he questioned her, his eyes hard as he seemed to search out her body for the right place.

She squirmed beneath that hard gaze, heating as if he touched her. "My upper arm." That was perfect because she rarely wore sleeveless gowns. When she did, she could drape a shawl around her shoulders to hide the mark. She would have to keep it covered for the rest of her life.

Blandly as if he didn't have a care about this topic, he began to speak, "Women who get tattoos don't put them on their upper arm. Their ankle is usually the most popular. However, the back of a shoulder or, if they truly want to be discreet...and this is what I'd recommend in your case if I were going to make a recommendation, which I'm not...a breast." He finished the statement staring at her as if he saw the tattoo on her breast, as if he remembered seeing her breasts totally bare.

She hissed in a sudden desperate cry for air. That single word brought all that went on between them back in a blinding rush. The feel of the silk sliding down her body, the heat of his lips following the secret glide of fabric, the pull of his teeth on her nipple. She quivered.

Evan knew exactly what his wicked words did to her. She saw no remorse in his eyes, just a devilish glint of retribution.

"You don't say?" She forced a sip of tea that caught going down the wrong way. She coughed trying to hide what was all too obvious, "Well, I'm certain you have more experience in this matter than I."

"You're still furious about last night, aren't you."

"Of course not. I've forgotten all about it. I've put what you did to the back of my mind. You should also."

He grinned then looked at her with boyish seriousness. "Fill in the spaces for me. The way I see you is that you're a very sweet unmarried lady who has made it clear to this man she would like a little sexual play before she returns to her boring life as well as her even more boring lovers in London. Absolutely normal. Continuing with this theory, you've got to admit that when you're in London, you've got a certain reputation to uphold. You're not free to explore different avenues of your sexuality. Here in Scotland, you're a free woman. Nobody knows you or cares if you experiment. The tale will never get past the outskirts of Glasgow if that far. Now, what I need to understand is this. What difference does it make whether I happen to be an escort or a professor or a financial wizard? I've got all the necessary male equipment you need to fulfill that wicked little dream of yours. I'd be pleased to let you use all my apparatuses."

Her face flamed while she tried to digest his outrageous suggestion. "You're far too big-hearted. That was a very kind suggestion. The fact remains...I wouldn't let you touch me again if you were the last man on earth."

The moment the words blurted from her mouth she knew she was in trouble. This lazy fool, who wasn't a fool or lazy, made his living by competing in markets far more flammable and dangerous than she. Unless she was wrong, she caught the light of a challenge in his sizzling golden gaze.

"Uh—huh...we will just have to see about that. Now won't we, Miss Betsy Darling? The last man you say? I'll have to give that a test."

Thankfully the waitress appeared at that moment with their food. Betsy ate most of her fruit but could barely push down the rest of what was ordered. He had this disarming way of making her stomach roll, of unsettling her to such a degree she couldn't eat. Evan finished his eggs and bacon then dug into what she pushed aside.

"That's not...well it's not done. You might get sick."

She was watching him eat, wishing she could also put food in her skittish stomach.

He set the fork down to look at her once more. A second echoed past them before he began to talk. "We already traded kisses last night, so I'm not too worried about sharing food. If I was going to catch anything from you, I have already."

She pushed thoughts of his slow deep kisses aside, the feel of his lips along those sensitive parts of her he uncovered, parts she'd never thought about before Evan. Thinking about them only served to tie her nerves in knots as well as send heat racing to all the places he caressed, all the parts of her she wanted him to touch again. Just thinking about him her nipples were hardening while other parts ached with the flaming rush of blood to them.

"If you won't help me, find a place to get a tattoo, I'll simply take a cab to the docks. In the meantime, I need to go to a modiste. I'm in need of gowns more suitable for me than what I packed."

"Thought you were here on research."

"I am. Research won't take up all my time though. I do want to spend a few hours this afternoon in the university library. Perhaps we can visit a museum."

"So, tell me more about this queen consort you're researching. Seems a big topic to take on. Is there information on someone born so long ago. Wouldn't it be more interesting to pick someone different? A man who might have been more important?"

Visibly, she recoiled at the all-male statement men were more important than women. "Mary of Guise...sure you want to know? Most people would find the topic boring."

"Not me." He sat back his arms crossed in front of his chest. "Hit me with all you got."

"Oh, well, I could tell you more later. Should get going as soon as possible. Do you know of a good modiste?"

He would most likely. Probably where he purchased that negligée she wore last night for such a short time. She groaned as more thoughts of his heated caresses, the warmth of his tongue, the gliding rake of his teeth dabbled into her mind. She shivered, moving her hands along her arms.

"You cold?" he asked his large hand at the small of her back as he ushered her from the restaurant to the phaeton. His fingers rested just above her bottom, seemed to slip lower before he glided his hand back to the original spot.

"No."

When she saw the grin he was sporting, she knew that he knew why she shivered.

Barely able to speak, she tried, her voice whisper soft even while she forced the words. "Do you know of a good dress shop? I'd like one where I might be able to purchase a few gowns that are ready made."

"Yes. My least favorite places are dress shops," he ground out sounding irritated with her even while his large hand roamed her back to settle on the curve of her hip to squeeze gently.

She tried to move away. Smoothly, he pulled her back. So close now, she felt the radiant heat from his body flow outward.

Well, that was just too bad if he didn't like dress shops. He would have to learn to live with it as long as she held the winning hand. Just to antagonize him, she pointed her parasol toward the phaeton. "This way."

Before she could blink or defend herself, he snatched it from her then pitched the offending article outside. It landed smack dab in the middle of a thorny rose bush settling deep into the thicket. She couldn't retrieve it without suffering a wealth of scratches.

"That wasn't very nice," she blustered at him, enraged knowing she wasn't going to risk the scratches. "I'll just buy another one at the dress shop."

Gratification swept through her at the wealth of curses following. "I'll do the same to any parasol you buy."

Comprehending he won this round, she took off. Betsy was headed for the phaeton before she realized Evan wasn't following her. Irritated, she turned.

He was moving in that slow, lazy way that was becoming all too familiar to her. Watching him with annoyance, she tapped her toe impatiently waiting for whatever caused his attention to vanish. He was doing this just to exasperate her.

With that charming smile of his, he greeted two men, probably a pair of professors, then stopped to admire another rose bush, bending down to smell the flower. He plucked a petal from the bush then rubbed it sensuously across his cheek.

Her breath swept from her lungs in a sudden rush. He was infuriating. If she lost her temper again, she certainly didn't know what would happen. She'd probably end up naked somewhere, his pawn to do with as he pleased. If that happened, he would take every advantage he could. She counted backward from ten. After she finished, she did it again then another time. Finally, that blasted temper of her wasn't ready to erupt.

Ultimately, he made it to the phaeton, helped her up. "You positive you want to go shopping today?" he asked as he slipped inside then gathered the reins in his hands.

His thigh pushed against hers. She moved hers. His followed. He tucked her chin between his thumb and finger in order to make her look at him. In that soft sexy voice of his he invited, "We could go for a drive. Stop at one of the parks. Take a walk. Kiss. You started to learn how I like to kiss last night. I could continue the lesson until you got the task down to perfection. I do enjoy a perfect kiss. Don't you?"

"Yes, wherever you think is best. I'll trust you with this decision."

He lulled her. She caught herself. "No! No, lessons."

This was about the only decision she could afford to rely on him for, of course the tattoo also.

He grinned knowingly. "All I can go on is the place Caro shops. I'll take you there. Not going to make any guarantees if they'll have anything you'll like. It's expensive, that I can guarantee. Just buy what you want and charge it to me."

"No! I can't do that!"

"Why get self-righteous now? You didn't object to that fifty pounds a day you're forcing me to pay to keep your mouth shut."

"One hundred pounds a day. No, It was two hundred. You

understand fully it's blackmail money, so, that money is different. Isn't it?" She looked at him haughtily. "You owe me for keeping quiet when it would be so easy to run to Caro with what you did."

His knowing, heated gaze swept over her again. The nerve of the man. She understood what he was most likely thinking. His gaze rested on her bosom. She took solace in the fact the gown she wore was modest. She touched the lace around her neck before running her hands down the elbow length sleeves. The silk negligée was anything but modest. Her body quivered at his blatant perusal.

"The gown becomes you. What do you need more of? You've a trunk full at my place."

"Thank you."

This wasn't a conversation she wanted to have with him. He didn't care what she wore or didn't wear. Perhaps that wasn't entirely true.

After some time, they traveled into the heart of the city. He stopped in front of a dress shop. Moving quickly, he was on the other side of the phaeton before she could help herself down. Air slipped through into her lungs, though not enough. She tried to get down by herself, not wanting to risk his hands touching her again.

"No, you don't."

His hands wound around her waist as he plucked her from the seat with no effort what so ever. He pulled her against the length of his body. She felt all of him including that part of him that was all male and hungry.

Breath rushed out.

He set her feet on the ground but kept his hands tucked intimately around her backside. "Spending time picking out fabric along with fashion plates is not my favorite past time. I'm just dropping you off. Thought I would go over to Duncan's office and have a short tête-à-tête. I'll be back in a few hours."

"You can't leave. I know exactly what I want. Wait for me outside. This won't take very long."

Before he could reply she swept through the door. Once inside, she let her gaze wander around the room. Yes, there was a rack of ready-made gowns. She meant to purchase two if she could find ones that fit. She could almost hear his frustration along with his anger. Knew exactly what he was thinking. The last thing he wanted was to wait for her. Ah, he thought he had better things to occupy his time. Too bad. He was hers for the day.

Searching through the two racks of clothing she found some gowns to try on. With four in her arms the modiste showed her to a room. Quickly, she tried on all four. Decided on the two she wanted. These would be perfect for dissuading Lord Oliver. If he saw her in these, he would turn tail then run all the way back to London. She could only pray.

With the parcels tucked beneath her arm, she ventured outside. She found him leaning idly against the phaeton, his hands stuffed into the pockets of his trousers. His lids lowered sleepily over his golden eyes. He seemed to sense when she approached. He graced her with one of his lazy smiles that sent heat rebounding through her. She couldn't let the man get to her. If she did...she didn't want to be reminded of the consequences.

"Now the tattoo." Her plan was finally coming together. The feeling of relief that swept through her was tangible. "Did you figure out where I could go?"

Without speaking, she prayed he wouldn't give his opinion again, they were traveling through the city. She wasn't at all certain where they were going. The direction certainly wasn't toward the waterfront.

"You're serious about this. This tattoo thing?"

"Perfectly."

He seemed to be thinking hard. His brows were furrowed again. "All right, if you're dead set, I'll help you. It's going to take some time though to find a place where you can be sure they are using clean needles. Don't want..."

"Needles?" Panic shot to her stomach. She didn't know what she'd thought or how it would happen. Her naivety must be showing through as he grinned at her question. "You're not teasing me again, are you?"

"How do you think they put those tattoos on? Permanent? It's not with a colored pencil." Idly, he touched her upper arm where she said she wanted it put. "Hmm...your delicious and very curvaceous backside would be a good place for one. There are other places I would enjoy kissing while admiring said tattoo. Now that I've come to accept the fact you are getting a tattoo, I've several ideas."

"Yes, well..." She caught her lip beneath her teeth, certain she'd never thought that far ahead. *Her backside?* "I know they use needles. I read all about how it's done. It was just the way you said the word."

"Sure, you do. Second thoughts?" One of his dark brows lifted as if he was hoping she would change her mind. That wasn't going to happen. "You know it hurts. If you can't take the pain..." he left the thought hanging for her to mull over.

"It won't be that painful."

His snort wasn't encouraging.

~ * ~

The devil, the little innocent had no idea what she was getting herself into. Well, he did have a few plans up his sleeve. He had some ideas that would put her in her place quicker than any arguments he could dream up. If he had his way, and he damn sure meant to, she wasn't going have anything on her perfect creamy flesh to mar her beauty.

Perhaps he'd been right when he decided it would take two to three days to seduce Miss Betsy Darling into his bed. Today, he meant to tease her every chance he could make for himself. He would let her off at the library to research this woman she wanted to write about while he researched the woman he had in mind to give her the tattoo. Yes, he would go find the Black Widow on the docks who was renowned for her tattoos. Evan wasn't at all certain why she was called the Black Widow. He imagined the name was one she liked. The needles brought rough tough sailors to their knees sometimes. Yes, the tattoo would hurt but he had something else in mind for sweet, impulsive Betsy. He wasn't about to allow her to get a tattoo under his watch. He wasn't at all certain why he cared. She'd be out of his life in a month or two.

Shocked for a moment that thought left him first depressed then elated and after that, furious she would dare go back to London. The ever-changing emotions left him off kilter. This was not what he expected today. Seeing her with that man, Jasper, this morning left him boiling even though he immediately understood the man was just a messenger.

Who the hell was she running from. The information was something he meant to garner before too much more time passed. She would tell him. First though, tonight he would have a bit of fun with her.

He missed seeing her eyes cross.

When she saw the tattoo she was going to get on her breast just where he wanted it, her temper would flare. In this instance, he wasn't going to give her a say. No, everything would be left up to him. Once that happened, she would be under his thumb once more.

In front of the university library, he reined in. "I'll be back to pick you up in exactly three hours. Be right here."

"That sounds like a threat," she said her chin moving up at least a notch possibly two. "Will you be on time?"

His smile didn't appear to reassure her. "Oh, one more thing."

He pulled her to him, embraced her so tightly she couldn't move away. Staring into those startling blue eyes, he watched them dilate, grow darker with hungry desire. His lips closed over hers, his tongue pushing the sweet, warm plumpness of her mouth to part. Silken warmth, ardent desire, the taste of instant passion greeted him. A small broken sound caught in the back of her throat. Her hands pressed against his chest then clung. The sultry dance between them sent a lightning bolt of need straight to those masculine parts he offered earlier. Yes, he did possess all the right apparatuses. He needed to use what he had.

After several seconds he slowly pulled away. Moisture coated her rose colored lips; her eyes dazed with slightly lowered lids. She was arching in his arms offering her neck, her shoulders. Now he could imagine the rosy tips of her breasts that needed to be touched as well as tasted. The quick rise of her passion left him breathless and clearly pleased. The instantaneous growth of passion that happened last evening was still there waiting to be flamed to life.

He ran a fingertip across her eyebrows then down her nose to touch her lip as he traced the dewy softness left behind from the smoldering taste of his kiss. "There will be more of that later tonight."

When he let her go, she swayed slightly, her fingers touching her lips where his had been. With one last, lingering look, he leapt into the phaeton. He set the horse to a fast pace, in a hurry now to make arrangements for the evening.

The waiting would be difficult.

In the end, she would be his.

The Black Widow was in her salon when he entered. She stood, smiling at him as if she expected him. "What do I owe the pleasure of your company, Mr. Murray? It must be a woman. You look all tied up in knots. Is it a massage you are after? Just go on into the back room. Don't have a client at this time. I'll have you relaxed back to normal in a flash."

Evan hooted with pleasure. "You are always unpredictable. While a massage would be nice, I've need of a bit of secrecy between the two of us as well as some of your other talents."

He paused in thought wondering how much he dared tell this woman who always took the woman's cause in matters of the heart. This was not a matter of the heart. This was a decision that needed altering.

Perhaps he should tell her as little as possible.

"Brandy?" she asked even while she was at the sideboard pouring them both a drink. "By the look in your eyes, I've a feeling you might need more than one." She handed over the crystal glass.

He cleared his throat while he thought on all the necessary details. He didn't want to leave room for error. "First of all, do you still own that little shack on the dock where you give tattoos to the randy sailors who come into port?"

Looking cautiously at him, "You haven't given into the current rage, have you? Are you asking me for a tattoo?"

"No, my favored lady at this moment wants one. If I have my way, which I will, she isn't going to get one."

"I see." She sat down, tapping her fingernail on the glass, her brows furrowed together as if trying to put sense to his words.

"Probably not."

He chuckled. The Black Widow would understand soon enough.

"Why don't you want her to have one? They are all the craze, quite in fashion even among women, the aristos." She sipped, keeping an eye on him over the rim.

The question was good. Yes, indeed, perhaps he didn't want her to get one because of his gut reaction that she would regret what she did.

For a conservative woman, Betsy was far too impulsive for her own good. As far as he was concerned, though, her impulsiveness would get her into his bed coupled with that wonderful temper that he was coming to adore. Bedding her had been his ultimate mission as soon as he reconciled with her one fetish, that of pointing her parasol at him or directing him with it. Perhaps there were two. She had this burning need to give orders.

"Too conservative."

One of her dark eyebrows rose an inch. "You with a conservative lady? I'd like to see that."

She downed the rest of her brandy. The Black Widow was the largest woman he'd ever known or seen for that matter. Even though she possessed a wealth of womanly curves, her breasts full, her hips wide. Nothing about her besides her woman parts was soft. She possessed muscles, large muscles in her forearms as well as her thighs. Her eyes were steel-blue, searching, unforgiving. For most of her life, she worked alongside grown men on the docks.

"If you're willing to do my bidding, you will come to understand. I'll bring her to the shack down by the docks at eight."

He was so ecstatic by the look in the woman's eyes that he nearly rubbed his hands together.

"Willing to do what? If the price is right, I'll do most anything except murder. Won't murder anyone for you. By the way, heard about your little *faux pas* at the university."

His grimace didn't go unnoticed by the woman. "Wasn't so little. Won't apologize for something that wasn't my fault. So, don't see myself getting reinstated anytime soon. I'm entertaining myself with a woman who, well, she's so damn naïve I can't stop teasing her."

She is so damn innocent; she will fall into my plans with a little bit of sweet talking.

"That doesn't sound like you either. What does she hold over your head?"

"How the hell did you know I'm being blackmailed?"

"By the little woman?" She ventured a guess that was spot on then erupted in heaving guffaws that left him swearing beneath his breath.

"Not for long. After tonight, if you're with me, I'll hold the winning cards. So..."

"I'm intrigued with this plan of yours and I haven't even heard it yet. What is my part in this sensual play? You understand I won't do anything I believe will harm this woman even though it's you doing the asking."

Once he had every little detail in place, he left with a smile on his lips. The black widow had been more than happy to see his plans come to fruition. She agreed to be at the shack at eight o'clock sharp with all the necessary paraphernalia to give her a tattoo that would cross Betsy's eyes the moment she saw the intricate design. Evan even told her exactly what he wanted as well as where. Betsy would think she was in control. She wouldn't be.

Setting the phaeton to a brisk place he headed toward the university. Traffic was heavy, congested in places. He didn't care. She'd be tapping her toes impatiently. He pulled up where he told her he would pick her up. She was nowhere in sight. The devil, he didn't think she would be late. He was the one who didn't care about time, not prim and proper Miss Betsy Darling. There was no sign of her.

He leapt from the phaeton. Searching the walkway, he didn't see anyone. She was doing this to aggravate him. Her ploy was working. Ah, but he thought about tonight. Her eyes would pop right out of their sockets just after they crossed, temper would flare. He would sit back and enjoy the show. Rubbing his hands together, he could hardly wait.

What would she do?

His imagination worked double time. He pulled his watch from his pocket.

Fifteen minutes late. Damn... He wanted to go home before he took her to dinner. Needed to change into something more appropriate for walking along the docks in one of the worst parts of the city. She left her packages from the dressmaker in the phaeton. He was tempted to look to see what she purchased.

"Mr. Murray?" She called out to him waving her hand as she hustled down the walkway smiling sweetly at him. She lifted her skirts as she picked up the pace. Her ankles were the prettiest damn ankles he'd ever seen. "There you are. I was certain you wouldn't be on time. What happened?"

While she walked swiftly, her breasts swayed invitingly beneath the soft fabric of her gown. Her skirt swirled around her feet showing glimpses of the sweet ankles he wanted to taste. Because of the exertion a rosy glow painted her cheeks. The pink was an entirely different color from the times he embarrassed her. Both colors were nice.

"You're late," he said his voice flat.

Breathlessly, she began to speak. "After yesterday, thought you would be late. Didn't want to waste my time if I had to stand around expecting your imminent arrival."

"You thought it would be fine if my time was wasted instead." Both annoyed as well as bemused at the sight of her heaving bosom, he tapped her on the nose. "Next time don't be late. If you are, there will be consequences."

"What? Consequences?"

Another challenge she wouldn't win. Once more his Betsy was playing nicely into his hands. "You'll find out. Don't test me. You might not like the results." Before she could protest, his hands were around her waist. She was sitting in the phaeton. "We'll go to my place then on to dinner."

"Did you arrange for my tattoo?" she asked, a bit breathless from her rush down the long walkway.

If he'd worn his hat, he would have tipped it her direction. "Everything your heart desires." He jumped in beside her. "I would like to know about this man you're running from. Is he in town? Or is it just his man servant, Jasper?"

The rosy blush from exertion paled. He watched her swallow hard. "You don't need to know about him. He's not your business."

The devi, he did. In time, just be patient and all will follow.

He brushed her arm with his. "So, thought you would object to going to my place." He turned so he could watch her, expectation high. The expression on her lovely face was one he'd never seen before. He didn't like what he saw.

"No objections. We can pack my trunk into your carriage since I'll be returning to the cottage after my tattoo." She spoke as the prim and very proper woman she was meant to be, showing no sign of the rebel beneath the surface.

"No."

"No? Is that all? Not even an attempt at discussion? This decision is not yours to make." Her voice shook with her rising anger. Tiny, clenched fists settled waspishly on her wide hips. She looked ready for battle. He would wage war with her. One he would win.

"No, simply because you need a safe place to sleep. Caro's cottage without me in it with you does not appear to be safe. I won't stay the night there because my bed here is much larger and much nicer for me...and..."

He wanted to say for his plans. Kept his words behind his teeth hoping the rest of the evening would go without argument. He'd much rather kiss her than argue with her.

"Oh..." She looked blindsided.

This was a rare event, Betsy with nothing to say. The rest of the trip passed by with silence. He meant to enjoy the peace that would eventually erupt with dissension, then passion and if he had his way, with amazing pleasure.

Alexander opened the door for them. "Your trunk is still in the bedroom next to mine. Would you enjoy sharing another bath with me before dinner?" He grinned thinking she would say no. Her hesitation surprised him. "Naked of course."

"Of course, no."

Her earlier agitation in the face of the enemy turned to calm serenity. She seemed to school her face, showing no emotion. He knew he could trigger the temper that was a hair's breath away from exploding. If she lost the calm serenity she was trying to present him with, what would she do?

"You didn't get a bath this morning. Perhaps after your tattoo. Before we go to bed together. Warm water would take away the pain, would calm then relax your nerves." So far this was just a dream. He would see. "I'll meet you downstairs. Don't take long. Your appointment is at eight sharp. Wouldn't do to be late. The woman might move on to another customer then where would you be? Without your tattoo."

"Woman?" Her eyelids blinked a couple of times as if she heard him wrong.

"Yes, didn't think you would want to bare any part of you to any man except me."

He didn't want her to bare any part of her to a man other than him. When did he get so possessive? He didn't like the notion. There it was though. Staring him in the face.

"No, no I wouldn't. Thank you."

In the hall upstairs they parted ways. Quickly, he dressed in buckskins and a white shirt. He pulled on his boots. The night was warm. He wasn't going to need a frock coat. However, he grabbed one. He took the steps two at a time as he raced down the stairs eager for the ensuing events to unfold. Pouring them both a pre-dinner drink, he waited. He slipped a tiny bit of a sleep potion the Black Widow gave him into her drink. He had more for later. She would sleep through most of the adventure. Unfortunately, she would wake to a blinding headache.

For a few minutes he stared out the window toward the street, thinking about his plans. Just a whisper of a noise caught his attention. When he turned to see Betsy, his mouth dropped open. If he'd been holding one of the drinks, he felt certain he would have dropped the glass. After that and for the longest time, his heart forgot that it needed to beat.

When he finally found his voice, he yelled. "You're not going anywhere in that!"

The devil, the woman was wearing a whore's gown. The fabric dipped so slow in front he could almost see the soft pink surrounding her nipples. It was cinched tight at the waist, the skirt flaring. The top was what needed fixing. He wanted to put his fingers in the fabric then pull the top up until the gown reached her neck. He had the feeling that would do nothing to solve her problem. Her lushly full breasts were spilling from the corsage in a beautiful display for anyone who cared to look.

"You've painted your face!" That was the second revelation as he hastily then more slowly took in her appearance. "Go upstairs and wash." He gritted out between clenched teeth knowing full well she wouldn't heed his command.

She smiled at him, twirled until the gown was billowing sweetly around her slender legs. "It's fabulous, isn't it? Thought you would like the dress. Didn't expect that reaction. I wore coloring on my face yesterday. So, what's wrong with it today?"

"You didn't have the appearance of a painted harlot yesterday!"

His temper flared more with each passing second. After a few moments of rage and despite the fact she was underdressed, he realized the gown suited his purpose tonight. The tattoo as planned would be blatantly obvious to everyone she saw. How sweet. How *verra, verra* sweet. He couldn't have asked for anything better. He also realized that he and the Black Widow were the only two people who would see her lavish charms.

"I don't look like a harlot," she said without blinking, her stance stiff, her feet firmly set apart as if she meant to do battle. The argument did not hold water with him.

In a complete turn about which left her appearing confused, he held out his arm for her to take. "Come along, sweetheart, I'm famished. Unless you ate something while we were apart today, you've eaten nothing in the short time I've known you. Hopefully, you will have an appetite for dinner."

His gaze dropped to the valley between her breasts which was so obvious, his eyes nearly crossed. When she moved just the right way, he could see pink surrounding her nipples. What the devil was her intention with this horrible gown? He didn't believe for one moment she meant to entice him. So far today she tried to keep her distance.

Before they left, he dropped a shawl around her shoulders taking the opportunity to brush the back of his hands across her breasts while touching a tender nipple with a finger. At the brief contact, she sifted in air. He'd been in such a rage about the gown, he didn't give her time to drink the brandy. Tonight, instead of the phaeton he decided to take the carriage. He wanted her all to himself so he could use the opportunity to get closer.

Alexander opened the carriage door after they were inside. "Seems the two of you forgot your drinks." The man winked at him as he handed Betsy the one he poured for her. He certainly hoped that the drinks weren't mixed up. Unable to take a chance he decided to wait and see if there were any visible affects taking place after Betsy drank hers down.

"Thank you," Evan said as he watched Betsy sip the potent liquid. "Your ardent attention is much appreciated."

Alexander *kenned* a bit of what he was about tonight though not the details.

He didn't want her to fall asleep too soon. Not until after they reached the tattoo shack down on the docks. When they arrived, he would fix her another drink which would put her out cold. She would have no recollection of what she told the Black Widow. When she woke, he would make certain she understood the permanence of what she did.

He grinned.

"You've the silliest grin on your face," she said slurring her words just a tiny bit while she seemed to be staring at his lips. Leaving a damp trail behind, she leisurely sent her tongue across her mouth.

Unhurriedly he sipped his brandy. The carriage started.

Her hand on her head, she sighed leaning in his direction. "Oh, my...I'm a bit dizzy. What do you think? I probably shouldn't finish the drink."

Quickly, he slipped to her side of the carriage, his arm around her. "Lean on me then finish the drink. You'll be fine. If you drink that down, the tattoo won't hurt so much."

Perhaps he gave her too much. Despite all her beautiful curves, she was not a large lady.

She complied without one word of scorn. The sounds of the horses' hooves along with her deep breaths was all he heard for a short distance. Sluggishly, she pushed away, her eyes slightly dazed looking into his. "You're not going to seduce me?" She sounded disappointed.

"We will see," he murmured, tenderly brushing a tendril of hair behind her ear, taking the opportunity to outline the lobe with his fingertip then feel her sultry response. "Are you hungry?"

"Will you be highhanded and order for me again. What if I don't like what you choose?" she questioned her eyes flashing dangerously. "I don't like a man to choose my food for me."

"If you will eat, you can order anything you want."

His fingertip crept down her neck enjoying the silken skin. He ran his thumb across her lower lip, pulling on it slightly so he could dip his thumb inside the heat of her mouth.

Moments passed in bliss. He couldn't belief his luck. She didn't refuse any of his advances. Instead, she leaned into him seeming to absorb the sensations. He'd give just about anything to learn what she was thinking. What he gave her to calm her was not potent enough to take away all her inhibitions. He would never do that to a woman as he had enough confidence in his sexuality. Seducing a woman never gave him problems.

They stopped at one of his favorite restaurants. She ordered for herself, except for the wine which he insisted on ordering for both.

After she put up a hand to cover her glass, "No more."

"Yes, more. You're going to get a tattoo. The needles are painful. They are sharp and pointed. You need to be half-drunk so you won't run shrieking onto the docks with whatever part of you bared. I couldn't stand for sailors to see you naked or even half naked."

She removed her hand. He filled the glass. She did eat her dinner. Did drink most of the wine. They did speak briefly about his reinstatement to the university. In Evan's mind what happened wasn't any of her business. To his surprise she seemed to care about the incident. Was surprisingly on his side. No one he knew, even his brother was on his side.

He ordered dessert, a peach confection that was delicious. She must have a sweet tooth. He watched her devour all of hers then half of his. Perhaps it was the wine giving her the appetite. He'd never seen her eat so much. Maybe she was nervous. Maybe she wasn't. Last night she was nervous and she didn't eat.

When they finally left the restaurant, she was a bit unsteady on her feet. This was perfect for his plans. Wrapping an arm around her, he helped her to the carriage where he sat next to her. The drive was short. He planned both destinations well. Taking two long would only serve to sober her up. She needed to fall asleep while the tattoo was being administered. In the end she would thank him.

~ * ~

The Black Widow watched with narrowed eyes as Evan Murray led the slight girl into her shop. She was too damn little for the likes of a man the size of Evan. She reminded herself that she didn't ask questions or give opinions. Evan paid with good English pounds. What more could a working woman want. Before they arrived, she'd given tattoos to two young men off one of the merchant ships that pulled into the harbor yesterday afternoon. They'd cried out when the needle went to work, pansy's both of them. She scowled. Men should act like men.

"You have everything ready?" Evan asked while he escorted Betsy, his arm around her waist as if holding her up. "Betsy," he turned to her, lifting her chin up so she could see the woman. "This is the Black Widow. This is Betsy."

You're newest conquest? She asked silently. It wasn't her place to judge. The woman was beautiful though small. Her dress was not what she expected to be worn in front of a man such as Evan Murray. The woman's breasts were spilling from the low-cut corsage. She looked more like a woman of the evening than a woman who Evan would be interested in. From first-hand experience, looks could be deceiving.

Evan seemed to catch the drift of her thoughts. "She doesn't usually wear gowns like this one. She bought it for tonight so you would have easy access to her body parts."

The Black Widow nodded in understanding. She snorted, laughter in her eyes. "She wants the tattoo on her breast?"

Betsy looked up appearing startled. "Breast?" she asked appearing confused, her eyes so dark they looked as velvet as midnight.

"A little parrot." The Black Widow laughed as she led the way into the back room where the procedure would take place. She pulled out two wicked looking needles, held them up to the light in the room.

Betsy gasped, obviously pushing against her escort. The sound told the Black Widow that she made her point with the needles just as Evan had asked her.

Evan pulled out a chair for her. "One more drink before we get started. What do you say?" he asked grinning. "You won't feel a thing. I promise. The drink will ease the pain."

"D-do-don't y-you." She sent her tongue spinning across her

143

bottom lip. "Enough..." she finished.

"Enough wine? Not yet, the needles hurt," he reminded her while the Black Widow turned her back on them, readying her equipment. "It's your choice. A bit more wine or pain. What do you say? You can always change your mind." Funny thing was, he didn't want her to decide against the tattoo.

Betsy was nodding her head, licking her lips. "More wine then."

"I'll get it for you."

He went to stand by the Black Widow who handed him a glass. Quickly, he poured the wine then added the sleeping potion that would put her out for about an hour, possibly more. The Black Widow wasn't certain. Except for certain strategic places she was tiny. They would be back to the townhouse by the time she woke. There would be nothing she could do to change what would happen here...or there. She wouldn't do this if she didn't believe Evan to be honorable.

Hell, he was a man. She was a beautiful woman. Where was honorable in this scenario?

A few seconds later he stood beside her handing her the wine. The Black Widow watched the couple, laughing inside at Evan's antics. She would normally play this out in the way the woman wished. In this case, she had to agree with Evan. A real tattoo would be regretted for the rest of her life. This woman was adorable, just the handful for a man like Evan Murray.

Evan was honest enough to explain to her his guesses. She was running from something or someone. She had this crazy idea a tattoo would dissuade this unknown man. Him, because Evan felt certain a man was behind her change of character.

After Betsy downed the contents of her wine, she began the questioning. The Black Widow asked, "What would you like me to draw? The design?"

Laughter would not suit. Betsy's eyes were so wide. She was staring at the needle she laid by the table where Betsy was going to lie down.

"What do I want?"

She turned to Evan as if the man would give her the courage to go through with this.

"A rose is always nice...or a heart."

His smile was bland. That was not what they discussed earlier.

"A cross?" she asked shaking her head as if she had second thoughts.

"Are you religious?"

"A heart...a small one." She blurted quickly as if she had to make the decision this moment. "On my arm."

Well, she did, but the Black Widow didn't think she'd given serious thought to the matter. "A heart it is. Are you certain? Once it is done there is no changing your mind. Perhaps something that has more significance. A name..."

She was falling asleep in the chair. Her head was lolling to one side. "No...a ros..."

"A heart or a rose?" the black widow insisted. "Where?"

"I..." Her head jerked up. "Evan! Not on my backside! Evan please. I want Evan." she was able to put forth with a bit more strength than the Black Widow thought she possessed. "Evan it is."

Evan caught her before she crumpled to the floor, a wide grin sporting even white teeth flashed at her. Picking her up as if she weighed no more than the rose she spoke of, Evan laid her on the table.

The Black Widow held the block of wood with the design covered in ink. "Good thing she didn't see this; she might have had a heart attack. She did play into your hands rather nicely. If she remembers anything, she might remember insisting on your name."

"Probably will when we get back to my place after her first look in the mirror," Evan was smiling like a besotted fool.

There would be hell to pay.

Chapter Six

She woke to the sound of running water. For the longest time, she ran her fingers across the sheets. Wondering where she was, she heard other sounds she didn't recognize. When she lay on her back, looking overhead, the crack across her ceiling wasn't there. After she turned to her side again, the stained blue wall on the far side of the room was egg shell white. Nothing was familiar. When she opened her eyes again, she saw the dark blue draperies, the blue Aubusson carpet. Closing her eyes, Betsy took in the scent of...Evan! She sat up so quickly, the sheet pulled around her waist, her naked waist. Her breasts were bare as was the rest of her. The negligée from the first night when he seduced her lay at the end of the bed.

No!...no...no...she didn't did she? Wouldn't she remember such a momentous occasion? Looking to the door to the bathing room, she heard him whistling. Quickly, on all fours she groped for the gown at the foot of the bed. With jerky movements, she slipped the silk fabric over her head. The fabric covered her but she could also see all of her. She groaned softly as she realized her body ached everywhere.

Bloody hell! What happened. She groaned as the pounding in her head grew. Her hand went to her left breast.

Needles!

A tattoo, she did it. She had a tattoo put on her body. She didn't want to look. Never asked for the tattoo to go on her breast, did she? While her head throbbed, so did her breast. "Oh...oh...no..." Needles. She shouldn't have gone through with this adventure. He told her she would regret having it done. Why did she have the black, the black...she rubbed her temples unable to think of the rest of the woman's name. She'd had too much to drink or she would have never had the tattoo put on her breast. On her breast, dear God. She didn't want the blasted drawing on

146

her breast. Her arm. She wanted the design on her arm.

Reassuring herself that the mark was small, she would make certain Oliver heard about it. Would he insist on seeing the design? No...he would not, could not look at her breast. She couldn't allow him to do so. A tiny moan left her lips only to grow into a louder one. That's one of the reasons she purchased those two gowns. When she wore the dress the next time she met with Oliver, he would see the tattoo. Did she mean all along to have the mark on her breast?

What had she done?

Confusion rattled her aching brain. There was good as well as bad here. The blame for this outrageousness couldn't even be put on Evan's shoulders. He tried to talk her out of the tattoo. Tried to talk her out of wearing that horrible gown. If Oliver continued his pursuit, she would have to wear the harlot dress again. She couldn't think straight. She placed the heels of her hands on her temples, pushing, massaging.

His men, had one of Oliver's men seen her as she went into that shack to get the tattoo? She hoped and prayed that was true. Just as Oliver knew she was at Caro's the night before, he would learn where she slept last night. He would learn she now had a tattoo. He knew everything about her.

This morning...last night...she was in Evan's big bed.

Naked.

Did she, do it? Did he take her virginity and she didn't even remember? He must have. She couldn't think of any other reason for her to be naked in his bed while he was nonchalantly whistling in the bathing room as if nothing momentous happened.

More room to maneuver.

She didn't feel different. What did she know? She wanted to see her tattoo. She didn't want to see it. The flesh burned where the needle punctured her skin. This wasn't a small heart or a rose. What did she tell the Black Widow? At this moment, remembering was impossible. Now she felt the same burning on her backside.

A tap on the door. "Come in," Evan called out.

She slid beneath the covers. Alexander walked in with a breakfast tray. She wasn't hungry. Nonetheless, her stomach grumbled then began to rebel. The coffee smelled hot. She never liked coffee. Alexander ignored her then set the tray on a table between two chairs. He poured two cups of coffee. She wanted to ask for tea. Didn't dare draw attention to herself. Evan's servant would know she was here. Of course, he knew. There were two cups.

"Thank you, Alexander."

His man bowed toward the bathing room before leaving. This was a nightmare of her making. She should have never agreed to come here with him. Did she agree? Nothing made sense. Her mind was blank. The evening was a total washout. All she could remember was seeing the needles. That was the last of her memory.

She woke up here, in Evan's bed.

"Good morning," Evan called out cheerfully and way too loud. "You certainly don't hold your wine. I had to carry you up the steps. You blacked out the moment you saw the needles sitting on her table. I hope you're happy with the tattoos."

Tattoos? As in plural?

"I told you to stop pouring," she retorted then immediately regretted the outburst as the pounding in her head escalated.

He told her she needed a cushion of alcohol so the needle wouldn't hurt. His ploy certainly worked. Not only did she not feel anything, she didn't remember the night.

"True."

He stepped into the room, his unfastened buckskins hanging around his trim waist and narrow hips. "You would have felt the needle. I don't like tears. Wanted you knocked out cold before she started."

"I don't cry!" Her temper flared. "I don't like surprises either," she mumbled positive he would have something to say about that. For the sake of her head, she needed to keep her temper in check.

"What surprise?" He was towel drying his hair. At the table where breakfast was delivered, he sipped some of the coffee. "Everything was done just as you directed."

The bristling of her body started as a slow simmer began to work its way to full-blown proportions. With him, she needed to be angry, furious. Somehow, she couldn't quite muster that emotion. Mortification suffused the anger she should feel. "Why am I here? That's the surprise. Why didn't you take me to the cottage?"

A look of astonishment crossed his face as he tilted his head slightly in seeming confusion. "Ah, you don't remember asking to come home with me? You wanted me to give you a woman's pleasure. You asked me. Begged me. How can I, a mere man, refuse such a beautiful plea? Tell me."

"No!" The crux of the problem was that she didn't recollect anything at all. She couldn't possibly have asked him to take her virginity. Not after the night before. "You didn't!"

He could tell her whatever he wanted. She would have to believe him. So far, he hadn't said anything she wished to consider.

He was tsking and shaking head as if she was a recalcitrant child in need of an explanation. Well, she did need an explanation, more than anything. "Would you like coffee? It's a particular favorite of mine ever since I visited Baltimore." Once more he took a drink. "Delicious."

"Tea would suit me better."

"Try some." Half-naked he was walking toward her carrying two cups of coffee. "It's really very good. I could put some milk and sugar in yours if you would prefer. Won't be quite so bitter. It's works much better for a hangover than tea."

Bitter, yes, she was bitter, humiliated, torn with conflicting emotions. He took her virginity and she didn't recall anything. What she would prefer would be to remember what happened last night. It was all a black mess, a jumble in her muddled brain. She accepted the coffee, sipped. "It will do."

"Food?"

She couldn't possibly eat. Her stomach turned over. Bile rose. Naked, unable to stop, she rushed to the bathing room, to empty the contents of her stomach. He stood over her, holding the length of her hair behind her head. She wretched again. Soon nothing was coming from her. Groaning, she started to slump to the floor. He caught her up, carrying her back to the bed running his hand along her back in soothing motions.

"You really can't hold your drink. In the future, I'll try to remember that about you. You are much smaller than I thought.

Hopefully, you won't want another tattoo since you did get three last night."

Three?

She jerked up, confused. She'd only signed up for one. "There won't be a future," she shot at him. Wishing what she was saying would turn out to be true. She wanted to ask about the three tattoos. Was terrified to discover the truth. He wouldn't joke about something like that.

Three tattoos...oh dear God.

Two steps from the bed he turned. Looked to the basin where she lost the contents of her stomach then back to her. "You're not pregnant, are you? Now, I was certain it was the excessive drink that caused this but one never knows."

Pregnant?

Was he daft? No, he thought she had lovers, old lovers, men who couldn't give her pleasure in bed. She didn't quite understand his reasoning. That was why she was interested in him. She didn't do anything to change his mind about her. Wasn't about to now. Nonetheless, she wasn't going to let him think she might be carrying some man's child.

"No."

"Positive?" One of his dark brows launched toward the ceiling in apparent disbelief. "If one plays then sometimes one has to pay the consequences."

Ignoring his question, she sipped, letting the heat of the coffee soothe her stomach. Tea would have worked better, not that she ever in her life needed something for a splitting headache. She never had a headache before. Never drank too much either or allowed a man she hardly knew to make love to her. Never got a tattoo before either or wore a gown befitting a harlot.

"Positive?" he repeated as he sat down on the bed a plate of toast in his hand.

One couldn't get much blander than dry toast. The wretch knew she'd be sick, must have ordered this before she woke. He held the tray to her. Reluctantly she picked up one piece, took a small bite.

"Good girl. I take it you're not pregnant."

Couldn't be.

"Not pregnant." She was shaking her head, giving him more reason she hoped to believe her.

"Been that long since you took a lover?"

What more could she say? Sheepishly she answered, "Yes."

"Glad to hear that. Now, would you like to see your tattoos? I was quite pleased when you finally told the Black Widow that you wanted her to put one on your breast. A man doesn't expect anything like that from a woman he's just recently met. You must have been smitten with me from the moment you first saw me. Was surprised, too, when you asked for two more to be put on your adorable backside."

"Something like what? My backside?" All of her heaved, her breast swaying provocatively.

He laughed, brushing her hair from her face with a tender hand. "You are adorably sweet. Little parrot again. You don't remember what tattoo you requested? You truly don't recall anything about last night, do you?"

Her entire body shuddered as she closed her eyes as if the image was burned behind her eyelids. "After I saw the needles, I don't remember anything. Did I pass out?"

She felt the slow burn of her temper. For some reason she was trying to lay the blame for this on his shoulders. It wasn't working. He wasn't at fault here. She was.

"Oh!" he sounded surprised. "You were quite vocal as well as adamant about your wishes. Guess you took my suggestion to heart about the best place for a tattoo was on the breast. I didn't even suggest the location to you when we were there. Who is it you want to shock with the tattoo? I'm quite certain when this person sees the top of your breast, the tattoo will do what it is meant to do."

"Lord Oliver..."

She saw the narrowing of his eyes as the information settled into his head. She didn't mean to blurt that out. Her mind just wasn't working this morning.

Stroking his chin thoughtfully, he went on to say, "Thought it was a man you were running from. What does he want with you?"

After she turned away from him, he took her chin with his fingers, turned her so she had to look at him, his eyes penetrating her. This wasn't his business. He didn't have a right to know. "Marriage. He wants to make me his wife."

"I take it you don't want the same thing." He whistled softly still looking intently at her, seeming to absorb the reason for her bizarre behavior. He stared at her naked body seeming amazed she made no attempt to clothe herself. "Have you tried telling him no? Often that word works the best in situations that need agreement."

"Not in this case. The man doesn't take no for an answer." Truly, he didn't. She told him 'no' one day before she left for Glasgow. So, what does he do? He follows me.

"Uh--huh?" His speculation was obvious. He didn't understand her plight.

"If I don't tell him, yes, I'll never work again in London or anywhere close. No one will hire me as a nanny or a tutor."

Moisture was beginning to cloud in her eyes. Nevertheless, she saw the sudden rise of fury in Evan's eyes. While he was a man who took what he wanted, he didn't seem to think other men should do the same. Perhaps he wouldn't take something from her that would cost her so dear.

What of hers did he take that he wanted? Her virginity. Now Oliver wouldn't want her. If she'd known what would happen moments after her tattoo, she wouldn't have gotten one. As her father would have told her, the event was now water under the bridge. She couldn't turn back time.

Well, she wanted that to happen, practically begged him to do just that last night.

"I will tell him no for you. Just tell me where he is staying. I'll pay the man a visit after I drop you off."

"No. you can't interfere. That wouldn't be smart. He can bury you."

She didn't want to think of Lord Oliver hurting this man. Oliver was ruthless when it came to getting what he wanted. He possessed the money along with the power to make Evan Murray's life a miserable one.

"Perhaps. That never stopped me confronting someone who is doing harm to a person I care about."

He cares about me?

"I must do this myself. I need to be the one to make him believe that I want nothing to do with him." Desperation sank into her as if talons raked her flesh. "At the moment, he still thinks he can wear me down. He can't." She sipped the coffee, ate another bite of toast. Thought that maybe the morsel would stay down. Tired of morose thoughts she meant to change the topic. "I want to see my tattoos," she told him wishing he would leave her in privacy for the unveiling.

"I can't tell you how pleased I am to hear that." He stood extending his hand to her. "I'll go with you. I'm certain..." He left off the rest of the comment unfinished.

She didn't want to fill in the blank. For seconds, she held back from him. "Privacy for the first look?" she asked feeling sheepish.

She would have to bear herself. Even though she spent the night with him, she didn't recall.

"If you wish."

His voice took on a harsh note. Obviously, he wasn't happy with her request. She imagined he would want to see the first reaction. He could see the second.

After she rose from the bed, she smoothed the fabric of the sheer gown she wore understanding he could see through to her nakedness. She held her hand over that part of her that was tattooed. Odd that the negligée did not fall as low as the two gowns she purchased the day before. The fabric was so sheer it didn't need to reveal more than it already did.

As she walked the short distance to the bathing room, she felt the heat of his masculine gaze burn her. The steps seemed to take forever. Finally, standing in front of the huge mirror, she undid the ties at her shoulder allowing the gown to reveal what she did.

For the longest time she looked at herself in shock. Her breathing stopped as did her heart. When she finally sipped a drink of air and her heart began to pulse, she swallowed down the cry of horror that hovered in the back of her throat.

She could hold the scream back no longer. The shriek following her first sight brought Evan running to her. He stood behind her, his hands on her shoulders. His grin swept from one ear to the other.

"Do you like it as much as I do?" he asked her eagerly waiting for her answer. "When you told the Black Widow you wanted to have my name tattooed on your breast, I was surprised. It's splendid. The color is spectacular."

He cupped the bared breast with his hand, holding the mound so his name was bold just above the pink of her aureole. "I held you like this when she put my name here." His breath caressed her nape. Her response was quick and heated.

"No..."

"I couldn't have asked for a more perfect gift. Here." He was pulling up the skirt of the negligée. She was doing nothing to stop him. "I'll show you the other tattoos." To put her back to the mirror, he turned her holding the gown above her waist.

He held my breast in his hand when the needles spelled out his name.

He could see all of her. She was so mortified about the tattoo on her breast that she didn't care she was all but naked to his eyes. He'd seen her before, touched her, put his lips on her.

"See..."

Peering over her shoulder she stared at her rump. On either side close to her spine just as her hips were beginning to flare there was a rose on one side and a heart on the other side. Light-headed she leaned into him, her head against his chest. Her heart fluttering. She heard the pounding of his heart. Hers was racing out of control.

Dear God, how was she going to get rid of his name on her breast? The other two were bad enough. She couldn't show them to Oliver. Never in a million years could she do something so daring. Although Evan's name boldly written on her chest might do the trick of dissuading the man. All she would have to do was wear one of her new gowns. Even Lord Oliver would think long and hard about asking a woman to wed him who had another man's name spelled out boldly on her breast. A woman who gave herself to that man.

She looked into his laughing eyes. She wanted to smack the silly grin off his face. She cut to the most important question, tilting her chin defiantly. "How do I get rid of them?"

"You don't. Tattoos are permanent. You do recall my telling you just that yesterday before you insisted I find someone to do the job. You will wear my name the rest of your life." He paused with dramatic affect. "I did tell you that. You told me you understood and still wanted one. If you recall, I did my best to dissuade you."

"Why didn't you tell the Black Widow I would never want your name permanently on me?" She wanted to beat on him, needed to make sure he understood how angry she was.

"I did, my sweet Little Bit. You insisted. I was so flattered, I finally agreed."

"Evan! Evan, you taking a bath? I'm going to barge in."

"Fletcher, no!" Evan left her standing in front of the mirror, staring at her backside. Her temper began to simmer out of control. Time seemed to stand still before everything burst into confusion. *Who was Fletcher?*

"Evan?" Fletcher's deep baritone slowly began to make its way into her senses.

The man stood in the doorway to the bathing room. The dark of his eyes focused on her. For all practical purposes, she was naked. A man she'd never met before stared at her, grinning from one ear to the other.

"You can't be in here." Evan said dryly as he seemed to realize it was too late to undo the damage. "Go on downstairs. I'll meet you as soon as I take care of Betsy."

When she gasped then whirled, she understood her predicament. While from one view her backside was blatantly in clear view of this man named Fletcher who resembled Evan a bit, the second view was of her breast with Evan's name boldly scrawled across the top.

"The man wasn't following Evan's directions.

Quickly, she pulled the gown up and dropped the skirt, not that the action did much good. She tried to cover herself with her hands. Her hands didn't cover much of her as she learned earlier. Fletcher was clearly enjoying the show she was putting on for him. A towel dropped around her shoulders.

"Go into your bedroom," Evan whispered, his mouth so close to her ear his breath sent a heated wave of pleasure through her despite the situation.

Dazed, she nodded.

Once she disappeared into the other bedroom and with the door closed firmly behind her, she put her head in her hands. Tears wouldn't fall. She had no reason to cry. Except for his name on her for the rest of her life, he gave her exactly what she asked for. Her mother also told her a body needed to be careful about what they wished for. She imagined in this case those words were true.

Dear God, how could this all turn out so badly. After she walked to the door, she heard the rumble of masculine voices blend into words she didn't understand. They weren't arguing as she thought they might. No, there was laughter. They were probably talking about her along with the tattoos. Her predicament amused them. Being the source of male amusement was not to her liking. She threw the towel on the floor then whisked the gown over her head before tossing it aside.

Looking at her trunk, she walked to it. A few minutes later she set clothing out and dressed. If she could figure out how to do so, she would leave. After the immediate need to flee, rational thought set in. She had nowhere to go as well as no way to get there. She couldn't go to Oliver even though he would accept her until he saw what she'd done. Giving him reason to hope for something that would never be, disgusted her even more so than the tattoos.

Confronting this man who saw her naked was also something she couldn't do. No matter, she would tilt up her chin, in the process pretend nothing happened. She walked out the door then down the stairs. In the drawing room, Alexander brought her a cup of tea.

"Is your stomach feeling better, Miss Darling? Your head?" he asked pleasantly the fine lines of his narrow face drawn with concern. "I would get anything you need."

"That toast worked wonders. Thank you," she murmured as she added things to her tea.

"Thought it might. When my late wife drank too much, bland toast was all she could handle afterword."

He smiled as if recalling a memorable moment.

"Who is that man?" Her voice wavered uncontrollably when she asked

Alexander shot a look up the steps. "Fletcher Murray, a younger brother; not the youngest though. He has three brothers."

"That's what I thought. He saw me naked. Saw all three tattoos."

Betsy didn't understand why she was telling Alexander this newest humiliation. It seemed to her the man was always there to see to her needs or Evan's. Without even trying, he endeared himself with his tender caring. She could get used to his codling.

"Evan will explain everything to him. No need to worry," he said, his words taking on a soothing tone calmed her seething nerves as well as her befuddled mind.

With a deep breath, "Yes, well, that's easy for you to say. He didn't see you naked or the humiliating tattoos that I guess I begged for."

No man ever saw her naked until she came to Glasgow. Now, within the span of two days two men saw her with nothing on. If anyone besides these three men of her acquaintance knew, she'd be ruined. No one else knew. Lord Oliver needed to know. How to go about telling him, she didn't know.

Voices coming down the stairs stopped her musing along with her conversation with Alexander who vanished. Heat rushed to her face as soon as she saw Evan's knowing grin then Fletcher's. She would never recover from the mortification. Felt a surge of heat to her face. They both looked at her as if they'd seen what was beneath her clothing. Ah, they both had.

She sipped in a long drink of air waiting for more of what she wasn't at all certain. There were certain intimate details she needed to speak with Evan about. Fletcher was in the way. The brother didn't appear to be going anywhere.

"Betsy, this is my brother, Fletcher. He says he closed his eyes."

Evan had a look of a man who was holding back his laughter.

She turned away, her hands on her face as she tried to sooth the flames burning on her cheeks. When she turned back, he still grinned at her. Speaking stiffly, she began, "I'd like to say it's nice to meet you but it isn't. Perhaps under different circumstances."

The man didn't close his eyes, not one tiny little bit. He looked at her now as if imagining her naked.

"These circumstances suited me just fine." His grin was more lecherous than Evan's. "You're quite beautiful. Told Evan he was a very lucky man. If you get bored with the stuffy man here, let me know. I'll take over where he's left off."

Now she turned on Evan, her voice discordant. "How could you let me do this?"

She was fuming from the inside out. He should have stopped her. "Well, now uh...let's just take a quick look back on last night."

~ * ~

"The tattoo has character," Fletcher spouted his opinion with a sideways smirk when he looked at her briefly. "The only thing better would have been my name. Would have had to take up both breasts since my moniker is longer. I could have held them both in my hands while that needle did its work."

To Evan's delight she looked as if she wanted to throw her cup of tea, saucer, and all. She just didn't know who should be the recipient, him or his brother. He could hardly wait until she let lose all that simmering fury. When she would explode, she would tackle him instead of throwing things at him. He just needed to prod the dragon a bit more. He also needed to wait until Fletcher left for the full onslaught to come to its proper conclusion. His little brother was amused with the situation. It wasn't everyday a man was unexpectedly greeted by a nearly naked woman. He would be amused as well as pleased. Nonetheless, Betsy was his not his brother's to look at. For the time being, he would lay claim to her.

"Fletcher, don't you have better places to be?" Evan asked while he studied this situation, which turned out better than he ever could have expected.

Taking a few seconds, he studied his nails.

"Alexander offered me breakfast." Fletcher said blandly. "Don't have to be at the university until noon. After what I saw in your lavish bathing room, thought I might stick around for a bit just to see what else might happen."

"Fletcher works in the philosophy department," Evan explained to Betsy. "He truly does need to get to work."

"I still have a job so I'm a much better escort than my brother, much more reliable," Fletcher added with a wink. "Did you know even Duncan has said he can't work in the firm until he apologizes. Who do you think will give in first? Evan or the big brother?"

"When hell freezes over," Evan mumbled.

She was now dressed in one of her normal gowns that went clear to her chin. He was beginning to prefer the harlot gown. He wanted to see how his name moved when she sipped in air. When her anger flashed to fury. No, he wanted to get her naked in bed, so he could watch his name when she climaxed beneath him, on top of him, in front of him. A soft groan rumbled up from his chest. He didn't think he could get her back in the bedroom before this evening. However, he had time to work on this new challenge.

"Guess you better count on making your own way. Your savings won't last forever," Fletcher taunted him with the loss of both jobs. "By the way, have you seen this morning's paper? You should try not to create scandal everywhere you go." Fletcher took the newest edition from his breast pocket handing it over to Evan.

"Thought you were a financial wizard. Didn't you just make some fantastic investment that made you a great deal of money." Betsy looked to him as if she'd been lied to again. After she spoke her attention seemed to follow the paper. "What is that?"

"Part of that goes to the firm," Fletcher said appearing amused by stirring the rivalry between the two of them. "He doesn't receive all the groats. Did he tell you differently?"

"You and I both know we've more groats than we can spend in a lifetime." Evan stood nodding toward the dining room, ignoring Betsy along with the headlines about his visit to the tattoo parlor. "If you're going to stay for breakfast, let's eat. Betsy has research. Don't you, Little Bit?" He was in a hurry to get her all to himself, close quarters in the phaeton. He also didn't think she'd be too pleased with the headline now that the boldly printed topic concerned her. Though no one would know it was her since her name was never mentioned. Thank God. It wouldn't take long though for someone to figure out who he was escorting to places like tattoo shacks located on the docks. Sooner or later her name would mingle with his.

"Evan!"

"Later, sweetheart."

He liked the way she bristled when he called her sweetheart. He'd have to think of an appropriate pet name that would be just for her. Sweetheart wasn't good enough for her unique personality. Little Bit had potential.

Once again, she ate little. He imagined her head still hurt. Her stomach seemed to have recovered somewhat. He didn't have regrets. If he could do it again, he would. The henna would wear off in a couple of weeks. Until her tattoos started fading, she wouldn't know they weren't permanent. He wasn't going to tell her different.

Fletcher left after about an hour saying his goodbyes from the dining room and telling Betsy he would take her to the next university ball. There would be one in a few months. He hoped Betsy would still be in Glasgow. She told him a month or two.

Evan didn't understand why he felt the loss if she left. He wanted her to stay. He supposed he should discover a bit more about Lord Oliver. If he could arrange a meeting, he would. The best time would be when he dropped her at the university. It would be easy for him to take a detour to the hotel. Taking the measure of the man would give him a bit more insight into how he was going to help Betsy rid herself of the unwanted baggage.

Once Betsy sat next to him in the phaeton, and after a few minutes of silence, she turned to him, her tiny fists clenched in her lap. He wanted to laugh. He didn't dare. "You can hit me if you like. I know it will make you feel better. Do your worst or, well, maybe your best. What do you think? If you punched me in the nose, would you feel better?"

"Hitting you wouldn't serve one purpose. Nor would it make me feel better. I'd more than likely hurt my hand," she pouted prettily.

Usually, he didn't enjoy a woman's pout or sulk. He thought this one might be contrived. Perhaps for his benefit, she was trying to show her displeasure with him.

"You don't want to hit me?" He set his hand on her thigh, ran the length from her knee to her hip then back. "Maybe you want to go to bed with me again. Last night you did howl your pleasure. Would that help ease your anger? A little exercise. Ah, that will have to wait until you've been to the library. If you want to visit the Black Widow again, I could arrange another tattoo. One on the other breast, my middle name or..."

She gave him a look that would send him straight to hell if she had the power. "What I want," she bit out coldly, "is to get rid of the ones I have. Now, tell me about the paper. It had something to do with me. Didn't it?"

"Ah, I did enjoy kissing the heart as well as the rose. Your backside is almost as delicious as your front side. The article didn't mention your name. Though it did bring up the question of the lady I escorted to the tattoo shack."

A rosy blush tinted her delicate features. He liked making her blush almost as much as he enjoyed kissing her or seeing the flare of her temper. Watching his name sway on her breast was becoming the first, number one enjoyment of his.

Her bristling body delighted him. "As you well know, I don't remember last night. All I know is what you tell me. Did it say anything about the tattoo? What it was?"

"You were a little wildcat, clawing, scratching, begging me for more then more. You writhed delightfully beneath me. When you cried out my name, well, that makes a man feel *verra* proud about what he's about. Means he's doing everything just right."

"I did not." She straightened again. "I wouldn't do that. I don't."

"Oh, but you did. Before we even got into the bedroom, you were ripping your clothes off as well as mine. I had to send Alexander away so he wouldn't see you naked. Have you never cried out the names of your other lovers before? You cried out my name more than once when I gave you your pleasure."

He needed to kiss her. Needed to find a nice secluded place away from prying eyes so he could do more than just kiss. Since he pretty much invented last night, he wanted to see if she would be a wildcat in bed. He'd already tasted some of her passion and fire. He needed more so he could make a valid assessment.

Her eyes darkened; a moment later they crossed. She hit his chest with her reticule. "I did not. I wouldn't. That's not like me."

"You did. Do you feel better now that you hit me?" He turned the horse down a side street. Branches of trees nearly grew together over the road. It was dark, perfect for a short dalliance with the woman that would soon grace his bed. He wanted to feel more of her appetites for love. Feel the raw hunger bubble up from deep inside. A kiss right now would be more than nice. He spent the entire night lying next to her, holding her, feeling her nakedness pressed against him, the curve of her enticing breasts against his chest unable to do anything. She was passed out drunk on the wine along with the sleeping potion. He never took a woman who wasn't conscious. He hadn't meant to get her quite so drunk that she wouldn't wake up until the morning. Thought he would have the night with her.

"No." She looked behind her then in front. "Where are we?"

"A place where I can teach you how to kiss. Your first lesson was nice. You were adequate. Last night, well, your kisses left me needing to teach you a bit more. Nonetheless, you can do better when you are not intoxicated."

"Lesson? Kiss? No, I'm not going to kiss you."

"Uh—huh, you are." He pulled her onto his lap. Her body pressed closed to his. Tonight, he would take a closer look at those beautiful breasts of hers. Tonight, he would not make a tactical error that would send her running away from him. "Now, where to start?"

He pushed back a few tendrils of hair that had fallen free, studying her. He was pleased with what he saw.

She wiggled against him. Stopped when she must have felt the male part he told her she could use anytime she wished.

"Really, Evan, wasn't last night enough for you?" Her sweet pink tongue the one he wanted to dally with left moisture behind on her bottom lip.

"You comfortable?" he asked as his hand wrapped around her waist, inching higher to settle beneath the swell of her breast. He ran his thumb along the bottom, wishing she didn't have fabric shielding her from his questing fingers.

She wiggled again, adjusting herself. The soft roundness of her breast pushed against his chest. "Yes...no...I don't want to sit on your lap." She was staring at him, the cornflower blue of her eyes darkening with the burgeoning flames of passion she was just beginning to recognize.

His thumb traced her bottom lip. "You're so soft." Her tongue flicked out to touch the pad of his thumb. "Moist. Wet. You do want me to kiss you, you just don't want to admit to the fact. Don't deny us our pleasure. What have you got to go home to? Lord Oliver or your archaic lovers. They won't give you a woman's pleasure."

"You are going to ruin me?" she sighed out breathlessly then stiffened.

She must not have admitted to a fact he figured out this morning when she mentioned the man she didn't want. Her eyes were closed now. Her little sighs coupled with the broken sound in the back of her throat spoke of pleasure. She responded so quickly. His lips met hers in a brief slow caress that quickened her. With just her secret breath mingling with his, he touched her lip with the tip of his tongue, teasing her to give him more of her passion. She moved on his legs. He hardened even more. The devil take the afternoon. He didn't have a need to go anywhere. Neither did she. Research could wait for another day. With the tiniest kiss this woman set him on fire, flames blazed, his body wrestled with the instant need for her.

His hands at her waist he lifted then turned her so she sat astride him. He ran his hands along the ladder of her ribs to her breasts then back to her waist. Squeezed. "Thought you wanted me to ruin you," he murmured softly, his lips touching her lips that were slightly parted. "Can't do that unless we start at the beginning. Got to learn how to give a proper kiss to the man who's going to make all your dreams come true."

"Yes..." she sighed softly snuggling against him as he took her breath into his mouth, sipping. Tasting her woman-scent.

"Kiss me, Betsy," he told her, his voice husky with the rampant desire she flamed to life.

Her hands wrapped around his neck, her tiny little nails raking heated flesh. She touched his mouth with hers, leaning against him as she tried to close the distance. Seeming to experiment, she swept her tongue across his bottom lip before pushing slightly inside. She was going to kill him if she kept up this half-hearted exchange. Her thighs pushed against his. The heat and dampness of her woman's folds seared through his pants to touch him, arouse him fully.

Unable to stop himself, he enclosed her mouth with the heat of his. Searching, seeking the sultry heat inside her body, he pushed his tongue inside. Deeply he played with her, sucking then exploring. More flames ignited as her hips moved across his hardening body. When he turned her, he managed to pull her dress up around her legs. The opening of her pantalets was against him. Damp heat pressed against his arousal. It would not take much to open his trousers then thrust inside her.

He pulled back slightly. Their first time together he wanted her in his bed. Husky feminine sighs filtered from the back of her throat. Her back arched as he left the heat of her mouth to rake his teeth along her neck. She was hanging on to him allowing his hands to roam. He found the softness of her ankle then the back of her knees. He glided his fingers to the soft thatch between her legs. Parting the pantalets, he caressed the folds at the apex of her thighs. She jerked then gave over to the intimate caress. Hot and wet the sultry rain of her hunger poured onto his questing fingers.

She was so passionate he thought he might die if he couldn't have her. She seemed to spark out of control. He found the hard satin jewel hidden between the folds that were ready for him, waiting for his entrance to her velvet sheath. Sometime before his first taste of her and now, she'd unfastened his shirt. Her fingers spread across his chest, running across his rapidly hardening nipples.

"You want it right here, right now. Don't you, Betsy?"

She was so hot with her desire. He thought he must have died and gone to heaven. Again, he told himself this was not the place or time for their first hungry joining.

"Evan..." her voice was a thin wail. "Please..."

Now she was begging. Moaning. Heaving. She arched. Swearing at himself, cursing softly that he started something he couldn't finish. She seemed to unravel with each caress, each rake of his teeth. He wanted to taste her again, needed to taste the sweet rain between her legs. His lips met hers while he fumbled with the fasteners of her dress. His fingers closed around her breast, his thumb flicking across the hardened tip.

The sound of horses, a carriage somewhere down the long rarely used road, brought him to his senses. "We can't...company coming." He pulled her dress together. Didn't do anything about her position astride him. A distant thought that there might be another article in the paper tomorrow. Someone was following him.

She made a slow sound of displeasure. "Evan, please..."

"I understand. Tonight we will come together as you want. You were such a little wanton last evening. There was no doubt you needed me. Seems I forgot how fast you detonate with just a kiss."

Her head fell against his chest, her breath sifting frantically across his muscles. They heated, rippling with the soft caress of her secret awakening. She aroused him with just the whisper of her heated breath. The afternoon would last an eternity. The last few days he spent hard, wanting to be sheathed in her core.

"I..."

She didn't move for the longest time. Her fingers flexed spasmodically against his shoulders while she clung to him.

Slowly, he brought her skirts to pool around her, his hands settling back on her waist. He turned her so she sat next to him on the phaeton. He felt the absolute cad leaving her in need. When he looked at her, Betsy's eyes were glazed, her body trembling with the pleasure he almost gave her. Next time she would know ecstasy. He'd never touched a woman who responded so quickly or so intensely. She was everything he ever dreamed of, sweet, impulsive, passionate, ripe with raw hunger.

"Tonight, sweetheart. Tonight. Can you wait?" The devil there wasn't a choice unless he drove home and carried her to his bed. "For now, I'm going to take you to the university. Need to see someone while you research that queen consort of yours."

He needed to tell Lord Oliver she was his. He couldn't have her. Best he go home to London since he was wasting his time in Glasgow.

"I don't want to wait." She was still dazed, her breathing shallow as she tried to recover from the intensity of the recent encounter.

He didn't want her to wait either. Though in a few minutes once the passion died, she'd tell him she didn't want anything to do with him. Her denials were expected as well as ridiculous. This woman wanted sex as powerfully as she wanted to breathe. He was certain she almost climaxed in his arms just now. Another few seconds and her core would have been pulsing, throbbing hotly with ecstasy.

Tonight. *Ce soir.*

With his finger he touched her beneath her chin. "How are you feeling?" he asked his voice soft, seeing that she was beginning to find her way from the harsh jaws of desire unfulfilled.

There were so many ways and so many places he'd like to take her after the bed. Twice, he kissed her and barely touched her intimately. She nearly climaxed both times.

She didn't answer right away. He chuckled softly. His hands stroked her arm then the length of her hair that had come undone. She must have to think over the question.

If she gave herself to this Lord Oliver, no wonder he didn't want to lose her. How could any man suffer the loss of such a wanton lover? The thought of her in another man's arms left him with Gaelic curses simmering in the back of his throat.

The carriage he heard earlier slowly passed them by. The driver slanted them a curious look. Evan tapped her on the nose. "You, okay?" he asked again, hoping she was on the path to recovery.

With a soft sigh that she let sift slowly from her still moist lips. "Never better."

She would be fine in a few more minutes. "Good, I saw the tattoo on your breast. Tonight, I'll outline each letter of my name with kisses. Would you like that? Afterword, I'll turn you over, slip my tongue across the heart as well as the rose."

She moaned, a soft broken sound cascading once more from her soft lips. He didn't truly understand the emotions filling him. This woman was unique, touching him tenderly even when she could also send him to such levels of frustration, he wanted to shake her.

Denying her sexuality wasn't what he expected from a woman who'd had numerous lovers. When he touched her, her hunger exploded, her passion discharged. Sometimes she acted as if she was an innocent, then, when she flew so quickly and so high in such a short time the fact told him she was experienced. Once he touched her, she never denied him, never once told him no, never a gasp of surprise when he stroked her intimately. Had expected the first time and even the second time he caressed her sultry feminine petals she would have been shocked. The only gasp, the only broken sound he heard were ones of pleasure. Most women would have stopped him. Her elderly lovers would never have stroked her intimately or tasted her using their tongue on her secret parts.

She wasn't shocked or horrified of his bold caresses. Betsy welcomed her into the promised inferno of her body with willing abandon.

She seemed to want those strokes as much as he wanted to give them. In the bath she'd looked beneath the water. She must have seen the evidence of his growing desire for her. Unexpectedly, she touched parts in him no woman ever affected before her. He didn't think he'd ever grow bored with her in his arms, his bed, his life.

He lifted her chin. Placed a brief brushing of his lips on hers. She lowered her eyelashes as if embarrassed by her rapid rise of passion. Once again, the pulse at the base of her neck leapt begging eagerly for more.

"You don't want me?" Her mint scented question whispered across his lips. "I'm sorry. I didn't know what I was doing."

She looked at the floor seeming to find immediate fascination with her feet. "You should take me to the library before I do or say something we'll both regret."

He should. She couldn't do or say anything he would regret unless she denied him. "I don't want to. To me, Little Bit, you knew very well what you were doing. My arousal was swift as well as potent. Don't deny your experience. If you try to pretend you are a virgin, I will see through the ploy. No virgin can respond as you do. No innocent can send the inferno so swiftly to me, heating me from the inside out."

"As you say," she murmured looking straight ahead, her expression a mask now.

Her voice was stiff with meaning he didn't understand. He wished to be inside her head. She couldn't still intend to fob herself off as an untried innocent. As soon as he thrust into the silken flames of her sheathe, he would know the truth. A woman could hide the fact of her innocence to only her first lover. As far as he could tell, this woman had many.

Her seeming denial infuriated him. Honesty was of utmost importance in a lasting relationship. He soothed his shattered nerves with long deep breaths. "Yes, as I say, don't pretend to be someone you are not." He spoke softly, watching as her eyes slowly slid to meet his gaze.

"You're angry with me."

To deny the anger seemed inexcusable. Pursuing a different topic seemed the best way to proceed. "Tell me more about your Lord Oliver." The command in his voice almost made him cringe. He had to know. After he dropped her off, he was going to meet the man. He wanted some idea who he was about to confront.

"What do you want to learn about the man?" She asked while she played with the fasteners on her gown. The yellow fabric reminded him of sunshine just as her hair did, golden sunshine for him to bask in the heat.

"Everything, anything that comes to mind." He wasn't certain that she would say what he wanted to hear. "Why does he want to marry you instead of some younger woman? If he's titled with money, he can have the pick of all the debutantes coming to London for a season."

Shaking her head, the hint of a smile on her lips, "To torment me." She lifted her shoulders in a feminine shrug of disbelief. "Truly, I don't know why. He has had his eyes set on me for two years now. For some time, I've dodged his advances. I don't have wealth or a title. Don't have anything he could possibly want. I'm too old. For some reason he thinks I'll take good care of his girls because I'm such a stellar, conservative woman. I have to make him see I'm not."

"He wants you as his wife? Not as his mistress? Interesting." The fact staring him in the face astounded him. After the question arose in his mind.

What would he want? What did he want? A mistress or a wife? That would depend on the woman.

"Believe he understands I would never be any man's mistress. So, the only way he can have me would be as his wife. I don't understand his reasoning either. I'm not terribly attractive. There are so many young beauties in London."

"Have you looked at yourself? You are stunning."

"I am?"

She appeared totally astounded by his compliment. The thought of her becoming the wife to anyone but him sent a primal rage of jealousy piercing through him. "Yes, you are. You don't want to be his wife. Why not? If he has wealth as well as a title, what woman would not want that for her future husband?"

She shivered, her revulsion at the notion clearly an integral part of her. "Would you want to bed a man who resembled King Henry VIII?" Her voice shook with disdain coupled with loathing. "I could not go to bed with that man for all the wealth in the world."

His hoot of laughter seemed to surprise her. He watched her eyebrows narrow. She looked as if she wanted to hit him again. With a slowness of words that surprised her, he calmly pointed out, "I wouldn't want to bed any man."

After she hit him in the chest with her tiny fist, he set the phaeton to moving at a quick clip. He was eager to get on with the afternoon. Once they moved into the traffic, he glanced at her waiting for her to respond.

"You know what I mean."

He nodded. "Is that the only reason?"

"No, he's loathsome, his personality not only his body. He acts intitled. Arrogant. Self-centered. Pompous." She pointed down the road. "That carriage that just passed us is most likely one of his men spying on me."

"On us," he corrected realizing his loathing might be growing. "He knew where you were when you slept in Caro's cottage. He followed you from my townhouse." He was certain the man was behind the tattoo article as well. At this revelation, he wasn't positive what to think. Was the man trying to ruin the woman he wanted to wed? If so, her attempts to malign her character were only going to help him. The next most prevalent question in his mind; was someone trying to ruin him? That was also possible. Except, he didn't believe he had an enemy at least not one of that caliber.

"He most likely had spies following us when I got my tattoo."

She confirmed his thoughts. "In London, he always knew where I was as well as what I was about. If he disapproved of something I did, he would tell me. The notion he knew all about me both infuriated as well as terrified." Visibly, she shuddered. The distaste for the man still evident in the expression on her sweet face.

"You're doing this, acting unlike yourself to scare him away." He didn't like the fact Betsy was using him to suit her purposes. "If he thinks you bedded me, he will turn away from you. Is that it? What about your other lovers?" he was quick to ask as he wanted answers. "They don't matter to the man?"

"He doesn't know about them." She hid her face from him.

Evan wanted to swear at the sun. He also wanted to believe all that passion he felt a few moments ago was only for him. Not for a reason to get rid of the man who wanted to be her husband. "If he has you followed everywhere, doesn't it make sense that he would also know about your lovers?"

She paled, her lips drawn into a thin line.

They turned onto a busy street. He tried to still his raging thoughts with calm rationality. "Why don't you just tell him about the men you've slept with? If you're right about Lord Tindell, the facts should send him packing." The question was simple enough. Straight forward.

"He wouldn't believe me. He believes I'm stellar, beyond reproach. Perfect to be the mother for his girls."

The sense she made was fleeting. After his meeting with Lord Oliver, it was time for him to slip away to the country home. His parents were in Edinburgh for the next month. They wouldn't be requesting a conversation. A dinner one night with Caro along with Duncan would help him get back in Duncan's good graces. He would have time with her alone to discover if there was more between them than mere lust.

Although experiencing her lust would be heaven sent. He would evade the scandal her presence seemed to be creating in his life. If he continued in this vein, he would never find himself reinstated at the university or at his brother's firm. Evan didn't understand why, but he wanted something more from her. He meant to get it. At what cost? He didn't truly care.

~ * ~

Evan was headed to the Grand Hotel. That was where she told him that Lord Oliver Tindell was staying. He tapped his fingers on the reins. Too much, there was just too much he didn't know, too many conflicting facts to set his mind at ease. Nonetheless, what he did know was that he wanted Lord Tindell out of both their lives. He didn't care how he managed to convince the old reprobate but he would. Intitled, all lords felt enabled to some degree. Self-centered, of course. Arrogant, the characteristic went with the entitlement. From what Betsy told him, Tindell felt the emotion more than most. The man had the gumption to have her followed. Still, the thought the man didn't know about her other lovers didn't make sense to him unless he was blind where Betsy was concerned. She told him he followed her. He might think he was Betsy's lover or was he so blind where she was concerned, he didn't see who she actually was?

He wasn't blind with his relationship with Betsy.

He handed the reins over to the valet at the front of the hotel. Walking purposely into the elegant hotel, he slipped his gloves off, idly slapping them on his thigh as he waited to be accosted by one of his spies. He was certain this Lord Tindell knew exactly where he was.

Sitting down on a plush chair in the waiting room, he picked up the Glasgow Harold. Before, when Fletcher handed him the paper, he didn't read the entire article. The thought of the words condemning Betsy sent his stomach into a tailspin. He drank in a long draught of air, soothing the rattling nerves that skittered around inside. The damn lord was doing things no one else had ever done to him. He needed to put a halt to the shenanigans before he was a madman.

Focusing on the article, he read every word. With each sentence, he realized so far the Black Widow revealed nothing about Betsy or the tattoos she administered. As far as anyone knew, he might have been the recipient of the tattoos. Good, let everyone think he got her name printed permanently in ink on him. The thought of her name on his breast presented a startling pleasant thought.

In front of him a man cleared his throat. He saw the well-polished boots. Slowly looked up. "Lord Tindell wants to see you."

"What about?"

Just as he expected. The man's eyes had been on him from the moment he walked through the door then found a comfortable chair by a potted palm tree. He would not be as easy a mark as Betsy Darling was. Although he didn't have the vaguest notion how he would dissuade this man without telling secrets that shouldn't be told. Betsy deserved her privacy. Whatever she wished to reveal about her relationship with him was up to Betsy. Maybe she did have the right plan. Possibly, he was poking his nose into something that wasn't his business. Too many convoluted thoughts spun in his muddled brain, which was never scrambled until he met Betsy Darling. What he did know was that knowledge was power.

"I'm certain he'll let you know."

Well, the time to turn around and leave passed a few seconds ago. The man evidently knew he was coming to see him. He was led to a plush room on the first floor that was obviously used for meetings of this sort. A small table accompanied by two velvet covered chairs sat in front of a fireplace, which blazed despite the weather outside and the fact it was summer. Though the room still held a decided chill coupled with a musty odor that sparked of disuse.

On the table a platter of finger foods sat accompanied by a bottle of brandy and two glasses. He poured himself a generous amount then sat back to watch the flames, resting his hands holding the crystal on his stomach. Not too much time passed before he heard the door behind him open then the slow tread of footsteps across the wood floor. The sound changed when Lord Tindell walked on the carpet.

Out of the corner of his eye he saw her nemesis, Henry the VIII indeed. She was accurate on his appearance. The man sat down, poured his own brandy before asking, his voice accusatory. "What do you want with Miss Darling?"

"I'm here on behalf of Betsy Darling. To speak for her."

He knew then he was wasting his time. Still, he would use the opportunity, if possible, to gain some sense of the man as well as the type of relationship that existed between them.

No comment followed. Lord Tindell ate one of the tiny cakes, leaving not one crumb behind. Meticulously, he wiped his mouth as well as hands with one of the white napkins that were set nearby.

"You need to leave her alone."

Evan's frustration level along with his temper climbed. Betsy wouldn't have anything kind to say to him when she learned of his interference. Nevertheless, he could no more leave this alone than he could stop breathing.

"I always thought the woman possessed a mind of her own. She's asked you to see me? I find that fact hard to believe." He questioned seeming to take exception to his earlier suggestion.

No, of course not. He wasn't going to tell him that. "Has Betsy told you 'No' to the proposition of marriage?" he asked accepting the fact he wasn't going to get anywhere with this man who had a well-orchestrated agenda where Betsy was concerned.

Tindell cleared his throat, taking a momentary pause to think, "Betsy is spreading her wings, testing herself before she commits to me. That fact is not unexpected. I'm here to keep her from hurting herself."

Once again, he examined the tray of sweets, slowly picking out a new one.

That part might be true. Did the man have any idea what he said? If so, he needed to reevaluate his wishes for the woman. The part about spreading her wings was definitely going to be true this evening.

The thought that what Lord Tindell implied might be valid. Perhaps she was using him. Well, hell, he knew from nearly the first moment between them that fact was true. He was using her too. They each wanted something that only the other could give. Presently, she was wearily circling him. He was pulling the string tight.

"What else did my Betsy tell you?"

"She doesn't want to marry you," he blurted something that should be abundantly clear to the man. "Betsy would like you to leave her alone. She is not the conservative governess you think her to be."

He couldn't tell him about the tattoo or his plans for this evening. Those pertinent facts were up to her to elaborate on if she so wished.

"There is no choice for her but to accept. If she doesn't marry me, she won't have a single farthing to her name. When she evaluates her finances, the fact will become abundantly clear." With the neatest precision Lord Tindell devoured the favored morsel in the same manner as the first one.

That comment stopped Evan cold. She told him he would refuse to give her references not that somehow, he manipulated all her money. He'd convince her to borrow money from him so he could invest it for her. In no time, she'd be richer than Midas.

"Blackmail?" Evan's gut turned over. He was outraged by the insinuation. Hell, what he said was no implication. Tindell was more despicable than he previously believed.

"No. Never that. Never resort to something so underhanded."

"What then?"

"She owes me quite a bit of money though she doesn't know it. I will forgive the debts if she marries me, if not, she will have to pay the funds back or go to debtor's prison. So, you see, she truly has no choice in this matter."

Evan's anger nearly exploded. He fought for control. Lord Tindell manipulated Betsy to his own ends. He didn't understand how the lord could do such a thing. However, he believed all the man said was true. He would have to return the favor.

"How much?" he bit out still trying to remain calm. He would pay whatever debts she owed. How to do it without either Tindell or Betsy learning about it was the question.

"Now that is between Betsy and myself. Don't you think?" He swirled the brandy in his glass while he looked over the crystal rim, smugly confident.

Chapter Seven

Just by looking at Evan, Betsy could tell there was some underlying friction between them. He appeared decidedly guilty about something. She didn't understand what could have him stretched so thin she thought he might explode. Several times he tried to speak to her then seemed to change his mind. He snapped at Alexander the moment they walked into his home. Alexander merely bowed then poured him a snifter of brandy. When the butler looked at her as if questioning, she nodded indicating he could pour her brandy also. She didn't know what was wrong with Evan.

All the way home from the university Evan was surly. Every word that came out of his mouth brusque. At first his attitude amused her. After that she figured his irritation must have something to do with her. Betsy wished he'd just tell her. In the process, end the conflict between them. She wasn't brave enough to ask outright.

"You should try to relax," she told him forgetting the way he manipulated her. She'd been thinking of the huge tub he had upstairs. This afternoon when he kissed her beneath the canopy of trees on the nearly deserted lane, he implied they would make love this evening. She thought of the tub as a way to ease into the sensual heat he meant to create tonight. If she suggested that, he would insist she join him. Her body flooded with heat. She still had to figure out a way to make certain he would make love to her. She didn't know how to seduce or charm. She didn't recall last night. Certainly, if they made love, he would have discovered she was a virgin. Which brought her to the conclusion he lied to her.

When he discovered she wasn't as he thought she was, he'd most likely be furious. Men didn't appreciate being deceived by a woman. She didn't do so intentionally. Evan made assumptions that weren't true. She didn't correct him. That wasn't lying. Was it? She certainly didn't have the answer.

"How, pray tell, am I going to go about relaxing?"

He swiveled on his boot heel, stared at her as if she was a crazy person.

Nodding to the drink he held, "More brandy?" She lifted both eyebrows in speculation. "Enough to make you forget whatever it is that is bothering you. Perhaps you can drink enough that you won't remember." Her suggestion left him prowling the room again.

His footsteps sent him to the foot of the steps before he headed back to her. Stopping in front of the fireplace he downed what was left in the snifter. He filled his glass then topped off hers. "I've a better idea."

Before she knew what was happening, he held her by her free hand. They were walking up the steps. Mercuric heat rushed through her. Betsy was quite certain she held an inkling of what his better idea might be. At the same time, she wasn't at all certain she was ready to share another bath with him or his bed. Her breath caught in the back of her throat. She'd known this was coming.

"What is that idea?" her voice sounded weak, quivery as breathless as she felt.

She didn't like the weakness sifting through her at the thought of seeing him naked. She did not see him at all the other night. The first night, she'd seen him. He was a magnificent specimen. Nothing like King Henry VIII.

"Hot water, lots of hot water. Soothing hot water to relax. You in my arms. The tip of your breast in my mouth." He continued into the bathing room with her still in tow. She stumbled, balanced herself, ever watchful.

What had she expected? Exactly that.

Alexander was by the tub pouring hot water then refilling the kettles to place on the burners behind the tub for future use.

He let her go. She stood back debating with herself. He would want her naked. This was what she wished for. The reason she came to Glasgow. Wasn't it? She understood by getting into this bath with Evan she was committing to him for the night.

They would make love.

She would no longer be a virgin. It was what she wanted.

He would know the truth about her.

By the time she made up her mind Evan was sitting in the chest high water, his arms stretched across the rim of the tub. His eyes were closed. He appeared contended for the time being. She didn't think the water would work that quickly to soothe his nerves. Just staring at the water, thinking about disrobing, she was becoming more anxious, panicky.

Turning her back on him, she slipped from her clothing including her chemise. She understood within a time frame the cloth would be gone. Before she turned to climb into the steaming heat of the tub, she drank in a breath of air. Once more, she sat across from him watching him watch her.

"I'm pleased you recalled my rule." His deep throaty voice sent sensual vibrations through her, heating her. "That way I won't have to disrobe you. I allowed you some leniency the first time."

"Rule? I don't under..." But she did, all too well. No, at first, she forgot but now she remembered what he told her that first time only a few days ago. Everyone who came into the bath with him had to be naked.

"Are you playing coy?" he asked, his eyes closed again. "The time spent in here would be more pleasant as well as relaxing if you weren't sitting so far away. You should come sit next to me."

That was most likely true for him. For her, sitting next to him would be far from tranquil. With this distance between them she was a bundle of seething nerves. "N-not p-playing at anything."

Her body was shaking, her nerves stretching while she flamed just thinking about his hands on her. She had to stop thinking.

"Come over here." he told her, splashing the water to show her where he wanted her. His smile untamed.

She was pressing her thumbs across the palms of her hands, massaging. All the while she tried to tell herself this was what she wanted. "I..." she swallowed the lump of apprehension that was suddenly stuck in her throat. Second along with third thoughts sent her mind spinning. If she could move, she might jump from the tub.

"I?" he queried softly opening one eye to lazily stare at her.

"Can't move..."

"Would you like me to help you?" She heard the chuckle in his voice. He was enjoying her discomfit.

"N...no."

Betsy found herself staring at her toes beneath the water, listening to the soft sounds of liquid lapping gently on the sides of the tub when either one of them moved. She did want to move to him. Felt the corporeal tug from his eyes as they darkened. Could not bring herself to be so brazen. He thought she was a well-practiced woman with numerous lovers. No wonder he thought she was playing coy.

Damn!

When he was suddenly beside her, she gasped softly startled by the erotic feel of the skin-on-skin contact. In a moment she was on his lap, once more astride his big body just as she'd been this afternoon in the phaeton. This time she felt him boldly, intimately as the most masculine part of him rose to press against her belly.

"I didn't know what was taking you so long. Thought I would remedy the problem," he murmured close to her ear. She felt the whisper of his breath flutter along her cheek.

He bit gently touched his tongue upon her.

"Oh...oh..." she moaned.

Her hips arched. She felt him rise hard against the softness of her belly. *So, this was it. It was happening.*

His lips leisurely formed across her mouth, touched caressed softly, stroked with fire. Heat flooded her. She touched him, reciprocating, played with his tongue. "Evan," she murmured softly. She wanted to tell him the truth.

"Oh!"

His hand cupped her breast, his thumb lightly flicking across her nipple. This was just as she remembered. The heat the fire, the curling ache between her legs. A soft fragmented sound, a sigh, a murmur followed as his hands explored the length of her. She closed her eyes, enjoying all the wonderous sensations he created within her. She wanted as much of him as possible. All fears vanished with the first silken caress of his tongue between her lips.

"You're so soft, smooth, warm," he told her as he continued his assault to her senses.

"You're so hard."

She drank in a breath of air.

Her arms wound around his neck as she pushed her breasts against his chest. The rough hair on his chest teased her nipples. The slight water barrier seemed to make the sensations more erotic, more desperate as flames within exploded into an inferno.

"How do you make me burn so fast?"

His teeth left her mouth to rake down her neck. He stopped where her heart thundered to suck lazily on the flesh that formed a small barrier between his questing lips and her pulse.

"I'm burning too," she murmured as she tilted her head back to give him easier contact. "You make me feel...oh..." Her sigh turned into a soft moan of pleasure.

"Good, a man wants to hear that. More than all your other lovers?" His teeth closed over a nipple, bit gently.

She stiffened at his words then melted as she burst into another round of flames. She was reminded of the same instant response to his attention to the tight hard buds. "All my lovers combined."

He did as he told her he would do. Beginning with the E of his name, he laved kisses along her breast, kisses along with gentle bites, until she thought she would certainly not last another minute. The sweet delight went on and on. Her body reached for something more than he was giving her. Fundamentally, she wanted him inside her body. Needed to feel him deep inside. Filling her.

Still, he teased her, sent sporadic bursts of fire through her. She touched him, intimately. Ran her hand along his penis. Cupped him before caressing his length again. He held her hand away. With a soft curse, "No, not yet. I want you to beg for me," he told her continuing to caress, to explore her. "Need to have you writhing beneath me before I give you what you so desperately want."

Her nails bit into his shoulders when he stroked the cleft between her legs. She gulped for air, never understanding that he would do so. She knew she should tell him to stop. Knew if she did, she would remain a virgin. If she stopped him, he would be angry with her. He wanted her to beg.

Once more she reminded herself she needed to act as if she'd had all those lovers he thought she had. She couldn't. This was all so very new to her. Only he touched her. Knew her so well. He kissed her again, deeper, harder than ever before. His tongue pushed into her just as he touched her more intimately between her thighs. She lurched upward, seeking, her body beginning to pulse and throb. The pulsations pounding and vibrating deep in her core. He sucked her tongue deep inside his mouth, sucked hard. One hand toyed with a nipple, drawing it so tight and so hard that she was about to shatter into thousands of pieces. While the other hand continued the erotic assault in her most secret place.

"I wanted to do this, too, that first time I was with you," he told her. "I wanted to feel your body all bare against mine with only the warm water between us."

Her nails bit into his shoulders. He groaned deep in the back of his throat. His body as rock hard as his arousal pulsing against her.

"Evan, did I hurt you?"

His laugh was as fragmented as his breathing.

"No, sweetheart," you're killing me but you're not hurting me.

Her sigh washed over his moist, sensitive skin sending a visible vibration of pleasure through him. A soft catch, a break in her breathing, a moan then a mewl of pleasure.

"You're killing me," she spoke as she kissed then bit along his shoulder. She wished she could see all of him, feast her eyes upon the splendor of the man. "I'm burning up for you because of the way you're touching me. Still, I want more. Need—"

He slipped a finger inside her which caused her to gasp again, her breath shattering from her lungs. A second finger entered inside her. "Evan..." his name was whisper soft, shattered as the sound wept from her lips.

"Do you like this?" Slowly he moved within her, teaching her that there was indeed more to love making than kissing. His thumb continued to massage that spot that was bringing her to this point of no return. She was going to explode in a few seconds.

"Y...yes, Evan, I, you've got to finish or I'm—"

"I'll decide when you climax. You might have told all your other lovers when and how but you won't dictate to me."

He was sipping on her breasts now, alternating sucking them so deep inside his mouth she thought he must hold all of the one inside. When his lips were settled on one breast, his fingers fondled the other. His other fingers continued the assault at the apex of her thighs.

She was reaching higher and higher. Something was happening to her body "No...truly...Evan!" She was overwhelmed by the onslaught of indescribable pleasure that seemed to go on and on. For a moment her world turned black then a crescendo of lights invaded her mind. She was moving, tugging on him, vibrating against his hand. Arching against him. Coiling from the inside out. Moaning. Her body pulsed and throbbed. She lost all control. Didn't stop for seconds upon seconds. Slowly she began to ease. His hand roamed along her back. Soothing. Calming.

"I guess you were right," he murmured, his lips touching upon her ear, her neck, across her collarbone then down to the tattoo.

An instant later, she was in his arms. He was striding from the bathing chamber to his bed. After he set her down, he stood in front of her casting his gaze over her. He was seemingly admiring her. "You came so quickly. I'm going to come inside you now, pleasure you again. This time I'll join you in the ecstasy."

With a slow motion, he spread her legs then came down between them. He kissed her ankle then continued to place soft kisses then sharp little bites along her leg until he reached the juncture of her thighs. He wound his fingers through the dark honey hair of her mound before moving down her other leg. After he reached her ankles, touched, and kissed each of the delicate toes, he came over her again. His forearms by her sides, he looked at her, his gaze seemingly focused on her eyes.

"You are very lovely."

She couldn't speak. Didn't have anything to say. He was going to do this again and she hoped again after that. Her body trembled at the image of him above her, stroking her, kissing her. His eyes dark with desire. She gasped softly with each knew caress. Fragmented, shattered with each ragged breath.

Before she understood his attentions, his lips suckled the folds between her legs, his teeth nibbled on that place where his fingers massaged that sent her body soaring, flaming to burst on fire to come back to earth before soaring like the phoenix again to the heavens above. She screamed. Her fingers wound into his hair, tugged frantic with raw hunger while she arched against him, moving wildly, curving, reaching toward him, begging as he'd wanted.

"Are you going to climax again before I come inside you?" he asked laughing softly as his nimble fingers moved over her. "I'll have to hold back a bit to keep you grounded. Don't want you flying without me. I want to burn together."

She heard the soft laughter in his voice. Knew he was right. Though she could not hold back the blinding inferno he so easily created. "I—I just might."

"This time you're not going to leave me behind. You're a delight, Betsy, your body delicious, your scent divine, the taste of you more than I ever imagined. I had no idea. Your sweet honey is raining down on me even as we speak, passionately drenching my lips, my fingers. Now, sweetheart. Keep your eyes open. They've darkened to the color of precious gems, sapphires. I want to watch you when you climb ever higher. I want to feel your silken core kiss my length with the vibrations of your ecstasy."

Spreading her legs farther, he came over her then thrust inside. She gasped out when he broke through the barrier until this moment, only she knew existed. It hurt, but not that much. He held still. She felt his anger simmering on his moist flesh as her hands traveled across his shoulders. He held himself tight seeming to restrain himself. He seemed to struggle for control while he waited for her to look at him. She didn't want to do so.

When he finally spoke, his voice was soft, almost a sultry purr, "Why didn't you tell me?" He was holding still while her body trembled with a burning need she now understood. She was no longer a virgin.

Her hands were on his shoulders while he held himself aloof. He was so hard inside her. Even while he seemed to wait for the answer, he began to move inside her, slowly at first. She clung to him. He filled her, stretched her. Not seeming to want to know the truth, at least not at this moment, his rhythm changed. He was driving faster and harder, filling her, touching deeper with each thrust.

Above her she felt his body stiffen, the lines in his face taut with the sensations. She discovered the shattering pulses that signaled the beginning of her fulfillment. It seemed he felt it too. Suddenly, for a second time she felt the blinding climax to their love making. Above her, he cried out as he thrust one more time deeply, so very hard he buried himself inside her. His seed filled her, warmed her. A few more hard strokes then he fell upon her, his weight a wonderful blanket of pleasure on top of her. He rolled over bracing himself on an elbow. He played with the hard tip of her breast.

After several minutes ticked by, "Betsy," he began as if tried for patience, his hand now tenderly cupping her breast, his thumb idly flicking across the rigid tip. "Why didn't you tell me? I would have proceeded in a different manner. Treated you with more gentleness."

Was his anger vanquished? She couldn't tell. She closed her eyes thinking for a few seconds, knowing she should have been more explicit when they spoke. It was just that he held so many assumptions about her. He was so cocky and self-assured that she'd had many lovers. The only viable answer to his question came to her. "Would you have believed me?"

After she spoke, he ran his thumb along her bottom lip. Her mouth still felt damp from his previous kisses. Bending lower, lightly he scored the tip of one breast his teeth. He stared down at her again. Almost reluctantly, he told her, "I suppose not."

Relief flooded her. "As you just learned, I was a virgin. It did hurt when you believed me capable of having many lovers. I'm not a whore. That is what you implied by your assumptions. Your thought also didn't make sense that Oliver wouldn't know about all the imagined lovers since he followed me everywhere. He hounded me in London just as he is doing here."

"Did I hurt you?"

He pushed damp hair from her forehead. Ran his finger along her cheekbone before gliding down her neck.

"Not much. Just the stretching and the first, you know."

Betsy wanted to learn his thoughts about her. Needed to know if he was going to be her escort after this. Now that she was no longer innocent, she didn't need him. She wanted him though.

"I know." He rose from the bed to enter the bathing room coming back with a basin along with a cloth.

She felt sticky between her legs. Knew the feel of his seed on her thighs. She might become pregnant. So, she supposed this should be the last time between them. "We shouldn't make love again. Now that the deed is done, Oliver won't want me. I've accomplished the task I came here for."

Those were the last words she wanted to say to him. Her self-confidence was at a low ebb. The thought of never seeing him again created a gigantic lump in her throat. Tears threatened.

After sitting on the bed, he spread her legs then began to wash her, cleanse his seed along with her blood from her legs. She didn't protest. The strokes were gentle, so very tender just like the man. "This won't be the last time." His voice held a harsh note as he spoke to her. "Don't ever think that. I'm not letting you go, Betsy Darling. As long as you still want me, you're mine."

She looked up at him, startled not so much as by what he said but how the words came out. He washed the blood from himself. After that he padded to a tray that Alexander must have brought to them when they were in the other room. Deftly, he poured two glasses of wine setting them on the tables on either side of his big bed. He followed with a plate of food. They were both still naked. Her clothing lay in piles in the other room. She felt an urgent need to cover herself. When she reached for a blanket, he stopped her with his hand coupled with a gentle smile.

"I can't do this again," she told him in the firmest voice she could muster. "This is...well...this is not supposed to keep happening. I..." She swallowed hard, clearing the moisture clogging her throat along with her mind. "I won't be your mistress."

"Why?" He bit into an apple slice before holding the slice out for her to do the same. "Don't recall asking. You're not actually mistress material. You're too commanding, too opinionated to be a mistress who is supposed to be all things biddable. You would fail miserably in that role."

For a few seconds she looked down, embarrassed by her forward-thinking assumption. She didn't want to meet his eyes. They both understood what would happen if they continued to see each other. She couldn't tell him no. "I might become pregnant. What would we do then? How would I go on? I don't want to be a single mother, have a child without a father. Don't want any baby of mine to be a bastard."

She didn't understand what she was trying to say. Didn't understand her feelings. The ones she could come to terms with she didn't want to acknowledge.

He was nodding his head, sipping his wine, eating as if she wasn't quaking with anxiety. She wanted to know what was in his head. Needed to understand what complexity he could be thinking about when the concept was obvious to anyone and everyone who knew anything about procreation. The concept so very simple.

Finally, he spoke what seemed to be his feelings. "Don't worry your pretty head about the problem, I will take precautions."

She didn't like the condescension in his tone. *Pretty head.* Bloody hell, she was more than that. She couldn't let go. He needed to tell her what he would do if the precautions didn't work. Even she understood that nothing about what they were doing was one hundred percent. "What if it happened this time?"

"We'll take care of any problems that might arise. I will take care of you along with any child of mine."

She stiffened at his words. She'd never needed help since she turned sixteen. Since that time, she'd been on her own. This trip was all about asserting herself, showing Oliver she didn't need him. She didn't need or want Evan to take care of her either.

"I can take care of myself!" she shot out understanding that by his standards she was lacking financially.

"That's the problem, Betsy. You can't. A woman alone cannot raise a child by herself. Besides, if the *bairn* is mine, I want him or her to have everything they deserve in life. A single mother, no matter how stubborn, cannot do that."

His words sounded so certain. A black cloud of foreboding swept down upon her. She wanted to be able to tell him how wrong he was. There was something in the way he looked at her that told her his words weren't nonsense. "What do you mean?"

"Have an apple slice."

He held one out to her holding it between two fingers. His golden-brown eyes blazed, shimmered with the light slanting across them.

Uncomfortable, she shifted the air in her lungs. "I'm not letting this go. What do you mean, I can't take care of myself?"

A long rush of air followed her question. "I didn't want to get to this so soon. I spent the afternoon with your Lord Tindell. He's been a very crafty and underhanded man. He's done things you will find difficult to believe."

Anger flared then annoyance at his audacity. All she heard was that Evan paid Oliver a call. "You had no right!"

As if avoiding her questions, he leaned back against the headboard. His glass of wine in his hand rested on his hard belly. His eyes were closed, his breathing even as if he didn't have a single care. She looked at all of him. His form was magnificent, nothing like Oliver's. She'd never seen Oliver naked. Didn't want to. The thought was revolting.

"You're right. I couldn't help myself. Needed to learn more about him as well as why he was diligently pursuing a woman who didn't want him." He opened his eyes to look at her. "I'm feeling a bit protective of you." He traced his name on her breast before gazing at her again. "Since you will have my name on a very appealing part of your anatomy for the rest of your life, need to make certain nothing untoward happens to you."

His words as well as his voice were so tender, her breath shattered in her throat. Before he could see the seething emotions in her eyes, she looked away. "I don't need protecting. I will always make my own way."

"I think not." When she started to argue, he placed a finger lightly on her lips. "Hush, there are things you don't know. Matters Lord Oliver Tindell stole from you in order to keep you under his thumb. Obviously, he didn't steal your heart. I find I'm very glad of that fact."

No, Oliver didn't steal her heart. She had the sinking feeling that perhaps Evan was stealing hers. She might not regret the tattoo. "What is it he stole? Why did you speak with him?"

He lifted his broad masculine shoulder in a slight shrug, a smile on his face. "Nothing better to do while you were in the library. Would you like to go to the country? I have a nice home there. The place is private. Your Oliver will learn where we are but he won't be able to intrude."

"He's not my Oliver!" She fisted her hands.

"Uh—huh. Drink some wine. The alcohol will relax you."

She couldn't stop shaking her head. He wasn't going to answer any of her questions or maybe he would but on his time and when he felt like it. "What would I do in the country?"

"Enjoy the fresh air. Make love to me." He ran another apple slice along her lips, parting them. "Take a bite. Don't want you to starve. For what I have in mind, you'll need energy."

Unable to do anything else, she bit, touched the tips of his fingers with her teeth. He finished the slice she chewed, withdrawing somewhat from the conversation. There was nothing Oliver stole from her. She didn't have anything of value except her savings. Her eyes crossed. "No!"

"You guessed? He does have control of your money? All of it. Enough so he can rob you blind?" his voice turned harsh.

She sensed he wasn't angry with her. "I don't know. Yes. He was making financial decisions for me."

~ * ~

That wasn't the answer he wished to hear. The devil, Oliver would do as he said unless he interfered. He would have to figure out how to do so without her knowledge. Would have to make certain Lord Tindell could never get at the money that would be in her name. The irony of the situation didn't elude him. His brother stole all his wife's money along with her property so she would marry him. He was going to do the opposite. Almost the opposite. He didn't want Lord Tindell to hold that kind of power over her.

"Yes is not the word I wanted to hear. You gave him the power to access all your money." He would rectify this. "That was not very smart of you. Did you trust him that much?"

"Yes."

"He understood loyalty. Also understood his brother's firm held complete financial control over many of their clients. They were a reputable firm except in that one instance. In this case, there would be a second instance. "We can fix the problem. Another reason to travel to the country. Duncan is there now."

"Stupidly, as it turns out. What is it he told you about the money? My money?"

"That you are in his debt too such a degree that if you don't pay him back, he will see you in debtor's prison. Or..." He pinched the bridge of his nose thinking of some other solution. "...or marry him and the debts will be forgiven."

The devil, he didn't want her to feel as if she had to marry that man.

He watched as she closed her eyes, waited as she appeared to get her breathing under control. Still naked, her breasts swayed with each inhalation. On a swift breath of air, she shouted, her tiny fist shaking in the space over his head. "The beast! Possibly, I'm not angry with your visit. I don't know what to do. I can't marry him. I won't!"

She sifted in another broken piece of air before softly sighing the breath from her lungs.

She inhaled another frantic breath. Her breasts heaving in a delightful way, he tried to temper his rising passion to focus on a solution to her plight. One she would be able to accept. He would put his proposition out there. While he didn't have one doubt she would refuse him, he needed to offer. After the rejection, he had to figure out how to fix her dilemma. His brother was residing in the country, delegating most of the firm's business to his three younger brothers. Duncan would understand the complexities. Duncan would be able to set her finances on the proper course. She might have to agree to borrow money from him. Betsy wouldn't like that. Eventually, she would see there was no other way.

Evan didn't mean to give her a choice in this matter. Once she learned everything, she would be able to make good decisions. Until then, he would make the choices for her, take the problem from her long slender fingers. "You're going to travel to the country with me. I can give you enough money to invest. With the profits you can pay Oliver what is owed."

"No!"

He knew she would answer negatively. In time, she would see this issue his way since his way produced the only possible positive outcome. "That's the stupidest word I've heard your sweetly kissable lips utter. You have to rely on me. I won't threaten marriage. I won't steal you blind. My only motive is to keep you out of the clutches of your Lord Oliver." The thought of marriage did have a certain ring to it. The thought appealed to him. "Think about letting me help you. Duncan can help too. In fact, he will be the brains behind outwitting Lord Oliver."

"How? I don't have any money."

"You do have the groats I'm paying you to keep my secrets."

He hadn't thought of that at first. Under his brother's expertise, it would not take long for her to double the money. Without her knowledge, he could pay her extra for his services. He could make certain he overpaid her directly to Duncan. If she discovered the ruse, he could feign innocence.

"I do. Don't I?"

The smile on her mouth told him she was beginning to fall into his plans. She now had a way out of her dilemma and would still be able to maintain her pride.

Evan could almost see the wheels spinning in her pretty little head. He wanted her again. The sexual need she provoked in him, intense. Needed to feel the heat of her secrets enclose him, burn him alive. "Drink your wine down, sweetheart. We've more things to do together this evening."

He reached across her, his arm sweeping the tips of her breasts to retrieve the glass. Handing the drink to her, he enjoyed the way she sipped. That plump bottom lip of hers, damp with the wine, called to him to taste. He wanted to drink the tiny red drops that were left behind.

"When do you want to leave?" she asked as she watched him over the rim of the crystal, her eyes alight with what he thought was mischief.

"Right now, I want to make love to you. After that, sleep with you nestled close to me, your head in the hollow of my shoulder, he can follow later in the day. When we reach my home, we will have the vast estate all to ourselves for hours."

"All right." shoulder. Want to hold you through the night. After the sun rises, will be soon enough to make plans to leave the city. I will make up a list for Alexander. With the chef

Once again, he blanketed her. His large body covered hers. He adored the way she felt beneath him. Kissed her. Kissed every part of her until she begged him. Only a few minutes later, she climaxed beneath him with a tiny mewl of pleasure, the sounds broken with the power of her culmination. He thrust deep and hard, sending his seed once more inside her. As he fell asleep, he realized he forgot to withdraw. The devil he didn't think he could ever take himself out of her hot tight sheathe before he found the ecstasy inside her he sought. He would have to figure out another way.

If she increased with his child, he would marry her. In his mind, there was no question. Any child of his would have a father along with a loving home. He would love his child. Never in his sexual life had he put a woman at risk of pregnancy. As far as he knew, he had no illegitimate children. He found himself thinking he might want to father a child with Betsy. The notion both terrified him and thrilled him. Thought of Duncan's child, a delightful little boy. Since he wasn't in need of an heir for the earldom, a little girl would be wonderful.

He woke to Betsy's, wandering fingers. They made their way from the tips of his nipples lower to more sensual spots. She held his heavy arousal in one small hand, stroked him. Squeezed gently. Startling him, her lips touched upon the tip, circled with the moist pressure of her mouth. At the unexpected sensation, he nearly jumped out of his skin. His ragged breaths, the pounding of his heart, sent him reeling. His fingers wound into her hair, slipped through the tendrils. The strands were silken heat to his hands. He spread her hair across his belly and thighs as her lips worked their magic.

Strung tight, he understood he would embarrass himself if she continued. "Enough!"

He pulled her up, letting her straddle him. He wanted this encounter to last for more than a few seconds. He wanted to bring her to such heights she would writhe within his arms. Even though their encounters had been few, he understood her body. Already, with very little provocation, she was reaching that point where she would lose control, where she would climax before he wanted her to. He didn't know how he was going to slow her down, pulling back nearly impossible. Everything he did sent her to greater heights. He needed to figure out how to regain the control he was known for. How to slow her down.

She impaled herself on his hard length. He brought his hands to her hips, holding her still. The picture that now greeted him was something he'd cock up his toes remembering. Her luscious breasts stood out impudently. His name written across the fullness of one, enticed every sinew he possessed. They were swinging slightly with each ragged breath of air she inhaled. He wasn't going to let her have control until he was good and ready. Their bodies were joined. The sight, one that thrilled him.

As if she guessed his mind, she bent over, the hardened tips rested against his mouth. She moved slightly, treating his lips to the hesitant pressure of her nipples brushing across them, teasing, tantalizing. With his tongue he touched each one when the tip passed along the crevice. In the back of his throat, he groaned.

"You're burning me alive," he murmured softly enjoying each sweet pass of her tight hard buds across his lips.

"Evan? Please..."

He sucked one breast deep into his mouth drinking its softness, teasing, tasting the secrets of this alluring woman. When she tried to move on his arousal, he held her still. "Not yet. Soon, sweetheart, soon. I want this to last, to savor the moments we share."

"Please..."

Her eyes were closed, her head tilted back. Wantonly her posture incited every part of him.

At one point, he told her she would beg. Had never expected that moment to come only minutes after the seduction began. He wanted to try to hold on for at least another minute. His mouth switched to her other breast. He allowed his hands to wander along the ladder of her ribs then back down to the rise of her hips. The feel of her heat, the passion, the raw desire inflamed him. When he touched the tiny hard jewel between her secret folds, shattered sounds erupted from her lips, splintering into the madness of the night. Her head was tossed back as he slid his finger between the cleft paying more attention to the part of her that would send her spinning once more.

Her tight core was pulsing, kissing his length, vibrating, burning him alive. She seemed to be fighting the climax.

"Ride me."

He let go of her hips giving her free rein. She moved on him, conducting the seduction to her will. She set the raging tempo. So very slowly moving, tempting him, arousing him, stripping him to his basest needs. He closed his eyes tight, fighting to maintain himself. She tightened then relaxed, tightened her muscles again, the movements rippling along his shaft. He thought he would explode when he felt the beginning tremors of her climax. She cried out, moving faster and harder until he shuddered and his seed filled her. His hands rested on top her thighs. His breaths so ragged he gulped the needed oxygen while his heart thundered against his ribs.

When she relaxed against him, her skin was moist, slick, and shiny with the exertion of their mating. He ran his hands along her back, counting the vertebrae, stilling when he touched the spots where her heart and rose tattoos resided. He smiled, remembering how beautiful she was lying on her stomach while the henna was applied to her white flesh. Even more delightful was holding her breast in his hand, keeping the soft white flesh from movement while the Black Widow printed his name on her breast. This was a memory he would hold dear for his entire life.

If the tattoos were permanent, he wouldn't mind. Disconcerted by his strange thoughts, he touched the tip of her nose with a fingertip. "Time to get up."

Lazily, she rolled over to look at him. Her smile promised more sensual delights. He groaned, discovering he wanted her again then again after that. He could willingly spend the day in bed with her. If they made love now, they would be later to the country if they managed to leave the house at all. He wanted to reach his destination before the sun set. As it stood now there was plenty of time. If he couldn't rouse her from his bed, they would be delayed for another day.

Sifting in a deep breath, ignoring the thrusting perfection of her breasts, he rose. He wanted to look out at the day. Test the weather. If it wasn't to his liking, the scene would give him a reason to join her in his bed. Sunshine poured through the window after he pushed the curtains aside. At the sight below on his front lawn, his breath caught in the back of his throat. His heart lurched.

"The devil, what is going on now?"

At the sound of the loud knock at his door, he pulled on a dressing gown. Looked to see if Betsy heard the noise. He chuckled when he saw that she slipped beneath the covers, only the honey of her hair poking above the sheets and blankets. She was delightful.

"Alexander?"

He opened the door for his butler, concern in his voice. This had to have something to do with the people occupying his front lawn. "What is it? I don't like the look."

His butler handed a newspaper to him. "You've seen the reporters below? It will be hard to get in or out of the house with them swarming over the lawn. If you can manage to ignore all their questions, you might be able to slip away from the chaos. If I remember correctly, in your brother's case after the scandal at the ball, very few followed all the way to the country home."

Evan was reminded of the scandal his older brother created with Caro. He didn't know what possible scandal was created with Betsy. He could make a few guesses though. "We were going to leave for the country estate. Still intend to do so. As soon as we can get ready. Is there hot water on the stove?"

"Yes, it has been heating for an hour. Anticipated your needs. As usual, went into the chamber from the servant's entrance. As to the reporters, you will have to find a way to the carriage house. They we will be on top of you as soon as you set foot out of the door," Alexander reminded him. "Before you decide what to do, look at the paper."

On the front page was a drawing then a headline.

EVAN MURRAY WITH HIS FAVORITE WOMAN OF THE MOMENT.

He closed his eyes, understanding that one of them had an enemy. Lord Oliver, if that passing carriage had been one of his men spying, would stop at nothing to drive Betsy into his arms. By stopping on that tree lined drive, he played into Oliver's hands. He didn't believe anything except the debt would drive Betsy into Oliver's arms. No, she loathed the man. Soon there would be no more debt.

"Does the man think he can frighten me away by creating more scandal? Except where it will concern Betsy, I don't care what he prints about me." Evan slapped the now folded paper against his leg. "If anything, it reinforces my plans. No woman, especially one as trusting as Betsy, should be at the mercy of someone like Lord Tindell."

"What are you going to do?" Alexander asked as his gaze shifted to the bed then back to him. "Obviously, this is not just about you. The man thinks to ruin you as well as the girl. Is this a case of petty revenge?"

"He will have to work a great deal harder to ruin me. As to revenge? I don't have the answer to that question. Lord Tindell has no idea of my net worth. Even if I never worked at the university again, I would never starve, now, would I?" Evan couldn't help the laughter he tried unsuccessfully to keep behind his teeth. "Perhaps Duncan and I can find a way to ruin that man. He deserves to feel some of the pain he dishes out and more. The arrogant bastard!" Plans were taking shape. He had ideas of ways to handle Lord Tindell. Before he left he would have a message delivered to Duncan.

Evan never in his past felt loathing for another human. He did now. The financial ruin of Lord Oliver Tindell was his objective. He hoped Betsy would agree with his plans.

"You would like me to pack your things then follow you to your country home?" Alexander asked.

"You read my mind. Betsy's trunk is in the adjoining room. We will leave as soon as we've bathed and dressed."

He thought he would like a bath first. Maybe Betsy would share the water. When he stepped inside the bathing room, the buckets

Alexander always kept filled were on the stove just as he told him.

"Everything is ready for you and your woman."

Stiffly, true to his position in the household, Alexander backed from the room, a wry smile on his stoic face.

His woman. Yes, for the time being she was his. She would have to acknowledge that fact soon enough. She would have to lean on him in order to defeat the machinations of Tindell. Kneeling beside the bed, grinning besotted with the delectable woman, he stroked her head. "It's safe. You can come up for air now. We're all alone."

"You positive?" Her voice was paper thin, wide-eyed her gaze sweeping the room as if she didn't completely trust him. The question already answered.

"He's gone. I wouldn't lie. Don't want anyone else seeing you in the buff."

She lifted her head slightly. He could see her beautiful blue eyes, much lighter now that she wasn't in the throes of passion. Ah...he could get used to this. Never thought he would find a woman he'd want to spend this much time entertaining in his bed as well as elsewhere. A woman he'd like to sample for a second course along with a third.

"Evan? Who is on the front lawn?" Her question surprised him. She must have overheard his conversation with Alexander.

Not quite ready to answer her enquiry, he conveniently changed the subject. "Would you like to share a bath before we leave?" As soon as he committed the words to verbal use, he regretted them. He didn't dare share a bath this morning.

Her eyes widened growing a bit darker. "I'm not sure. I'm a bit..." As if she realized what he suggested. "No..."

There was just enough hesitation in her voice to please him. Obvious to him, she wanted him again as much possibly as he wanted her.

"Sticky?" he asked knowing exactly why. "I promise to keep my hands to myself. If I don't, we will never get off today."

He didn't know if he should show her the article coupled with the drawing of them. He imagined he should. She deserved to learn about all the obstacles Tindell was tossing into her path. Once she learned, she would come over to his way of thinking. When they left, he couldn't keep her from seeing the hovering reporters. To his mind, knowledge was power in this world. She needed to discover the man's weakness. Evan believed at least one was wealth, another would be control. With his brother's help, legally he would dissolve both where it concerned Lord Tindell. If his plans came to fruition, he would reduce him to nothing.

"Don't want to share." Slowly, she sat up, keeping the covers beneath her arms acting shy. "You go first."

"Have to share." He kissed the tip of her nose before brushing his lips softly across hers. "Don't have enough time for two baths. We must be on our way as soon as possible." He hoped to lose the reporters with a quick getaway.

Cocking her head slightly to one side, her head shaking while her hair splayed around her body. "What do you mean?"

Tossing the paper on the bed, he stood up. "I'm getting in the bath. Take a look at the article then join me as soon as possible. As I told you, I'll keep my hands to myself. Can't touch or we won't leave. Staying here is not a good option under the circumstances."

He turned, striding toward the bathing room, hoping she would follow as soon as she read enough of the article to appease her curiosity.

Slipping into the hot water he breathed in the scented steam. Wonderful heat assuaged his muscles. He picked up the sponge to begin washing. Was surprised to see her standing naked in the doorway, her face a pale mask. He saw her fear along with uncertainty. She wavered slightly. After she pushed her hair from her face, she strode to the tub, sitting once more opposite him.

Alexander must have left her different soap. Without looking at him again, she began to wash. The jasmine scented soap mingled with the spicey scent of his. Alexander was a marvel. She seemed to be staring at him through lowered lashes. Although he needed to hear her take on the article, he decided he would wait until she was ready to talk. The carriage ride could be long. Unless they found a way to spend the time, the trip would turn out boring. He could think of several ways to change that.

She looked as if her nerves were stretched to a breaking point. He didn't like that look. Explanations were in order but not now. "Would you like me to wash your hair."

When she looked up, he thought he saw her lips twitch in amusement. "Thought you were going to keep your hands to yourself. I can do it."

"Of course you can. I just wondered if it would be easier."

Probably not. She was right. If he touched her that would be the end to their trip today. They might not leave the heated water until their skin wrinkled.

She stared at him with wide eyes while she continued to remember he told her he would keep his hands to himself. Her decision was obviously for the best.

"We both know what will happen if you come over here, wash my hair, touch me. You wanted to leave as soon as possible. Didn't you? Besides, I am a bit...I could use some respite..." She made the same point he did repeatedly both verbally as well as in his head.

"You're right."

He ducked under the water to rinse completely. She was attempting to tell him, he used her too well last night and this morning. He had indeed.

"I'll wait for you in the breakfast room. Come down as soon as you are done." Quickly, he rose from the heated water. It wouldn't do for him to linger a moment longer than necessary. As it was, the instant she walked naked into the room, he grew at an astounding rate. He imagined they would discuss the paper along with the path to outwit Lord Tindell when they were alone in the carriage for the long ride to the country.

When he stepped into the breakfast room, hot scones along with a pot of tea sat on the table. Before he left the bedroom, he picked up the paper to read the article again. Plans were beginning to form in his head. Most of the strategies would have to be approved by Betsy then initiated by Duncan. His brother would know how to go about finalizing the deceptions. Lord Tindell would rue the day he sought to blackmail Betsy into wedding him. The day he decided to rob her of her savings in order to bring her into his control would haunt him for the rest of his life. The man intended to dominate her.

He was finishing a scone when he heard Betsy speaking to

Alexander. When she stepped into the breakfast room, he stood then seated her. She was silent, her face still too pale for his comfort. The article had that effect on her. He was certain Tindell wanted to unnerve her. The man wouldn't understand how his efforts were unraveling second by second until it would be too late to change the course. If possible, Evan wanted to see Lord Oliver Tindell walked into Newgate Prison as a debtor.

Debtor's prison. He deserved that and more.

For a few seconds, Betsy stared at the plate he dished up for her. After a moment of reflection, she smothered the scone in the strawberry jam that was set on the table. She didn't appear hungry. A bite later, she set the scone on the plate then stared at him, her eyes huge.

"We do need to talk. Maybe later I'll be able to eat. Can we take some food with us? Eventually my stomach will want something inside it when and if it ever settles."

His heart went out to her. She didn't deserve this behavior from a man who had all the privileges a person could have. He didn't want her to be a victim to his greed. "We can take whatever you would like. Alexander has packed a lunch for us to eat later when we are hungry. You do need to keep up your strength." He waggled his eyebrows at her hoping to put some levity into this situation knowing tonight she would once again be in his bed, beneath him, on top of him.

He was well pleased when he saw her smile at his antics. For a few seconds, she toyed with her fork. Pulled a small piece of the scone off then ate chewing slowly.

"Did you have any idea that would happen? The article? Is it Oliver who is behind those words? That picture?" Her face flushed a beautiful rose color as she must be remembering how she straddled him, how he fondled her. "Why would he want to humiliate me?"

"Probably. Can't think of anyone else who would go to the trouble to create scandal for me. Believe he wants to drive you into his arms by painting me as a cad. Possibly believes more scandal circling me will end my reinstatement at the university. There are a vast number of scenarios. What he doesn't know is that I don't need employment. I work there because I enjoy doing so. He cannot connect my brother's firm to the family."

She sipped her tea, her mouth forming a thin line. "Nothing would drive me into his arms. I would starve before I would go to bed with that man." She visibly cringed at the notion. "While your face was pictured very accurately, mine was not. Do you imagine he didn't know it was me you were kissing?"

"I've no idea. He understood I was escorting you. Any sensible and logical man would conclude I was, indeed, kissing you, Betsy Darling. I am the one he is after. Not you. With me absent from your life, he believes you would cling to him."

"What are we going to do?" She set the tea cup on the saucer.

"Ah...a lady who comes straight to the point. With my groats coupled with Duncan's financial wizardry, we are going to send your Lord Tindell to debtor's prison. He will be the one walking through those hallowed doors. Not you."

He was pleased with his plan until he noticed her reaction, the narrowing of her brows, the thinning of her lips.

Her gasp of despair or outrage, he wasn't certain which, startled him. "You can't!" She was shaking her head, her face a pale mask. "You can't do something so reprehensible."

He didn't like the sound of that. She was too sweet as well as too kind. With his hands, he formed a steeple beneath his chin. "Why not, pray tell? The man deserves it for what he's contrived against you. He has only his interest at heart, cares nothing for you."

She drank in a huge gulp of air. Her eyes wide circles in her pale face. "Yes, you're right about Oliver. As far as that man is concerned, I don't care what you do. However, if you ruin him, his girls would suffer. That can't happen. They are innocent of all wrong doing. They would be turned over to the state. They would go to workhouses. Likely they would become whores."

Possibly he liked her sweetness, her willingness to look the other way. She was correct, the children should not be put at risk. The revenge he plotted would go too far. Too bad. Conversely, he could put a substantial debt in Oliver's investments. The man would have to act quickly to stop the downward spiral. A man of his significant means would be able to do that. A bit of panic on his ruddy face would be delightful. He would speak more about different options with Duncan.

"What would you do then?" he asked hoping she would at least agree to using his money to dig herself out of the hole Tindell put her in. "This is up to you."

"I don't know. Talk to him. Explain to the man I would not make him happy. He wouldn't enjoy being married to me. Could tell him I'm no longer what he wants, a virgin. He might not believe me. If all else fails, tell him I refuse again. I can always start over in another city or country if necessary."

"You are far too naïve. You realize, of course, by marrying the man he would have access to your delightful body. You couldn't tell him firmly enough for him to believe you don't want him. That is what the man wants. You."

It wasn't her intellect that drew Tindell to her. No, it was her delightful woman's body along with her beautiful face. Of course, that was what first drew him. Now, he understood more about her, although now...

The thought of another man making love to her infuriated every male part of him.

What the devil! Now what? She burned him alive. Sex with her was the best he'd ever had. He didn't want to lose that. He tried to be honest with himself. He wanted to tell himself there was more to their fledgling relationship than the instant flaming of their bodies when they touched. The problem was, he didn't know if there was more or how soon the lust would burn out.

Until he knew her better.

He held out his arm. "It's time to leave. We can talk more once we pass the reporters."

She looked stunned. "Reporters?"

"Ah, you didn't look outside. The people on the lawn you questioned me about. We have a bevy of reporters in our front yard, or would it be a gaggle of them. Nonetheless, passing them by without confrontation will be difficult to navigate. Don't say anything to their questions. Keep your head down. I will simply respond when necessary."

"What will you say?"

He grinned at her almost relishing the short trip from side door to carriage. "Why...no comment of course."

~ * ~

Lord Oliver Tindell sat, his legs crossed, while he studied the drawing of his fiancée along with the man he considered the worst nemesis of his life. That man dared to kiss her, touch her, in public no less. His actions were a travesty of good taste. Only a commoner would do such a thing. Didn't matter that he was second in line. The spare as some would call him. He would have this Murray fellow on his knees before he finished with him.

What seemed even worse to him was that his Betsy allowed him the intimacies that were meant for him alone. According to his sources, they spent the night together in the man's home. He would have to act quickly or Betsy would no longer be a virgin. Oliver felt certain her moral values coupled with her conservative nature would enable her to hold off against the reprobate's seduction for a little while longer. She was not in trouble of being deflowered unless she spent more time with the man. What would he do if that happened? Bloody eyes, if that happened, he still wanted her but not as a wife. As a mistress, she could satisfy his need to possess her. He would still control her money. At least he was certain, he would figure out how to do so.

He stared at the drawing.

Possibly not. If the rendering was accurate, Betsy was in the throes of intense passion. The artist caught her body language exquisitely. At the sight of her, her head thrown back allowing the cad access to her white neck, had him standing at attention. Bloody Hell! He rose, adjusted his clothing. Stepped around the room. A caged lion could have appeared more desperate than the way he felt.

The sound of footsteps shifted his attention from his dark musings to the man walking into the room. "What is it, Duckett? Didn't want to be disturbed. Have some serious thinking to do, plan to orchestrate a few ideas."

Duckett cleared his throat, "Sorry sir, wouldn't have disturbed you if I didn't feel it necessary. The young couple..."

If he had his way, and he would they weren't ever going to be a couple. He fisted his hands, determined to end this travesty before it went any farther. This unexpected relationship had already gone too far. "Well?" Oliver snapped at his man.

His gut churned, understanding there was something terribly wrong.

"The man who reports to me hourly tells me the two have left town. They headed out about an hour ago."

"Where are they going?" Oliver understood this man wouldn't know, at least not yet. "Are they on a trip of some sort? Her research?"

What a crock of bull. Betsy was no more doing research than he was. He wasn't about to let her get away with that nonsense.

"Strumose along with Wellesley are following at a discreet distance. They will report back as soon as they learn anything of value. Until then you will have to wait."

He wasn't used to waiting. Patience wasn't necessarily his strong suit. With Betsy that seemed all he did was wait for her. "If you have to guess..." Oliver, put it out there. His need to know burning a hole in his belly.

Obviously uneasy, the man shifted on his feet. "There were about twenty reporters on his front lawn this morning. The article did the trick, created scandal Murray would have to explain to the dean at the university. Who knows until this is all said and done. They left, fighting their way through the reporters refusing to answer questions. Yes, if I must guess, the pair are off to another home. I've done a bit of research. His family owns land about thirty miles out of the city limits. They each have their own gated home. Will be impossible to gain entrance."

Oliver let out a heavy sigh. Isolated, they would be together. The man would seduce, charm, and sweet-talk. He was well aware of the man's reputation with the ladies. He didn't want them to flee the city. He needed Evan Murray here so he could create more and more scandal around the man lowering his name even farther. So much so, Betsy would look at him with more favor in her beautiful blue eyes. She would see this

Murray fellow as he was, a man of lose morals, a man who seduced women, taking what he could before tossing them in the garbage. It would only be a matter of time before Murray would set her aside.

What he did know was that he meant to ruin Evan Murray's reputation along with his financial security. He didn't know how he was going to go about doing it. He was. Perhaps finding an advisor of the financial sort here in Glasgow should be his next order of business.

He strode to his desk. Sorted through various papers he'd requested while he idled his way in Glasgow. He made requests to several financial firms. Found himself directed by more than one satisfied customer to a special one located here in Glasgow. Halstead & Family was the name of the firm. He would contact them. See what they could do for him. He knew for certain that he would never return Betsy's savings until she was his wife. If she didn't agree to his proposal, she would starve or find herself forced on the streets.

He rang for Duckett.

He would put his plans into operation this very afternoon.

Sitting back, his hands folded over his belly, he grinned, a self-satisfied grin.

Chapter Eight

Betsy had a lot to think over. Evan gave her little chance to speak her opinion about driving to his country home. Before she could voice an objection or agreement, he had her bundled up and within the carriage. If he gave her time, she didn't know what she would have said. Torn between conflicting thoughts, she would have eventually conceded to his wishes. The thing of it was, Evan made certain she understood they didn't have time to deliberate or negotiate. If she accompanied him, there needed to be terms.

The reporters surrounding them both frightened as well as piqued her curiosity. She read most of the article. Understood the words written in the Glasgow Herald were Oliver's work. What the man didn't understand about her was that she couldn't be coerced so easily. An article that denigrated Evan would not force her to be with a man she despised. In this instance, she was as much at fault as Evan. If she didn't melt in his arms so easily, there would be no ongoing commentary.

She should explain to Evan she didn't care, but Evan might. It was his face that was made obvious in the drawing. His name that was prominent in the words written as well as the bold headline. However, Betsy was beginning to think Evan wasn't touched by gossip or rumors any more than she was. He didn't care what other people said or thought about him. He was his own man. She liked that about him. In this, his thoughts mirrored hers as she realized blackmail was not something that would coerce her.

Betsy was pleased Evan was the man she gave her innocence to. Nevertheless, she no longer knew how to proceed where he was involved. Evan Murray would never marry her. Not that marriage mattered to her. Years ago, she resigned herself to spinsterhood. Until recently she'd been a long-in-the-tooth virgin. Now her title was just spinster. She was fine by that. She decided she would enjoy every moment with this man as long as she could.

At her age, harboring thoughts about marriage was ridiculous. What man would wish to wed a woman of her great age? Not a man who was as attractive and wealthy as Evan Murray. What she needed to do was enjoy Evan for as long as they wanted each other. When she no longer wished to be in his arms, if he hadn't already, she would cry off. She wasn't going to allow him all the power along with the control to direct this relationship.

Sitting back on the comfortable seat, she closed her eyes, thinking of the wonderful night they spent together. Oh...the magical things he did to her body. The way he stroked her, caressed every part of her. The soft sigh whispering from her lips was oh, so pleasant. Just thinking about him, her body thrummed with the wild intoxicating pleasure she recalled.

When she finally opened her eyes, he was sitting across from her staring at her. His eyes sparkled as if he knew what she'd been thinking about. Blood oozed to her face. Her resulting smile wavered slightly under his ardent perusal. "What is it? Is there something wrong?"

She looked out the window then back to him. The act gave her a moment to gather her wits about her.

"I was going to ask you the same question. Seems you've been lost in thought for the last ten minutes." He leaned forward, resting his forearms on his muscled thighs, his fingertips close to her legs. "What were you thinking about? Last night? This morning? How you felt when we made love? Should we repeat the performance? What do you think? Making love in the carriage would shorten the trip."

Betsy thought that was a lot of questions. She was shocked he would even think of making love here. "I..."

She swept her tongue across her bottom lip; immediately understood she should not have done that when his grin widened. His look wicked. His golden eyes changed to dark honey.

More heat rose swiftly and instantly to her cheeks. He chuckled seeming to reaffirm the direction of her thoughts. "Been thinking about us? Together? I have."

Slowly, he ran one long fingertip up her leg then back to her knee.

Even through the fabric of her gown she felt the searing heat from the light touch. She quivered, fixating on the tips of her slippers while she knew her cheeks were growing redder by the second. The man delighted in shocking her with what seemed to be casual attention. Answering him would embarrass her further while the answer, if she chose to tell the truth, would raise his ego at least another level. Beneath her lashes she tried to see him, needed to see if he still grinned. He did, understanding the discomfort she felt was orchestrated by his sensual and suggestive words.

"Tell me, Betsy."

He wasn't going to let her off the hook without an answer no matter how she tried to change the topic of conversation. She didn't mean to provide the answer. Determined to have her way, he could guess until he stuck his spoon in the wall. Distressing herself further was not going to happen. Perhaps she could change the subject. Her musings were private.

"Oliver is a fool," she told him her voice shaking while she thought of Evan's intention to ruin him financially.

As far as it went his was a good idea. How he would do the deed, was impossible for her to imagine.

"No, he's a very bright man. Oliver is no man's fool. Do you understand why I wanted to ruin him?" He ran a finger along her arm. "His ruination might be the only way he will stop pursuing you. If you follow my directions, you will be a rich woman before the year is out and Oliver will have nothing."

She found herself shaking her head while she mulled over his words. "You haven't yet explained your strategies. Perhaps I'll change my mind about your suggestion. If there is some way to protect Virgie and Poppet, I would like to see him left with nothing. The thought is amazing, intriguing."

She thought of the sweet girls, Virgie, and Poppet. They didn't deserve to have their lives turned into a nightmare. Evan would have to protect them. She loved the little girls who were nothing like their father.

"Your Oliver has stolen your money. He told me he would send you to debtor's prison if you refused to marry him. Believe I said something to that affect earlier. Did you not listen or believe Tindell would do something that horrible?"

He sounded angry, his hand slashing through the air.

She sat back startled by the emotion she witnessed. On some level Evan did care about her. Didn't love but cared. "I don't remember. How would he go about such a thing? The money is in my name. He can't just take it without my permission." Betsy was baffled yet she imagined something like that could be done. She wondered if somehow she didn't sign something, inadvertently turning her capital over to Oliver. From time to time, he did give her documents to put her name to. Until now, she always trusted him.

"Underhanded bastard," Evan mumbled. "My brother did much the same with his wife before they were wed. His reasons were better. Though it didn't justify what he did. He took everything she owned, all her substantial fortune, putting the documents of ownership in his name. She owned two homes, both of which he confiscated. Duncan left Caroline with nothing. She had to marry him or go homeless. Duncan was ruthless in getting what he wanted. Seems your Lord Tindell is proceeding much in the same fashion. The difference here is that Caroline was trying to keep Duncan's child from him. If she had not betrayed him, he would have never gone to such drastic and underhanded measures to belittle her."

"How?" She felt her jaw open with his words. She found herself gaping at him. "I didn't have much. Didn't own anything of importance. My savings were meager."

Evan sat back, his grin feral. "My brother, unbeknownst to her, was her financial advisor. In that case he had no trouble transferring funds from her account to his. Even without her signature on each document he was successful in his endeavor. She gave him *carte blanch* with her finances by signing one paper and one paper only. That fact impowered him to do anything he wanted."

"Why?"

"Over the years her investments grew in leaps and bounds. She was extremely wealthy. Most customers give him that much leeway so Duncan can invest without consultation. Sometimes deals can't wait for retrospections. He's trusted in the financial community. You see. Many of his clients have the same agreement with him. In most cases, he contacts his patrons as soon as possible."

"No, not that much. Don't understand. Oliver didn't have that arrangement with me."

She didn't see at all. Seemed ludicrous that one man held so much authority. "I never gave Oliver *carte blanch*. Not knowingly."

"Think about it. He must have had some way to get into your saving, an identification of some sort. What did he know about you?"

"Pretty much everything."

She lifted her shoulder shrugging even when she didn't feel at all nonchalant about Oliver. At the notion he stole from her, her stomach somersaulted.

"More than I know?" Once more Evan sounded angry, even impatient with her. "You should tell me what I need to know. I still plan on giving Tindell a taste of what he's wrought on you. The man cannot be allowed to get away with no repercussions."

He sat back now, his arms spread across the back of the seat, stretching from one side to the other.

"The girls can't be hurt. Their futures need to remain secure. The two of them are sweet and innocent. They don't deserve to lose everything just because their father is a backstabbing thief."

On that point she was adamant. Would never change her mind. "You have to figure out something that won't affect them."

"I've a plan for that too. Perhaps an untouchable dowry would do the trick. Duncan can make certain the way the groats in each girl's dowry will be invested will grow over time. He's the best with funds. The girls will be rich ladies by the time they reach their majority."

"All right." She could imagine something along those lines. "What makes you think you can ruin Oliver. I'd wager my lifesavings if I still possessed it, that he is thinking along the same lines where you are concerned. He means to ruin you. This is my fault. If I didn't ask for your escort, none of this would happen to you."

His arms crossed over his chest looking pleased with his ideas. "We will see. A financial battle of the big guns is blooming. Duncan will win, of that I've no doubt."

"I thought you were also a genius?" she said thinking about that first paper she read that was sitting on his bedside table.

His soft chuckle caught her off guard. "No, Duncan is the genius. I dabble. Get lucky sometimes. Always take my big brother's advice on matters concerning finances. He seems to know what is good as well what is not. His timing is impeccable. It's almost as if he has a crystal ball."

"I'm in over my head. It is not logical to think I would understand anything you and your brother scheme. I'm going to put my trust in you. Make certain Virgie and Poppet have a sizable dowry that Oliver cannot access or if it becomes necessary a legal guardian I approve of and I'll be pleased. As far as I'm concerned after what you told me, I'd like to see him put in Newgate or sent to one of those penal colonies for criminals."

"What is it that Tindell knows about you that I do not?" He changed the topic back to her.

It seemed he wasn't going to let that question drop. He was persistent. She lifted her slim shoulders, a bleak feeling swamping her. "Don't like to speak of my past. That's what it is, my past. None of what happened has anything to do with the present or even why Oliver, out of the blue, wanted to marry me."

"I'm certain what Tindell holds over you has everything to do with his expectations. If I'm going to protect you, you need to tell me all your secrets. Surprises will only serve to get in the way."

His eyes were hooded, dark lashes lowered slightly over the golden-brown tiger eyes.

"Surprises to who?" She stiffened her back, determined to keep her secrets. "I've nothing to hide. What do you want to know?"

He leaned forward, taking her hands in his. He was warm. The sensations both calmed her and set her heart spinning. This man held her life in the palm of his hands. He could forget about her. Could go on his way without a care in the world. He owed her nothing yet for a reason she couldn't fathom, he wanted to help her.

"Surprises to me," he spoke softly. "I have to learn all I can about your past in order to see you through this."

"You know Oliver was my guardian from the time of my parents passing. He did everything to make my life better. He sent me to the best schools. He purchased fashionable clothing for me. His intentions toward me were always good. Until they weren't. Until my refusal of marriage." She looked up realizing there were tears in her eyes. "For the longest time, I thought he was a saint. I worshipped the ground he walked on."

"What happened to change that?"

He was rubbing tiny circles on the underside of her wrists, seducing while they rode in the carriage. She understood she could change the tenor of their conversation by letting him charm her with his sweettalking. He might forget his questions at least for the moment. With that tiny contact her breathing changed. Hitched. Broke.

"He..."

She didn't want to tell him that Oliver kissed her, forced her lips apart. Touched her. She loathed the few contacts between them. They were nothing like when Evan did the same. They were not mercuric, never sent her mind along with her body spiraling through time. Somehow, she understood telling him would never be prudent or wise.

"What, Betsy? What did he try to do?" His large hands squeezed hers, giving her confidence she shouldn't feel.

Once again, it seemed he had little trouble seeing into her mind. "When I turned eighteen, the way he looked at me, spoke to me, changed. He found me my first position in the home of a wealthy gentleman. I thanked him. He wanted me to thank him with more than words as did the gentleman I was supposed to be working for."

She watched as Evan sucked in his breath. She knew what she said would anger him. He would also understand what she didn't want to say.

"Go on..." His voice was still soft, calm. When she saw the anger flare in the changing color of his eyes, she knew different.

After she looked up a lone tear slipped down her cheek. "I didn't know what was expected of me. What I did understand was that I didn't want either of the men touching me. My employer tossed me on my bed then came down on top of me. The only reason he didn't take me right at that moment was the fact his eight-year-old daughter came to see me in my third story room. You see, she had an urgent question. Imagine I was fortunate." She paused thinking, "I would not have needed you to take my virginity nor would I have sought a tattoo."

"I like your tattoo. Love to see my name on your breast."

"Evan." She didn't want to think about that tattoo. His name would be written on her for the rest of her life, until she stuck her spoon in the wall.

"Then..." Evan tugged her onto his lap, holding her head in the hollow of his shoulder. His heartbeat against her cheek was loud, strong, comforting. She felt the expansion of his lungs each time he breathed.

Enfolded in his arms, she felt secure, safe, loved. She'd not felt love since her parents passed away. He didn't love her. This was just a passing feeling. "I heard the servants talking. He made a bargain with Oliver when he hired me. The thing was, I left that night, packed all my belongings in the one valise I owned. Had enough money to rent a small apartment until I found employment, which I did."

"Why did you start to trust Tindell again? After what he did to you, seems he would be the last person to rely on." He brushed away a tear with his thumb.

"Not right away. About a year later he sent me a message. He knew where I lived, knew who employed me. He wanted my forgiveness. Told me he'd made a mistake. Followed with the words that I was a beautiful woman and that I shouldn't begrudge the fact he was enthralled with me. The woman who employed me was a widow with two small children. I was more a nanny than a tutor though we did read as well as practice writing. Taught them some history too."

One of his large hands settled on the curve of her hip. "So...you made your own way in the world. You were very brave, Betsy. Did Oliver make amends to you then get your trust back?" He soothed her, running his hand along her back. "Did you forgive then forget?"

"I never trusted him again. Don't understand why he suddenly wanted to marry me."

"Hmm...Tindell must have discovered something about you that even you don't know. Nonetheless, you are a beautiful woman. That was a fact he was right about. Expanding on the conversation, he continued. There must have been something about your past? Your father? What do you think?" His large warm hand continued to soothe her shattered nerves.

Betsy inhaled a long deep breath. The tears seemed to go away. She set her hand on his chest, ran her fingers down to his waist band. Smiled when she heard the sudden intake of his breath. His hand closed over hers. She imagined she now understood how to seduce him. She did know how as well as where he liked her to touch him.

"Why don't you tell me something about you? Anything. Why did you become a professor of biology? You must not make a lot of money."

"Why would I care about groats when I've more than I can spend in a lifetime since my big brother started investing? I did what I enjoyed. Are you enjoying this?"

His hand cupped her breast, flicked lightly across her clothed nipple. His lips brushed the corners of her mouth, so light the caress was barely there, a moment in time that left her wishing for more.

"Yes...with you I imagine I'll enjoy everything we decide to do. Not in the carriage though. You wouldn't..." Her comment was stopped when his thumb touched her lips.

"Don't say anything more. If we start this, we'll finish it in the carriage. What do you think? Do you want to make love in this transport? If you don't want me, tell me no now while I'm able to stop myself."

Before she realized what happened, the bodice of her gown was unfastened, her breasts free from restraint. A fragmented breath whispered across his neck. The heat from his touch burned instantly. She squirmed trying to get more comfortable on his thighs. The hard length of him pushed against her bottom.

"It's only been a few hours." She pulled up his shirttails so she could touch his chest, run her hands across his naked skin, revel in the hard planes. "Do you think you are up to the task?"

There was laughter in her voice. The moments of despair from her past vanished with the enchanting inferno he ignited.

"Can't you feel me? If you do, you know I'm up for whatever you have in store for me."

Her tears gone, she giggled. "You're incorrigible."

"As are you. Should I take all your clothing off? That could be dangerous if there was an accident of any sort." His hand ran the length of her leg, exploring, sending mercuric sensations to all of her. He reached her pantalettes. His hand at the waist band, he tugged. "We do need to remove these." With a sudden lift to her hips, they fell on the floor.

"You." She forced in air when he found a delicate place, a tender spot. His hands explored, enticed, found so many secret sensitive places. A shattered sound, a soft sigh a mewl of sweet sensual pleasure rippled in fine ribbons from the back of her throat.

"Yes..." He touched the pulse at the base of her throat with the tip of his tongue. His teeth grazed along the length of her neck. Moving higher he found the sultry evocative zone behind her ear.

"Evan..." she sighed his name, the whisper floated across his cheek. Her fingers wove into his hair, parted the fine silken strands, sifted through the length.

"We..."

"Can't you talk, *lassie*?"

He laughed softly as he explored across her shoulder with his most seductive moves.

"No..."

"You need to tell me what you want me to do. My poor man's brain is blank. What does a woman want from her man? Her lover? A bit of this? A bit of that? A touch here. Maybe one there. Lower. Intimate. Secretive." He followed his words with teeth along with his tongue. "Where should I touch you next?"

"Y...you know."

His head shot up, the look on his face was one of scandalized surprise. He arched a dark eyebrow. With a startled expression, he asked, "I do?" Gently, his lips brushed across her mouth, once then twice. He slipped his tongue along the fissure between her lips. She opened for him. Felt the shiver of his tongue as he glided inside moving slowly in then out to repeat then repeat again. He propped his forehead on hers, staring into her eyes. "*Dinna* tease me, *lass*. Tell me what you want me to do. How to proceed to give you the most pleasure. I want to bring you to your sweet ecstasy."

His fingers caressed the inside of her thigh, gently pressing them open. Cool air caressed intimately. She gasped in air as his nimble fingers moved ever higher. She couldn't tell him what she wanted, what she needed. The act would be too decadent, too brazen. She was too new to this game of love he played.

"I'm," she swallowed hard, wishing she could do as he asked. "I'm not teasing."

Her voice was whisper thin as he toyed with her, his fingers dancing anywhere, everywhere that pleased him, that pleased her. He knew just how to make her burn, the inferno building with each pass of his hand.

"Think about last night or this morning. What did you like best. I want to satisfy you, Betsy. Let me know."

He didn't have trouble pleasuring her. Her head fell back, she arched toward him. His fingers on that place between her legs that sent her higher then higher still were doing just that. She cried out as he filled her with two of his long fingers doing to her the same as his tongue was dancing within her mouth. Slowly, evocatively, his fingers glided into her then out while his thumb played with that sensitive spot, driving her wild.

She turned her face into his chest. Her fingers raked across his shoulders. Suddenly, he withdrew from her.

"What am I to do with you? You can't even wait for me to come along with you. I'm not even inside you. I feel your body reaching for that pleasure point. Betsy, you must learn to wait for me."

He sipped on her exposed breast, laving the nipple, scraping his teeth across the tight bud before closing his teeth delicately over the tender flesh. He ran his tongue along the tattoo featuring his name, leaving dewy moisture behind. His fingers vanished from inside her. She would have climaxed in the next second if he'd not withdrawn. Her nails raked across his shoulders.

"Evan...please...please..."

"Naughty girl. If you wish to be a good girl, you must wait for me. Pause a moment for the man who is your source of gratification." He turned her so she straddled him. "You must unfasten my buckskins. After that we will see how to proceed. Fast or slow you will wait for me in all things, Betsy. Tell me you agree."

She stared at him, stunned by his male arrogance which knew no bounds. She wasn't about to agree to something so ludicrous. This was just like a man to set down rules about their love play. He wanted to command, demand obedience in all things.

"No. I don't agree to anything you've said."

His hand covered her mound, slicked the wetness between her legs before leaving her panting with her woman's need once more. "Evan..." she wailed softly, her forehead resting at the base of his neck. "You..."

"Yes. Will you wait for me to be sated? I want to find pleasure with you. Not before. Not after. At the same time if possible." He brought his hand that had been between her legs, touching, stimulating until her heart pounded and she could barely breathe, to her cheek. "This is your woman's pleasure. Your warm, luscious honey rained down on my hand when I was inside your delicate sheathe." Following his words there was a long pause while he regarded her pensively. "You haven't told me what you want. I can't go on until you explain to me how to give you the most pleasure possible."

Betsy sucked air. "You know what I need."

"No...no, I don't, tell me," he repeated the order.

He was insufferable. He would persist until he had his way. She sucked in a deep breath of air. I want you inside of me."

"I've been inside you. Was that not good enough to make you purr with delight? For your breath to hitch. My tongue, my fingers. What more is there?" he teased, his grin crooked, a half-smile as he watched her.

"You know bloody well what I want!" Beneath her ribs, her heart thundered. With every soft caress of his lips, she writhed against him. He was poised to enter. Why hadn't he done so.

"Sweet, sweet Betsy. I know you can tell me. Swearing isn't necessary. You won't get surcease until you speak the words, the right words. Be specific now or your pleasure will seethe within you until you speak. We will proceed as I wish."

Furious with the insufferable brute she shot back. "Neither will you! You need me just as much as I need you."

"Do I?" he laughed as he stroked a breast with his tongue fondled the tight, hard bud with his teeth.

Her body shuddered against him. She arched, quivering with her need. "Evan what is it you want?"

"For you to tell me exactly what it is you so desire. I want to see to all your needs. A man is so at loss unless his partner is explicitly exact."

"You've never done this before."

She could barely breathe. Each sip of air was a fine granule that did nothing for her.

"You were learning what you liked. Once, you were too shy. No longer. Tell me, Betsy. What do you want? What will give you the greatest fulfillment?"

She didn't want to be exact. Didn't want to say exactly what she wanted. She was quivering, almost climaxing just with the play of words between them. She wanted to feel all those exquisite feelings he could orchestrate.

"Bloody, bloody hell, Evan! I want your penis inside me! Now!"

His hoot of laughter infuriated her. "Well, I suppose I couldn't have asked for anything more exact than that. No euphemisms for my shy one. Well, no longer shy. Straight to the point. I knew you could do the required task."

Before she could blink his britches were unfastened. He was deep inside her. She tried to rise, his hands on her hips held her still.

She looked at him, confused with what was happening. Her body pulsed with need. "What?"

"I'm inside you, Betsy. Now what?" he asked, his voice bland.

She hit him hard on his shoulder. He grunted. Still, he didn't move. She found herself shaking her head as to what he wanted. "I don't understand." Her breaths panted in short spurts. Her body squeezed against his length, delightfully kissing him.

"What is it that you would like now?" he asked softly. "My penis is inside your vagina. Tell me everything or nothing. If it's nothing, we stop here since I don't know yet how to proceed."

"Cad! I want you to move or let me move on you. I want you to touch that place that makes me spiral out of control. What do you want?" she tossed the question back at him. "Be exact."

"Everything you do. The problem, however, remains that we cannot do what you want. We are very nearly at my home. The driver would catch us in the most private of moments if we were to act on your demands."

"Demands! You made me tell you everything. We could have finished this minutes ago. We both would be sated."

~ * ~

She was so right. He cooked his goose, hoisted by his petard never thinking they were almost to his home. Somehow, he would have to figure out how to make this right for her. If he didn't guess wrong, she was so stimulated she would climax the moment he moved inside her. He wasn't ready, though her pulsing core would send him over the top in a flash of ecstasy. He didn't know if that would happen before the driver opened the door for them or after. In this, her privacy, he wasn't a gambling man. No one would watch her climax except him. No one save him would see the sweet expressions flash across her finely sculpted face.

After he set her aside, he smoothed her skirts then fastened her corsage. She stared at him with a pained express on her lovely face. Her brows were drawn together, her lips tightly honed in a smooth thin very kissable line. Kissing those lips until they were both swelled and plump from his attention was next on his agenda. With a heart-felt sigh, he picked up her pantalettes slipping them into the pocket of his frock coat. The notion she was naked beneath her skirt was indeed, enjoyable. Perhaps he could find the first empty room. That shouldn't be too hard. He groaned.

"I'm sorry," he whispered, more than she would ever know. "You'll have to wait for your pleasure, sweetheart. Soon, I promise."

He smoothed the damp tendrils of hair from her face before running his thumb across the plane of her eyebrows. She was so beautiful when she neared her climax, the culmination they both sought. Her face, her eyes, in the throes of her gratification would forever be etched in his mind.

Even as he spoke, the carriage slowed. The gate in front of the long drive to his home was opened. Only minutes would pass before they reached the front porch. He checked her bodice just to be certain nothing was askew, before smoothing her skirts one more time. Her eyes slightly dazed from passion were adorable, her lips as she began to relax, enlarged so round... There was nothing to be done to change the pretty picture she made. She had the appearance of a woman well loved. After he introduced her to the few servants at the home, he would carry her upstairs to the master chamber so he could finish what they started here.

"Evan." She reached out a trembling hand. "What are you doing to me?"

"Going to love you tenderly as soon as we have the privacy needed. You'll meet the housekeeper as well as my chef. As you know Alexander will be here later this afternoon." He leapt from the carriage.

When she poked her head out the door, he held on to her waist then swung her down to the immaculately mowed lawn. Introductions were made. Lydia, the maid, curtsied prettily. Claude, the French chef he employed, bowed to her.

He brought her to his home for several valid reasons. Evan never thought she would be viewed in a scandalous manner when he introduced her. She was not his wife or fiancée. She would sleep with him, cementing these peoples view of her.

Alexander never judged. He never brought a woman to his home to stay the night. Until Betsy, entertaining a woman for an entire night was not something he did. Now Betsy was going to live for an undisclosed time with him. She would lie in his bed chamber, in his bed, for an unnamed amount of time. What the devil was he doing?

Claude was thin as well as short. He wore an apron that covered him from the top of his chest to his knees. A handlebar mustache graced the top of his lip. While they spoke, he twirled the end between two fingers.

Lydia was plump and red faced. She beamed at them. Her hands were small, fingers short. Her salt and pepper hair was tied back in a tight bun, a net covering her head to keep the strands in place. She was always laughing.

"Dinner?" Claude asked, a pleasant smile. "I could have

something prepared in an hour or if you wish something lighter, I can get it ready in say a half hour. What would you like sir?"

"Lighter fare. He turned to look at Betsy asking with a look if that was fine with her. After he took care of other matters, they would explore his estate from the top to the bottom.

She nodded, her body still appearing to be stressed with her need. He held out his hand for her. Once he found her fingers enclosed with his, he strode quickly to the stairs, tugging her with him, impatient to reach privacy. After she stumbled the first time, he swept her into his arms. Before she had time to say a single word, her clothing along with his were strewn across the floor in his chambers. While they weren't completely naked, it was enough.

On top of her on his big bed, not wasting a precious moment, he thrust inside her. No seducing this time was necessary. She was hot and slick. Almost the moment he sheathed himself, she cried out his name as she reached that pulsing high they both craved. He growled hoarsely; a shot of sheer ecstasy then spent his seed inside her secret core.

"Is that what you wanted?" she breathed softly, her arms still around his back. "We could try something else but you'd have to tell me what you want? Perhaps a bit of this? A bit of that? A touch here. A touch there."

With a breathy voice, she teased him with his words.

Again, he traced his name on her breast. He would look into getting the Black Widow to put a permanent tattoo in place of the henna. He was growing quite accustomed to this one, didn't want to see his name gone from her body. Most likely he would have to get her drunk again.

Bracing himself above her, he grinned down, staring into her lovely eyes. "You did nicely. You told me just what you wanted. I'm proud of you."

He was solicitous, wanted her to yell at him. Wished to do this again and again until he stuck his spoon in the wall. Forever. Growing bored with this woman would never happen. So, how would he change the way his servants looked at her? If he had his way, she would always live with him. He imagined his parents would have something to say about this relationship. In the end though, he made all his decision. He would please her. She would please him. They would be happy.

Letting her go...no, that wouldn't happen in this lifetime.

Not ever!

"We can't continue like this," she told him while she ran her hands across his shoulders, pushing at his shirt as if she wanted him to remove it.

"Why the bloody not?" He traced the tip of her nose, then the line of her jaw down to the beating pulse at the base of her neck that told him she was still breathing heavily. "Time to rid yourself of your skirts. Want to feast my eyes on all your lovely white flesh. Need to watch the tight pink buds on your breasts grow tight with excitement. Watch the way my name moves when you climax."

"Because..." she stopped, looking hesitant. "It's just not done. I cannot live in your home, sleep in your bed without talk." She ran her fingertip across his lips down to his chin crying out for him to kiss her again. "I don't want to see your reputation damaged."

He liked the fact she thought about him, yet her words did not bode well for them. He would have some convincing to manage. She wasn't leaving for any ridiculous reason that she spouted. "Thought you didn't care about rumors, about what other people say. Was I wrong?" He sounded harsh even to his ears. Wasn't surprised when she visibly flinched at the sound of his voice.

"It's you I'm worried about. Your status. Mine is already tarnished. After this is finished here, I can return to London with no one the wiser." She touched him, caressed his mouth another time. "I love your kisses. If I had a choice, I would always stay with you. However," there was a long pause. "Eventually, you will want someone else. I'm not the type of woman a man of your station could be with. A man like you couldn't marry me."

Startled by the conviction in her statements, he sought more valid words. Instead, he uttered commands. "You are not going back to London. Not ever unless you go with me." The thoughts simmering in his brain were unusual for him. With each new one, he wondered what was happening to him. Betsy touched a part of him he never knew existed.

"I cannot stay here forever," she sounded wistful.

"Aren't you happy here? With me?" he asked while he watched her turn from him.

If she would only speak her feelings, he would understand how to deal with her, how to cope with whatever she was afraid of.

"I'm happy, too happy. Don't want this time with you to end." her soft murmur was enlightening.

Perhaps she had some regrets. He did take her innocence, did tease her with the fake tattoos. As of this moment, she didn't *ken* the markings were fake.

So, far, their relationship was all about sex, nothing more...or was it more? What did she offer that would enhance his life? None of that mattered as long as she came to his bed in the same delightful way with the wild abandon he yearned for. He had a lot to think about concerning Betsy. What would happen when Oliver was no longer a problem in her life? The independent woman she was would no longer need him.

Was Betsy just a diversion to his otherwise boring life? He wanted answers.

"One cannot be too happy."

By her winsome smile, he understood she didn't agree. "What will we do now? You said you would show me around your home."

"I'm going to love you again. After that, if we have the stamina, we'll eat that dinner Claude is making. When we finish the meal, I'll show you my estate. We can then go to my brother's home. If my parents were not in Edinburgh, I would introduce you to them."

He thought of the beautiful lake, the secluded spot he loved. Making love to her there in the summertime would be exquisite.

"An introduction to your parents would not be appropriate," she told him stiffly rising from the bed to dress.

She slipped into the bathing room to wash. With lust in his mind, he watched her beautiful backside. The sway of her hips mesmerized. He could take her again right now. His thirst for her would never be sated.

Of course she was right. She was wrong as well. They wouldn't judge her. No, his parents would only judge him. They would tell him he couldn't keep his doxies at his home. He would tell his mother what he did was no longer her business yet he would listen to her opinion then do exactly as he pleased.

Briefly, the thought of making this relationship with Betsy permanent crossed his mind. The thought that he wasn't the marrying kind replaced the brief moment of insanity on his part. A man who harbored the intention of keeping one woman in his bed for eternity might be the marrying kind.

After she emerged, she dressed then tossed his clothes at him. "I'm hungry," she told him smartly. "...and this time it's not for your penis."

He howled with laughter never expecting her to say something so brazen. Well, he did spend the better part of the drive here teasing her. She rose to the occasion. No, he rose to the occasion. Now, it seemed he opened the floodgates. Loving the notion she could be so bold with him, he dressed. He could hardly wait to see what the next round with her would bring. "I could change that feeling with one kiss."

She turned on him, disappearing out the door. He saw her look over her shoulder as if to be certain he would follow. The door shut. He heard the sound of her slippers as she walked away. Beneath his breath he swore softly.

By the time she reached the first floor, he caught up with her. "Do you know where to go? You should have waited for me."

"No, but I'm certain I can figure out which way to turn to get to the dining room. The scent of delicious aromas has already filtered through the house. I will simply follow my nose."

She started to walk again.

He caught her around her tiny waist, bringing her flush with him, her breasts pushing against his chest. While he had her attention, he brushed a light kiss across her lips. "I'll show you how to proceed."

She grunted.

Claude's dinner was fabulous. All types of seasonal fruit and vegetables were set out along with warm, fresh bread. There were three different types of cheeses coupled with ham along with roasted chicken.

"I am hungry," she murmured while she chewed on a piece of cheese. "What will your brother and Caro think about my staying with you? They couldn't possibly approve. They will tell me I've got to go.

They will inform you how much an idiot you are."

"Caro will suggest you stay with them. You won't."

One more time he left her with no choice. Where the *lasses* he slept with were concerned, he never cared before. If his sister-in-law wanted to dictate some other living arrangement for them, she would find a heated argument brewing that she wouldn't win.

"So, you've become a dictator. Why?"

"I want you in my arms as well as in my bed." He needed to examine his reasons more thoroughly. She could even now be pregnant with his child. Would he do as his brother when faced with a bastard? If she wasn't pregnant now, she would be soon. He knew for certain if he had a child, he would be a father in every way. Hells bells, possibly the solution to her problem with Oliver could be had in a proposal of marriage from him. If he wed her, there would be no way Tindell could set the marriage aside. An annulment would never be possible. He'd had her hard and deep many times. Would continue to do so. Determined, he set his mind on a course he wouldn't deviate from.

She might have conceived his child. In another few weeks she would. The idea kept reverberating, bouncing around in his head. He would have to do something about that possibility. There was no way he could withdraw from her to prevent a pregnancy. No way.

Betsy would have to agree to marry him.

He hoped so. Perhaps he needed to try a *wee* bit harder, stay inside her longer so his seed could take root. That was probably a bit of nonsense. Nevertheless, doing so would never be counterproductive to his goals, would undoubtedly be quite enjoyable. Would lead to more lovemaking. If she discovered she was increasing, she would have to concede to his plans. Tapping his fingers, he smiled, pleased with his new ideas to cement their relationship for all time.

"We both understand that scenario will not happen. To make a living, I will have to return to London. I can't possibly remain here."

"You can tutor in Glasgow. I do have contacts. Know a lot of people who might need the service of an instructor for young children as well as a nanny. Duncan and Caroline could use you, could afford to pay you well. No, you can just as easily work here as there."

He mentally patted himself on the back with his ingenuity. His brother lived only a ten-minute ride from his home. The set up was perfect for his needs. That fact still didn't change the promise of a bastard. He would have to change that prospect. If she tied the knot with him, she wouldn't have to work. He would provide for her.

"I would never want to impose on your brother and Caroline. Would like them to remain friends."

"You'd be working for them, not imposing. You love children. At least I assume you do."

He made a mental note to have a large tub installed in his bathing room at his country estate. When she moved in with him, there would have to be other considerations and changes made to his home. She would want to decorate. The house would need a feminine touch.

"Seems you have an answer for everything." She sounded upset.

Except for one question. He would have to garner his courage if he truly meant to propose. If he didn't want a bastard, he would need to do just that. He wondered how Duncan handled the proposal. Recalling the situation, he decided bringing the minister to the house then insisting she say yes might not be the best tactic for them. It was something to consider. With Caroline and Duncan there was no other choice. Caroline had to fall into his plans. Without Duncan's support, she was destitute.

Unable to separate his thoughts from words, he blurted with astounding force. "You will marry me!"

Hearing his proposal in the form of a demand, she flinched. Her brows drew together, defiance written clearly in the shimmer of those beautiful cornflower blue eyes. That wasn't a good sign. "Are you daft? We barely know each other."

Evan didn't expect either comment to fly from her sweetly kissable lips. Lips he needed to kiss right now. A bit of sweettalking might be necessary to convince her. "I've seen, tasted and explored all of you. How much better do I need to know you? My name is tattooed forever on your breast." He was proud of his answers. Even went so far as to puff up his chest. She didn't appear to be buying his response. "You *ken* what kind of man I am. What more do you need learn about me?"

"You don't love me." Her voice held a hint of ice while her words shot icicles his way her jaw clenched tight.

What did love have to do with marriage? He felt befuddled by her accusation. Wasn't lust enough to sustain a marriage through eternity. If they continued to want each other, life would be fine. "You don't love me." He told her with more sincerity than he meant.

For some reason he suddenly discovered he might want her to love him as he thought of his brother and Caroline. They obviously love each other.

"I rest my case."

She crossed her arms beneath her breasts pushing up her lovely bosom. His mouth watered. The arctic expression vanished. Now, she just looked relieved that the conversation would end.

"No, love, you don't have a case to rest. We both want what is best for us. In so many ways I couldn't possibly count, we're best for each other. By marrying, we solve both our dilemmas." He nailed that argument on the head.

"I don't understand. What is your dilemma?" She stood, walked around the table then out the door. Looking over her shoulder, she said. "It's time for you to show me around the premises. We can visit your brother later when you have your bizarre emotions under control. Is he expecting us? Are we going to show up on his doorstep unannounced."

"Duncan is expecting us this afternoon. By the time I show you the lake then ride back the time will be right. Do you swim?"

Evan thought a diversion might be appropriate. After all she would need some time to think over his sudden suggestion. She was correct in the fact they had not known each other for long. How did length of time make a difference? He could know her for years and years. He would still feel the same.

"I swim like a fish," she told him continuing to the foyer. Without a backward glance she stepped through the door.

Betsy wouldn't have any idea where to go yet there she was acting as if she did, leading the way. All she needed now was her damn rain napper to point. "Do you now?" he asked suspecting her swimming skills were more on the level of her riding expertise. Lacking in every aspect.

"Guess you'll have to wait to find out. By the way, I'm quite proficient sitting a mount."

His yowl of laughter didn't stop her strides. She wouldn't understand the double meaning. He raced to catch up with her taking her by an arm. In any case, she told him when they were in Glasgow that she didn't ride. Never had the opportunity to learn. He would let her ride Venus, the most biddable mare in his stable.

"Come along."

He held her by her waist pulling her closer. He would always enjoy the feel of her body warmly nestled against his.

"Saddle Venus and Zeus," he called to the stablemaster. "We'll be gone for several hours."

When they walked their horses toward the lake, he knew he chose the perfect horse for her. "So, you can sit a mount proficiently?" he challenged her. "Does this tell me about your aquatic skills? Will I need to hold you up in the water?"

She nudged her horse as if she wanted to get away from him. Venus would have nothing to do with her urging. Evan settled for watching. She would be sore when they returned. He thought of massaging liniment into her thighs. The task would be quite enjoyable.

"This way."

He pointed toward the trail that would take them to the lake. She turned Venus. He followed.

When they crested the hill, the water shimmered with the sunlight hitting the silver-colored liquid. A startled crane rose from the edge of the lake. The day was quiet. No breeze, no ripples to mar the surface. The lake would be cool against the heat of their bodies.

After dismounting, he helped her down. "Are you sore, *lass*?"

He held her close, his hands cupping her delectable rear. This was heaven. Even if she couldn't swim, he knew his favorite place a short distance from where they stopped. "Let's walk."

If she didn't like to swim, they could make love on the moss nearby.

Taking her hand in his, he led the way. They skirted the lake for about a quarter mile. She leaned against him. His hand settled on the curve of her hip.

"I do swim a little," she confessed.

"That's what I thought. I will have to hold you up."

For what he planned, she didn't need to swim. He had other ideas besides swimming. There was this shelf where he could sit. She could mount him as she suggested she was good at doing. The slim barrier of water between them would be all that separated them. The thought was erotic, the most sensual notion he'd had since this afternoon in the carriage.

"I do my best underwater," she murmured while his hand drifted higher, fiddling with the buttons of her gown.

How could he always want her? Only an hour ago, he thought he was sated. The feeling, he was certain, would last the afternoon. Beneath the fabric of her gown his fingers glided to cup the soft flesh of her breast. The tips of his fingers played with one hard tip.

"Do you want me, *lass*?"

"Is that question for real?" Her breath whispered from her lips with a soft sound. "You know I do."

He stopped, finished undressing her. Quickly, he slipped from his clothes. Holding her in his arms, he stepped into the water. "Don't actually care if you can swim."

She gasped when the water hit her body. He sat on the rock. She straddled him. Seconds later, she was crying out his name.

"Little Bit...you unman me. What am I going to do with you? Will you marry me?"

At the time, the question seemed appropriate. He wasn't going to bring up the fact she might carry his child, their child not until there were no other arguments. He didn't want her to have second thoughts about the delightful sexual games they played.

Betsy, set her forehead on his. "You know I cannot."

Why ever the bloody hell not? He wanted to yell at her, shake her until she agreed. This was the best as well as the only option they had. "I'll keep asking until you agree." He'd keep asking until she was left with no choice.

"So, you're saying I should just accept." She let out a long sigh. "When I was a little girl, I dreamed of finding a man who would love me, who would put me first in his life. I told myself I would never settle for less. Even though I've never found that man, I won't settle. We both know you aren't that man."

"With me, you don't have to settle. I will always put you first in my thoughts and deeds."

His words were the truth. In asking her to marry him, he was putting her first in his life, the unborn child as well. He wanted the best for all of them.

"Perhaps today, even tomorrow. Forever though?" She asked wistfully. "We should see your brother. You and Duncan can discuss how you wish to proceed with Oliver. I'd like to speak with Caroline. I've a few questions for her. It seems an eternity since I've seen her."

He heard a note of sadness in her voice. It wasn't the first time. She refused to tell him what was wrong. If he was a guessing man, he figured it had something to do with the fact he didn't love her. What was so glorious about love? It was just a word of endearment. To his way of thinking, commitment and loyalty were so much more important.

"We will lay out a strategy that will send Tindell reeling. You can talk girl-talk with Caroline. Perhaps she will convince you marriage to me is the only solution to your issue with Oliver. If you agreed with me, Lord Tindell could not go forth unscathed. It wouldn't matter if he gave back your savings. I'd be willing with your approval to allow him a few funds."

"You must allow him to keep the house. Without that the girls will have nowhere to live. No matter how much I want him to pay for what he's done to me, Virgie and Poppet need a father, even a terrible one."

"You're shivering..." He ran his hands along her arms. "We will do whatever you want." He needed to get her out of the cold water.

~ * ~

Lord Tindell sat, waiting for an interview. This firm was the best in Scotland, he was told. His mission was to ruin Evan Murray. With this man's help all would be taken care of. The task should not be too difficult. The professor couldn't possibly have much to steal. After all, he was a lowly instructor.

After shaking hands, the man whose name was Gordan sat down behind the large cherry wood desk. Gordan was a handsome man, tall, broad of shoulders. He didn't appear to be a man who would become an advisor of finances. Ah, he looked more like a man who would compete in the caber toss. Tindell imagined a woman might find him attractive. What he cared about was intelligence.

"What is it you want to accomplish here?" Gordan asked while he twirled the pen between his long fingers. His golden flecked eyes were hard.

This was the tricky part. He was told this firm was discreet. They would do things no one else would. With a bit of money under the table it was rumored the employees here would orchestrate deals that might change a man's life. The owner even ruined the woman who he later married. Did it because of a child. These were exactly the type of people he needed. Intelligent. Unscrupulous. Willing to skirt the edge of the law.

His reason was just as sound. "I need to get Evan Murray out of my way. As my situation exists now, he stands between me and the woman I wish to marry. Can you help me?"

"Can help anyone for the right price. Since you are here, I assume you wish to have his funds vanish. Do I have this right?" Gordan asked, his voice harsh.

The sound pleased Oliver. He felt a weight lifted off his shoulders. He would have his vengeance as well as Betsy. What could be better? "How long will this take?"

He found he was eager to get on with his life. He didn't even care if Murray took her innocence. The more he was away from her the more he wanted her. Coupled with what she could give him, she was the woman of his fondest dreams.

"Not long. Mr. Murray will begin to feel the sting soon, possibly as soon as tomorrow. I understand he is no longer employed at the university."

"True. You did some research on the man."

"Yes, I wanted to make certain I had all the necessary paperwork when we met. Once these documents are signed, you won't have to return.

When all is said and done, I'll have *carte blanch* with his finances."

Oliver wasn't at all certain he understood how his signature would give this man free reign over Evan Murray. He suffered a moment of doubt.

As if Gordan understood his concern, he spoke up. "Murray will be called into the firm for a consultation. I've arranged this. He will also set his name on a few documents. Trust me. I've everything under control. This will transpire just as I've planned." Gordan tapped the end of the pen on his desktop. "If you have reservations, now is the time to say *yeah* or *nay*. Once the scenario is put into play, changing the scope of our strategy will be difficult if not impossible."

"Will you provide me with updates?"

"Absolutely. Anything for such a fine outstanding client. We wish to please." Gordan rose, extending his hand. "This is concluded then. If I have anything else that needs to be signed, I will send a message for you to return."

Oliver left, feeling well-pleased. He was satisfied now that Betsy would leave the fraud behind. She would choose him, a man who could give her all she wanted over a man who would be left penniless with nowhere to live. With no job as well as no financial means to survive, Murray would become dependent on his family.

Ah...the amazing feelings swamping him. This was just as life should be. He'd waited a long time for Betsy. Soon, she would be his along with all she owned.

At home he meant to celebrate. Possibly, he should return to London. No, he would wait until Betsy came to him, agreed to the marriage. He would return her savings to her. Virgie and Poppet would be pleased. They cared a great deal for the woman. For the life of him, he didn't understand their feelings. Well, a man would do what he had to in order to acquire a fortune. While he was able to steal her small savings, he couldn't put his hands on her dowry. He needed her small treasure to pay for his mistress along with the other pleasant diversions he'd become fond of. She would give him an heir then he'd be done with the woman.

When her father passed away, he didn't completely trust him. The way the dowry was written the man made it impossible for him to get his hands on the funds. Years ago, Betsy could have had the money. When she turned twenty-one, the groats were hers. She would have never needed him for anything. Now, when she wed him, the money would automatically be his. Unable to help himself, he rubbed his hands together in silent glee.

Chapter Nine

Three days passed before they met with Evan's brother. Duncan's home was lovely. Betsy immediately felt comfortable. She was in the sewing room with Caroline. She didn't know what to expect, a lecture perhaps. A reason to give up this crazy scheme. She would not dismiss the idea. Oliver deserved whatever the two men doled out.

"You can stay with us." The words came from Caroline's heart. "You don't have to live with Evan."

Betsy understood the silent recriminations. Caroline truly didn't believe she could judge so she held back her disapproval to a small degree. "I understand you want to be hospitable. I cannot stay here. Don't judge me. At least I'm not deceiving Evan." By that last statement, she implied so much. She watched as Caroline looked away for a moment. "I'm sorry. That was not well said of me."

"The truth sometimes can hurt. You're right. At least you have been open and honest with my brother-in-law."

"I need to continue on that same vein."

She would probably have to come up with a reason for refusing her friend's hospitality. The simplicity of it all was that Evan wouldn't allow her to stay anywhere except with him. How he would go about that she didn't know. What she did comprehend was that he would find a means. Deep in her heart, she admitted that for as long as possible she wanted to live with him, love him. She did love the blasted man.

"Why?" Caroline poured tea then offered cream and sugar.

Though Betsy knew the question was coming, she didn't want to answer. She picked up a lavender tea cake bit then chewed slowly. Instead of putting this at Evan's feet, she lifted her shoulders to tell her more than she needed to know, "I don't want to leave him even if the house is ten minutes away." A long pause followed her statement while she sipped her tea. "He has become special to me. I won't have much longer to be here with him. I need to enjoy every exceptional moment we can find together."

Caroline made a face, her brows drawing together. "What if you're increasing? Rejecting Evan will not be so easy. You will be ostracized no matter where you go. If he is anything like his brother, he won't let his child be labeled."

Her cup clashed down on the saucer, some of the liquid slipping out to splatter in the saucer as well as on the table. She'd not thought that far ahead.

"What did you say?" Blood drained from her. She touched her hands to her cold cheeks. While she wasn't stupid, she never truly thought of the possibility with clarity. She stiffened, thinking quickly, perhaps too quickly. "You didn't care. You didn't think twice about raising a bastard. I won't either."

"I wasn't thinking straight at the time. All I knew was that I wanted a child." She pushed flyaway hair from her face, her lips thinned in a fine line. "You heard me. Have either of you taken precautions?" Caroline didn't appear to let this topic go. She was knowledgeable. Knew so very much. "When was your last flow?

"No, no I wasn't. I..." she murmured, pleating the folds of her skirt with her fingers.

Less than an hour ago, the gown was on the soft green moss near the lake. He was within her, pleasuring her. They could have conceived then along with the numerous times before that one. "Maybe a week or two weeks. I never kept track, never needed to." Her brows drew together, concentrating.

"Has Evan mentioned the possibility to you? Has he? You need to be treated with the respect you deserve. He should make certain you understand the consequences of what the two of you are doing. A marriage for the two of you is the only way to make this right." Caroline sounded adamant. "I know how the Murray men react to the possibility of a child. He won't let you go if you are pregnant. Just as Duncan was relentless, Evan will also pursue this. They intend to be fathers to their children. The way I read this situation, Evan decided he wanted you as his wife. He will never relent."

Possibly that was why he asked her to marry him every day. He expected her to conceive. In the discussions afterward they never found their way past the main reason, they didn't love each other. She didn't know what to say. The possibility was more than sound. At the notion of marrying Evan, her pulse leapt.

I do love him.

"I gave the question no real thought until you mentioned the possibility. I couldn't saddle him with me. If he was forced in any way or for any reason, he would hate me for the rest of his life. I'm too old to be considered as marriageable."

"You have belittled yourself too many times. You're a beautiful woman any man would be pleased to call his wife. You haven't been with him that long," Caroline pointed out. "However, I can tell by the look on your face as well as your reaction to my question the two of you have been intimate. Do you love the man? Is that why you gave yourself to him."

Betsy could do nothing save nod. Before she knew him well there was another significant reason. Oliver Tindell. The lies were too complicated, turning to a muddled mess now that she understood her feelings for Evan.

"Your situation is different than mine. I set out to get pregnant. I purposely deceived Duncan. Never intended to see him a second time. After that, I didn't plan on a third encounter. Whatever you do be honest with Evan. When you are positive you are with child, tell him. He will want to know. I expect the man has thought of the possibilities or he wouldn't have proposed."

She nodded again. "I imagine that is one of the reasons he offered marriage. I thought the offer was to stop the gossip from affecting me. I didn't want his reputation tarnished. After the article, well, I worried about him. It was his face that was depicted in the newspaper. He doesn't seem to care if the dean reinstates him at the university. Told me he doesn't have to work."

"He doesn't," Caroline said softly. "He, as do all the brothers, have more money than they could ever spend. If they were gamblers, perhaps. None of them care to risk their fortune on anything expect the financial deals Duncan discovers. Duncan is a wizard. Are you going to reconsider his proposal?"

"I would wait..." Thoughtfully she stirred the tea in front of her. Even if she waited, if she continued to sleep with the man, it was just a matter of time before she conceived. Her head was filled with conflicting emotions.

"Wise thought," Caroline's voice was mocking. "I waited. Didn't believe I conceived the first time, the night I presented myself as his birthday present. On my second try, it created a huge scandal. Even Evan was disgusted with his brother."

"What did he do?" Betsy asked seeing that Caroline was laughing. "There is a twinkle in your eyes at the memory. The memory could not have been too bad."

With a little giggle, "He was horrible. He wanted me so desperately. He tossed me over his shoulder. Carried me straight to his bedroom then locked the door. His brothers followed. Pounded on the door while they begged him to return to the ballroom at least until people started to leave. He refused."

Betsy mulled over Caroline's story. "Did he love you?"

"Lust is not such a bad thing to have in a marriage. In the beginning, we could not keep our hands off each other. I was desolate when I had to move away from him. Tried and failed to hide in Edinburgh. I left Glasgow while he was in London on business."

"He found you."

"Yes." Caroline had this dreamy look in her eyes. "Yes, he discovered where I was then insisted I marry him."

"We do lust for each other, Evan, and me. Will that feeling turn to love?"

Oh, how she wanted it to do just that. Needed to feel loved. Not since her father and mother had she felt love. That emotion was something she coveted.

"Time will tell." Caroline reached over to touch her hand. "Evan has never acted possessive with another woman. Has never brought her to the country home. Has never asked a woman to marry him. You must be very special to him. It's possible he loves you and doesn't even *ken* the emotion."

"Never? Never to all that?" Betsy queried, her mind running in too many different directions to count.

Caroline was convincing. A baby without a father was not ideal. Even though it was doable. Other women survived the scandal. She looked up to see Caroline smiling at her. "He wants me to work for you. Told him the idea was ridiculous."

"Doing what?" Caroline acted surprised, her eyes narrowing. "You..." she stopped as if trying to figure out what position she could fill.

"He thinks I could be your nanny while I live with him. I told him I would never impose in that way." She laughed softly at the thought. "Although I wouldn't have to worry about Duncan attacking me. That would be a plus."

She was shaking her head reliving other times, other positions. She would have to work for someone.

"Ten minutes away. Very convenient for your man. I do hope you didn't agree. Not that I don't think you would make an excellent nanny or tutor for my little one. I would be furious with Evan if he didn't ask you to marry him."

"If he asks again, he'll have to give me a solid reason, one I can believe."

Only a few months ago she thought she would never entertain thoughts such as this one.

"Isn't the possibility of a child a good enough motive for marriage?" Caroline asked, her voice softening now. "Do you truly want your child to be a bastard?"

"Not really..."

Betsy still wanted love. She needed to have a man put her before him. While Evan told her he would do that very thing, she didn't know yet if his words were a lie. Taking a chance by saying yes was a huge risk by her way of thinking. "I need more from the man I marry than lust coupled with financial security."

"Keep in mind the Murray men are persistent. I've never known one of them to back off from something they want. He will never stand down no matter how many times you tell him no. You should just agree to disagree then marry the man. You'll be a lot happier when this is resolved."

"I understand."

She did understand what Caroline was saying. He would never let her go without pulling out all the stops. He couldn't make her financially dependent on him. She didn't have any money to take from her. No, that was what Oliver did.

"Do you? You will end up wed to the man if he truly wants you. What do you think? Wouldn't it be easier to say yes now rather than later."

Caroline was making many relevant arguments. "Possibly. We need to talk over all the issues before I can—"

"What issues?" Evan asked as he strode into the sewing room, Duncan behind him. "Issues between the two of us? Tell me."

He plucked her up from her chair then kissed her hard. His tongue glided between her lips, parting them. She thought she should protest. She could not do so. Instead, she moaned softly with the pleasure he gave her.

"Private issues," she said, gasping for air, when he finally set her on his lap. "You can get your own chair."

He held onto her, his hands on the curve of her hips. He wasn't going to move or find a place to sit for himself. Just as Caroline told her, once a Murray made up his mind, he would never back off.

"Don't think so," he said as he ran his hand along her rib cage. "Want to sit right here with my soon to be wife." Moving closer, he whispered to her. "Caroline has convinced you of all the benefits of marriage. Tonight, we can wed."

There was nothing to do but glower at him. She tried to flatten her lips into a thin line. In front of his brother and his wife, she wasn't going to argue. He was acting outrageous. On the positive side, Duncan seemed to be doing the same to Caroline. They were not paying attention to them.

"I can get a minister here by this evening," Duncan said turning his focus away from his wife as he seemed to now be studying both of them. He was looking over Caroline's head. While he stroked her arm, touched her hip, his large hand resting possessively on the curves.

"What did the two of you talk about besides Oliver's demise?" she queried.

His hand fanned across her belly. He knew she was with child. He was telling her not so subtly that he thought she was pregnant or would be soon. She wanted to cosh him over the head. It seemed he wanted to make love to her. He was seducing, charming, sweettalking all without one word being said.

"You," Evan said with that half-smile that told her he was keeping something back from her.

"Your upcoming marriage to my brother," Duncan said softly as he sent his gaze toward Betsy. "You do want to marry my brother. If I do say so myself, he's a fine catch. Intelligent. Handsome. Resourceful."

"What did you talk about?" Evan asked. "Me? I would like that. You were at least talking to Caroline about us." He paused for a moment. "About issues we'll talk about in private. They wouldn't have something to do with my baby you're carrying inside your womb."

She hissed in air. So much for speaking in private. Did the whole world know his thoughts? "No."

"No what?" He nipped the back of her neck.

She fidgeted. That tiny contact sent an inferno sweeping inside her. "I believe it's time to go. I..."

Evan smiled at his brother. "We can be back in time for the ceremony. Believe my Betsy has some more convincing before she agrees. Is there a room where we can talk?"

"You can go into my office for the privacy you need. By the way, Oliver will be taken care of. He's seen Gordan. Just this afternoon, I believe. The documents we need have been signed. Everything he owns will be divided between his girls equally. Gordan will be the trustee of both girls' estates. Oliver will not be able to touch his money. Ah, I suppose it is the girl's groats now. Though I'm certain the two girls will do the best they can under the circumstances. The matter was taken care of so quickly because Evan wrote a letter about the circumstances you found yourself in along with how you would like the money settled. I received the missive yesterday afternoon then put to work the details to see this through. Oliver will rue the day he followed you to Scotland.

When I visited Lord Oliver the first time, something he said got me thinking. I made a few inquiries then guesses, all panned out. You didn't need to tell me about your savings. I figured that much out during the times you were researching your queen consort."

Mouth slightly open she stared at him. He smiled widely, his even white teeth showing as the grin widened. "I knew you wouldn't want Virgie or Poppet hurt even before you told me. You'd never hurt children. You love them. You will also love ours."

His audacity unnerved as well as jolted her sensibilities. "You took matters into your hands without consulting me!" Furious with his arrogance she didn't know how to tell him he didn't have that right. How did he know her so well? He seemed to read her as easily as he would an open book.

"I did exactly as you would have wished," he sounded a bit defensive. "I'm confused as to why you are so angry."

In Betsy's mind, he should grovel at her feet and apologize, not look so smug as well as self-satisfied. "Behind my back," she bit out while she tried to calm the escalating fury. This was all too much. Just too much. She tried to push off his lap. He held her securely.

"Time was of the essence. I had to set the wheels in motion," he said, his voice lowering. "As we've talked about, he was trying to ruin me. Expected that to happen from the first article that was written. This scenario wasn't just about you. He wanted to take my entire fortune. Instead, he will feel the financial pain. Not I."

He stood, picking her up. Without asking if she wanted to talk, he strode to his brother's office. Embarrassed, she hid her face in his shoulder.

Once inside, he slid her down the length of his hard body, cupping her bottom in his hands. His heavy arousal pulsed against her belly. "We are not—"

His mouth on hers cut off her comment. When he looked up, "We are getting married today. You will say yes. We are not going home until we tie the knot. Now, we both *ken* you might have my baby growing inside you. If you don't at this moment you will within the next few weeks. What are these issues you are seeming to have?"

She felt defeated. Ambushed. He set the path in the direction he wanted to follow. Not where she thought to travel. "I don't know. We don't know if I'm pregnant."

"You will be. Think of the child."

He was adamant. Just as Caro told her, he would never change his mind. Walls seemed to close in around her.

"How will the baby feel when she discovers her parents don't love each other?" Her words were a thin wail that held little to no conviction.

"How will the baby feel when he finds out his parents didn't care if he was born a bastard. I won't have that label attached to a child of mine. I will love all my children."

"B...but..."

To no avail she fought the moisture clogging her throat, rushing to her eyes. A sob then a hiccup followed. He pulled her into his arms, holding her tight. "Don't cry. I have the devil's own time when a woman cries. You won't regret becoming my wife. I promise you that. I will take care of you, worship you. Put you first." His voice so sincere he stole her heart.

"I-I'm...n-not crying."

"Uh-huh...that's good you're not crying. Don't want my bride to have red eyes. Now," he held her slightly away from him. "You will say yes? Do you need more convincing?"

She nodded, wiping her eyes before she shook her head. His hands framed her face. With his thumbs he brushed away the tears slipping down her cheeks. "Betsy?"

"Yes...I better be pregnant. If not, I want an annulment!" She wasn't making sense.

His hoot of laughter unnerved her. "No, my dear, there can be no annulment. I've been inside you, took your maidenhead. You bare my name on your soft breast. There are no grounds for dissolving this marriage, besides I would never sign the papers."

"All right. What now?"

She didn't like to think of herself as meek or timid. At this moment, that was exactly how she was. If she admitted the truth to herself, she wanted the marriage. Would love to be his wife. Never thought to have a proposal.

"We tell my brother and Caroline that we will get married as soon as the minister arrives. After that, we'll go home. I've written an announcement for the paper that Alexander will take tonight so it can be in the Harold first thing in the morning. I will also send a missive to Tindell that you are my wife. Not that it will matter."

"Now that I've agreed, does it have to be this instant?"

Betsy never thought to marry. Now that the event would take place, she would like a few...she would like it to be nicer, not just some rapidly put together event.

His finger was under her chin, lifting. She looked into the golden shimmer of his eyes. They were warm, heated with the raw hunger she began to recognize. "Now, would be nice. I've the feeling you're holding something back from me. I'd know—"

She was shaking her head. "Never mind. It's not important."

"Thought we should go about this honestly. How can I help if you don't tell me." He stepped back, accessing, maybe thinking. "Always honest, that's what I would have for the rest of our lives."

"You'll think I'm being foolish. Evan...no...I'll talk to Caroline. Maybe she can help."

She looked at her dress. It was soiled from when it lay on the moss. She needed a bath to freshen herself. A dress that was clean would be nice Until now, she thought she would be fine.

"Together we'll tell them what we've decided. Possibly, I've been hasty. Just focused on your agreement more than the wedding. You want to have a real wedding, don't you? I would say friends that would be here. Don't know if you have any...friends, except Caro and Letty. Duncan will give you away. If you like, that is."

He was walking in circles, threading his hair through his fingers as his long strides circled the small office. "I'm fine. There is nothing I need." Except you. The decision was taken out of her hands.

Holding his hand out to her, "Come here."

She came to him. He tugged her through the door. "Caroline!" he called out. Appeared surprised to see her almost as soon as the words were uttered. Both Caroline and Duncan waited what seemed to be anxiously.

"Evan, you don't have to holler your head off. Come along, Betsy, I believe we have some preparations to take care." She looked to Evan with a moment of hesitation then back to her friend. "Betsy did agree?"

Evan nodded wondering what his sister-in-law was up to now. "Yes, she said, yes. She will say I do to the minister. Everything has been taken care of."

Caroline was grinning, clearly pleased with the last-minute effort on Evan's part. Good, leave us. Not everything. We're leaving the men. They can have a drink while they wait." She turned to the two men. "We will be in the master chamber."

With Betsy in tow, Caroline headed upstairs continuing to talk. She stopped on the first step to speak to the men again. "Betsy and I are close enough to the same size. I've my wedding gown, worn only once, hanging in the armoire. We might have to make a few tucks here and there, let out the seams in certain places. She will be beautiful. If you talk to our chef, he'll put together a wedding cake for the happy occasion. Your siblings will be here if you send for them. Send a message to Letty also. If she can get here, I'm certain she will."

"Your wedding dress? You don't have to do that." The emptiness she felt earlier began to disappear. The love she needed seemed to be within a heartbeat. In a few short minutes, they came together to do things for her. The caring was new to her.

Three hours later, Betsy stood in front of the minister. Duncan gave her away. Fletcher, one of his brothers, served as best man. Gordan, his youngest sibling, along with Letty, were witnesses. Caroline was her matron of honor. Fletcher brought her a lovely bouquet of roses from Glasgow. His parents arrived in time to witness the ceremony.

They said their vows. It was done. She was married to the man she loved. There was no turning back. Her life was irrevocably changed. She wanted to believe he loved her. Her love for him had to be enough.

They drank champagne. He waltzed her to a corner then kissed her. "Are you happy, *lass*?" he whispered close to her ear.

"Are you?" she said back to him refusing to make herself more vulnerable than she already was.

Truth be told, she couldn't want for much more. Never expected to marry a handsome man, one who was also wealthy beyond comprehension.

When they left in the carriage supplied by Duncan, she was just a *wee* bit tipsy and Evan told her he enjoyed her that way. She acted different. "Different good or bad?"

"Very good," he chuckled softly, running his knuckles along her cheek. "The differences are pleasing. I like you both ways. You said some wild things after you got your tattoo."

She sighed softly her breath whispering into the evening air. There it was, the 'like' word when she wanted to hear another word, a different word.

During the ten-minute journey to their home, he held her while she felt protected. She expected him to seduce her as he did the last time they journeyed together. He did not. When his hand stilled on the curve of her hip, she pulled in a breath of air. That was all though. Nothing more.

Exhausted, she fell asleep, nestled into his warmth thinking of the swimming hole. When the carriage stopped, she woke. He grinned at her. "You fell asleep on our wedding night. Must have been all that champagne you drank." He kissed her forehead then her nose. "Well, Mrs. Murray, that will not be a tale we will repeat to our grandchildren A woman just doesn't fall asleep when her new husband is hoping to pursue different directions."

Grandchildren? He seemed to jump ahead. They didn't have children yet. She touched her belly thinking about the child she might carry. His hand closed over hers. She swallowed hard.

"I thought you would..." she murmured.

"Seduce you?" One of his finely chiseled eyebrows lifted to the sky. "If that frown on your beautiful face is thinking I've grown tired of you, rest assured I have not. I plan on keeping you awake all night, loving every part of you. Thought you might need a tiny bit of rest before I carried you upstairs." With that said, he did just that. Once they were in the bedroom, he set her on the bed, slowly disrobed her. She was naked except for her stockings and garters. He perused her from head to toe, his gaze approving. The borrowed wedding gown, he set on a chair. "You are so beautiful. I can hardly wait to see you increase, to feel our son move within you. I will take good care of you, Betsy. Nothing bad will happen to you or our child. You can have anything you wish for."

The warmth of his words filled her with both happiness and longing. Maybe this wasn't a love match made in heaven, but he did offer security...lust...he offered mercuric pleasure. "I pray you never grow tired of me." She feared that more than anything.

"Betsy." He sat down beside her while he pulled his shirt over his head. His shoulders broad, his muscles flexing as he moved to finish undressing. "You need to look at yourself in the mirror. You're exquisite." He ran his fingertip along his name where it was etched on her breast. When he looked at her, his expression saddened. "This..." He repeated the tracing of his name seeming to regard the shivers he created. "This is not a permanent tattoo. I wish it was. I love looking at my name engraved on your breast. The others are not real either."

Her breath gushed from her lungs. "Not real?" Both relief along with curiosity filled her. She was getting used to the idea of his name being there forever. Now that they were married, she liked the idea. Curiously, she tipped her head to one side, "I..."

"Would you consider making this tattoo permanent? I'm certain I can have the Black Widow use the needle this time." He was tracing then retracing his name, sending shivers of desire swamping her body

"The needle? This time?" She shivered with thoughts of seeing the needle again. The first time she didn't do so well.

"Yes, I deceived you." His trousers hit the floor. Naked, he was beside her, touching her, stroking her. "At the time I felt the deception was necessary to protect you from yourself."

His strong good looks never ceased to amaze her. His arousal was obvious. She sucked in a long deep breath, her body responding quickly. She knew that whatever he wanted he would get. "As long as you drug me again. Yes, I know that what you gave me was more than necessary. Don't want to feel the needle. I'm terrified of them."

"You're not angry?" He appeared shocked yet the smile touching his lips swept more heat into her. "I thought..."

"I should be angry, furiously so. I'm glad you told me, though a bit late. Happy you protected me from myself, from the impulsiveness that is so much a part of me. What you did was thoughtful. Under different circumstances, I would have regretted the marking. I thought the only way to rid myself of Oliver was to prove to him I was not what he thought."

"The man is an idiot."

"He needed an heir."

"Don't defend him."

"No, you're right. The man acted horribly."

"Perhaps that is true about the heir, but he also coveted your dowry. At least that is what Gordan discovered. Seems your father left you substantial wealth. Near the end of his life, he must not have trusted Tindell as much as he did in his earlier years. Your father, with your best interest at heart, put multiple codicils on your dowry to the extent that Tindell could not touch it even though he was still named your guardian. You, on the other hand, could have retrieved your dowry when you turned twenty-one."

"My dowry? Is that why you wanted to marry me?"

The sudden spurt of anger surprised her. She thought it was lust not greed that spurred him to the marriage bed. Somehow to Betsy, lust was better than greed.

"Sweetheart, I've no need of your dowry. Gordan made sure all your money stays in your name. Now, as your husband, technically it is mine. I don't want the groats or as you well know need them." He placed a finger to her lips as he must have guessed she was about to protest. "I don't want the money. We can do what you want with it. Leave it to our children? Invest? What is done with the groats is up to you."

"What if he ruins you? What if Oliver wins this game the two of you play?"

She was afraid now for him. Not for herself. She'd seen hard times. She didn't think Evan ever felt uncertain financially.

"Do we have to talk about this on our wedding night?"

Her stomach was churning as she nodded her head.

He cleared his throat, "Very well, if that is what will make you feel better, Gordan is Tindell's financial advisor. While some fraud was involved in order to make our plans work. Everything was clear as well as precise. The man didn't read the papers. He signed. That is all anyone needs to know. He has all the necessary documents pointing to Tindell's guilt in his effort to swindle you of your money. Oliver will never try to harm the firm since he will put himself into the same position. Since we are not doing enough harm to send him to debtor's prison, he will keep his mouth shut."

"He can't hurt you?"

"No."

~ * ~

Evan and Betsy spent the next two weeks in his country home. They divided their time between his bedroom, the breakfast nook, and the mossy covered glade so close to the little pool. When they weren't making love in the pool, she learned to float. He took delight in watching the rosy tips of her breasts peek above the surface of the water when she was on her back. When she floated on her stomach, he would kiss the two tattoos on her delectable backside. He couldn't get his fill of his darling wife. It seemed he wanted her night and day, wherever he saw her. If there were no servants in sight, locking the door behind them he would make love to her in whatever room he found her.

"Has Tindell left Glasgow? I would hope that when we return, he will no longer haunt our footsteps."

The day was exquisite, the sky a lovely shade of blue. The clouds building on the horizon would end in a thunder storm. It was the time of day he loved as it was full of electricity. When the storm hit, the sky would sizzle and boom. Tonight, if the storm crashed as it was threatening now, they would dine on the veranda. The Guinness would be chilled, the meal satisfying, his woman hot...spicey. She was always ready for him.

"No, not yet. He's been to see Gordan several times this last week. Doesn't understand why he no longer has accesses to certain accounts. The noose is tightening. He will come to me soon. Perhaps he will try to see you. He cannot get to you here. In town, it will be much easier though

Alexander will never allow him in the door."

She plucked at her gown, staring at the folds. He understood she had more questions that needed answers. He wasn't certain he could give her those answers. Gordan was the source they needed to seek.

They were sitting in the breakfast room eating a light luncheon of fruits along with an assortment of cheeses. When she looked at him, her expression was unreadable. He interpreted what he saw from what he was beginning to learn about his new wife. "Good God, you don't feel sorry for that man?"

Looking at him, she tossed him a hesitant smile. "Oliver will not understand. He is such an arrogant, proud peacock. He will never believe he's been bested."

A bit too harsh for his taste, he said, "Of course, he understands. He ruined you. After that he tried to ruin me. He will certainly comprehend the ramifications of all he singlehandedly set in motion."

"When he discovers he was conned, he's going to be furious." She buttered the warm piece of fresh bread. "He will seek retribution." She pointed at him with her bread. "You need to be ready for whatever he tries."

"Yes."

"Are we going to go back to the city?"

It seemed she was hunting for answers since he was not forthcoming.

Her questions bothered him. He realized she cared for this man, Lord Tindell. While she didn't want to marry him, did all she could think of to deny him what he wanted, she was now feeling bad for him. Evan didn't want her to feel regrets. She should be dancing with delight.

"I was notified I could begin teaching again. Guess there was a petition from some of my students. Would you like that? Would you enjoy living in the city?" He wondered what she would want to do. She no longer needed to work. What he wasn't telling her was that there was a condition to his reinstatement. The apology he was unwilling to give coupled with a challenge by his older brother. The challenge also wasn't acceptable.

"Is there a catch to that? You haven't apologized nor do I believe you intend to." When she looked at him her brows were drawn together, concentrating it seemed on the entire picture.

"Yes," he told her. "If I'm to go to work again for Duncan as well as the university the stipulation remains in place. While I want to return to lecturing, the apology sticks in my craw." He was drumming his fingers on the table, agitated by all that he wasn't telling her, all that he needed to point out. Unbeknownst to her, her talents or lack thereof were an integral part of the challenge issued by his brother.

"Would apologizing be so hard?" Her voice was very quiet. She looked as if she wished he could do that very thing.

Rubbing the back of his neck, he tried to give her the answer she looked for. He could not. "Yes. Apologizing is impossible. I've gone over that in my head more times than I care to admit. I was not in the wrong. The young man needs to beg forgiveness of me."

"Duncan says I'm too arrogant and cocky. He also tells me I need to come down a peg or two from the pedestal I put myself on. My brother is wrong. I'm no more arrogant than he is. The university is siding with the student on this issue. Believes I don't care enough about what is important. Also believes if I wanted to continue teaching, I would come to them crawling and begging for the position. I won't do that."

"Your brother actually thinks that about you?" Betsy sounded surprised, more than surprised. "He thinks you're arrogant?"

"He's right. I'm also too stubborn. Have a temper. Stubborn pride is what he's calling my refusal. Can't go back to work for him or the university." Pausing, Evan battled with himself. Telling her the next part wouldn't be easy. He'd put it off for two weeks. He should have told her sooner. "He has given me a way out of this predicament."

"Are you going to take this offering of piece Duncan is handing you?" She stopped to focus on him. "What is it? This opportunity?"

"I can guarantee you aren't going to like it. I've put off answering my brother for these two weeks. When you and Caroline were working on the wedding gown, Duncan was giving me the terms of my reinstatement. At first, I couldn't believe his nerve. He told me it was time to consider new priorities now that I would have a wife. Duncan went on to say I was also selfish, I needed to consider someone other than myself.

I told you I would always put you first. Told Duncan I said that. He laughed at me. Told me if my statement was true, I'd agree to the contest."

"Why on earth wouldn't I like the terms. They don't have anything to do with me, do they?"

"Yes." He withdrew slightly into himself. "You don't play tennis, do you?"

"Tennis? Lawn tennis?"

"That's what I thought. You don't know anything about the game, do you? Well, he's challenged us to a tennis match. Us against them."

"Them? Caroline and Duncan?" Both surprise coupled with horror were written clearly on her lovely face. "I'm supposed to play tennis?" She blinked a few times, as if that would help her digest his brother's proposition.

"Yes. If I agree, the doubles match will take place in one week. I've seven days to teach you how to play the game well enough that we can defeat them. Can you do it?"

He didn't believe anyone could do so.

"You do care if you're reinstated and you're afraid that I'll hurt your chances of winning." She visibly bristled appearing to be angry with him. "Once again, you've come to the right conclusion. If I go out there and try to play tennis, I'll be humiliated. Possibly, I'll take the decision from your hands. I can decline to play the game."

"Caroline isn't very good either. Though Duncan taught her a long time ago. They play often enough when the weather is nice. She can hold her own. She doesn't have to cover the entire court."

"I could just stand on the sideline and allow you to play. Can one player win against two?" Her question was valid.

To his ears, she sounded bitter. "Yes, but in this case I would lose. Duncan is a very good player. If he had help, he would defeat me. I could probably win all my serves. When you serve, however, he will poach then return the ball not allowing Caroline to do so."

He didn't want this. His brother was tying his hands. He needed to apologize. If he won, his deed would be automatically excused. Evan still didn't understand why his apology was so important to his reinstatement.

The devil, he wasn't at fault here. He could never get over the truth.

"Can't you do the same? Poach?" she queried with a hint of indignation in her voice. He didn't blame her. "You understand I would try my best. Can't help the fact I never learned how to ride, or swim, or play tennis. I don't know how to golf either." She studied her fingernails. "You think I'm lacking."

"Not in what is most necessary." He couldn't stop from winking at her. "The best you can do will not be good enough. We will lose. I will lose."

In an attempt to keep his thoughts from escalating to a dangerous point, he strode from the breakfast room hands fisted. He needed to run or hit something. The thought that Duncan orchestrated this scenario knowing full well his wife would be at a loss. One week, he had one week to teach her a few things. She would never be able to return a hard-hit ball. Never be able to place a serve in the correct square.

"Can't you just apologize?"

He heard her question as he entered the foyer, leaving the blasted conversation. He passed Alexander and nodded. "See to my wife."

Once he hit the driveway he ran. He didn't know how far he ran. He ran until there was a stitch in his side. After that he walked. With no conscious thought, he found himself standing at the family tennis court. For a generation at least, tennis had been a favorite hobby with the Murray's. They all played from time to time. He was the best of the lot. That was why Duncan picked that game. His brother understood how humiliated he would feel when he lost. In any other circumstance he wouldn't lose.

He opened a metal box that protected the equipment during the spring through the fall. Bending over he located his favorite racket. The game was first played in France in the twelfth century. The people hit the ball with their hand. At the time, the game was called *jeu de paume*. Later they began to wear gloves when they played. Evan wasn't certain when the rackets came into use.

Ah, but the game of tennis changed. The nice lawn court near his parent's home was perfectly cropped so the balls would bounce. He pulled from the box a bucket of balls. He needed to expend some energy, so he would stop thinking about the upcoming loss then the ensuing apology. An apology for something...the devil he'd do it again, would defend himself. What did the administration at the university expect? What did his brother expect from him? That he would stand by and let the young man pummel him?

Evan felt as if he'd been wronged a second time by his brother.

For the next hour he hit balls, practiced his serve. Every time he hit the little white ball, he felt his anger grow. His brother manipulated him. He wouldn't have known Betsy never played before. Duncan made an assumption. He was right. He'd wager Betsy had no idea what the game of tennis entailed. He wasn't going to waste time teaching her how to score each game as he understood, he would have to explain why zero points was called love. He groaned thinking add-in and add-out then deuce.

In her very sweet way, she asked questions. She would want to understand everything.

"See you're getting ready for the big game. Did your new wife agree?" Duncan was standing beside him now. His smug expression coupled with his all-knowing tone of voice sent the fury that had been slowly coming under control to an explosive level.

Evan hit another ball, pretending he was aiming at Duncan. Too bad Duncan would just stand at the net. He would have his brother dodging balls as fast as he could hit them.

"You taking your anger out on that little white ball?" Duncan hooted his laughter once more setting his blood boiling.

The need to answer his brother wasn't paramount in his mind. For the moment he didn't want to talk. If he remained silent, possibly Duncan would go away. That would be too sweet. Evan felt sure that Duncan was here to taunt him with the impending loss.

"One week from today. The die will be cast. If you could have rousted yourself from your bed and your pretty little wife sooner, you would have had three weeks for her to learn the game. As it stands now you whittled your time down to nearly nonexistent."

Evan hit another ball, a perfect serve. He ignored his brother while he continued. There were a few things he could teach her. First, of course, would be how to serve. He would negotiate for more tries at serving. While the number couldn't be limitless, she needed to get more than two tries. There was no way she would be able to learn a real serve in one week. She wouldn't get any into the court let alone the correct place. Betsy would be lucky to land an underhand serve. What would he do if Duncan insisted on playing by all the rules?

He didn't want her to play close to the net. The devil, she would get hurt. Could get hit by the ball. Duncan wouldn't play any different with her in the game than he did with just the two of them. By all that was holy, what was his brother thinking?

This would be a fiasco. While he didn't have to work for a living, he wanted to work. With work there were challenges to be met. Learning was important to him. Working at the university stimulated his mind. He loved teaching the young students. Over the last month, he'd been occupied entirely with Betsy. He didn't miss teaching until the prospect of losing this second love for the rest of his life became more apparent. His brother wouldn't even allow him to work at the firm unless he asked for forgiveness.

The devil!

He hit the ball out of the court. Thought it would soar over the fence surrounding the playing field. To play a good game of tennis it wouldn't do to lose his temper.

No matter what he did, Caroline and Duncan would beat them soundly.

"Best you bring Betsy out in the morning before it gets too hot. She's got a lot to learn," Duncan called out, howling with laughter as he left. The laughter changed to a whistle as he strode away.

His brother so cock-sure of himself...whistled. Inhaling a deep lung full of air, Evan held the air in his lungs for a few seconds. Yes, his brother gave good advice. The morning, tomorrow morning would be her first lesson. First, he would teach her how to hit the ball. Second, he would teach her how to hit the elusive little thing back. He would leave the serve to last.

For now, he needed to make it through the night. He had to let her rest so she would be at her best. He stayed another hour thinking about the quickest way to teach her. This would not be as nice as teaching her how to swim. In this endeavor, he would have to do his best to keep his hands to himself, in the process not lose patience. He would have to touch her to help her with her swing.

When he walked into the house, he didn't see her at first. She might have left. After all, she wasn't pleased with the position he put her in. No, Betsy would never leave over a game of tennis. He knew she didn't want to talk about the challenge. Tomorrow morning would arrive soon enough. He would see how quickly she would learn. In other endeavors she'd been quick to absorb the concept.

In a dark corner, he found her curled up reading a book. After he saw the title, he almost laughed. With great control he managed to hold the crack of laughter behind his teeth. The book was all about tennis. She was reading to help him. His heart did a small flip. He sat down next to her taking the book from her hands before setting it on the table. Knowledge of the game wouldn't help the practical application.

"Thank you," he spoke softly bent close to brush a quick kiss across her lips. "I do appreciate the effort you are making in my behalf. You don't need to know any of these facts that are written here. Learning how to score is not necessary, neither are all the different terms. What you need to do is to be able to hit the ball; practical application, not theory."

She looked startled along with confused. Her pretty brows drawn tight her lips thinned as much as they could be considering how plump they were. "Thank you? Whatever for? You're my husband. I told you I would do my best. You don't have to thank me."

"Caring," he murmured, his voice low, close to that part of her he needed to kiss senseless. "Thank you for caring about my feelings. Tomorrow, I'll start your lessons."

He hoped she would learn to play this game as quickly as she did swimming and riding. Perhaps she was a natural athlete. Just because Betsy never had a chance to learn, didn't mean she couldn't catch on quickly. There was a small chance they could surprise Duncan.

Betsy slanted him a half-hearted smile then with a resigned lift of her delicate shoulders. "I'm sorry you're angry with me. I don't want to be the reason you lose. It seems there is no other choice for you. Duncan is a nasty brother."

Those were exactly his sentiments. He cupped her chin in the palm of his hand. "Caroline is not good. When we play a match, I always send Duncan home defeated. Maybe this will turn out fine. Who knows. I'm not giving up without a fight."

"You think so?"

She appeared a bit less forlorn. Her smile brightened with his words of encouragement.

No, he didn't. What she didn't know might give her confidence when she needed it the most. "We will practice then hope for the best. You will have to learn how to serve. To play at the net. To return volleys." Her look of chagrin stopped him. Caroline could do all that. Not well, but she could return the easier shots. He would have to direct his volleys at Caroline just as Duncan would focus on his weak spot, Betsy. His stomach flipped. He didn't want her playing in an intense match. A game on a Sunday afternoon should be all she played. He would never forgive his brother if he hurt her.

His emotions buffeted one against the other. The devil, he didn't want to lose. The tightness in his body, in all his muscles blindsided him. Losing wasn't acceptable. Deep in his heart, he understood he would never win this game. His brother manipulated him to that exact end. They didn't stand a chance. If he wasn't so competitive, he would swallow his pride then apologize. At that thought his teeth clamped tight.

Now Betsy was staring at him, watching him, wanting to understand what he was considering. He watched her bosom heave as she sipped in a long, deep breath of air. Knowing what she was going to say would not help.

He held up his hands. "Don't! I don't...I won't..." He'd made up his mind, cast his destiny with the game.

Instantly, she appeared confused. Her head cocked to one side, her tongue sliding along her bottom lip. The gesture telling him she was thinking perhaps more than thinking. She might seduce. She understood what would tempt him. She would comprehend he knew what she would say. Possibly, at this point, it would be wise to change the subject to something that wasn't a topic now. He needed her to contemplate the possibility of pregnancy.

"You haven't had your monthly." He regarded her closely watching her face for any signs that she understood what he was getting at. Would she know that lack of this would signify her conception of his seed. She was such an innocent. Literally grew up without a mother.

Her cheeks flamed then she frowned. What he could see of the tops of her breasts also colored prettily. She turned away from him clearly discomfited by his bald statement. He grinned, touching his chin to turn her. To see into her eyes his objective. A woman needed to understand she should be able to speak to her husband about female issues. In time, this might not embarrass her.

"That wasn't a question, sweetheart. A man knows, particularly a man who has had you more than once each day for the last thirty days. No," he paused as if taking a moment to count backward. "Believe it's been more than thirty days since I first made love to you. I know your body."

Her expression suddenly changed, a subtle difference. "If I'm increasing does that mean the challenge is off?" she asked, a mischievous grin on her face. Her embarrassment didn't last that long.

"No," he said his tone curt. "If it did, the fact would only put off the challenge for a year. This needs to be settled in a timely fashion. Want to be reinstated by the next semester."

"Do you think...?"

"Yes, I was positive from the very beginning. From the first time I had you beneath me, thrust deep inside your warmth. Your honey rained on me even that first time we made love."

"Very well," she said, "You must be a potent man. We only needed to make love once. You must be pleased."

"Yes, we will hold our first child in our arms in about eight months. Yes, that pleases me immensely."

"Rogue!" She hit him on the arm, laughing. "You are so arrogant. Your brother is right. He's no different than you. Neither of you have any right to judge each other. You are both cut from the same cloth."

He chuckled softly understanding full well the fact she was increasing had nothing to do with potency. He held out his hand, "Should we retire for the night? The morning along with your first tennis lesson will be here before you know it." He was both eager to see what she could do on the court as well as fearful that she would be a complete disaster.

"Not yet. I want to know what you've heard about Oliver. I understand Gordan keeps all of you informed. You need to tell me everything you learn when you hear about it. All of this, my marrying you, having your baby came about because of him. In a way, I should be grateful he pursued me."

"Lord Tindell visited Gordan the other day. The man is furious. He says he must have signed the wrong documents. Gordan then asked him if he read what he signed. One must always read contracts that are binding. Gordan lectured him. He went on to tell Lord Tindell that in everything mistakes can be made. In this business many costly mistakes."

"He has no money."

"Oliver has only the allowance that Gordan decided to grant in Virgie and Poppet's name." Evan stroked his chin. "Believe that allowance is the ripe sum of two hundred pounds a month. It is enough for food as well as rent. If the girls allow him to stay in one of their homes, he has no need of rent or food. He will have a small amount of spending money. At the moment, he doesn't have the means to return to London. Before he can do that, he will have to wait for another allowance to be doled out."

She seemed to think that over for a short time. For a few moments, she fidgeted with her skirt. When she finally looked up to speak to him, she asked, "You? Have you lost anything in all this? Have you checked?"

He took her hand into his, kissed the top then the palm. Was pleased to see her immediate response "No. I've lost nothing and gained everything, you." He wanted her to believe he meant what he said. "Now, my sweet, is there anything at all left to talk over. I want you in my bed."

~ * ~

The rumors about the firm were all true. They were all cutthroat, ruthless, without shame. He would find his revenge. It might take him time, but he would recoup his losses then seek these men out. All that he owned, all he coveted was lost to him. A man didn't weep. No, a man found his retaliation. If he couldn't ruin Evan Murray, he'd take his wife from him. Betsy was supposed to be his, her dowry his. She would give him his heir.

All he had now were two little girls, two rich little girls who wouldn't inherit his title. No, to gain an heir was why he sought Betsy. She would have made a fine outstanding wife. Now, he was dependent on his girls for everything. All he got was a measly two hundred pounds once a month. His fist hit his hand. Hit the wall next to him. Two hundred pounds wasn't enough to pay for his mistress. It wasn't enough to pay his gambling debts or his tailor. His man left him the moment he couldn't divvy up his salary. He would have to use his first allowance to begin to pay the people he owed. If he didn't, he would end up in prison, debtors' prison. Bloody, bloody eyes! He didn't have the fare to return to London. Didn't own a bloody sou. In less than a few days, he spent the measly allowance he was granted. He would have to learn.

Even if he wrote to Virgie, she couldn't send him anymore money until next month. Lord Oliver Tindell knocked on the door, begging entrance, begging to see Gordan Murray, not knowing he was Evan's brother. If he had known the Murray family owned this firm, he would have never gone to them. He needed the executor of what once was his estate to lend him an advance so he could either go home or pay for a place to live while he began to recoup his loses. He was feeling both furious as well as desperate.

Gordan didn't bother to stand when he walked in. "What can I do for you?" His insolent voice grated on Oliver's nerves. "There is nothing more for us to talk over. Because of your signature on the documents, nothing can be negotiated differently. If you had read..."

Gordan had the audacity to shrug his broad shoulders. A man employed by a financial firm should not have the physical beauty this one did. He remembered how that thought flited through his head the first time he saw this man.

Oliver's throat was parched, he poured himself a glass of water before sitting. He sipped then cleared his throat. He needed more courage. "I want an advance on next month's allowance. Need to pay rent. You understand. A man must have a roof over his head."

He understood he needed to be bold to tell this man who conned him exactly what was necessary for his immediate survival. He didn't have any doubts that he could eventually turn his circumstances around. Doing so would take time along with a great deal of ingenuity.

Gordan clasped his hands under his chin. With his elbows on the table, he leaned forward a smile on his smug face. "I can do that. How much do you need? You do understand that you do not have sufficient funds to maintain your room in the hotel where you now reside. You will have to find some other place to live. Have you thought that your lifestyle has changed. Do you have someone in London who would lend you money."

Even though Oliver understood that as a fact, he was reluctant to acknowledge his change of status. The upheaval in his life didn't sit well. There was no one he knew who would not charge him huge interest on the loan. "I will find other lodging." Indeed, he'd done so already. Had done so immediately after understanding he somehow lost his battle of revenge. Lost for the time being, he'd amended. He would not be out done.

"You also understand that an advance now will only serve to deplete next month's allotment." Gordan leaned back in his chair, tapping his chin with one finger. "If I allotted twenty-five pounds, you should be able to secure a room in a boarding house which would also feed you. Room and board for twenty-five pounds. Yes, those extra groats should be doable. In that case your groats wouldn't be depleted to such an extent you will be asking for another advance next month. You do realize eventually I'd have to refuse the request. If you're not careful your allowance could dwindle to nothing for one month. You cannot continue to borrow on the next month's stipends."

Chastised, humiliated, Oliver nodded. He realized this man was enjoying himself. He didn't appreciate entirely why Gordan would be so pleased. "I understand completely about borrowing. I won't be back again." If he decided on retribution earlier, he was now more committed to the notion.

"Good then we are finished." This time Gordan Murray stood, his hands behind his back. "My secretary will see to the funds. Gordan handed him the message that would give him twenty-five miserable pounds. He was used to dealing in thousands a week. How the bloody hell was he going to survive on so much less?

When Oliver thought to shake hands, Gordan made no attempt to facilitate the intent. "Thank you." Those two words stuck in his craw. He wasn't thankful for anything.

He had to wait for more than thirty minutes for the money. The wait wasn't entirely wasted time. He learned second hand about the tennis match that was going to be played in less than a week. Betsy couldn't play tennis. He also learned about a challenge that would be getting Evan's job back. A bit of amusement did sit well on his bruised ego. He imagined Evan would lose. He wanted to see the man embarrassed. After that he would find Betsy so he could exact his revenge. He would convince her an annulment or perhaps a divorce would be necessary In this case it was her best course. When that happened she would marry him. After all, he would then be in possession of her dowry.

Whistling, feeling much better about his situation, he walked from the office then down the street. He found a place to stay earlier. The woman running the boarding house was almost forty, a widow. She was amenable to a few pleasantries. She would warm his bed for free. This new situation wasn't as bad as he thought it might be.

Ah, it wasn't just room and board. His stay included long, luxurious nights of sex. He wasn't too particular. However, this woman possessed all the amazing attributes he cherished in a woman.

~ * ~

"You didn't!" Caroline was appalled at her husband's antics. "What if I refuse to play? Would that stop your blind need to put Evan in his place? He shouldn't have to apologize as you well know. At first you defended him. You deserve to sleep on the couch. What made you change your mind?"

"A man should be able to hold in his temper. Evan should have held back. Should have controlled himself until someone else could interrupt the fracas."

"You changed your mind," she bit out again obviously furious with him. "What you said may be true. What would you have done?"

"It's not that I want to put him in his place. I want him to take over a few hot-tempered clients. He needs to take charge of his emotions. He's too stubborn, too arrogant. In addition, the man misses his classes, the young adults he interacts with. They are important to him. What difference would a simple apology make?"

"Obviously to your brother a hell of a lot. I know you well enough that you could have stepped in a month ago. If you'd done so, he'd be teaching now." She was waiving, pointing her finger at him.

"Uh-huh. Would he have found Betsy if I did. He would never have agreed to escort her if he'd been employed. Evan would have snorted at the very thought. You knew he would fall in love with her. You're such a little matchmaker."

Caroline bristled at what he told her even though it was the truth. Not willing to admit anything to him, inwardly she grinned. It was exactly what she intended. She did think they would like each other. Didn't expect the attraction to be so potent and fast. Well, she hoped this would happen. Never expected these events to end in a tennis match.

"Betsy doesn't know anything about tennis. She cannot play. Will not be able to do well in a week. You planned this. Perhaps you would like the couch for a month."

"They would have had three weeks to practice," he defended himself. "A couch is not tenable, as well you know."

"Do you remember how you acted when we were first wed, before we were wed? you couldn't keep your hands off me. Evan is no different with Betsy. Do you think your other brothers will be the same when they find the woman for them? Perhaps I should look for a woman for Fletcher."

"You loved every moment. Should we make cinnamon rolls?" He waggled his dark eyebrows at her.

"No." Just to shock the man she should tell him yes. "That

wouldn't absolve you from the couch."

"Then we'll go to bed without our melted cinnamon and sugar." It seemed he wasn't going to allow further argument. He swept her into his arms, his mouth framing hers, their tongues mating as if they were newlyweds.

Chapter Ten.

Six in the morning came too soon for Betsy. When he tried to wake her, she rolled over and pulled the covers over her head with a soft moan of distress. Squinting her eyes, she saw sunlight dancing on the carpet along with a few dust motes. After that she recognized his feet. He was not wearing his usual well-shined boots but what looked like lightweight shoes.

She didn't like to get up this early. When she recalled why they were getting up with the sun, she groaned. "No."

She was not looking forward to this. At one point she hoped this tennis thing was all a bad dream. When she woke up, he would tell her he lied to her. Was teasing.

"Time to learn a few things about tennis."

He tapped her on her bottom after pulling the covers from her, traced both tattoos with a fingertip. He chuckled when her body quivered from the light touch.

She'd rather stay in bed with him, seduce him. If she had to be awake, she'd rather play with him. "It's cold. Evan no, I need sleep. You kept me up all night," she moaned turning over once more trying to take the covers with her. No one should have that much energy. "Go away. If you don't want to stay in bed, come back in a few hours."

"It will be too hot in a few hours." Once more, he tugged on the covers laughing as he watched her struggle. "When we're done, we can go to our favorite place on the lake."

"Let's wait another day."

She couldn't think of arguments to sway a determined man. Learning to play tennis was not on her list of things to experience.

"Dress in a lightweight gown. You want to be able to run. No corset. Keep your attire simple. You don't want to be weighted down.

This isn't a fashion show."

He didn't sound like himself. His voice was distant, vague.

Did she have a lightweight gown? She never tried to be in the height of fashion, rarely wore a corset. A dress she could run in. Dresses weren't made that way. She hated running. She remembered the stakes. Groaning she rolled over, determined to prove herself to him. "If I must. I'll be down shortly. Can we eat first. I'm starving. This time it's not for you. You left me quite sated last night."

"Don't take long."

He left the room.

He was going to leave her alone. If she wouldn't feel so terribly guilty, she could curl up with the covers over her head. He'd be furious with her. Bloody eyes, she didn't like him much right now. He was stubborn, determined. At her expense she was doing this for him, the man she loved. Quickly, she washed and dressed. In less than ten minutes she was in the breakfast nook with him.

He pushed a hot cup of tea her way, a blueberry scone on a small plate. "Should never eat a big breakfast before we play. It will stay in your stomach, make you sluggish." He sipped his tea, regarding her. "You dressed appropriately."

"I don't run."

"Most likely you won't have to." His broad shoulders rose a fraction. "There is an off chance though."

Her glower went unnoticed. No, she shouldn't be sluggish. If she had to run, her dress would tangle around her feet. What she'd seen of most tennis matches they were more a means to meet someone of the opposite sex. It was called lawn tennis for a reason. None were actually a competition.

He seemed to be focused on one thing, tennis, and the practice court. She ate quickly. The scone landed in the pit of her stomach as if it was a brick. She was positive it would stay there. Positive she would be sluggish. When she finished, she brushed her skirts then stood thinking the sooner she got this first day over the better.

He looked at her, a strange expression on his face. It appeared for a moment that he was looking forward to this as much as she was which was not at all.

At that second, her attitude changed again. The resentment lessening as she watched the stiffness of his shoulders, the tight thin line of his lips. His brother forced him. Evan was a man who didn't like having a bad hand dealt to him. She was his bad hand, his losing hand. She wanted to tell him he could apologize. After he made the attempt to soothe her twisted nerves over the situation he inadvertently became part of, he'd be done, reestablished, lecturing. He shouldn't have to lose to his brother. A long heavy breath of air left her mouth.

She knew better than to say anything.

After this was all said and done, they would laugh. They could tell their grandchildren about the contest. The stories would amuse everyone.

When they arrived at the tennis court, the sun warmed the day. She was hot, sweaty. So far, they'd done nothing except swing the racket; no balls, nothing came her way. He had to stand behind her, his hand on hers to teach her. Now he showed her how to drop the ball then hit it over the net. When he did it, the task looked easy. When he attempted with her, the task seemed doable.

When she tried by herself, she missed the ball. "Maybe if it was a different color, I could hit the blasted thing?" she told him thinking she was funny. "A yellow color would show up better. Be easier to hit. Maybe lime green."

"Balls only come white," his gruff reply startled her for a moment. He bounced one of the white balls on the grass turf.

She slanted him a lopsided grin. He scowled, understanding what she was thinking but not saying anything in return. When she finally hit one over the net, she dropped the racket then jumped up clapping her hands. "I did it! I did it!"

She turned toward him thinking he would praise her. She grinned until she saw his expression. Her heart plummeted while she wondered what she did wrong this time.

"You can't do that when you play."

"Why?"

"You need to stay focused. Odds are the ball will come back fast. If you don't have the racket in your hand, the ball might hit you."

Well, that put the situation bluntly and in specific terms.

His ensuing heavy sigh made her rethink this situation. She could still refuse. Of course, she couldn't back out of the game. She owed it to him. He could at least attempt to make her feel as if she made progress. With no effort he made her both self-conscious and lacking in skills. Well, she did lack skills where tennis was concerned. She didn't volunteer for this difficult task. Instead of her fury directed at Evan, she should be extra annoyed with his brother who orchestrated Evan's humiliation.

How dare the man? What he did was unconscionable. Why, Duncan was more stubborn as well as arrogant than his brother. She should ride over there then give him a piece of her mind. Another hour passed while she dropped the ball to hit over the net. For some strange reason, Evan decided she was getting better. She didn't agree. Though now she was successful more than not.

He walked to the opposite side of the court. "I'm going to return the balls you hit over the net. See if you can get it back. I'll return as long as you do."

Her arm was sore and her legs ached.

"You want me to do what?" she asked, her racket, hanging limp from her hand, sweat dripping down her forehead.

She couldn't possibly return anything.

"I'll hit it easy. You can do anything you set your mind to. Focus on the ball. Remember how to swing."

She watched him inhale a deep breath of air then reminded herself he was just as frustrated as she was. He wanted her to learn everything in one day. The man should realize by now that wasn't going to happen. She drank in a gulp of air. Practiced her swing a couple of times. "What happens if the ball come to my left side? Do I just run around it. Seems like it might be easier..."

"I'll teach you how to hit a backhand tomorrow. I won't hit anything to your left side today." He sounded angry.

"You don't have to be—"

He held up his hand to stop her. "I'm not angry. You're doing extremely well. Better than could be expected."

His first praise. Sort of. Better than expected. He doesn't have much hope for me.

"Are you ready?" She mimicked him, tossing the ball on the ground a few times before she hit the blasted thing with her racket. Each time he hit the ball gently and straight to her, she couldn't hit it back.

The first time she was forced to run for the ball she tripped on her skirt, fell to her knees. For several seconds she stayed in that position. She sipped in air, wishing she could take a bath, wishing she wouldn't find her hands scraped along with her knees. Trying to keep the threatening tears from her eyes. Her body shook. She couldn't breathe. Sweat dripped in rivulets between her breasts, down her back.

"You're just fine." His voice boomed from across the net. "Get up then let's hit a few more. If you get one back, we can quit for the day."

It was easy for him to say. He wasn't the one who fell. After she finally stood, she leered at him, shaking her racket in his direction. "Tomorrow I'm going to play in britches. Have had it with this skirt." That was an empty threat, one she probably couldn't stand by. She didn't own a pair. Certainly, she could send Alexander into the village to buy a pair for her. She wouldn't have to play with a handicap. If she tripped, it would be because she was clumsy not because her skirts wound around her legs.

"No! You're not wearing pants!" His voice thundered across the net.

Betsy couldn't believe what she heard. What say did he have in this? She stiffened her shoulders bracing for the argument that was certain to follow. "I won't play in a dress. If you won't allow me to put on britches, why...then...I won't play at all." She hoped he would understand the logic of her declaration. She could blackmail him. "Or...or...I can play in my pantalettes and chemise."

Or...she could cut off one of her dresses to just below her knees. That might work. He wouldn't like the fact her ankles would show as would the lower part of her legs. Damnation, he didn't have to be pleased. She did. She was doing this for him. All this was about...him.

He jumped over the net, striding to her, wrapping his arm around her shoulder. "It's the heat. You're just hysterical."

Hysterical!

"We'll discuss this later. You won't wear pants though we might be able to think of something else. Winning this match is important to me. If we can get a *wee* bit of an advantage, I would never be adverse."

She lost all perspective. She didn't want to have a conversation about this later. She wanted to resolve the disagreement now. He'd never agree to a short dress either. "Ass!"

She swung her racket at him. Hit him on the shoulder with good force. His shoulder was a better target than the *wee* ball. He swore at her.

He had the nerve to swear at her. "I'm going home." Exasperated, she threw the racket on the grass.

"No, you're not!"

The blind command hit her behind the shoulder blades as she walked away. He would be obeyed. She sat down on the grass. "I'm done. I'm hungry as well as scraped up. I've had it with this lesson as well as the entire game of tennis. Shouldn't there be some fun in this?"

To her chagrin a tear slipped down her cheek then another one, another after that. Before she knew it, she was sobbing.

He squatted down in front of her. Lifted her chin so she had to look at him. His thumb brushed some moisture from her cheek. "Maybe it won't be quite so hot tomorrow morning. We can come back this evening."

"I won't be able to see the ball at night. You big oaf, it will be dark. We can't practice at night."

At least she wouldn't get sunstroke. Maybe it would be cooler. She would have to take a nap or she'd never make it an hour He would want to practice at least two possibly three hours.

"Imagine I'll have to get you up earlier. Let me see your hands." He crouched down beside her, taking her hands in his. "They are not too bad." Without blinking an eye, he pulled up her dress to look at her knees.

"A tiny bit grass stained is all. Come here."

He held out his arms for her to come to him. While he waited, he smiled.

She shook her head. After all she went through for him, he was acting as if nothing happened. "No." She felt defiant as well as belligerent. Wasn't going to give in to all his commands and demands.

She wasn't going to be treated this way. She wanted to cool off. Needed to eat something before she fainted from starvation. Needed a long drink of water.

His hand was still held out to her. "I'm going home. Do you wish to stay at the tennis court? You could walk back. If you like, we can visit the lake." He seemed to have a change of heart when he mentioned the lake.

To Betsy's ears he almost sounded wistful as if she'd agree. She'd rather visit the lake than play tennis or go home. When she looked at him, she tried not to look too pleased. "The lake would be cool, refreshing." Her voice was soft sounding a little sultry.

"Is that what you want?" his voice was gruff, whiskey smooth, just as he sounded when he made love to her.

So, now he was asking her for an opinion. "Yes. Yes, I would like to go to the lake, among other things."

It seemed to her he was of like mind. They needed to make up, to mend the anger from the lesson.

This time when he extended a hand, she accepted. He helped her mount the horse. His hands around her waist tightened. When she sat astride, his fingers trailed the length of her leg, stopping at her ankle.

They rode.

The cool breeze from the ride dried the perspiration on her skin. She breathed deeply of the early fall air. The scent of heather filled her. A fox ran across her path. Some of the trees were beginning to change color. The day was starting to look better. When she lived in London, she rarely was able to go outside the city.

She still had tomorrow's tennis lesson to look forward to as well as the ones after that. *Oh joy!* What would he try to pound into her head on the next day or the next? He said he would teach her another way to swing her racquet. Well, that would be an experience. They would also practice hitting the ball to each other. The next days they would keep practicing. He would teach her about serving the ball, the start of play. She would have to get it over the net first time. No, he said she got more than one try but not too many.

When they reached the lake, it seemed the day was renewed. She breathed more easily. He helped her dismount, holding her close, pressing her against him. She felt his heavy arousal, found she was instantly inspired.

Seconds later she was naked. He followed suit then caried her into the lake.

"Hold your breath, *lass*."

She did.

They were promptly submerged. After he rose to the surface he smiled softly at her, pushing the damp tendrils of hair from her face. "I'm sorry if I pushed you too hard. I'll try better in the next days."

Moisture clogged her throat again. She didn't want to cry. All her frustration as well as her anger vanished with his words. He couldn't help his intensity. That was who he was. She would have to learn to cope. "Thank you," she murmured knowing with those few words he was instantly forgiven.

After they made love in the cool waters of the lake, he sat on the shelf, she on his lap. Betsy rested her head on his shoulder. His hand soothed along her arms. Sometimes she thought the moments after they made love were just as nice or nicer. When he held her so close to his heart, she felt loved as well as protected. Felt as if there might be hope for them. Possibly someday he would love her.

Getting her hopes in that direction would not be worth the time it took to think the words. He ran his hand across her back then down to her tattoos. When she looked at him, his eyes were closed, his brows drawn harshly together. He looked so very serious. What was happening now?

She knew that look. Recognized the tension whenever he thought of the game that would decide so much, his fate with his brother as well as the university. In her mind, this wasn't the time to talk about the game. She needed to put tennis in the back of her mind until tomorrow morning when they started this all over. She ran her finger down his chest. "I don't want to talk tennis," she blurted the words before she had time to think. "This afternoon has been nice. While I know tomorrow morning will come before I want it to, I'd rather not think about it now. Want to concentrate on you and how nice you make me feel when you love me."

"I'm sorry." He kissed his way across the back of her shoulders causing another rippling of desire. It seemed she was always hungry for him. "I'll try to be more patient with you. I'm proud of you. Have I told you that? No, don't suppose I have. Now that we're off the court and I look back on the lesson, I *ken* you did a fabulous job. No one else could learn so quickly. You're a natural."

"What will we have for dinner?"

It was all she could think of to say. She'd told him she didn't want to talk about the game. He told her she did well. Still, the conversation was not a desirable one.

"How should I know?" he said harshly, seeming to forget the few moments of bliss they just enjoyed together.

Ah, that went well. He said he would be patient. She wasn't giving him a chance. It didn't change the fact he treated her like a child when she fell. Alexander would buy her britches if he didn't know Evan forbade them. If that was refused her, she would cut off one of her dresses. She thought that a splendid notion.

The next day progressed better as did the next ones. She knew it was just a matter of time before she would humiliate herself on the court even though she seemed to pick up the game quite easily. She learned how to serve. Returning softly hit balls didn't go beyond her skill level. He told her she might be able to return some of Caroline's shots. As of yet, she'd not dared to put on the cut off dress. Decided she would wait until the day of the big game when he couldn't do anything about what she wore. Alexander also bought her a pair flannel trousers. She would keep those on hold as a just in case the dress was forbidden. She would give him a choice. He would think what he was deciding on was no choice at all.

She was terrified that Duncan would direct hard and fast balls her way. Evan told her if he did, to get out of the way and not try to hit the ball back. He didn't want her hurt. She could imagine a ball hit hard on her face. On his serve she wouldn't play close to the net. She would have to stand back. That would also give them a disadvantage. However, he believed Caroline would play the same. Duncan would not want her hurt either. If these two brothers would stop a moment to think they would understand just how ridiculous this was.

The night before he went over more strategy with her. He also promised not to yell at her, at least he would try not to yell. She understood what he wanted her to do. In simple terms as little as possible. She was to try to hit only the balls he wouldn't be able to reach. He felt certain Duncan would tell Caroline the same. During the week the men negotiated a few rules. The women would be given extra balls to serve. They would not be held to just two tries.

"The big game is tomorrow, *Lass*," he told her while he poured her a glass of wine. "Are you ready?"

"Well, you are my coach. Am I ready?" she tossed the question back to him, angry that he persisted in speaking about the match.

She wasn't ready. For that matter, she would never be ready. The thought of the match sent her stomach turning somersaults. She was so nervous. This seemed to rest square on her shoulders. She didn't appreciate that fact.

She didn't welcome the grimace on his face as she understood what he was thinking. When he saw her flinch, he immediately softened his expression. "You've worked hard this week. I drove you past your endurance several of the days."

"We are going to lose. Aren't we? Would that be so bad? All our losing means is that you will have to apologize. I've never understood how that can be so difficult. This stubborn pride must be a male thing."

He sat back in the chair, closing his eyes. When he opened them and started to speak, "Yes. I've spent the last weeks trying to come to terms with the pending loss coupled with the ensuing apology. Cannot do it. The game depends on you." He held up his hands. "I'm not trying to pressure you. I understand you played for only a week. Nonetheless, you are doing exceptionally well." After a long pause, he continued. "Caro is not that good."

Betsy understood he wouldn't compliment her unless he meant it. She also knew there was a "but" in his words. But she'd only played for a week. She still had a lot to learn. Caroline was much better at the game. In any case...the list would continue to grow while he thought of new reasons they would lose.

"You learn quickly. I did see Caroline play about a year ago. She was not very good. Duncan is very patient with her when they play. I'm certain her skills have improved. For both of us our game is partially dependent on our wives."

"It's still a game between you and your brother. The rest of it is how many mistakes I will make versus the number Caroline makes. I fail to understand why just the two of you can't play with the same outcome."

"Yes, if you can keep your errors to a minimum, we stand a chance of winning. No, Duncan and I can't play a singles game because I will win. He knows that for a fact. If he wishes to have his way, he will never challenge me. This all comes down to more than just a game of tennis. Duncan is attempting to teach me a lesson, one of humility and arrogance."

"You don't think we will win." If he was so much better than his brother, why didn't they have a better chance. Ah, she knew it was her lack of talent that would sway the game. The thought didn't make her feel better. She didn't want to be the cause. Didn't want to know that because of her, he would be made to do something he loathed.

"No, I don't believe we will. Should we go for a walk. The air is cool. I want to breathe deeply of the fresh flower-scented air."

"You just want to walk to the gazebo."

"True. Don't you?"

"As long as the conversation doesn't revolve around tennis. I believe when this over, I never want to see one of those little white balls again."

~ * ~

Evan understood the importance of concentration. He shouldn't allow her feelings to sway him. He did need her in every way to be one hundred percent his partner. Even though he planned to take as many of her shots as possible.

The night was cloudy. Thunderheads were building on the horizon. If it rained tonight, the court would be terrible, sluggish. Might be better for the girls. Duncan would be sure to have his gardener trim the grass close. He wouldn't want to have it too damp. The sun would come out early, possibly dry the turf.

"Let's sit on the porch. The gazebo isn't protected enough. There is a threat of a storm." Evan swept her off her feet. Carried her to the large chair that would hold them both. He had plans for the evening, big plans for them. Promising himself he wouldn't mention tennis, he thought on more delightful pursuits.

His hand settled on the curve of her hip then around to her belly. Once this match was over, he would concentrate on his wife along with the child she carried in her womb. Tonight, he wasn't in a hurry to make love with his wife. They would take their time. "When this is over what would you like to do? Would you enjoy working in Glasgow? You don't have to work though. We've plenty of groats for you to be a wife of leisure."

She pushed slightly away from him. "You would allow me to tutor children or take on a job as a nanny?" she questioned him, studying his face. "It would have to be for a widow with children. I vowed after my first employer attacked me, I would never work for a man." She paused for a moment, tapping one finger on her chin, "I don't believe I do want to work. I want to be a wife and mother. Need to concentrate on being a good mother as well as wife."

"One way or another, I will be teaching again. We will have to live in the city. I don't want you to be bored. What would you do with your extra time." He paused in thought, his fingertip running along her arm. "Do babies take up much time? Don't know much about the *wee* beings."

"Babies, yes, they take a lot of time. You've forgotten about my research?" she laughed, punching him in the chest. "We never made it to the library in Edinburgh or any of the museums here in Glasgow. You still need to finish escorting me. With the new semester, you won't have the time. Possibly we could take a wedding trip to Edinburgh."

"I did forget. You aren't actually planning an article or a book. The research was just a ruse. Wasn't it?"

His hand slid along her ribcage rested beneath her breast. He felt her quicken. She was hungry for him. His desire for her raged. He tamped the seething passion to a simmer. Again, he told himself he wished to take this slowly. With Betsy the passion rose to a crescendo too quickly for desire to build with the finesse he so wanted to utilize. Her passion was explosive almost from the first second he touched her. Tonight would be different.

"A ruse..." she murmured leaning into him. "As you well know I needed to get away from London. Oliver followed me here intending to bend me to his will. You showed up to ruin all his carefully constructed plans." She sat up distancing herself from him. "Where is Oliver?"

"After he lost everything, he landed firmly on the ground with both feet. Seems he found a boarding house to live in which provides him with extras. Well, yes, he did appear to have a knack except when it came to dealing with the Murrays of Glasgow."

"Extras? What kind of extras?" Her eyes widened in surprise. "I don't understand what you're talking about."

"Uh—huh, perhaps I'll give you a clue."

One at a time, he pulled pins from her lovely hair, needing to wind the silken strands through his fingers. His intent tonight was to seduce her slowly, very slowly. She would climax when he decided she would do so. Not a moment before.

"My lovely innocent wife. Extras...a willing woman to warm his bed. One he doesn't have to pay for services rendered." He watched her eyes widen again. She really was lovely. He fell in love with her plump lower lip. The moment he saw it, he knew he had to taste her sweetness. After that he noticed the cornflower blue eyes that drug him to her as if she was a magnet reeling him toward her. Her breasts, so lush, even covered he knew they would be sweet as nectar to taste. He never expected her to reach that point of ecstasy that there was no returning so quickly. She was his heaven, his angel, his dream come true. She was good for him, so very good.

"Oh..." She punched him again, her eyes glaring. "You cad. How was I supposed to know something like that."

His grin caused her brows to furrow together. He kissed the tip of her nose then brushed an easy kiss across her lips. Leaning back, he smiled at her. "I for one am pleased you don't know a lot of things, sexual things. A man likes his wife to be innocent. He wants to teach her about love, about *amour*."

"That's a man's point of view. I for one would be pleased to know everything. Knowledge is power. Women should understand what a man is thinking when he looks at her and his eyes darken with hungry passion. I want to know how you feel when I touch you, or caress certain parts of you. Don't want to hurt you."

His laughter barked loudly. "About sex? You couldn't hurt me if you tried." His hand cupped her breast. He wasn't about to touch tender bare flesh until they were in bed. If she kicked him in a certain place, he supposed she would hurt him. He would never provoke her to do so.

"Yes. Sex. It would be nice to learn everything." Her pert little chin lifted into the air. "When are we returning to Glasgow."

"Day after tomorrow." Lazily, he stroked the tight hard bud that stiffened when he swept his hand across its tip. Enjoyed the vivid shuddering of her body. In another second she would weep for him. He would need to control the momentum if he wanted to dictate the terms of her pleasure.

"Cannot go with you to the university. Oh my..." He continued the easy dance on her breasts, one then the other. He watched her close her eyes while she gulped air. "I don't know what I'll do with my days. I don't know anyone. Don't want to work. Could I work for you?"

That question gave him reason to pause. He would need another secretary. His last one was now working for Professor Lind. "Uh-huh..." He loved the way her body twisted and arched with each lazy stroke of his fingers. He understood she was having trouble containing herself. The hunger would build and build. "You can meet the wives of the other men in my department. We can have dinner for them. Would you like that?" His lips claimed her mouth before she could answer. He plunged inside, dueling entering the sultry inner sanctum. Lust swamped him, hardened his body.

"Ev—ev—an." She was having trouble forming words. Her gasp pleased him. "I don't know. Would...I? Are...are they nice p—people?"

Her voice shattered slightly when he squeezed the tip of one breast. He moved on to do the same to the other.

"Yes, very nice. You will like them all." His masculine pleasure was apparent in his voice.

She was his, only his and she was very, very good.

"Oh..." she sighed softly. Her hand rested on his chest played with the tight hair poking from the opening. "Are you going to take your shirt off? I want to touch you like you...oh...are doing to m—me."

"No, not until I take you to our bed. Not until you've climaxed at least once without me touching you intimately."

He stroked her breast, twisted the tip then stroked again and again. Once more his mouth touched upon hers. He kissed her hard and deep, over then over until her breathy voice mewled with the pleasure he so skillfully composed. She let out a long breath of air that broke in a soft sob of need.

"You know that won't happen." He continued his play, his fingers dancing along her clothed body.

He was very pleased with her reaction. Wanted to see if her honey was spilling from between her tender folds. The wait would be hard for him to endure. He wanted to watch the thunderstorm, see the lightning spear across the sky, hear the loud booms as the storm escalated. He meant to bring her to that magical place amidst the tempest. Her eyes darkened as her passion grew to a mercuric level. She ran her palm across his chest, hesitating on each nipple.

A tempest in her body coupled with the tempest in the sky raged as he encouraged her to the highest summit. Her tiny butt wriggled against him sending waves of hunger instantly to his groin. He was hard and pulsing for entry. The devil he needed her. Possibly this was not the best idea. Still, he meant to see it through. This was a challenge to him.

"I'll come close."

He found her ankle. Ran his hand along her leg to the garters holding up her stockings. Higher still then higher his goal so close. She trembled, shuddering as her hunger grew more with each stroke across her inner thigh. Anticipating his caress, she opened for him, offering her sweet warmth.

She buried her head on the hollow of his shoulder. She pulled his shirt tails from his trousers. Her hand found its way beneath his shirt. He supposed that was fine. The contact was minimal. He hissed in a breath of air when she played with his nipple, flicked with her thumb, fondled with her tongue, raked her teeth across the tip. Air hissed from his lungs. If he wasn't careful, she would seduce him. He would embarrass himself. He couldn't let her have *carte blanch* with his body. He lifted her head from his chest, tugging down his shirt with his free hand.

She looked at him. He saw the disappointment in her eyes. Watched as she swept her tongue across her dewy lip leaving more tempting moisture behind. She cleared her throat, seeming to concentrate on her words. "Back to the wives. Do you think they will like me."

After he removed her hand from his chest her fingers seemed to possess a will of their own traveling to the waistband of his pants. If he was going to succeed, he couldn't allow her to touch him.

She pushed the tails away from his body after unfastening the shirt that seemed to be a hindrance to her plans, her hand swept up his torso. That was fine unless she explored lower. He wasn't a randy boy. He could command his body. She wouldn't take charge here. He decided he needed to give her a small taste of delight. He wasn't going to touch her where she would detonate. He was going to gradually glide his hand ever so close then closer still to her sleek wet petals waiting for more attention. He wanted her writhing with her need.

Sliding his hand along the silken expanse of her thigh, he came to the apex of her thighs so very close to her woman's mound. In anticipation, she spread her legs wider. Opening. Expecting. He meant to disappoint, at least for now. He wasn't going to give her her pleasure so soon.

"Evan..." his name was broken, fragmented as she reached for that pinnacle of raw and raging passion. She was very close so close she would be able to feel as if her climax was but a moment away. All she needed now was a small caress that would send her over the edge.

"Not yet, sweetheart. We need to wait for the storm. I want you to reach that delightful peak with the lightening coupled with the thunder."

"The storm?" The two words were a breathy thin wail into the sultry air.

Good, she was confused. She was lost in her building desire, the raging passion along with the mercuric ecstasy. His hand slid back to her ankle. She moaned low in the back of her throat. He understood she was disappointed he didn't touch her more intimately. Decided to cast his attentions on her other leg. Repeating the process, he came so close he could almost feel the dewy moisture along with the heat waiting for his caress for the touch of his fingers where she wanted to feel him. Then he did feel the wetness on her upper thighs.

The first rain drops hit the porch. The devil he loved a howling storm. He wanted Betsy to scream her pleasure, to yell his name when her body writhed with her completion. He could time her release to erupt with the lighting coupled with the thunder. At times they were so close together a body couldn't tell one from the other. All he needed to do at this point was touch the jewel hidden between her sensitive folds. He wanted to see if she would reach her pleasure with these tender seductive caresses.

This time when his hand moved upward, the palm of his hand skimmed against the slick folds. He wouldn't enter nor would he touch the wonderful pearl that brought her to a crescendo so quickly the speed always amazed him.

"Please, Evan..."

"Not yet. You don't need me enough. You don't need me as much as I need you." He brought his hand back to her ribs, smoothed her skirts along her legs. Though her clothing he played with the tip of one breast then the other. He kissed her again, over, and over, hard as well as deep. His mouth didn't leave hers until she panted for air. "You are almost there. Aren't you. What do I have to do? Tell me what you want."

In this case he did know exactly what she wanted. She wasn't going to get it until they were in his bed and she was writhing against him once more.

"You're wrong," she spoke very slowly as if she tried to gather her thoughts.

He chuckled knowing her need was indeed more intense than his. Again, his lips closed over hers. She met his tongue with hers opening for him. Her legs were spread nicely, wider than before. She arched against him. Her fingers gripped his shoulders then his neck. She ran her hands through his hair then rubbed her sensitized breasts against his chest.

This was torture for him. No, he needed to wait. Discipline was the thing here. He would teach her how to control her body. She arched against him when his fingers tightened over her nipple. He kissed the marvelous pink bud that caused her so much pleasure when he suckled her. Through the fabric of her corsage, he bit lightly.

A mewl, a scrappy sound, a cry for release rippled across his cheek from the exhale of her breath. He brought his hand along her leg again settling it on her belly, imagining his child growing there. He massaged, slipped lower so he caressed the soft hair shielding her woman's mound. Delved lower to touch her damp petals once more. He spread his fingers, fondling lightly, just barely a caress, over then over again. He teased. His hands taunted her. She arched against him. He bent to bite each nipple, moving from one to the other then back to her mouth.

"Are you there, almost ready to shriek and wail your ecstasy? I want to hear my name. Need to see your eyes when you reach that point of no return," he queried still lightly brushing her petals while his mouth sucked as well as bit on her plump lower lip.

"You know I am."

The storm chose that moment to bellow and rage above them. "Now, sweetheart." Lightening slashed across the sky. "Now..." He bit the tip of her breast once more, brushed the soft folds, played with her inner thigh. Slipped a finger along the crevice between her legs.

He knew the moment she reached her pleasure. She cried out, surging against him. "I want you inside me!"

"Not quite yet." He felt the escalation of her response, "Now." He played her body for second upon second until her body stopped arching and trembling, until her head rested on his shoulder and he heard the sharp breaths of air gradually slow to near normal.

"Wine?" he asked.

Not giving her a chance to answer, he set her aside. In a few minutes, he was back with two glasses along with a bottle of wine. He was well pleased. She was always such a joy.

She sipped looking over the rim of the crystal, licked a drop of that was sliding down the side. Her eyes were wary. Suspicious. "What are you planning?"

"A glass of wine first then bed. Six o'clock will come early. Imagine it's a good thing that we've been rising at the crack of dawn all week. You are now used to the morning hour." He lifted his glass in salute. "To my wife, to you, Betsy."

"Whatever happens tomorrow do you promise not to be angry with me?"

"Whatever happens," he agreed, then downed a large amount of his wine.

She sipped. "I'm having a hard time. Do you also promise not to yell at me? I don't like it when you lose patience. You do understand that I'm not purposely trying to sabotage what you do."

"All I can promise is to try."

"Very well then," she sipped more.

Lightening sizzled across the sky in blue-white streaks. Thunder boomed above them while rain pelted the roof of the deck.

"Come here." He wrapped a blanket around her shoulders pulling her close. Now was the time to slowly disrobe her. Before they left for the bed, she would be naked as would he. They could gather their discarded clothing in the morning.

"I don't trust you," she murmured watching him, studying him.

He wanted to laugh, to hoot with the notion she was hesitating in the sensual game they played. "Is that anyway to talk to your husband, sweetheart." He toyed with the buttons of her corsage, flicking them open one by one with the back of his hand caressing tender, sensitive flesh, delighting in the tiny shivers he created.

"What are you doing now?"

The cool air was stroking her breasts. He let the blanket float open before he closed it again. Watched the hardening of the tight hard buds he wanted to taste to savor.

"What do you think?" he growled the words, his voice husky with desire. Her fingers wrapped around his neck. He needed to feel her breasts pushed against him. With one hand she played with the opening to his shirt until she could push the fabric aside.

"That's what I thought." A disjointed sound followed then a small mewl of pleasure slipped from her.

He nipped her ear then laved the sensitive spot behind the lobe. His teeth grazed slowly down her neck until he reached that point where her pulse pounded, leaping with each caress of his lips. Minutes later, her bodice gaped open. He set to work on the little blue ties to her chemise. She didn't wear a corset. When the cool breeze from the storm touched upon her, she shivered, her rosy nipples tightening even more.

His hand roamed down her ribcage to the waistband of her skirt. Adept at the closures, he had the skirt from her body with ease. All she wore were her stockings now. Lazily he peeled them from her, down her legs, touching as much tender flesh as he could. His lust spiraled, increased with the tempo of the storm raging around them.

Her clothing lay upon the floor. His followed. Naked, she pressed herself against him. He swept her into his arms to carry her to their bedroom, everything left behind. She snuggled against his chest. Her sweet sultry purrs ruffled across him.

Tonight, would not last forever. He understood her fears, the dread of the next day coming. He would lose patience with her. He might yell at her when she failed to hit a ball that he knew she could.

For several hours, he lay awake, Betsy pressed against his chest. They made love two more times before he was finally able to stop. Her sleep was essential. When this was all done, before the new semester, he would take her on a wedding trip. They needed to discover each other more completely. Needed to be together when there was no outside pressure thrust upon them.

He too dreaded the match. In so many ways his brother was right about him. Nonetheless, it was not up to Duncan to teach him a lesson or put him in his place. Eventually, on his own terms he would have come to the same conclusion that his brother orchestrated. However, he would not have been reinstated this semester.

Possibly, he should swallow his pride, go to the president of the university along with the dean of students. If he apologized, Betsy would not have to play. Tomorrow, he could forfeit the match. Even while staring at the ceiling that was bathed in moonlight after the end of the storm, he could not will himself to do so. Not as long as there was the slightest chance of a win.

When he finally fell asleep, he was more determined than ever to see this through to the end. Whatever would happen would happen. By the time sunlight woke him, he was eager to see what the morning would bring.

Today Betsy rose before him. A strange sensation filled him when he smoothed her place with his hand and she wasn't beside him. They had been a couple for more than a month. She was always there when he woke.

Ah...she was nervous. He heard her in the bathing room. Stretching, scratching his belly, he rose from the bed then padded softly to see her. A morning kiss was mandatory. He would never forego the first kiss of the day.

When he stepped through the door to the room, he stopped, his mouth falling open. She turned, a look of concern gracing her beautiful features. He choked back the yell of disapproval. As if reading his mind, she stiffened her shoulders, her breasts pushed out in front of her in delightful display, one he wasn't interested in now.

"You're not wearing that!"

He pointed, his finger shaking. The words tore from him without conscious thought. What she wore was outrageous, scandalous.

"It's either the dress or these." She held up the flannel trousers Alexander bought for her. "If my opinion counts for anything, I prefer the dress."

"Where did you get those?" Disapproval swamped him as he stared at the trousers. Suddenly, he looked at her, "What did you say?"

"You heard me." She waved the trousers in the air, a smirk painted on her lovely features. "I'm going to wear one or the other."

"Neither," he murmured softly as he tried to hide his anger with the bland tone of his voice. "Neither is suitable. You will wear a different dress. One that will not show your legs to the world. Something only I should see."

"If that is what you choose for me, I won't play." She appeared to be determined to stand her ground. "I can't run in a regular dress. We will lose for certain. This dress or the trousers might give us the advantage we need."

Evan didn't quite know what was worse, everyone seeing her ankles or the sweet curve of her butt then on down her thighs. What was his to see no one else would get a crack at. His temper simmered at her audacity.

He had to concede or she might not play at all. Even after such a short amount of time with her, he recognized the determined look on her face. In this she was not about to give in to his wishes. He would have to choose one or the other. "Very well, the dress would be more suitable. You will still look like a woman."

He wasn't going to say lady. No lady would wear that dress. The devil he could see her ankles and more leg than he wanted to think about."

"Knew you would choose wisely." She twirled grinning at his look of chagrin. She understood she won this round. Possibly that wasn't a bad thing.

He almost forgot his decision. The sight he beheld was far more than just her lovely ankles. His body hardened with the lust, the view of her lovely body created. "I'll meet you for breakfast."

Chapter Eleven

On the way to the courts neither spoke. She was too nervous. He seemed content to sit back with his eyes closed his hands resting on his belly. Betsy was surprised when he allowed her to wear the shortened gown. She preferred the gown to the trousers. The way the dress fell around her legs it was cool as well as comfortable. She didn't wear a corset, only her cotton chemise and pantalettes. Didn't understand why he gave in so easily. She imagined it might be because he pushed her so hard this week, he was afraid she would refuse to go onto the court. A bit of rebellion would have been right in line with her feelings.

When she stepped forward to speak to Caroline, Evan held her back. With whispered words, he apprised her of some unwritten rule she couldn't ever agree with. "We don't speak to the opponent before the match."

She wanted to ask if he made up that rule or if that was an actual statute set down in blood for all players to memorize. She didn't. Neither Evan or Duncan smiled. Caroline shrugged her shoulders when Evan stopped her then she flashed her an approving smile when she saw her dress.

Behind her Evan cleared his throat before speaking. She thought his voice sounded strained. For his sake she made a determined effort to remain positive. "Caroline can toss the coin. Betsy will call it."

Duncan held his racquet along with Caroline's seeming to wait for the call. She didn't understand the reason. This was something he neglected to tell her. She called out heads. That was the way the coin landed.

"What does that mean?" Betsy asked clearly confused.

She should have kept reading the tennis manual he took from her. If she had, she'd know a lot more about this game she didn't want anything to do with. "You never—"

Impatiently he held up his hands to stop her. "It's one of those aspects of the game you didn't need to know. If we win the flip of the coin, we have the choice to serve first or to decide which court we want to begin play with. As we progress, I'll explain what different things mean. Otherwise, you don't need to know."

Once again, his impatience with her was shining through. It was obvious to her that he didn't wish to take any more time than necessary with her. "Oh...oh then—"

"We will serve first," Evan said interrupting her. "I will begin." He walked to the end of the court Duncan chose for them.

She hoped winning the flip of the coin was a good thing. Possibly she did something right. Duncan began to swear softly beneath his breath.

When she looked up, she noticed carriages were coming down the lane. A few men were on horseback. Within a few minutes a crowd was beginning to form around the court. "What are they doing here? Who told them about the match?" Duncan was muttering and swearing as he paced across the court to the first carriage.

"The devil!" Evan said as he continued to curse, repeating his brother's sentiments. "Who told the press?"

He stared at Duncan as if he knew the answer. He lifted his shoulders slightly, to suggest he had no idea how this happened.

To give more evidence to his innocence, Duncan was shaking his head. "Not I. This was supposed to be a family affair. No one but us to be involved. I didn't even tell mother and father who would have chastised both of us."

Caroline's face paled when Duncan turned to her as if she might have been the gossip. She was also shaking her head. The perpetrator became clear when Oliver Tindell stepped from a carriage, grinning broadly, twirling the cane he carried. When he stopped, he wiped his hands together, the smile on his face gleeful. He strode forward.

Oliver's snicker didn't go unnoticed. "Well, well, well, heard there's to be a little challenge match, a friendly game to decide a man's fate. Someone's career as well as livelihood seems to be hanging in the balance. Ah, my dear Betsy, what will you do if the man doesn't get his job back? You'll starve. You won't have a bloody sou to your name."

Betsy stepped back appalled by his words. As far as she could tell, he had no reason to be here. No reason to assume she would be left penniless at the end of the game. Evan's arms wrapped around her. He spoke softly for only her ears, "Don't let him rattle you, sweetheart. He speaks of things he has no idea about. Since he lost so much, he is hoping I will too. Tindell seeks revenge. He sees this as his golden opportunity."

She nodded in understanding. Oliver had no idea the vast expanse of her husband's wealth. She kept her tongue behind her teeth. An argument would never be forthcoming. She wasn't going to defend her husband who was in no need of defending. Drinking in air, she pushed her back against Evan as she soaked up as much courage as possible. He held her against his huge hard body, so different from Oliver's. Before she knew Evan Murray, she never realized how lacking Lord Tindell was in every aspect.

Oliver turned waving his hand in the direction of the men milling around them. "Seems what the Murray brothers do is news to the people of Scotland. Visualize that. Imagine that people are interested in the earl, what he is about. Seems the controversy from the university is news again." He pulled open a chair as he walked to a spot right on the outside of the court across from the net. Setting it down, he sat, crossed his legs then his arms over his chest. "This will prove interesting."

Duncan took the lead, following Tindell to the place he chose to watch. "You will have to move that chair of yours back at least ten feet. Don't want you to get in the way of the game. Be it known, you are not welcome. You've not been invited. This is private property. If you get in the way, I'll have you removed from the premises along with all the reporters." Duncan's voice was harsh, his features tense with both irritation and annoyance.

This was not supposed to happen today. "Come along, Betsy," Evan said as he strode to the side of the court that was his to begin this game. She ran to keep up with his long strides. Since the sun wasn't shining brightly, it would not get in anyone's eyes. The side they played on made little difference to the outcome of the game. When he had the chance to explain, she understood winning the toss was important.

Because Evan had the first serve, they would have the first chance to get ahead.

"Should we get started?" Evan asked as he readied himself to serve to Caroline. She knew this would be their first point. Last night he did explain a bit about the scoring. She didn't have to remember because he would call out the score when it was her turn to serve. He'd told her it was the server's responsibility to say the score in a loud clear voice before they tossed the ball so there would be no confusion.

As expected, Evan served first to Caroline who was unable to return service. The serve was the one point the other player couldn't poach. Evan won the first point. When he served to Duncan, the ball traveled hard and fast. Duncan was taken by surprise. He barely got his racquet on the ball. When he hit it, he directed the ball to her. She was so startled by the speed she had only time to put her racquet in the air and in front of her face. The ball bounced fast and hard across the net directly at Caroline. She screeched then dodged the ball. Duncan had been racing cross court to reach it. He dove skidding along the ground but didn't get his racquet on the ball.

"Good girl," Evan told her before he called out the new score. He was smiling his delight, "Thirty to Love."

Love meant zero points she reminded herself. The next serve was to Caroline who missed again. Duncan swore at her. Caroline made a face at him sticking out her tongue in a childish gesture. They had the next point. The crowd of family on lockers roared their approval.

Now the score was forty to love. She remembered the way the points would be counted. If they won the next point on Evan's serve to Duncan, they would win the game. She felt confident he could place the ball the same as his first serve.

They didn't win the point. The ball flew at her. Evan raced the distance but his return hit the net then bounced on their side of the court. She heard him swear. Didn't think the curse was because of her failure. He'd known since he began to teach her; she would not be able to return a hard-hit ball.

When Duncan returned the serve the ball flew past her, whizzing by her ear. Evan raced. He returned the point. He couldn't direct the ball toward Caroline. Duncan returned the ball to her. It landed at her feet. "Oh my!" There was nothing she could do. Evan swore softly. She dug in, stiffening her backbone. After all, she committed to this. Understood how he would feel every time she missed.

The next serve went to Caroline who hit the ball to her. She couldn't return the ball. The score was now Forty to thirty. She understood she needed to be able to return the ball when Duncan sent the little white thing her direction.

Luck was on her side, Duncan's return of serve went to Evan who returned it right at Caroline's feet.

One of the negotiations was that they would switch sides after each set. They were playing the best two out of three.

By the time the first set ended, it was six games to four, hers and Evan's favor. He kissed her hard, running his hand possessively down her back to squeeze her bottom. He whispered for her ears only, "That's for Oliver. I hope he's green with jealousy. The gall of him to show up here, bringing reporters with him."

Betsy heard the anger in his voice. Understood his temper was on a thin thread. The day grew hotter by the second. The sky was overcast, the air humid. They drank water when they stopped before beginning the second set. She played this much time two days ago. Between stress, the heat as well as all the running, she was exhausted for a moment felt bile rise in her throat. She tamped the sensation back. Two more sets to go. Unless they won this one. Mentally she crossed her fingers.

The play had just begun for the second set.

Duncan won his serve. Now it was her turn to serve. She could get the ball across the net. The points she might win would be the ones to Caroline. Though she did well, she lost the serve. Duncan was able to poach shots from Caroline and Caroline was able to return most of the shots that came her way.

Evan seemed to understand her strength waned as the game continued. Her stomach rolled. She was certain it was because of the baby she carried. There were a few times she thought she shouldn't be doing this. As if to assuage his fears, Evan had a doctor stop by yesterday to check her out. The physician assured him that in the first month there would be no danger from the exercise. Still the fatigue increased in gargantuan proportions as the morning drudged by. All she wanted was for this to be done.

Betsy knew women in the first three months sometimes had morning sickness. It seemed hers started very early. Though if she conceived as Evan thought, she was over one month pregnant.

"You look a bit green in the face. Are you feeling well?" he asked her his voice soft. His concern rallied her. She didn't want to be a quitter though that was exactly how she felt.

Between deep gulps of air, she spoke softly, "Fine just ducky," she lied to him.

They couldn't call this off now. Evan would lose. He would have his fate determined for him instead of by him. She wasn't going to do that to him. If they lost, if she tried her best, she wouldn't feel as guilty. If she quit on him, he might never forgive her.

"Looking at you, makes it difficult to believe you. I know you aren't fine. Though I do appreciate the effort. If you need to stop, say the word. I will honor the request." He sounded so sincere, so attune to her needs she almost gave in and told him she couldn't do this one second more.

Duncan stood beside them, "Is she able to keep playing? If she can't we can resume with the same score tomorrow morning."

Bloody, bloody eyes, no! "Yes," she told him quickly. Yes, she could continue to play. Wanted to finish this today. Didn't want to put anything off to resume sometime in the future.

"Then let's see who can win the best out of three."

Duncan sauntered across the court to lead Caroline to their new side of court. Caroline slanted her a look that told Betsy she sympathized and wished she could change things for her.

The play continued. Duncan and Caroline won the second set. Sweat dripped, sliding between her breasts, down her cheeks and back. Betsy wanted nothing more than to ride to the clean, cool lake. She wanted to float in the crystal-clear water while Evan caressed her, spoke words of endearment to her. She sifted in a humid breath of air. Closing her eyes, she pushed the nausea somersaulting in her belly to the back of her mind. She didn't want to humiliate herself farther by tossing the contents of her stomach on the closely cropped lawn.

"We can do this," Evan whispered to her as they walked to the opposite court. Keep your eyes focused on the ball. Remember to swing through the ball. If it lands close to me, let me take the shot.

She leaned into him understanding it was easier for him to say the words than it would be for her to do what he asked. Caroline didn't look tired. She smiled and laughed with Duncan. So far, Evan only yelled at her twice. Each time he apologized. He did swear softly whenever she missed the ball. She imagined he was doing a noteworthy job of keeping his patience along with his formidable temper as she did miss several easy shots. Her excuse? Perspiration dripped into her eyes. She couldn't see.

The last set lasted what seemed to her an eternity. When the ball came to her, she was hard pressed to stick her racquet in front of it. Her arms were sore as well as tired. She didn't have one more particle of energy left in her body. She thought she would wilt. She thought to sit out then watch the two men battle it out. Seemed Caroline felt the same. Visibly, she drooped. By the third game in the third set they were both dragging their feet.

Except for the serve, the men played alone. Once the ball was put in motion, she stepped to the side of the court so Evan wouldn't have to run around her. As bad luck rose to nip her in the butt the match came down to her serve.

This was not supposed to happen. Her serve should not decide the outcome of the game. If it had been Caroline's serve, they would have won. As it was turning out now, Evan didn't have any chance at all. She wanted to throw down her racquet and give the match to Duncan and Caroline. When she turned to look at Evan, he gave her a nod of encouragement. She bounced the ball a few times before taking her first serve into Duncan's court. Duncan returned her soft lob straight to her. She go out of Evan's way. The game went back and forth several times. Finally, Caroline and Duncan won by sending the volley to a far corner of the court that Evan couldn't reach before the ball hit the ground a second time.

Defeated she let her racquet fall. Her hand on the small of her back, she walked to Evan, moisture forming in her eyes. She didn't want to cry. Didn't want to feel as if this was all her fault.

She did give this her best shot.

As expected, when it was her serve, she had lost. They lost the last set as well as the match. Duncan whooped his delight at the outcome. She sunk to the lawn, her head bowed resting in her hands. Evan's cursing didn't go unnoticed. She wanted to apologize. Knew she didn't need to excuse her tennis play. From the start, Evan understood the risk.

His pride would have to be swallowed.

"Ha! Now you're done for." Oliver called out as he strode onto the court. "See how it feels to lose everything. I know your kind." The man was shaking his finger at Evan, his grin piggish. "You'd rather live off your wife's dowry than work. Well, you have to say you're sorry in order to be reinstated. Heard they weren't going to take you back even if you said the words all on your knees and tell them how very sorry you are."

What was he talking about? Oliver didn't have a single clue as to what was going on in Evan's life. He seemed to make up stories. Duncan strode to the two men. Evan's fists were clenched tight. So far, he didn't speak. She saw the muscles in his jaw tick. Beneath the fine lawn shirt he wore, his muscles rippled. He was furious. Oliver continued to taunt.

"Betsy's going to be mine." He stared hard at her. "You're going to come to me. Come now, Betsy. Why wait?"

"Even if she decided you would make a better husband for her, I'll never let her go," Evan said smoothly. "Her dowry is mine. As we speak the money has been invested for our future children. In the last month, it's doubled in value. You will have nothing that is hers." Evan slowly lifted her to her feet. With his arms wrapped around her, he held her close.

The brothers closed ranks, Duncan, Fletcher and Gordan surrounded them. Oliver seemed to notice Gordan.

Oliver turned his attention to the youngest sibling, the man who oversaw his financial transaction. Seeming to recover some of his arrogance, he pointed, once more shaking his finger at the man, sputtering for a moment with no words coming from his mouth. Then... "What the bloody hell are you doing here? Who are you?" It seemed Oliver began drawing a few conclusions of his own.

Gordan stepped forward grinning his hands behind his back. He looked Oliver up then down seeming to scrutinize him unfavorably. "Me? Why, I belong here. What are you doing at my brother's lawn tennis court? Seems you just want to cause trouble. You should leave. Gloating can be so unsatisfying when you realize you've nothing to delight about."

"That's exactly what I want. I'm here to gloat to take joy in another man's downfall. Betsy won't want Evan Murray now that he lost. We all know he won't get reinstated. He has nothing. Now he won't have his wife either. Not a groat to his name. Penniless. Just the way he contrived to leave me."

"In case you are too blind as well as deaf, I'm also a Murray as is Fletcher."

He pointed to one of the brothers then Duncan. Duncan owns the firm you came to for advice, Halstead & Family. Named after our mother, in her honor. Much to our enjoyment we were able to make certain you didn't ruin Evan." Gordan paused for a breath of air as he seemed to think for a second. "Not that you had the means or the intelligence to ruin Evan or any Murray."

Oliver blubbered, sputtered, spittle flying from his thin lips, his oversized belly bouncing. "No!" His face turned red as a beet. "No...you couldn't, wouldn't."

"We did," Evan finally said something.

When Oliver first approached Evan, Betsy backed away from him. The scene terrified her. Now Betsy, watching everything, walked to Evan to stand behind him. She thought to touch him, needing to feel the security only he could offer. Instead, she stepped back from him.

Oliver swung at Evan. He leaned back. The blow missed. "Coward!" Oliver yelled as he charged, his head down as if to butt him in the stomach.

Once more Evan stepped aside. Oliver ran by him. This time, Evan gave him a push to send him on his way to the ground. Propelling his ample rear with both hands Oliver's speed increased. The man stumbled, tried to gain his footing. He was moving so fast he couldn't control his body.

With a yell, he plowed head first into Betsy, his head hitting her low on her belly.

"Oh!" She cried out, her body crumpling with the blow.

When she fell, her head hit the ground. She moaned softly. Tears of searing pain fell from her eyes. Her body screamed with the terrifying agony. She curled into a little ball while she whimpered. Cramps ripped around her one after the other. The spasms kept circling her body in frightening waves. She closed her eyes, willing the cramping to stop. It didn't.

Evan was beside her, stroking her damp forehead. "What happened? Are you alright?" there was fear in his voice. "You're not."

The brothers along with Caroline circled her. She didn't know what was wrong with her. She'd never felt such pain. "N—no..." she whimpered the word. "It w—won't g—go away. Oh..." she wrapped her arms tighter around her body. "Evan...!"

"Stand back. Let her breathe," Evan cried out as he stroked her back. He looked to Duncan, "I don't know what to do. I'm helpless...the feeling...I've never..."

Betsy heard people talking all around her. She held her eyes tightly closed trying to block out the wild chatter, the noise, the pain that felt as if it ripped her apart. Evan was touching her, his hands roaming along her legs, her arms then her ribs. She didn't hurt there.

"I'm trying to find out where you are hurt. Duncan, along with my brothers are trying to coral the reporters, get rid of them. Can you tell me if you hurt anywhere? Your ribs. You might have one or two bruised or broken. I didn't see where exactly his head butted you."

She shook her head. She wasn't at all certain where she hurt. At this moment she felt as if she hurt everywhere. Pain circled her. Gripped her. No, "My, my belly..."

"All right. Hang on. Duncan is bringing my carriage around. Fletcher has gone for a doctor. You'll be just fine."

"I don't think so." Her voice was broken, a thin wail that seemed to come from the last remnants of energy. She felt the moisture between her legs. The cramping continued along with the blinding pain.

"No!" She heard his cry of pain. Heard the sobs of despair rack his big body. "No, not this."

Betsy didn't understand. When she looked up to see him, tears slid down his face. "What?"

"You'll be fine," he repeated. "Just fine. I'll get you home. The doc will be there. You're going to be fine." He picked her up, carried her to the carriage.

"I'll come with you," Caroline's voice seemed to come to her in a fog. "You will need help once you're there."

"What is wrong with me?" What did they know she didn't?"

Evan didn't answer, neither did Caroline. Instead, he cradled her close, brought her head to the hollow of his shoulder. The steady beat of his heart next to her ear comforted.

Caroline was whispering to Evan while she drove the carriage. Betsy couldn't understand what she was saying. It seemed she floated between consciousness and sleep. She knew Evan cradled her all the way home. Also knew Caroline was there too. The pain wasn't as bad now. She felt a bit fuzzy-headed. The world seemed hazy.

When she reached their home, Evan barked orders. People all around her scurried from one place to the other. After he set her on their bed, he undressed her. Caroline brought her a dressing gown.

She saw blood on her thighs, her clothes. His hands were bloody. Confused, she looked at Evan. "You've lost the baby," he said softly, tears streaking down his face. "I'm going to take care of you. We must stop the bleeding. The doctor is here. He will see you now."

"No..."

She heard the wail of despair echo from her. Didn't recognize her voice. Still in a haze. People, her husband, the doctor along with Caroline tended to her.

He wanted the baby. Was so pleased with the conception. She felt empty inside. The precious being she caried for such a short time was gone, his son or daughter. She didn't want to live. Didn't know how she could continue each day. He would blame himself even though this was all Lord Tindell's doing.

When she woke, Evan held her, protected her. She was in their bed. He stroked her arm. The full realization of what happened to her crept into her head.

I lost the baby.

Tears slid down her cheeks. More tears then more followed, "I'm sorry," she told him wondering if he would now seek an annulment.

He didn't need to be wed to her. There was no reason for them to continue as a married couple. He barely knew her.

"You've nothing to apologize for. I'm an ass. If I hadn't been so damn stupid, arrogant, stubborn..." he inhaled deeply. "You would not have lost the infant. This is all my fault."

"No," she held a finger to his lips. "You're none of those things. You're loving, considerate, funny."

"This was my fault. I didn't hit him but I sent the bastard flying straight into you. My anger overpowered thought. I should have stopped him. The irony of it all is that if I'd hit him, it would have been Tindell we would be doctoring not you."

The doctor was standing in the door. "She needs to rest." After a lengthy pause, he said. "You two can have more children. You are young."

"I don't want another child. I want this one."

Even with all the determination she could bring up from the depths of her soul, her voice sounded weak.

I want this child.

~ * ~

"You can go now." Evan spoke to the doctor furious with his callous comment. "It's not time to think of more children. At least not until we mourn this one."

Evan cursed himself over then over again. Duncan had been right about him. He was a stubborn bastard. All he could be thankful about was the fact Betsy would recover. If he lost her...he didn't want to think about that.

For the next few hours, he held and supported her wishing the pain of the last day away. When he knew she was asleep, he left her to take a bath. He still wore her blood. It was a horrific reminder of what he did. While he'd washed his hands, her blood coated his trousers and shirt. Quickly, he stripped, staring at the hated clothing, clothing that symbolized the most horrific day of his life.

"Burn them," he told Alexander after he disrobed. "Won't have need of clothing for tennis ever again," he whispered softly wishing to take back time.

The clothing lay in a pile at the door to the bathing room. He soaked up the hot water. While the heat soothed his muscles, nothing could ease his mind. Alexander brought him fresh clothing. All the times he'd been with Betsy slipped through his head. He recalled her laughter, the beauty of her smile. He enjoyed the way she teased him. From the first moments he met her, she would put him first. He never put her first except in their sexual encounters. That wasn't good enough.

She adored children.

He prayed she would eventually want to try again. He wouldn't force her. If after this, she didn't want to have a child, he would take every precaution to keep her from conceiving.

Her tears for the unborn child they would never hold, shamed him. Because of him, they lost the most precious life in the world. Because of him, she would never hold the baby. Would never watch the child grow, become an adult. Because of his needs and wishes, the list went on seemingly forever.

He didn't know anything about children. Along with Betsy, he'd been willing to discover all their hidden intricacies. He relished the thought of learning. Perhaps in the morning, they could name the child. Ah, but they didn't know if the *wee bairn* was a boy or a girl. What did it matter? The babe needed a name. Needed to be remembered, know he or she was cherished. While he wanted an heir, he came to realize he would love a girl just as much as a boy. Maybe a name that could go both ways would be appealing. Perhaps Pat for Patrick or Patricia. It could be Nick for Nicole or Nicholas. There were many possibilities to choose from.

He would have a marker ordered, one that would remember the child, tell of the love both mother and father felt. They would put it by the lake or the gazebo. He didn't care. Whatever Betsy would like would suit him just fine.

After he finished with the bath, he strode downstairs. He wasn't hungry but knew they both needed to eat. Light fare would do nicely. He put a tray together; hot tea, fresh baked bread, and honey on plates. There was fresh fruit in a basket.

He looked at the food. None of it appealed to him. Doubted if Betsy cared.

Eating was necessary.

She needed strength to recover. He would see to it that she mended. Her heart like his would remain torn. The tear would last a lifetime. He would always wonder.

Except for the small breakfast this morning neither had eaten. The hour was well past seven in the evening. If she felt like dinner, he would have something ready for her. If she wished to talk, he would do so. If not, they could eat then sleep. He would hold her through the night. She would need to rest her body to heal. He felt as if he repeated his thoughts. Felt as though he was going through the motions of life without feelings. He was numb from the inside out.

When he saw her sitting up in bed, tears streaking her lovely face, he cursed silently again, berated himself along with his stubborn pride for causing this. The period of mourning would not be over quickly or easily. He set the tray on the table before slipping in beside her then pulling her into his arms. She was so delicate, sweet. Her body so small next to his. She didn't deserve this. No one did, but least of all Betsy.

She gave herself to him with her entire heart. What did he give to her?

Heartache. Unbearable pain. The loss of a beloved child.

Nothing, the answer was nothing good. All he did was take then take some more. He expected her to bend to his will. He bounced into her life because he was bereft, bored with no way to pass the day. Caroline knew Betsy. Thought escorting her around town would keep him busy as well as out of trouble. All he did was take. Enjoyed her innocence.

She did bend to his will without complaint. In escorting Betsy, he found love...

The thought rebounded in his head. He loved her.

The thought was new.

I love her...!

Evan looked at her with wonder. She was so precious. He watched the tears fall. Heard the soft sound of her despair. He would do anything if he could turn back time. Anything.

He would let her sob if she needed to do so until all the tears ran dry. Forever, he would remember this day, lesson learned but at what cost? The devil take him! This was too much to absorb. His mind wasn't dealing too well with all that happened. The day should be erased from history.

Duncan arrived to pick up Caroline an hour ago, telling him he would return as soon as she was settled. Caroline was silent when she left, tears still hiding in her moisture filled eyes. Duncan wrapped his arms around her letting her sob in his protective shelter. There were no words anyone could say that would ease the terrible ache in his heart. Evan understood they all grieved. No words to change the events as they transpired. A time machine would be nice. To go back then alter the transpiring events to something more amenable. The damn tennis match should have never been conceived. He should have apologized. Damn his stubborn hide. Duncan was right about him. His brother knew him so well.

When Betsy was ready, they would have a private memorial service. Moisture welled in his eyes. Perhaps it would be days or weeks before the ache would begin to numb to a point where there would be no more tears.

Long, slow minutes ticked by. Betsy's sobs eased momentarily. The flow of tears finally stopped. Her hand rested on his chest. He placed his fingers over her very small ones. They would be the last tears either of them shed for the tiny life that was no longer to be. Tenderly, he stroked her hair. Let the silken strands soothe his heartache. He rested his chin atop her head. Her breaths were slow as well as erratic. Her heart beat quickly.

Evan wasn't certain how to approach the subject or if his question would cause more pain. He cleared his throat then let his knuckles glide tenderly down her cheek. "Would you like to name the *bairn*?" he asked as she slowly pushed away from him to stare into his eyes.

Evan wasn't certain what he saw in the moisture filled depth. If she was pleased or angry, he couldn't tell. She appeared confused. He continued, his voice whisper soft, "We can put a marker by the lake or the gazebo with the babe's name as well as how much we loved him...or her. We don't know the gender. Would you like that?"

With a soft sob, she nodded closing her eyes for a moment as if she was willing herself to forget. "Yes," she breathed. "A name would be nice as will a marker. I didn't want the babe to die. I would have moved out of the way if I'd seen Oliver coming at me. I was so tired. I could barely stand. It all happened so fast. What happened to Oliver? Is he all right?"

Oliver...he didn't know nor did he care.

"Hush, sweetheart. I should never have shoved him. If I'd let him be, he would have stumbled a few feet. Oliver wouldn't have plowed into you. It's my ungodly temper. As to what happened to the man, I don't *ken*. I was too worried about you to pay attention to a man I loathed."

"No...he provoked you. What happened is not your fault. You did your best to ignore the obnoxious man when he taunted you about the pending reinstatement. Don't ever think to put this at your doorstep. What happened to me is not your burden."

He wished he could agree with her. All of this came full circle to him...the nonexistent apology...his temper, damn his stubborn hide. She was his responsibility. He didn't look out for her best interest. He told her she would be number one in his thoughts. For the moment, he needed to stop thinking. "Should we eat? Are you hungry?"

She graced him with a tiny smile before lifting her shoulders in an artless shrug. It seemed to him she was attempting to make him feel better. Nothing could do that.

"A little. Before the doctor left, he told me to eat, to sleep. It would aid the recovery. The thing of it is, I wish I were dead." The last words whispered nearly silently from her lips, shocking him to his core.

"No!" He panicked. She couldn't possibly wish that. Fear rolled within, terrifying. "Never say something like that. Your death would not bring the child we lost back."

He pulled her close trying to absorb the chill she cast with her words. To him the room took on a deathly gloom. The few candles burning did little to cheer. He would have to make certain she wasn't serious in her death wish. He would remain by her side. Watch over her until she came to terms with the loss. "No, don't ever think that. You are too precious. I could not go on living if you passed. You mean the world to me."

He knew that someday...they would have years and years together. She wasn't going to leave him now.

Now that he understood he loved her.

"Not as precious as the child we lost," she murmured softly, seeming to need some form of reassurance. "I know I should eat. Understand sleep is necessary. Nonetheless, if I fell asleep never to wake up, I would...I don't know what I'm thinking. I don't want to leave you." She paused for several seconds. When she looked at him again there were more tears in her eyes, "Now...now that there is no child, are you going to seek an annulment?"

"No!"

Once again, she shocked him. Perhaps it was time to lay all his feeling out in the open. He wanted the marriage. Needed to live with her, hold her, share dreams with her. Have a child together or more if that was acceptable to her.

I love you.

"I will eat something. Sleep. Won't speak of death."

"Good, we will take each ensuing moment one at a time." He poured the tea then handed her a large slice of bread. "Butter? Honey? Both?"

"Both."

Her smile didn't reach to her eyes. In what seemed like a daze to Evan, she ate and drank the tea that was laced with honey and milk. He should have put a liberal dose of brandy in the brew.

He ate too. The food was good. When she finished, he took the tray away, tucking the covers around her as she settled to go to sleep. "I'll join you in a few hours. I've a few things to attend to. Think of a good strong name for our child. We can decide in the morning. Once we settle on a name, I'll order the marker."

"Yes." She reached out to him as if she wanted him to stay with her. "Don't stay away too long," she murmured sleepily. Her drink had more milk and honey than tea. She should sleep for most of the night. He laced it with the laudanum the doctor gave him. They were supposed to go to Glasgow tomorrow. The trip would have to wait. For now, he had to speak with his brother. He hoped Duncan returned after taking Caroline home. If not, that conversation would need to wait until the morning.

The doctor told him it would be three days before she could travel. The man also told him a month before he could make love to her again. Her body needed time to heal. There might be complications. Although he didn't believe there would be. The doctor said he would examine her in a month. *Over his dead body.* He would read all the literature on miscarriages that he could find then he would do the examining. If he detected a possible problem, he would call in another physician or a renowned midwife. Caroline might know someone who would be better than this country doctor. If Caroline didn't, perhaps Letty or Tora at the escort service would have some idea who to call on.

He should treat Betsy gently. At the moment, he wasn't certain he wanted to sire another child to take the chance of losing the babe or losing his wife. When he was ecstatic with the fact Betsy carried his child, he never thought she might not carry the baby to term. The notion never crossed his mind. Now the idea of losing another child would haunt him. He heaved in a lungful of air hoping the oxygen would ease his deliberations.

Gently, he shut the door to the master chamber. Betsy was sleeping soundly. When he walked into his office, Duncan sat in a chair facing the fireplace. Fletcher sat in another chair. Gordan stood beside the fireplace. His brothers had helped themselves to the brandy as well as poured him a glass.

"How is she?" They all seemed to speak in unison.

Evan felt tears form in his eyes again. They loved each other. They were family and would stand beside each other forever. Their wives, Betsy and Caroline were part of that union along with the future wives of Fletcher and Gordan.

This debacle would stain the Murray name even more than his earlier *faux pas* with the university. The match was meant for Murrays only. No one else was to be involved. As it stood now, Lord Tindell involved the city of Glasgow. There would be headlines along with a drawing. He could picture it now.

"Tired, sad more than one could ever believe. It's as if a part of me, a part of her has been ripped away. I look back and tell myself all the things I could have done differently. I'm a fool as well as an ass." He wasn't about to tell his brothers of her death wish. The wish came about because of the deep love she felt for the child coupled with the loss. They both were empty. He didn't know how to explain the sensation. In time the feelings would pass. He prayed they would.

"We've no way to understand," Duncan said his voice soft. It seemed he empathized though. "We will do whatever we can."

While he expected his brothers to agree with him that the fault lay in his hands, they did not. "She will live. How she will live will be up to me. We will take each day one at a time. I appreciate the offered support."

"You will need assistance with her. More than you and Alexander can provide. Caro told me she wrote to Tora. Miss May would be perfect to come live with you. She will tend to Betsy while she recuperates. You cannot be there for all her needs," Duncan said. "Whatever you do, don't blame this on yourself. You are not responsible. I was pleased with the way you held your temper."

"My actions killed my child. Could have killed Betsy." Evan held up his hands signaling his brothers to let him finish. "You will deny that fact. Nonetheless, I *ken* the truth. Tell me there were other reasons. Deep in my heart I understand if I had just let Tindell stumble to the ground he would not have plowed into Betsy. But no, I had to give him some more incentive to leave me alone. I shoved with all the strength I possessed." All he said was the truth. Nothing would change that fact.

"You might want to ask about Oliver?" Gordan said as he sipped the brandy he poured. "I've taken care of the man. Thought you would want to see him vanish from the face of the earth. His disappearance from Glasgow was all I could arrange."

Evan looked up. Perhaps one wish would come to fruition this afternoon. If he never saw Lord Oliver Tindell again, that time would be too soon. He didn't need to contend with the man's petty need to seek vengeance if that was what he intended when he appeared uninvited at the tennis match bringing reporters with him.

"What did you do?"

"First, I made him promise a few things with his signature on certain documents. If he goes against those few stipulations I set forth, he will be immediately sent down under."

"Uh—huh, tell me what you did." Evan suddenly felt a slight burden lifted from his shoulders.

"Easy enough, I sent him home to London," Gordan said as he finished his brandy. "Understood what the man needed."

"Groats, lots of them," Fletcher laughed.

"The man can be bought," Duncan said agreeing with his younger brother.

"Sent him home in the lap of luxury with five thousand pounds. He finagled for more. Told him he was lucky to get that much. At first, I'd been inclined to give him a fifth of that. Decided to add the signatures as guarantees."

"Very well done of you," Evan said. "What did he sign? His life away, I hope."

"Not quite that drastic. Just that he would never return to any part of Scotland. Believe he was reluctant though to leave his widow lady behind. He'd only had her a few nights."

"For five thousand pounds," Fletcher said with a lift to his shoulders.

Evan looked around the room at his brothers. They were all so alike physically but so different in personality. He had the temper coupled with a lackadaisical manner. Wished he didn't.

"Believe he did care about Betsy. He seemed genuinely sorry about what happened to the child along with his part in it."

"His feelings about Betsy might be genuine, might not be. We'll never know now, will we? Not that I give a damn." Evan knew Betsy cared about him. None of this would have come about if she never felt the need to run from the man. If not for Oliver, he would have never married Betsy or lost a child. No matter how he figured this, Oliver played a big role in his life.

Now he would be gone.

A few hours later, he said goodbye to his brothers. When he stepped inside the bedchamber, Betsy slept soundly. After he climbed into bed, he pulled her close, holding onto her, listening to her breaths along with the beat of her heart.

The laudanum helped her sleep. He didn't think he would sleep.

He did.

When he woke, her head was on his chest, her hand running along his torso. His body ignited.

"We can't," he murmured as he kissed her forehead, ran his fingers through the length of her hair. He was heartily glad she wanted to touch him. It seemed to be a renewal of their life together.

One month was going to be a devil of a long time.

Epilogue

Almost five years later.

"You are so beautiful when you are carrying my child. I can't seem to ever get enough of you." He placed his hand on her swollen belly.

"I'm quite huge. Do you suppose we could be having twins this time?" Betsy laughed at the horrified look on her husband's face but she prayed she was not. "Twins would be so much work. You would love them so much."

"That would give us four children," Evan watched his boy play, tossing rocks into the lake. "I wouldn't mind four. What about you?"

"Look, Papa, that one splashed the most." His little boy waved his hand in the air showing them how high the water went.

Their second son dozed. There was a small bubble on his rosebud lips. His blanket spread out on the moss. The day wasn't too hot.

"Four children in less than four years is too much. You are so..." She paused trying to think of the right word to describe him.

"Exuberant in bed?" His hoot of laughter was solid, loud. The sound caught his son's attention. "That doesn't come close to describing you."

The little boy stopped what he was doing to stare at his mother and father. "What is it, Papa? Why are you laughing so hard?"

"Your mother and I were speaking of children. I thought she might be having two this time. What do you think? Would you like her to have two babies instead of one?"

"Mama is very big," the boy said with honest sincerity. "Very big. She waddles now and can't run after me or play chase."

"Men," she said softly as she thought how beautiful all her men were. The boy had his father's temper, much to Evan's chagrin. He was

305

bright. All the Murray's were brilliant in some field. They all managed their numbers with terrifying ease. Even now at the tender age of three and a half the boy could calculate small sums.

Betsy wished she could tell Evan how much she loved him. After more than five years, it seemed he might love her. He never said so. She didn't either. That was her only regret. She needed to tell him her feelings.

Evan was good with the children. He told her when she was increasing for the second time that he wanted to learn everything he could about the babies as well as each stage of their lives. He needed to know everything about childbirth.

An hour or so later, after playing with their little boy, he set him down for a nap near the baby. "What would you like to do now? I know what I would like." he asked as he smoothed his knuckles down her cheek then her neck. His fingertip traced a path just above her corsage, along her collarbone, dipping momentarily between her breasts.

"You know what I'd like? It's what I always want. Have you forgotten so soon?" Her breathy smile gave him reason to grin then dip his finger lower so it passed across her nipple once, then twice.

"I love your breasts. They are so much larger when you're pregnant. Of course, now, you are not only increasing but you are also nursing. That makes everything so much more delightful." He traced his name across her breast. He'd been so very pleased as well as surprised when she agreed to the real tattoo. Because of that she was pleased too.

"Evan...wait..."

Startled he looked up. "What is it?"

She ran her tongue across her bottom lip thinking she needed to say her feelings before he sidetracked her. Knowing, that after such a long time, she had to take the chance. She gulped a huge dose of oxygen. "I...well...I wanted to tell you something."

He looked a bit panicked. His eyebrows drew tightly together. "What?"

For a moment, she lowered her lashes. Sipping in another breath of air, she plunged ahead. "I...I love you. Have since the first time you teased me so about the escort service, since you made me get naked in your big tub. I should have told you a long time ago. Was too scared since you don't love me."

His smile grew with each word she spoke. "You love me? You truly do?"

She looked to him, touched the thundering pulse at the base of his neck. He wasn't saying anything more. She looked away, her smile vanishing, a chill slipping down her spine. Dread filled her heart. He loved her body but he didn't love her. She'd been a total fool to tell him her feelings.

"No, don't hide from me, Betsy, sweetheart. While I can't tell you I've loved you for that long, you fascinated me from the beginning. I was always attracted to you, especially your plump lower lip, including your baby doll cheeks along with your cornflower blue eyes. Imagine I might have loved you, just didn't know it."

"Yes..." She waited expectantly, hoping for some confirmation. She needed to hear the words, longed to hear them.

"I do love you, my sweet darling Betsy. Realized it when you lost our first child. Knew I couldn't live without you. Didn't want to spend a day without you in my bed. I love you more than life."

"You love me..." she breathed softly her eyes looking dreamy then darkening.

"Yes, for the longest time. You are my life. The rest of our life you better be good. Betsy be good, yes, I like the sound of that. Betsy be good to me and I'll be good to you."

The two prospered, loved and had more children. The final count was six. Four boys and two lovely girls. They were bright children. All would excel in math. The boys continued with the financial firm, Halstead & Family, started by Duncan.

The two girls found they wanted more from life than dealing with numbers while making transactions that would gain them more wealth. The oldest girl went on to become a reporter, of all things. She always vowed to tell the news as it should be told, the complete truth and nothing less.

The youngest girl became a midwife. She wanted to become a

physician. Unfortunately, there were no institutions she could find that would allow women in their hallowed doors. She studied every piece of literature on birthing she could find. Understood things many of the male doctors ignored. She was sought out as the best midwife in all of Scotland.

Betsy and Evan lived to love and be loved all their lives.

Coming Soon
By the Author
At Rogue Phoenix Press

Gracie

Chapter One

Glasgow 1827

"I love him," Gracie Seymore swore beneath her breath understanding she would have to leave the man. Even though she just now understood how desperately she loved her soon to be ex-fiancé, he would eventually kill her. "I want to marry him. He wants me as his wife." Her fingers curled around the diamond studded heart he gave her after the last time he hurt her. He always apologized. Always gave her an expensive gift. Always said he'd never hit her again as well as how very much he regretted his actions.

"So, he can have you beneath his thumb. You understand he doesn't want you to have a life except with him. Isn't that right? Every time you've done something without his permission, that is when he's turned his fury on you," Phoebe was tapping her long slender finger against her chin.

"Excepting all you say as the truth will not change my mind about Alex. He's so handsome. His blue eyes steal my breath and make my heart flutter. When he wraps his long arms around me, I always think I'm going to swoon. His kisses…well…let's just say they make me melt. I don't want to leave him."

"You have to," Phoebe stated flatly. "If you want to live, leaving is the only viable alternative. Today, even though the timing is all wrong. I don't like the thought that you will be riding alone through the night."

"I could take the carriage," Gracie reasoned thoughtfully.

"A carriage the man would recognize. No, you will have to ride as fast as you can. You can take a pistol for protection. You will take refuge with your uncles. They will protect you, shield you if he tries to force the issue."

"We both *ken* how to use a pistol. You're the better shot though," Gracie mused as she thought about their last competition. Her father had always wished for a boy. He taught her everything a male would have been taught. Not only did she shoot well, she also dabbled in sword play with her father.

Phoebe Killingworth, ever the practical one when relationships were considered, spoke softly appearing to understand the distress she felt. "You have to leave now. The message said he would be here early tomorrow morning. It is my best guess that your viscount has left Glasgow. If you are quick about it, you can be with your uncles in the city before he can form a protest or stop you. As I pointed out, they will protect you. They will not allow him inside the door."

"Yes…and they will lecture me about the viscount, the man I love. It's deucedly hard to hear. Over three months ago the two of them warned me to stay away. Told me he had a certain reputation where women were concerned. I didn't listen. Ignored their good counsel."

"You should have done so. If you had you would not have suffered at his touch. You wouldn't be hopelessly in love with an unsuitable man."

"You are going to lecture me too. I've quite heard enough."

Gracie inhaled a deep breath wishing Alexander would not explode with rage at the least little *faux pas*. So far in their tumultuous relationship, he had given her two black eyes and a broken rib. The broken rib was the reason she retired to the country for healing as well as thinking. She understood some decisions would need to be made. She was afraid to be around the man when his fury overcame his good sense.

"When Alex is not angry, he is so sweet and kind, so very considerate." She touched the necklace he gave her after the first blackeye. He had her name engraved on the back of the gold heart that was trimmed with diamonds. When she arrived here, she was indecisive. The two of them would never be suitable. She was too wild and willful. Alex needed a mate who would bend to his every whim. Her thoughts didn't change the fact that the decision was difficult to make. Didn't change the fact that when he was sweet, he was very, very sweet. She didn't think any woman could bend enough to escape his fists.

"You are dallying," Phoebe said with patience Gracie didn't see in her friend's eyes. "Please do not tell me you've changed your mind again. You are wearing me out."

"I have not. It's just that I'm...no everything will be fine. There have been no tales of highwaymen in these parts."

"It is safe. Many would say that you would prove more dangerous than the people you might encounter on the road." Phoebe was laughing at her jest yet her mouth pressed together in a thin line.

"I see nothing funny in what you say. I know I'm a bit wild. This isn't the first time I've ridden to Glasgow by myself. Most likely won't be the last," Gracie mumbled as she downed the last of her wine. The time would be after midnight when she arrived at her destination. That part was infinitely different. She sipped in a long breath of air as she marched to the window overlooking the gardens. The sun was still high on the horizon. It would not dip beneath the crags for another hour. She could cover quite a bit of the distance before darkness overtook the roads. Phoebe was right. She did need to hurry. The longer she dallied here, the longer she would have to ride in the dark.

Phoebe pointed a shaking finger at her, a smile now easing the thin line of her mouth. "Go upstairs. I'll help you pack a small bag you can take with you. I will have the rest of your clothing sent to your uncles' home. Go now! Go, before both of us experience a change of heart. If you are here when your soon to be ex-fiancé arrives, you will regret not leaving now."

Understanding she truly had to leave in the ensuing minutes even though the hour was growing late, hiking her skirts to her knees, Gracie ran upstairs. Winded, she surveyed her clothing, taking a few necessities. In a few minutes, she was downstairs, accepting good wishes from her friend along with the words that spoke of haste. "You are not to stop for any reason. Ride straight through as if the hounds of hell are on your heels. You must reach Glasgow before the sun rises."

"I love him," she said again as if the words would change her mind or her friend's feelings. They wouldn't. When she realized her thoughts for Alex, she had been filled with jubilation, thinking love was such a fine emotion. After that all her dreams exploded.

What was left for her? She was twenty-two. While she wasn't horse-faced, she was on the shelf. What male would want a woman of her advanced age? Perhaps she'd been too eager to fall into his waiting arms. Maybe she looked the other way when he first showed his true colors. Marrying for love had always been her dream. The last few years, she thought she would never meet a man she could fall in love with.

That was when Alex stepped into her life, all smiles and muscles, the gentlest soul she ever met. He was whipcord lean. His kisses melted her to the bone. His eyes always shimmered when he wanted to kiss her. Except for those few explosive times when he lost his temper, he'd always been tender.

Once more, Phoebe was shaking her finger at her, the look in her beautiful brown eyes stern. "You cannot afford to love that man. He will be the death of you. We both understand that for a fact. I cannot bear to be your nursemaid every time he loses his temper. You know the title means nothing to you." Phoebe sipped more air before she spoke again. "Now, stay off the main roads. With your eyes closed, you *ken* the way. If your fiancé has had a change of plans, you might run into him. That wouldn't be good. If you hear a carriage or another horse, get off the road then hide in the trees until the vehicle passes."

Gracie struggled with Phoebe's calm words. There was still a part of her that wished to accept his apology and believe he would never hurt her again. "When you're right, I hate it. I won't stop for any reason. Will take every care to avoid traffic." Gracie hugged her friend. A few minutes later she was saddled on her mare, headed toward the city. Her heart raced as she stared down the long drive that led from Phoebe's country home. The trip would take her most of the evening. If she didn't encounter problems, she should be at her uncle's shortly after midnight. She would have to explain to Jason and Jasper why she needed their help. They would be furious. She would also have to find a means to make certain neither uncle acted against the viscount.

What she did tonight was foolish. She and Phoebe both understood that this action was the lesser evil. She could not afford to have Alex take her back to the city. Could not afford to bring down his wrath again. If they stayed together, doing so was inevitable. She would always act impulsively, risking the anger that could rise swiftly. Despite all the apologies her fiancé gave her, he always hurt her when he grew incensed with something she did or said. He lashed out before he thought.

A soft sigh rippled from her lips as she urged her little mare into a brisk trot. If she kept her mind focused on the fact she had to stay strong, the journey might not take too long. She would be on the road for about six hours. As if she heard something or perhaps it was nerves, she turned to look back at the manor house. Only shadows whispered across the drive behind her. Phoebe's home was shadowed in darkness. Behind the stately mansion, white clouds billowed ever higher.

An eerie feeling catapulted through her. Shivers swept down her spine sending goose bumps to her arms. A premonition that something was about to go horribly awry swamped her. She berated herself. Tried to force the sensation out of her head. This was not the time to second guess herself or her intentions. Focusing on her future, she let her mind wander. Unfortunately, her mind didn't travel in the direction of the future. It circled around her until all she could think of was the haunting past that sent her riding down country roads in the middle of the night.

The image strong in her mind, she recalled the first time Alex hurt her. They were at the Ramsey's ball. He told her how beautiful she looked. She danced with him once then twice creating a murmur around the room. Dancing with a man twice was scandalous. She liked him. Never thought to fall in love. They'd walked in the park, met for tea. At the ball, Phoebe took her aside. Told her she could not dance with him again this evening. She stared at him, as he partnered woman after woman, holding them too close. Even though her dance card was full, she longed to be in his arms. Needed to feel his warmth and strength holding her. She only had eyes for Alex, Alexander McKenzie, Viscount of Belmond.

When Lawrence Littleton waltzed her into a corner to steal a kiss, she'd looked for Alex. Hoped he would come to her rescue. She understood exactly what Larry intended after he pushed her against the wall. Even told him she didn't want a kiss. The horrible man said her wishes didn't count for anything. She squirmed trying to dislodge the hold he had upon her. His strength was greater.

Gracie pushed on his chest, beat with her fists on his shoulders. He was immovable. His hand behind her head held her still. When his lips met hers, she gagged. This was not how Alex's kisses felt. Suddenly the man was wrenched away from her. Cold air wafted against her trembling body.

Her gaze met Alex's. He was angry at her. When he grabbed her wrist tugging her toward him, his fingers closed tightly. He yanked her forward, hissing at her, telling her what a little bitch she was. In hindsight, she should have known that very instant they would never suit. Alex pushed her to the coatroom, her hand behind her back. She was afraid to say anything or cry out for help. A scandal was not something she wanted to deal with. Moisture from the pain as well as the humiliation filled her eyes.

When his carriage arrived, he pushed her inside. To gain balance, her arms whirled. She landed hard on the floor, her one wrist breaking her fall. The bone cracked with a loud snap. She cried out, the pain blasting through her. Her wrist was broken. Now, she couldn't remember the tirade he graced her with as he ushered her home. What she did recall was that he blamed everything on her. Blamed her for tempting his friend. Blamed her for being too beautiful. Blamed her for just breathing, it seemed to her. She was always at fault.

The next day, he brought her a new pair of gloves to replace the ones she'd been wearing that had been torn.

The gust of wind caught her hat, tugging on the strings that were tied beneath her chin. One hand flew to her head to hold the hat down, the other tightened on the reins. She looked to the skies. They were dark, black clouds threatening rain. The sky had not been so dark when she left.

The white billowy clouds seemed to have vanished. A storm had been unexpected. She wouldn't find shelter before the storm hit. Gracie didn't have time to stop anywhere.

Urging her mare to a faster pace she hoped to race in front of the tempest, knowing she couldn't out run the wind and rain. Eventually, it would catch up to her. Gracie dallied too long at Phoebe's home. She should have left at noon when they first began to discuss what needed to be done. When they received the message Alex was on his way to meet her then bring her home, she should have left. Once more, he disapproved of her actions. He would hurt her. Rain never hurt anyone. True, she would be wet and cold by the time her uncles' home came into view. Nothing would be broken. Nor would any part of her sport bruises.

The first thing she would do would be to order a warm bath and some hot mulled wine…some food too. Her stomach growled needing sustenance. She'd not eaten lunch. Now, the time would be well past the dinner hour by the time she reached home.

Hindsight told her she should have packed bread and cheese to nibble on when she rode. Hindsight could tell her a great deal. One of which was that she should have called the engagement off with Alex before she fell in love with him. Should have cancelled it the first time he hit her. What she didn't understand was how she could ever fall in love with a man who physically hurt her. He abused her in other ways too. It was easier to discount his insults than it was the injuries to her person.

An hour later the rain hit, poured in what seemed like never-ending fat, icy drops. The wind seemed to whip the huge thick drops sideways to pelt her face. She drew her cloak around her, lifting the hood to settle atop her hat. All she could think of was the nice hot bath waiting for her and that cup of mulled wine. It was those thoughts that kept her going.

Turning off the side road she travelled earlier, she took another route. No one would see or find her here. The road was canopied by thick branches. While the rain still fell the drops no longer pelted her from the side. Another blast of wind caught her broadside causing Gracie to nearly slip from her horse. She clutched at the mare's mane, holding her breath. If she huddled close to the long neck, the wind was not so bad. All around her the howling of the night sent chills down her spine. An animal dashed across the road in front of her. The mare reared. Desperately, she clung to whatever she could grab hold of. By the time she calmed the animal, she was breathing hard, terrified of the night. She might come to regret this decision to venture forth by herself.

A bolt of lightning ripped through the dense foliage, hitting a nearby tree, splintering the trunk into two parts. Once more her horse reared, whinnied in fright. A loud crack brought a tree branch down across the road even while smoke and fire rimmed the tree. The roar of thunder followed, bombing through the dark night. Franny sidestepped, whickering her displeasure. The horse pranced nervously.

"Easy, girl." She ran her hand along the horse's neck. Dismounting she led Franny to what she hoped was a sheltered spot where the canopy of branches was thick. The next gust of wind sent her pummeling backward, arms whirling to keep her feet on the ground. Frantic to remain on her feet, she clung to the nearest tree. Another branch fell to the ground. As she moved to avoid the limb, she was struck hard from behind.

Blackness. Secret darkness surrounded her, enveloped her mind as she felt as if she floated in a whirl of clouds. She saw Alex. Watched as he moved so very slowly through the hazy space. She should have been able to duck. Should have avoided the blow that sent her head snapping to the side then spinning. This time she didn't understand his anger. What, besides speaking her mind, had she done wrong? Every little thing she said or did displeased him.

Speeding through her foggy brain, it seemed she saw all the times he hit her or kicked her after he tossed her to the ground. She cowered, knees drawn to her chest in fright. This was all wrong, horribly wrong. She should be almost to Glasgow. Should be warm and dry. If she stayed at Phoebe's... No staying at her friend's home was not a possibility. He knew how to find her if she remained there. She needed to hide in a safe place.

Slowly, she pushed off the cold soggy ground. Her head pounded. With eyes so bleary she could barely see, she stood on wobbly knees. Gracie braced herself against an oak tree, leaning against the rough bark while she waited for the strength needed to put one foot in front of the other.

Turning, so her back was against the tree, she called out. "Franny!" she called out in a hoarse voice. There was no resounding nicker, no sound of the clop of hooves. The only noise was the thundering of the storm around her.

Her mare was gone. Fled home, no doubt. She supposed Franny had gone back to Phoebe's for a dry stall as well as fresh oats. As she faced the sky, she discovered the rain had nearly ceased. That didn't particularly matter as she was soaked through to the skin as well as covered in mud. She must look affright. What was she to do now? She couldn't walk all the way to Glasgow.

Heading down the old rutted road, she understood she needed to keep moving. She walked and walked for what seemed as if hours passed. Far in the distance a light shone from a large building. The brightness beckoned to her, inviting her to its warmth. She wrapped her arms around her shivering wet and cold body.

Warmth…Heat…

Someplace dry. Nothing would stop her.

Soggy mud sucked at her boots. Twice she fell to her hands. Twice she wiped mud from her fingers using her cloak. When she reached the building the chatter of people told her she would find help. At least she prayed someone would come to her aide. All her money was in her saddlebag. What did she have that she could pay the proprietor with so she could purchase a room for the night? Nothing. She had nothing. As far as anyone here knew, she was destitute, poor, perhaps even homeless.

Hoping to avoid a wealth of questions, she walked to the back entrance thinking that in her condition it was best not to walk through the front door lest someone toss her out. She knocked. Then knocked again, hoping she would be heard this time.

A large woman with ruddy cheeks and gray streaked hair opened the door. Her hands were placed on her hips. She appeared angry with her. After a moment of staring at her, the woman pointed her stubby finger at her. "Tilly. You're late. Look at you. You're a mess. Before you can see to any customers, you need a bath. Why did you seek this position if you mean to be so slovenly. You won't get top dollar." The woman grabbed her elbow then ushered her to a corner of the kitchen.

Tilly, was that her name? She had no recollection but it didn't sound right.

Gracie knew she was a mess but she wasn't Tilly. Couldn't be Tilly. She started to explain but was stopped short when the woman began to undress her. Batting at the woman's hands, she tried to protest the treatment. She whirled her, starting with the fastenings on the back of her clothing. When her gown dropped to the floor, the woman turned her attention to her corset then her chemise. Heat flooded her face.

"No!" She cried out her protest but her strangled words didn't stop the woman from devesting her of all her clothing.

"Get some hot water," the lady yelled to another girl in the room as she continued her assault on her mud-stained person. "This one needs a bath before she can go out in the main room. Even though she is filthy, she's a looker. Look at that hair of hers. Her bubbies…oh my, she's going to get top dollar. Just as we were told. This little lady will provide a handsome income in her spare time. Now, we'll just finish with this bath then we'll get you into clothing that is more appropriate for your position. Got just the dress to show off your sweet bubbies. They are a nice size. Fill a man's hands, they will. A man can cradle these while he rocks you."

The hot bath was welcome. The location was not. Her clothing was tossed in a pile of rags near the back door then tossed outside with the garbage. She was pushed into the tub then handed soap. With wide eyes, she watched the enfolding scene as if it was part of the dream she had earlier.

"Wash yourself or I'll have him do it." She sent her thumb toward a man who leered at her from the doorway.

The woman stood back, her hands once more on her hips. Another man stopped to stare. "She seems a bit missive for a lady of her persuasion, don't you think?" he asked as he studied her. "Nice bubbies though."

Gracie sunk into the tub with her arms crossed over her breasts. She thought to find a way out of this mess. As far as she could tell, there was none. Without her clothing she could hardly run out of the home. This was not her intention when she saw the lights of the inn.

"Hurry up, Lil missy. Don't have time to act shy, now do we? We all know why you are here." The woman winked at her. "You can keep part of the money. The rest goes to me. You understand. Why of course you do. This isn't the first place where you've been the star attraction, now is it?"

Nodding, she wondered what it was she was supposed to understand. Gracie did finish with the bath. She wound the bath sheet she was handed around her looking for the garments she'd been wearing when she stepped inside the establishment. As far as she could tell, she had nothing to cover herself with except the towel.

"You're wearing this. The cost will be docked from your first night's income. Too bad you didn't bring extra clothing." The woman held out a gown. "Get dressed. You're serving the wealthy gentleman in the far corner over there. Make sure you please him. All you need remember is that you have to do whatever he asks. If he has any complaints, you won't get your pay."

Whatever he asks?

Turning her back on the kitchen help, she dressed. Mortified, she looked at herself. The gown was too small for her. Her breasts were spilling from the corsage, the rosy hue of her nipples quite evident peeking from behind the fabric. When she tried to pull the gown higher the lace didn't budge. It was too short, the hem in front reaching barely past her knees.

The woman was waving her hands at her a look of displeasure on her ruddy face. "Go on now. Treat him real nice. Want to get a nice fat reward for your behavior. If you're a sweet one, you might get a bonus for the night. Pleasure him the way you know how to do. Rewards come with good behavior."

Baffled as well as frightened, Gracie picked up the tray on the bar. Discovering this well-to-do man in the room that was filled with farmers and tradesmen was not difficult. The man stood out. He was reading papers. His shoulders broad, his body tall. When he looked up, his golden eyes startled her, drew her to him. Those eyes seemed to pierce right through her, mesmerized her. She felt as if he could see all the way to her soul. No, in this dress he could most likely see all the way to her bellybutton…or lower. She felt a sudden urge to cover herself with her hands. She couldn't.

"Set the tray down. Join me, Tilly? I was promised you were well versed and could see to my needs. Is that true?" he asked as he lifted the lid on one of the dishes. Smelled then covered the plate again. "You can join me if you're hungry. I don't mind sharing."

She was hungry. Didn't want to act too eager. "I don't know?" she began trying to recall what the woman told her. Do whatever he asked. Please him and there will be rewards. She didn't know what that entailed. Nonetheless, she liked to please people.

"You must."

A quick look to the bar told her along with the sight of the man who watched her in the tub staring at her gave her good reason to remember what she was told. Whatever he wants. Quickly she sat. "I..." She ran her tongue along her parched lips, trying to think of something clever to say. She was supposed to be sweet. She recalled that.

"I?" he queried, his smile charming her to talk when she felt certain she should remain mute. "You were going to tell me something?"

Nodding, she blurted, "I don't think my name is Tilly." She suddenly realized she had no idea what her name was imagining that Tilly was good enough for now. Why didn't she know her name? She didn't know anything about herself. Dear God, she couldn't remember anything.

"Oh? What is your name?" He asked as he uncovered the food again. "I'll call you whatever you wish. Give me a name."

Blinking a few times, she decided not to answer. He didn't seem to mind. The man dished a plate of food for her. Her stomach grumbled loudly. His soft chuckle surprised her. She liked the sound of his gentle voice.

"My name is Fletcher. Unlike you, I do recall my name. Can remember most everything. Won't ever forget the moment I looked up from my work to see your huge green eyes staring at me. Eat up. When you're finished, we can take a bottle of wine upstairs, along with those pastries for later. I'm looking forward to getting to know you, Tilly."

Gracie didn't like being called by the wrong name. However, in this circumstance she wasn't going to tell him again she didn't know her name. Did she already tell him? So flustered, she couldn't recall anything. Obviously from what she'd seen so far, this Tilly person was supposed to be here doing this job. The job she wasn't certain about. She didn't comprehend her duties. The job that would give her a roof over her head at least until they found out she wasn't Tilly. What if Tilly showed up?

No, she wasn't going to think about that possibility. She was here now. No one would usurp her place where there was food as well as a roof over her head. She would be Tilly until she cocked up her toes, if that would give her shelter along with food.

For the next few minutes, she pushed the food she' wanted so badly to eat only a few seconds previous around on her plate. The hunger she felt earlier seemed to turn sour in her stomach. Her hand trembled so hard; she could not hold her fork still. What the devil was she doing? While she didn't know why, this felt wrong. She was doing something she shouldn't be doing.

"Not hungry?" His deep voice cut through all her musings. "We can take a plate up to my room in case you change your mind. Don't want you so hungry I can't see to our pleasure. What do you think? Should we bring food and wine with us."

"I was…hungry," she said in all honesty. "When I sat down here my belly was making loud rumbling noises. When I smelled the food, it ached. Now…well I look at you and I wonder what to expect. I don't know…I'm supposed to please you. Do whatever you ask."

"Now you're not hungry? As to what I expect from you is only a night of mutual gratification. I will see to your pleasure. You will see to mine." he told her a hint of amusement tinging his deep throaty voice. He stacked the papers he'd been reading then shuffled them into a leather case. Pointedly he stared at her, seeming to assess what he viewed in front of him. "Shall we go?"

"No, my stomach seems to be doing somersaults. What am I supposed to be doing?" she blurted the question to receive a hoot of male laughter. "I *dinna ken* what you want? What this mutual pleasure is." She furrowed her brows together concentrating on his peculiar words.

His smile touched her heart. The dimple in the corner of his mouth sent an urgent message to her fingers. She wanted to touch the small inviting crease. She yearned for him to kiss her. Placing a fingertip on her mouth, she thought with strange certainty that she had been kissed before. Now, she yearned to taste this man's kiss.

"Shall we go upstairs then discuss your duties? I would like to make certain all expectation are clear. Don't want either of us to flounder. If I mention something you disagree with then let me know so I won't have expectations to the contrary." He stood, holding out a hand to her. His fingers were long and lean, his nails manicured and clean.

At this instant, she felt hesitant. Weariness gripped her. A voice reverberated in her head telling her to be cautious. *Cautious of what?* Something wasn't right about his proposal. She held no knowledge of what that could be. "If you wish," she placed her hand in his knowing at this second her survival might rest on his approval of her. The feel of his fingers enclosing hers was strong and warm. He locked his fingers around hers, encapsulating them. "Will you explain my duties? It seems I should understand what it is you do expect." She sipped air when he squeezed after that her tongue drifted across her parched lips, leaving dampness behind.

For some reason he stared at her mouth, his grin warming her to the tips of her toes, tightening parts of her she didn't understand. "Well, Tilly, I was told you were experienced. Is that not true?" His hand settled at the small of her back drifting lower as if he explored, guiding her up the stairs. "Tell me now how many men you've slept with."

"My mind is a complete blank tonight. Cannot answer your question," she murmured as they stopped in front of a door. She didn't know if she slept with any man. He kissed the nape of her neck sending a myriad of sensation coursing through her. He brought out his key then unlocked the room. Holding the door open, he gestured for her to go inside. She stepped through. Felt a moment of fear when the door closed behind her.

"Sometimes a person can forget the rest of the world when their mind is blank. Tell me, Tilly, why do you sell your body? What brought you to this low place where you have to give yourself to men for coin?" he turned her so she faced him. The golden shimmer of his eyes bored into her asking for honesty.

She stopped abruptly. *Sell my body?* Training her gaze on the man, curious as well as confused to him, she tilted her head as she pondered his words. "I'm selling my body…to you? I don't understand what you are expecting me to do. Are you paying me to be in this room with you? I didn't ask you to do so."

Moving slightly away from her, she heard him curse softly. "Well, it's quite obvious to me as the words should also be to you. I'm buying the goods you're offering me. Your breasts, your hips, your female parts so I might receive pleasure. Though, I also intend to give as much pleasure as I receive." He ran a finger along the column of her neck then across the top of her bodice, dipping between the valley separating her breasts. "If you don't wish to remain with me, tell me. You are free to go."

Heat flamed inside her. She wished she could remember who she was. Wished she could recall some reason for her to be here. He seemed to honestly answer her questions. She was told to do what he asked. Threatened with the fact she would be sent away if she failed. "What does that entail? The selling of my body? You will have to be more explicate."

Once again Fletcher hooted with laughter, his golden eyes gleaming when the candlelight flashed across them. "I intend to be. You're a rare gem, Tilly." His fingers stopped at the necklace she wore. He picked it up, fingered it for a few moments. Turned it so he could look at the back. He grunted but said nothing for a few seconds. "That was a gift from a man? Perhaps your last protector? Have you fallen on hard times, Tilly? Did you displease the man. Did he kick you out, leaving you penniless?"

Curious to understand more, she tilted her head a bit so she could see the small piece of jewelry he held while she thought on what he told her. She had no recollection of the necklace or who might have given it to her. "I don't know what you mean?" She backed up a step as if placing some distance between them would help her recall what should be the simplest of memories. There was a man. She sensed that fact with her entire being.

He followed her bringing the piece of jewelry nearer to her, tugging her closer. She was looking at the heart from a difficult vantage point. "This says to Gracie from Alex. Does Gracie sound more like your name?"

Without thinking twice, she was nodding her head, eager to agree. "Yes…" then she lifted her shoulders. "I don't know. When you say the name, it sounds right. I don't remember."

"Should I call you Gracie then? Would you like that name better? I can call you anything you wish. Anything that makes you more comfortable. What do you say. Are you Gracie or are you not?"

She looked down, saw the rose of her nipples bared from his nimble fingers. "Oh!" she stepped back again. "You can see…" Her horrified gaze flew to meet his eyes. She tried to cover herself with her hands. He held her back, gently rubbing his thumbs along her wrists. He brought her hands to his lips, lightly kissed the knuckles.

"They are beautiful, your breasts. Is the rest of you as gorgeous? I'd like to see all of you. Would you let me, Gracie? Let me look at you without this gown between you and my eyes." After unfastening his shirt, he sat down on the bed. Poured them both a glass of wine.

Speaking to him about her person was far beyond anything she could understand. Shaking her head, she wondered just how to proceed with that question. "I've no idea. I don't think I'd like to wear nothing at all when you are near me. The man downstairs watched me take a bath. I didn't like him staring at me. I tried to cover myself with the rag they gave me. Even though I was bathing I felt dirty, used. The feeling wasn't good."

"You've never looked at yourself in a mirror? Would you help me remove my boots? I believe it's time we both got more comfortable. Don't you think?"

"Comfortable?" Gracie didn't think she'd ever feel relaxed again. Her body burned in places she never thought about before. Didn't know why that was happening. She felt the melting of her legs when he touched her. This was so confusing, beyond her meager understanding.

"Boots?" he asked smiling once more revealing the tiny dimple she wished to explore thoroughly. With that random thought, once more, she believed she was trespassing on forbidden ground.

Suddenly, she realized he spoke to her, asked her a question. "Oh! Yes, of course, I'll help." She turned so her back was to him. Heard the soft chuckle from behind her. Felt his hands on her hips. After that, he explored her bottom, holding her, squeezing gently. She had the vague thought that she'd done this before, taken a man's boots from his feet. Couldn't remember exactly when or with who. With a few deft tugs, the boots were lying on the floor. She turned to face the man wondering what he would do or say next. So far, her mind was spinning.

He stretched out on the bed, patting the place beside him. His shirt hung unfastened from his shoulders baring a broad chest, heavily furred with dark black hair. "I'd like you to join me on the bed. We can explore your duties over a glass of wine. What do you think? Would you enjoy a glass of wine with me? Mayhap you have duties for me to perform."

Nodding, she realized she would partake of a glass. If nothing else it might relieve some of her strained nerves. When she stopped to ponder this evening's events, she didn't know what it was all about.

One glass. No more. Don't want you foxed. My woman should never get drunk. It's not ladylike.

Startled by the memory, Gracie looked at him. The words didn't come from Fletcher. They were in her head though, clouding her muddled brain further. Said by a deep male voice a voice that warned her. She felt the kick to her ribs as if it happened right now.

Fletcher spoke again, his tone held a wealth of concern. "Gracie, I'd like you to be comfortable. Come sit. Tell me what's on your mind. Did you remember something? That would be good. If you recall who you are, would you enlighten me?" Once again, he patted the spot beside him encouraging her to come to him.

He sounded so sincere, so sweet and kind. She wished to give to him whatever he asked of her. Something inside her rebelled at sitting on a bed with a man, not just this man but any man. Still, she felt compelled to do as he asked. She'd been told to do everything he requested. How could sitting on a bed hurt her? It was a question she had no answer for. "Imagine that sitting on the bed might not be that bad." Deep in the dark recesses of her brain, she came to the conclusion she'd never sat on a bed with a man. "I don't think I've done this before." Hesitantly, she plopped down beside him, curling her legs beneath her as she turned toward him.

After sitting down, she held herself aloof as well as stiffly away from the man. He handed her the glass of wine he poured earlier. "Drink up. Shall we go over some of your duties?" His voice was pleasant yet held an edge she didn't wish to explore. Perhaps he wished she would sit closer.

"Duties. Yes. I imagine I should know what they are." She sipped. The wine was delicious. It seemed to warm her empty stomach. She sipped again letting the heady brew heat her body all the way to the tips of her toes. "Need to know my duties," she murmured.

"First…you should kiss me."

Kiss the man…hmmm…she recalled kisses from another man. They were warm and sweet. She turned to liquid. After that she recalled pain. Where the thought came from, she had no idea. She dismissed the thought in favor of the first ones. "I like kissing. Imagine I can do that."

"Second. You should undress me."

The wine she swallowed sputtered from her mouth sending a cascade of droplets on his white shirt. Quickly, she used the hem of her dress to swipe at the droplets of wine. "Undress? As in make you naked?" There were no memories surfacing here. Gracie stopped what she was doing. "I'd like to see you naked." She giggled at the thought. He touched her smiling lips with a fingertip. Her tongue swept across her mouth as if following the path his finger traveled.

"As I would like to look upon you wearing nothing at all." His voice resonated with sincerity.

"I can't do that. Mother would roll over in her gra…" Where did that come from? Mother? Of course, she had a mother as well as a father. Once again that nagging voice inside her mind, screamed at her. Though she wasn't at all certain what it was telling her.

"You remembered something? Tell me."

"No, just a random thought about a mother and father I don't remember but know I must have them somewhere. Must have heard something like that before. Don't know where though." After she drank more wine, he refilled the glass.

"Third."

"There is a third job? That's a lot of duties."

~ * ~

"I'm just getting started, Gracie." Fletcher liked her name. "There will be more once we've accomplished the first ones. You will enjoy what we do together."

She was a curious piece of baggage, one moment innocent the next strangely brazen. This lass was advertised by the lady who owned this establishment as a well-seasoned whore. He would gamble his life savings that she wasn't. He would also gamble that she might well be innocent, a virgin. He wondered if at some point he should stop this seduction.

"How many can I have? Glasses?" she asked as she finished the glass of wine. Not blinking an eye, she spoke, "I'm not supposed to get foxed."

"Says who? The lady who sent you to me? Someone else? As far as I'm concerned as long as you can perform all your duties, I don't give a damn how much you drink. As much as you would like is my answer." He took the glass from her before setting it on the nearby table. "For now, we're going to start with a kiss. Is that alright with you? Am I wrong? Didn't you tell me you liked kisses? If you do this right, I'll pour you more wine."

"What if I don't?"

He lifted his shoulders in a decided shrug, "Well, then…I'll pour you more if you ask. Now, kiss me, Gracie."

She blinked a few times seeming to mull his words over in her agile female mind. "I did say that. Though I don't *ken* where those words came from. Cannot recall a man kissing me. Something inside me is screaming that one has." She heaved a long dramatic sigh, "I'd like to remember how to kiss. Don't have the foggiest of ideas."

Somewhere, somehow, she lost her identity. Either that or this was an elaborate ploy, one she would soon fail at. Clear to him now, he didn't believe she was Tilly, the experienced woman of the evening who was supposed to see to his needs tonight. This little piece of fluff was here in that woman's stead. This Gracie was beautiful. He wouldn't change this scene for another woman. Seeing how far she would carry the ruse would be fun.

"Like for you to remember me better than the last man who kissed you." He grinned as her brows creased together in concentration. "Now, you are to kiss me. I'm waiting patiently." He paused watching her carefully.

"Would rather you kissed me," she told him sounding sincere as she swept that sweet tongue of hers across her plump bottom lip. "Don't believe I've ever kissed a man unless he was kissing me first. How do I start?"

"No, we'll do this my way. Come here." He took her wrists then brought them so they were placed on his shoulder. Her mouth was temptingly close to his. Her breasts pressed against his chest. "Go ahead. Let your instincts take over."

He heard the soft groan. Wasn't at all certain if that was a good or bad sign. Her lips brushed his, the softness of her breasts pushed more thoroughly against his chest. He ran his hands along her back while she moved away from him seeming to think what she did was actually a real kiss.

When their gazes clashed, her eyes were a brilliant soft shade of green, mossy green. "That was hardly a kiss, Gracie," he said surprised at the gruffness of his voice. "You can do better. Try harder." Inwardly, he laughed, content with her eager innocence. Willing to take as much time with her initiation into love.

"How?" she sat back on her legs staring at him as if he lost his mind. Her hands rested on his chest then seemed to explore the expanse. It was a distraction he liked. He wanted to feel those fingers on other parts of his body.

"The devil," he said as he pulled her closer his hand behind her head bringing her against him. "Open for me. I'll show you everything you need to know. I promise you will enjoy yourself. Let me show you how kisses will be between us." His fingers wound into her hair, drawing her ever closer. So close, he caught the scent of a sweetly aroused woman.

Her lips against his were warm and soft, pliant as well as slightly damp. He touched his tongue upon her sealed mouth, ran the tip along the seam, hoping she would come to understand that which he wanted. The tiny mewl softly emanating from the back of her throat pleased him. The sweet sound wasn't enough. Once more, he pushed against her lips, parting them slightly, touching the smoothness of her teeth, the sensitive inside of her mouth.

"Oh!" came a startled response. Her breasts heaved against his chest. He felt the sudden rapid beat of her heart. The tips of her fingers scraped against his flesh. Heat surged to his loins. His body hardened with a simple need she created

Taking advantage, he pressed forward slipping inside the torrid heat of her mouth, tasting the sweet wine she drank earlier, savoring the essence of her. She seemed to understand, touched her tongue to his. Again, she purred softly from the back of her throat. Her fingers clenched against his chest, winding into his hair, tugging, moving as if she couldn't contain herself. Continuing the kiss, he found she followed his movements, touching her tongue inside his mouth, along his teeth finally to search farther inside. He sucked, nipped then flirted with what she presented him. He nibbled on her lower lip then placed tender kisses across her mouth. He was both gentle then hard.

Gracie ran her hands across his chest while their lips continued to collide in heated fashion against each other. Her palms fluttered hesitantly across his hardened nipples once then twice then a third time. She moved her hands to his shoulders, sliding the sharpness of her nails along the breadth of him, pushing at his open shirt as if she needed to feel more of him.

She pulled away, staring at him, her eyes slightly dazed. Her tongue danced across her bottom lip as if to sooth. "Was that better? Should I try again. I do wish to please you, Fletcher. It's my job to give you everything you ask for."

If it was any better, he would expire with the pleasure her tentative sexual play created. All he could do at the moment was nod because her soft fingertips were following the path of his hair to his waist band. He grew, swelled as heat flared pushing its way to his groin. She looked at him, questions in the soft green of her eyes. While she ran her fingers along the flesh just above his buckskins, he toyed with the ribbons that held her bodice together, deftly pulling them one at a time from the eyelets. Firsthand knowledge of her beautiful breasts was his ultimate goal. As a patient man, he could take his time, revel in the sweet unveiling. After all, she was his for the night.

Against his flesh her hand moved with hesitation, lingering on sensitive spots he didn't believe she knew anything about. When her fingers crept across his belly, his skin retracted. "You can look if you like? Do you wish to uncover me? Then do so," he told her barely able to keep the throaty need from the timbre of his voice or the chuckle at her curiosity. Feeling her tiny fingers wrap around him would be heaven of her making.

When next she looked at him her eyes were wide pools of green. "Oh, I could never do that," she paused smiling at him as she turned her head slightly. "Unless doing so is a duty. If it's a listed duty then I imagine I must uncover you." It seemed she flirted with him, teased with her statement.

"Making it a duty as of this second. Nonetheless, you need to choose. Before the evening is over, you will see all of me…when is the only question. Do you wish to see that which makes me so very different from you, now or later?" As far as he was concerned the sooner the better.

"I will?" Her well-manicured fingers were toying with the fastenings of his britches even while she questioned the validity of his statement. "I will see that part of you?" She caught her bottom lip beneath her teeth. "Like the statues in Italy? You're not David, are you?"

Hardly.

Her statement shocked him. She was no seasoned whore. Perhaps a rich man's plaything but no whore. "Go on…" he encouraged even while he slipped the last ribbon from its holder. Without a chemise to hinder his efforts, her breasts spilled into his hands. He held the rounded globes, tested their weight along with the softness. They were lush, so creamy, tipped with rose colored buds.

She gasped as her gaze shot to him. He was smiling at her, caressing the rosy tips while she swallowed, her lips still damp from his ardent attention. "Is that something you should be doing? I don't know what to think. It's not my duty?"

"No, this is my duty. Do you like what you're feeling? The way I make you feel when I touch you here?" She was too damn innocent for a whore. Again, he wondered if this was just a well-practiced act. Her words about seeing statues in Italy another ruse to lull him.

"*Aye.*" As if to keep from making eye contact, she bent her head, still playing with the fastenings to his pants. Suddenly he was free, standing at attention as she stared at him, her eyes wide. As if hungry to taste him, she licked her lips. Her gaze darted to meet his eyes. Inside the depth of those green circles, he read a wealth of things, discovery, curiosity, excitement and so much more as her expression changed.

He wanted to laugh at the surprise in her eyes. Without being told or asked, her fingers wrapped around him. He bucked at the sudden surge of heat to his loins. Her hands fell away, her eyes wider with what appeared to be concern.

She was a delight. His delight.

"Go ahead touch," he murmured as he pushed the fabric of her gown from her shoulders then down her arms. "You are lovely. Do you like what you see? I know I'm a man well pleased with the woman who is giving herself to me this night." She possessed marvelous breasts, lush, creamy. He needed to suckle, to taste. So far, he hadn't kissed her enough. Hadn't filled himself until sated with her sweet flavor. For these few minutes, all he needed was to stare at her, to soak in her beauty.

One more time her fingers curled around his penis, moving instinctively as if she knew what would please him. Perhaps she did. While she gave ardent attention to him, he lifted her, removing her gown from her legs then kicking the fabric to the floor. She would wear nothing for the rest of the night. He would hold her, find the magic between them. Relishing every part of her was his goal.

In all her glory she was naked, her breasts swaying slightly with each breath of air she inhaled. Her hands rose to cover herself. She didn't know where to put them. He grinned at her look of horror. Her waist was tiny, her hips flaring wide, ripe for holding. Hourglass came to his mind. Her woman's mound was gloriously dark and golden touched with flames. Almost the color of her hair. He wanted to be just as naked. In all his dalliances, he'd never seen a woman that struck him with as much need than this one. From the moment he saw her, he wanted her in his bed. Who was she? Where did she come from? He was positive she wasn't Tilly, that Gracie was indeed her name.

He lifted his hips to give aide. "Pull my buckskins off. When you do, we can enjoy each other much more thoroughly." She did. Over her shoulder she carelessly, as if she'd done the same a thousand times, tossed them to the floor. He didn't think he could wait one more second to possess her. Something stopped him from surging inside her heated core. The thought that possibly her innate shyness was no game. Her lost memory might not be a ruse. He needed to make this right for her. If she was a seasoned whore, it wouldn't make a difference if he proceeded slowly though it was killing him.

She is innocent.

A virgin. A virgin whore.

That might or might not be true. Regardless of anything she did or did not tell him, he didn't wish to hurt her. Fletcher knew in that moment tonight would not be his last sexual encounter with this woman. One night would never be enough for him. Tomorrow, he would take her home with him, keep her in the grounds keeper's cottage which stood empty. He wasn't at all ready for the world to see her or his brothers for that matter. He sure as hell wasn't ready to let her go after one night with her.

"Has a man ever entered your body?" he asked wondering what type of answer he would receive. One hand rested on the gentle curve of her hip, his thumb gently caressing the flatness of her belly. The other explored the ladder of her ribs. He settled himself exactly where he wanted to be.

Her legs were spread wide. He was between them, looking at her. "Bend your knees, sweetheart. I want to see all of you." He pushed her thighs farther apart, kissing her belly, wishing he dared go lower. Tasting the embodiment of her womanhood would come later. Frightening her was not part of his plan for the evening.

She wet her lips again. Her body arching against his with every secret touch of his hands. "I…I don't think so," her murmur was followed by a soft mewl of pleasure when his mouth closed over one breast, sucked and laved then sucked until the nipple was elongated, damp and shiny from his attention. His teeth flirted with the pinnacle until it was hard and longer still. He pulled back to look at his handiwork. The nipple was perfect. He blew watching the tip harden even more.

Her doubts surrounding who she was spurred him to treat her as the virgin he was beginning to believe she was. Perhaps in time she would regal him with the details that led to this event. He did have a driving need to understand why she found herself in this position though he was heartily glad she was. Pleased she fell so neatly into his hands. Happy that she was so willing to give herself to him. Ah, he would have to reward her very well. As it was now, she was his delight. He would accept the gift of her maidenhead wholeheartedly.

If the thin membrane wasn't there, he didn't care. He needed to experience all that Gracie was, all that she could be in his arms.

His kisses delved lower, across her belly, between her thighs, behind her knees. He enjoyed the arching of her body as he left no part of her untouched. With loving attention, one more time he bathed her toes with kisses, dallying, nipping enjoying the way her body coiled and arched with each new and different caress. He fondled her, charmed and enticed her to his will. He kissed her then he kissed her again, retracing the earlier path until she heaved and moaned, clasped him with her sharp little nails.

Moving slowly upward, relishing the feel of her soft curves, he covered her mouth with his, kissing, playing, flirting with her. He kissed her long and deep, hard and fast. Her hums of pleasure excited him. He was eager to feel her velvet sheathe encase him. She created a blazing inferno within his body, one he would never forget. Her fingers wound into his hair, tugging him closer. She was a burning need in his soul.

He was swollen and hard, needing relief. His restraint amazed him. His fingers delved into the cleft between her thighs. Hot and wet, her pleasure soaked his fingers, honey raining down as he moved within her core. He found the tiny jewel that would bring her so much pleasure she would cry out. Once that happened, he would ease himself inside her sultry heat. Unhurriedly, he would take his time, search out all her secrets. Uncover everything about her until he had no questions in his mind as to who she was.

The scent of her aroused and inflamed all his senses. Resting on his forearms, he watched as her body responded to the urgings of his nimble fingers. "Open your eyes, Gracie. I want to see the expression when you reach that sainted peak of ecstasy you're fast approaching. Want to watch you when I pleasure you. Are you happy, *lass*?" If she asked him to cease, he didn't know how he would ever stop.

"Ecstasy? Happy? Don't know. Yes…" she whimpered softly as her body vibrated with the sensual need he composed. She tensed, her tiny bottom rising off the bed. Her heels dug into the mattress. Her fingers biting into his shoulder. She cried out, responding with cries and moans. She pulsed and thrummed with her need. "Fletcher…please… Fletcher!" She cried. A broken sound caught in the back of her throat.

"I'm coming inside you now." He didn't want to inform her that if she was the innocent he thought her to be, this would hurt her. He would go easy. Move as slowly as possible. The tip of his member pressed against her softness. She was so small he didn't know how he would enter her without hurting her even though her wet, humid heat sent lightening striking his body. She was tight and hot and wet with her woman's nectar as he slowly sunk inside her. She was ready for him. Creeping forward as her core kissed the length of him still pulsing with the building climax.

Her maidenhead loomed upon him. He touched the sign of her virtue, groaned understanding this would cause pain. A moment of guilt swept him. He was taking something from her she didn't understand. While she was willing, she had no idea the gift she bestowed upon him. Of course, she understood. Her mother would have told her not to give herself to a man. She was in an establishment where she agreed to do whatever he said, had agreed to the giving of herself for money. In this pursuit of both their pleasure, he would not feel guilty. This would not sway him. Closing his eyes, waiting for the cry this time that would signal pain not pleasure, he thrust through the shield that would no longer be hers to give.

The little cry of pain surprised as well as pleased him. She wasn't sobbing. So perhaps he didn't hurt her too much. She clung to him. Held onto him as if she didn't wish him to leave her. Her nails bit into his shoulders.

He froze inside her, enjoying the rhythmic pulsing of her body kissing the length of him, sucking him deeper into the tightness of her. "You be alright, *lass*?" he asked his voice soft as he hung on steadfastly refusing to cause further pain. He pushed damp hair from her forehead, from her eyes, wishing to see into the depth of her soul.

"Didn't know it would hurt so. You didn't tell me." Her voice as well as her words held a wealth of accusations.

"Frightening you was not part of the plan. Didn't know I was about to invade virgin territory. You never told me that you were untried in the ways of sex. If you had done so, we could have talked about what was going to happen." He tried to assuage his guilt. She did tell him because she didn't know if she'd done this before. Found the notion far from adaptable since he was pleased, he was her first dalliance into carnal pleasures. For his benefit, he stated one more time, "You could have informed me."

Lightly, she bit his shoulder. "I didn't know. While I remembered kissing, I don't recall doing anything like this. Do you think a person could forget this. You are still inside me, Fletcher."

Yes, he was. He liked being within her body so very much. "Would like to finish then we can have more wine or talk of what you might be remembering. You can tell me how you came to the Sliver Nickel." Hesitantly, he moved within her, testing tender territory. He groaned when her hot body caressed him again and again. When she slowly arched against him, pressing all of herself higher. He found the tiny pearl hidden deep in her cleft, massaged until once again she was spinning out of control.

His thrusts grew harder and faster while she seemed to spiral with him. He knew the moment her climax took her even higher. He spewed his seed deep within her sultry heat. This was splendid. He collapsed atop her, feeling the pinnacles of her breasts against his chest, the whisper of each breath. The sound of her steady heartbeat caressed his senses.

When he braced himself above her, Gracie's eyes were closed. With her first as well as her second climax, he watched her eyes turn darker then darker still. Her creamy white skin was flushed with the heat of their encounter a soft rose color. Lightly, he traced her collarbone then forged a path along the sleek column of her neck, lower to touch upon the tips of her breasts. He wanted to taste all of her again.

"A penny for your thoughts, sweet one." He thought it would be wonderful to learn more about this woman. Rolling off her, Fletcher brought her so her head rested on his chest. Her small white hand splayed across his dark chest. "Tell me what you are thinking. I would know."

Her breath whispered, fluttered across him. She turned to look at him, "Is that a command or a duty?" she asked as she trailed her finger along his chest following the path of his dark hair to his belly then lower before she hesitated.

"Neither." What he wanted was her to remember who she was as well as why she sold herself to him. It didn't seem as if she did. He couldn't command the truth or her feelings.

She didn't move her hand farther. He thought he would like it if she was to be so bold. Pushing against him, she moved away, the tips of her breasts, touching barely on him. She smiled at him. Her grin broad as well as endearing. Her eyes shining.

"I enjoyed what we did if that is what you ask. I don't believe I've ever done that before," she began slowly as she settled against him again, playing with the hair on his chest. "If it suits you, I would do it again."

"That thought leaves this man well pleased. Later, after you have a bite to eat, mayhap another glass of wine. Would you like that?" He meant to ignore the fact that when he thrust through her maidenhead, he knew she'd never given herself to anyone before him.

"I am thirsty."

Fletcher sat up, pulling the sheets with him. She tried to cling to them, was thwarted. Candlelight danced across her breasts casting a golden glow. He didn't think he would ever grow tired of looking at her body. "A glass of wine for my sweet *lass*," he told her as he handed her the crystal. "In order to partake, you will have to sit."

The blush sweeping to her heated cheeks was endearing. She did sit, trying to keep the sheets covering her. Amused, he kept his chuckle to himself. Finally, she gave up. Her breasts moved invitingly under his perusal, the tips hardening as if beckoning to him. She wore nothing above the waist, below only the sheet. Sipping on the wine, the sight of her was branded in his head. He handed her a pastry then selected one for himself. Leaning against the headboard, he closed his eyes. Breathing deeply, he thought about what would happen in the near future.

"We will leave early in the morning. I wish to be at my home by noon." He was chewing thoughtfully waiting for her to answer.

"I am leaving with you?" she asked sounding confused. "Why would you do that. I've this notion I should be somewhere. Don't know where though. All I recall is the blinding headache when I awoke down the road. The rain was a fine mist but I was soaked through to my skin. All I knew was that I needed a roof over my head. The frigid night air seeped through my clothing. When I saw the building, I decided to go in through the back door. The lady who grabbed me told me I was late. She stripped me then set me in the bath to wash off all the mud. After that, when I was dressed, she sent me to you." She cast him a wan smile. "Besides what happened here, that's all I know about my life."

"Until you recall where that somewhere is, I intend to keep you with me. Don't want anything untoward to happen to you." Before she could ask, he spoke again. "Think of it as your duty to remain with me. For the sake of your safety, you cannot stay here."

"Why?"

"You know why. Do you wish to service every man the lady of this fine establishment tells you too? I doubt if you would enjoy the job."

The thought of her with another man as she was with him turned his stomach sour. For the time being, she was his. No other man was going to touch Gracie. He would take care of this lovely woman.

She blanched at his words. "I had not thought of that. How can I go with you? Won't my presence cause you trouble? What if I've done something wrong? I *ken* nothing about my past."

Perhaps it would. Maybe he would have to think about all the explanations he would have to make to his family. His brothers would take issue with her presence whether in his home or the cottage. Though the only one who hadn't done something equally outrageous was his youngest brother, Gordan. Gordan would laugh then tell him he was becoming just like his older brothers.

Duncan created a scandal when he couldn't leave the woman who now was his wife, alone. He carried her from a ballroom filled with people to his bedchamber. Evan hit a student who attacked him after discovering the young man making love to another student in a school closet. Evan refused to apologize. After that he escorted a woman around town who he kept in his home. They both had their reasons.

There was nothing he could do his brother's had not preceded him in accomplishing. While they might lecture him, he didn't have to listen. He would house her in the ground keeper's cottage, not his home. He would not install her in his bed as Evan did his. Openly, she would be his mistress. He would not deny himself of her sweet charms.

Fletcher thought about all the things he would have to consider. She didn't remember who she was. He would have to make certain she was taken care if he ever had to leave. There were the occasional trips to London to consider. Other than that, he was usually home for extended periods of time. Turning to her he spoke softly, realizing she might have worries as well as fears. "I will handle whatever issues might arise. No need for you to concern yourself." He told her as his gaze roamed across her breasts once more.

Gracie seemed to bristle at his words. Her beautiful rounded globes moving with her annoyance. He wondered what he said to cause the agitation he read in her eyes along with her body. Getting to know this woman would be his delight.

"Need to concern my pretty little head!" She punched him on the chest, clearly angry with his words. Her eyes flashed, moving to a darker shade. "I don't like thinking all I am is a bit of fluff for your use..." She fell off for a moment, clearly confused. When she addressed him again, "I think I've told someone that before. Those words seem vastly familiar. A person who never treated me as anything more than a decoration for his arm." She seemed to puzzle over her statement.

This was an opening he longed for. Her recalling her life could be as an advantage or a disadvantage. He had no idea her background. Her speech, her attitude about life, all spoke of a woman gently bred. That was true until she allowed him to bed her without a moment's concern. "You remembered something?" He meant to probe until she could tell him her full name as well as where she belonged. Perhaps he didn't want to know details. If he learned more about her, he might not be able to do whatever pleased the two of them. If she had people who would take issue with this fledgling relationship of theirs, he would have to temper his actions, act more the gentleman than the besotted fool.

Blinking a few times then taking a long hearty drink, she set the glass on the table beside her. "No, it's just a feeling I had, a thought rattling around in my haze filled brain. I feel as if a fog surrounds all that I am. Someone else said those words to me. Don't remember who or why. The way they spoke those words was degrading. I've a healthy mind. Can worry or make a decision that please me or not. Don't need a man to decide for me what is right or wrong. I think that is what he tried to do."

Fletcher liked the indignation he heard in her tone. What he didn't like was the thought there was another man out there waiting for her. One who seemed to have abused her, both mind as well as body. After she was naked, he didn't miss the bruised ribs. Couldn't overlook the slight flinch when he caressed one of the dark colored places on her body. She deserved better than what she'd received at the hands of this man.

"Who hurt you?" he blurted not intending to give away this knowledge he had of her past life. "I would confront the man. Clearly there has been a man in your life. Someone who has taken advantage of you." He was heartily glad, though, that the man had not taken the innocence she seemed eager to give to him.

Shaking her head, she drank of the wine once more before she addressed him with a wobble in her voice. "A man in my life? Why would you think that? I don't recall…" She paused, tugging at a few of the tangles in her hair. "I suppose so."

"From your thoughts. One, about kissing, two about what you just said. I believe you've had a bruised or broken rib. Only a man…" he stopped to think. There were a hundred different ways her ribs could have been hurt. "I believe a man did that to you. Hit you hard enough to leave a bruise.

It seemed his Gracie needed a change of subject. When she spoke after a lengthy period of silence, "Tell me more about where you are going to take me. Will I be pleased? I wish I could remember who I am."

Despite the guilt sweeping through him, drowning him, he didn't wish her to remember who she was any time soon. She nestled next to him, her refilled wine glass in her hand. Her beautiful face was flushed both from the wine as well as her slight embarrassment. The movement caused some of the wine to spill onto her. He grinned, needing as he also wished for the manner of conversation to take on a different tenor. Placing her wine glass back on the table, he touched one of the drops of burgundy with his tongue. At the small contact, she sipped air. He licked again, grazing soft flesh with his teeth.

This time, Gracie inhaled a sweeping gasp of air when his tongue curled then flicked across the tight crest of her breast. He drank dreamily on another drop. Licked with carefree abandon on the drops that slid along her belly. Followed the red trail down to her woman's mound. The little drone of pleasure that floated through the air gave him good reason to continue. Her fingers wound into his hair.

When he reached the soft petals of feminine flesh between her thighs, they were hot and wet with her honey, her nectar flowed sweet and true. She moved her legs apart as he settled between her thighs, licking, tasting her essence everything that she was. When she began to arch and heave, he thrust inside her, taking his time, moving quickly then slowly. Holding back his release until he felt the vibrations of her ecstasy along his shaft. When they finished, both sated she lay in his arms. He felt the slow movement of her lashes against his chest, the whisper of her breath, the beat of her heart as the cadence slowed. No, he wouldn't be pleased to lose her to her memory anytime soon.

This beautiful woman with no recollection to speak of, slept in his arms. Nothing felt better at that moment. He would clear the path for her. If Duncan wouldn't allow her to stay at the cottage, he would move her into his home. Betsy lived with Evan before the two lovers wed. Not one of his brothers cried foul at that time. There was little to no objection to that as far as he knew. Within a short time, they wed. Betsy was pregnant with Evan's child. She lost their first baby in a tragic miscommunication.

If Gracie became pregnant, he would do the same. He would marry her. His breath caught in the back of his throat. The thought was a heady one, one he'd never considered before.

Marriage…

She didn't know who she was. There was another man in her life. Who the hell was it? He meant to discover that fact as soon as possible.

~ * ~

Phoebe paced with quick sure strides in the drawing room of the twin's home, Gracie's uncles, the Kenworthys. To her dismay they didn't seem too nervous about their niece's disappearance. They continued to tell her she would show up in good time. Her horse came back riderless, seemingly spooked. The raging tempest the night before might have terrified the animal. The little mare might have thrown Gracie. Phoebe followed the roads they agreed on into town the next afternoon. There was no sign of her. No proof she traveled the same path.

When Alexander reached the house in the morning, Phoebe told him Gracie was no longer in residence. Told the odious man her friend left to avoid him. She no longer wanted anything to do with Alexander. For all she knew, Gracie might have gone to Paris. Alexander cursed. He shook his fist at her, swearing that she would regret hiding his fiancée. Thankfully, the man was bright enough to know he didn't dare hit her. While her father was a duke, Gracie's father was a well-known judge in Glasgow.

She wasn't smitten with him as Gracie was. If he hit her, she would hold him accountable. First, she would go to her father then the judge. He would never get away with abuse to her person. After Phoebe was certain Alex headed back into Glasgow, she collected a few items along with her driver then headed into the city to search out her friend.

Once at the front door of the Kenworthy's she used the gold plaited lion knocker to summon the butler or the uncles. She didn't care.

Their under butler ushered her into the drawing room to wait for Jason and Jasper. She sat down on a chair to stare into the flames leaping in the huge fireplace. The minutes ticked by slowly. She was certain no one gave the uncles the message they had a guest. When they entered the room, she jumped to attention prepared to blast her cannons at these two men.

The twins were gentle giants. They were tall, broad of shoulder. Both had eyes of the softest blue color that reminded her of a sunny summer morning just after the fog evaporated from the dew kissed ground.

"What has you in such a dither?" Jason asked as he stepped closer to her.

"Do have a seat," Jasper encouraged.

She sat again, wishing the two men weren't such sweethearts. Gracie came to them several times asking for advice. Much to her chagrin the men didn't believe that a man, the viscount, would physically abuse her. The third black eye had them beginning to change their mind. When Gracie came to them with the broken rib, they then encouraged her to cry off the engagement.

"A dither? A dither! You two are such fools. I can't believe your niece thought to come to you for help. The two of you are useless. After heading here…to this house…Gracie has disappeared and the two of you sit on your hands as if she will turn up if you clap your hands or snap your fingers. We've got to find her! Before something terrible happens to her, we have to find her. Before the viscount discovers where she is, we have to protect her. Oh," Phoebe was nearly shouting as she voiced her anger to the two men. After that she was ringing her hands then moaning. "I think something bad has already happened to her. We are too late."

The two brothers looked at each other then back to her. There was question as well as some concern in their eyes. "Might I point out she has disappeared before," Jason reminded her smoothly.

The argument was disconcerting but the words wouldn't keep her from her goal. "Only when Alexander hit her or belittled her," Phoebe said, her hands resting on her hips. She didn't think she could get angrier with these two men who seemed to take life at a snail's pace. She didn't know how to spur them to action. A fireplace poker in the rear might do the trick since her concern didn't have a noticeable effect on them.

"This time?" One of Jasper's red eyebrows lifted toward the ceiling seeming to speculate and perhaps consider a search. "He was not with her. You were when she left. Then you should *ken* what she planned."

"Finally, a few words that make sense. Of course, I knew her plans. As I told you the moment you walked into the drawing room, Gracie was headed here. She should have been here sometime around midnight last night. She should be just rising to face a new day, rested as well as relaxed." The air she tugged into her lungs was tobacco scented. She coughed, waving her hand in front of her face. "Would the two of you put those horrid cigars out!" She was yelling again, frustrated as well as annoyed by their lack of concern. Phoebe didn't know how to create some energy and concern into these two.

"Sorry," they mentioned in unison, quickly stuffing the offending articles into the ash trays then handing them to the servant who entered with a tray of sweet confections and tea. "Something to eat?"

"You should be sorry," Phoebe said indignation in her speech. She sniffed the air which was now scented with fresh pastries. "Those things will kill you. Now, back to Gracie. I'm worried about her. It's not like her to disappear even though you did mention she did that once before. The thing of it was, that time I knew where she was. She sent a message as soon as she reached her destination. So, for me, she didn't vanish without a trace. She had to get away from the viscount to save her life. She was deathly afraid he might kill her, his anger was so intense."

"This time?" Jasper asked as he arranged the tea cups then poured the hot brew into them.

"This time I was also privy to her intentions. As I told you, she was coming here for protection. I haven't heard from her. Gracie's horse returned to my stable *sans* its rider. We have to look for her." She was losing patience. "Can't you employ a detective to search for her. Something bad could have happened to her. Her horse came back to the stable riderless. The storm last night was fierce. Gracie could be wandering through the countryside." After repeating herself, she sat down with a plop in front of the tea. She was hungry, having raced from her country estate as soon as she was certain the viscount wouldn't discover her destination.

His hands behind his back, Jason rocked back on his heels. Beneath his breath, he grumbled a bit as if annoyed. "Fine idea. Just fine. I'll get on with it after we have tea. No," He placed a finger on his chin, "I'll send Bolton after the detective I've used before to search for Gracie. The time when you allowed me to make a fool of myself. The time when you knew she was in Paris getting a new wardrobe. That time, do you recall the situation?"

Phoebe had the good sense to blush. She felt heat rise from the tops of her breasts to sting her cheeks with warmth. "I promised not to tell a soul what she was about, lest Alexander discover her whereabouts then go after her. She actually wasn't there to enhance her wardrobe. She was there to heal the wounds he inflicted." The twins were right. Gracie should have called the engagement off the first time he hit her, the first time he belittled her with hateful words. Gracie did not. Now, she was missing, very truly missing.

She watched as Jasper sent the men.

"Will you stay for dinner?" Jasper asked as he spied her over the rim of her tea cup. "I will speak with my detective this afternoon if that can be arranged. Mr. Sawyer is his name."

"I'm expected at home this evening. I trust you will keep me apprised of the search." She wanted to stay. Phoebe wanted to be part of the meeting between the twins and Mr. Sawyer. She was afraid they would be too lackadaisical in employing this man. "Gracie could be anywhere between my home and yours. She could have been picked up by some scoundrel then whisked away." Her mind traveled over too many scenarios. She tried to draw a deep breath but accomplished bringing only a tiny trickle of air into her lungs.

Also by the Author
At Rogue Phoenix Press

Nick's Tender Rogue
Naughty book One

Once a McClellan lass

Beautiful, naughty and audaciously daring, young Nickie Gray is a McClellan princess through and through—as wild and reckless as the most incorrigible of her male cousins. Now that she has reached a marriageable age, Nickie has set her amorous sights on a most unsuitable male—the notorious rake and womanizer known to all mamas on the debutante scene in London as dangerous. When her chaperone tells her all rakes are off limits, she finds the challenge one she sets her mind to.

Always a McInnis rake

Not expecting to find a ravishing woman throwing herself at him yet blatantly willing to accept whatever overtures she makes, handsome Collin McInnis is thrilled by the brazen escapades of this naïve creature and is willing to experience her high-spirited advances with no expectations of commitment. On the high seas, he is bested by a vivacious beauty whose love of freedom and adventure rivals his own...and by an inescapable tidal wave of passion that threatens to engulf them both.

Dream About Lyssa
Naughty book One

When Lyssa Andrews sees the earl sitting behind his desk scowling, she knows she will someday put a smile on his face. The handsome brooding earl isn't playing the same game. He resists her outrageous comments and questions until she is ready to give up. Lyssa didn't come to London with the intent to find a man. Now, though, she is willing to chance love with the stodgy earl of Blackmore.

Raised by the Sioux when his father sought adventure then fell in love with a Sioux maiden, Kane has been betrayed once by a white woman. He isn't about to give his heart to another, especially one who is as white as newly fallen snow. Despite his best efforts, he can't deny Lyssa's intoxicating effect on him. Now Kane will risk his very life to protect the innocent beauty who has seduced him with her tender love.

Connal's Eternal Love
Sweet McKenna Book One

A few days shy of All Hallows' Eve Connal McKenna, Laird of Clan Chattan stands on the parapets of his castle. Bonfires line the hillsides while his clan prepares for the upcoming festivities. Drawn by the whispering of the wind, Connal McKenna feels a strange restlessness in his soul. Setting out to discover the wickedness that is calling to him, he discovers his mate. With gentle words and sensuous kisses, the auburn-eyed highlander conquers his mate, the beautiful, defiant Wynnie Adair who he comes upon during an evening ride. She must ultimately put her trust in the only man who can save her from the ruthless plans of her father and succumb to his gentle coaxing.

In Brady's Arms
Sweet McKenna Book Two

Forced to run from the only home she knows, beautiful,

headstrong Lillian Townsends seeks shelter in the wild highlands where the McKenna clan live. Trying to avoid a betrothal contract signed by her stepfather to an aging lord, she is desperate to find a means to sidestep the inevitable, including a marriage to the oldest son of the laird. Lilly is enamored of the young lord who pursues her with unrelenting determination flashing his devilishly handsome charms. She is hard pressed to resist.

Besotted from the first moment Brady McKenna sees Lilly, he is determined to find a means to coax her into his arms and bed. With only the promise of carnal pleasure as his mistress, Brady relentlessly pursues the woman who has unwittingly forged a place in his heart. She is like no other woman, proud, defiant and enchanting. Despite his father's advice to stay away from her, he cannot. He boldly seeks her out and makes her his own.

Nobody but Walker
Sweet McKenna Book Three

The Highland Lass...

She was brought up, adored and loved by a doting mother and father ardently protected by her brothers. She was everything sweet and innocent until she was faced with betrayal and an unexpected and out of wedlock pregnancy. When she gave her love to a man who couldn't return her passion and commitment, she was left devastated and furious. Faced with the loss of her child if she didn't comply to his demands, Crissie McKenna followed him to Belfast then on to his country home to discover he was already married.

...The Irishman

Stunned to find out his one and only encounter with the woman he wanted to love forever created a child, Walker Endicott, Earl of Briarwood, claimed his child as his only heir. Walker threatened all her previously held values even while he thrilled her senses. From the moment he first saw her to the second she ran after him begging him to make love to her, his captivating masculinity held her fascinated. In his arms she would know tempestuous passion, bitter despair, and a soaring joy that would humble them both before the power of love.

Roby's Moonlit Night
Sweet McKenna Book Four

Once she'd been a pampered child with high expectations for her future blessed with love. Then she became an innocent pawn in a terrible game of greed and power. Now, with a noose around her neck, Pippa was to hang before she had the chance to unveil the men who drove her from her home, before she had the chance to live.

Roby McKenna was a man blessed with endless charm and wit. While he searched for his eternal love across the Atlantic in a new land, he would have to come home to find her. His silver blue eyes could sparkle with amusement or harden to steel gray with displeasure. He had all the women a man could want or need. As he grew older, mistresses were not enough. A quirk of fate brought him to the gallows, a spark of destiny made him claim the condemned Pippa as his bride.

Made for Houston
Sweet McKenna Book Five

Leah Kennedy is as wary of people as she is strikingly beautiful. However, the shocking death of her father that forever changed her girlhood has left her terrified of the very love she desperately longs for. Only in the untamed splendor of the Scottish crags does she feel safe from the feelings she stirs in men and the cruel mockery of Selkirk's villagers.

Debonair, well-educated doctor Houston Stuart has turned his back on social privilege along with professional honors to set up a medical practice in the lowlands of Scotland. There, serving those who need him the most, he hopes to forget the bitter memories and disillusionment that disturb his days.

Coincidence brings the cultured doctor and this fey mountain girl together. Something as bizarre as destiny disrupts the obstacle of birth and breeding, stubborn pride and fear which has kept them apart...as each seeks to heal the other's wounds with a raw passion neither can deny and all the odds against them cannot defeat.

Say You Love Kit
Sweet McKenna Book Six

Fascinated...

When the woman stepped through the door of the pub, the sun setting her fiery red hair glowing around her delicate features, Kit Stuart finds himself captivated by the sight. The moment he sees her he knows she will be his. Convincing the fire-haired lady of that fact isn't easy. After she calls out another man's name when he kisses her that night, he is instantly enraged as well as jealous. The road they travel is fraught with secrets that neither can tell. Trust is an elusive quality that neither can give.

Intrigued...

Forced to run for her life, desperate and afraid, Aila MacDuff willingly enters into the Kinnel Stones, a mysterious place where people disappear then appear magically in different times. At the first sight of Kit, she finds herself inexplicably drawn to him. She's been told to search for her mate and that she will know when she finds him. Aila doesn't know what this man's name is or what he looks like. Nonetheless, she is certain he will be similar to her mate from one hundred years earlier. Despite the fact she is falling in love with Kit, he can't be her mate. Her mate is a shifter. Kit is not.

It Had to be Riley
Sweet McKenna Book Seven

Her anger assured retaliation...

Shawna's only concern with the contemptable scoundrel she had been forced to wed was the return of her dowry. She had not seen her husband in three years, and now Riley Stuart furiously repudiated there had ever been a marriage. He even went as far as to tell his family he'd never seen her before this day.

... Her passion promised love

In the heather clad hills of the beautiful Scottish crags surrounding the small village so near to the Mckenna keep, the ferocity of her loathing yields to the intense hunger of unquenched longing. In the powerful arms of the dark and handsome husband she thought she reviled, Shawna shivers with the honeyed torment of awakened desire and powerlessly submits to the wild, enchanting ecstasy of burning passion. Together they abandon themselves to the exquisite pleasure of the love their hearts cannot escape.

My Sweet Broc
Bad Boys Book One

He's a bad bad boy...
Broc Wallace is a fun-loving rake who never thought any beautiful woman could melt his heart. He lives life in the present enjoying the camaraderie of his friends and the pleasures of his mistress. When Bliss races into his life, he is ill prepared to deal with her secrets or give up the tenor of his life. When the truth is revealed, he finds himself unable to forgive and forget the betrayal.
...but she's sweet for him
Bliss MacTavish knows she's playing with fire when she refuses to tell this bad boy her name. He tempts her with sweet whispers of seduction knowing her innocent nature will be unable to refuse all he yearns to give her. Deciding to follow her heart, she finds the repercussions more than she bargains for when she gives herself to this bad boy.

Crazy for Cam
Bad Boys Book Two

He's a bad bad boy...

Lord Cam MacEwen, Viscount of Rosehill, tries his best to be proper and court the lady of his dreams in the acceptable way. The feat proves impossible when the lady in question uses every means at her disposal to tempt him. He fights his jealousy for another man as well as the need to make her his own, finally giving in to her irresistible passion.

...but she's crazy for him.

Chelsea MacTavish wants the bad boy she fell in love with and kissed just before her eighteenth birthday. With feminine wiles and irresistible allure, the sensuous lady plans to best Cam at his game of hearts and make him forget his need to court her properly.

Falling for Flynt
Bad Boys Book Three

He's a bad, bad boy...

Fascinated by Hope's loss of memory yet haunted by her sultry beauty, Flynt is irresistibly drawn to the stoic miss—and into her troubles with the sultan who wants her for himself. When he discovers she is the sister of his best friend, his pride keeps him from pursuing her and making her his.

...but she's falling for him.

Raised in a harem but now penniless, alone and without her memory, Hope must discover a way to remember all that she has lost. She finds a way to continue with her life as a servant in Flynt's home. The first sight of Flynt steals Hope's breath as well as her heart. Can she overcome her fears and give herself to the man she fell in love with.

Dancing With Donal
Bad Boys Book Four

He's a bad bad boy...

Once a bad boy always a bad boy, Donal Chamberlin's carefree ways come crashing down around him when he meets the ravishingly beautiful Daryl MacTavish, the innocent little sister of one of his best friends. He is determined to win her heart as he sets his sights on marriage and an heir. His past gets in the way of his quest when a woman he once loved threatens Daryl's life.

...but she's dancing with him.

Daryl has seen the control her sister's husbands hold over them. She yearns for a life where she makes decisions for herself. No man will have power over her. But no man kisses her the way Donal does. No man can make her forget all her goals leaving her helpless to give up her dreams. Yet Donal is determined to dance through all the barriers she thrust in front of him, pursuing her until she says yes.

Loving Leslie
Bad Boys Book Five

He's a bad bad boy...

Leslie Stewart, Duke of Southcliff is stoic, set in his ways, a spy who is used to having his life well ordered. He expects life to continue on in this perfectly conventional fashion. He assumes his bad boy status while keeping mamas and debutantes at arm's length. An heir is needed but Leslie has every intention of finding a woman who doesn't covet his wealth and tittle. He is irresistibly drawn to the headstrong young lady who becomes more beautiful as she develops into a woman.

...but she is loving him.

When Leslie kisses Lacie MacTavish, she knows even at the tender age of fifteen this is the man of her dreams. Forced to wait until she comes of age, Lacie withdraws into herself. Now she is eighteen and Leslie has returned from a mission for the British Government ready to claim her as his bride. She refuses him and he must find a way to seduce her and in the process create a burning passion within her, which she cannot deny.

Pleasing Arie
Bad Boys Book Six

He's a bad bad boy...

Arie Demir has never been denied anything in his life. He takes what he wants. What he undeniably yearns for is the beautiful redheaded spitfire he sees in a restaurant in Glasgow. At every turn, she confuses him by disputing his power over her. Alison refuses to accept the fact he owns her. While Arie tries desperately with patience and tenderness to drive her wild with new sensations, his scorching kisses ignite the fires of her very soul to make her understand he is all she will ever want.

...but is she pleasing him?

Alison Fletcher never expected to find herself kidnapped and sold to a whorehouse then bought by a Turkish sultan to become his slave. She vows to never surrender to the arrogant man who believes he owns her. She is stunned by the magnificently handsome man who awaits her compliance. Unexpectedly, she finds Arie the lesser of all the evils. The hidden depths of his mesmerizing dark brown eyes hold her into their power; his muscular embrace makes her weak with desire. She is his to do with as he wishes.

Graham's Wicked Kiss
Bad Boys Book Seven

He's a bad bad boy...

Graham Chamberlin is stunned to find three young boys dangling from the trees lining the drive to Runningmead Manner. On further inspection, he is astonished at their obsession to protect a young woman who has been brutalized by her pimp. The woman he discovers hiding in a third-floor attic room is gravely injured. He takes the silver haired stowaway under his wing. Clearly, Graham's new guest is a lady with many secrets. He is determined to unlock all the mysteries surrounding her.

...But she can't resist his wicked kiss.

The years since Ria left the convent where she was raised have been a nightmare. Her secrets are dangerous—as is the powerful man determined to find her. Handsome Graham Chamberlin is clearly a gentleman with secrets of his own, but staying with him could mean the difference between life and death for Ria. With each passing day, her handsome host turns Ria's convalescence into an increasingly sensual escape. Now her greatest challenge may be imagining anything less than a future in his arms.

Feeling Etienne's Love
Bad Boys Book Eight

He's a bad bad boy...

Etienne Dubois is the son of a wealthy vineyard owner who craves the excitement of putting his life on the line. Working with the French government and as a confidant of King Charles X give him reasons for living. An encounter with a beautiful young woman in a plush bordello in Paris has him rethinking his roguish ways. Etienne never expects to become a father especially from one encounter with an innocent prostitute who whispers his name and has him rethinking his well-ordered life.

...But she can't help feeling his love.

Elisa Moreau, the only daughter of Angelique Moreau, the owner of an exclusive bordello in Bordeaux, France, has loved Etienne Dubois since she was six. Unfortunately, until an unexpected encounter at a brothel in Paris puts the two of them in the same room, Etienne doesn't even know she exists. Confused but wanting Etienne and this chance meeting to never end, Elisa gives herself to the man who has held her heart in hands for what seems like her entire life

All I Want Is Link
Bad Boys Book Nine

He's a bad bad boy...

Merry Stewart is wildly unpredictable. Left alone to run wild over the Bordeaux and Scottish countryside she becomes impetuous and daringly bold. Over the years, she's found she can bedevil her softhearted brothers into allowing her exploits to go unnoticed. As a young woman she has learned she can do as she pleases when she pleases. Now, Merry has set her amorous sights on the Duke of Weston—a man she has never met but has every intention of marrying. No other suitor will satisfy her—especially not the exceptionally striking, horse breeder, Devlin Mathews.

...she's the woman of his desires.

Posing as commoner Devlin Mathews to escape a potentially fatal confrontation, Devlin is enthralled and infuriated by the audacious, duke-hunting dark haired vixen. Bedeviled at every opportunity, he finds dealing with the tiny she-devil exasperating as well as intriguing. Without revealing his true identify, the infamous rogue pledges to thwart Merry's plans to wed the man of her dream-never imagining the bewitching strategist would turn out to be the only woman he would ever dream of marrying.

Devlin's Angel
Bad Boys Book Ten

He's a bad bad boy...

Merry Stewart is wildly unpredictable. Left alone to run wild over the Bordeaux and Scottish countryside she becomes impetuous and daringly bold. Over the years, she's found she can bedevil her softhearted brothers into allowing her exploits to go unnoticed. As a young woman she has learned she can do as she pleases when she pleases. Now, Merry has set her amorous sights on the Duke of Weston—a man she has never met but has every intention of marrying. No other suitor will satisfy her—especially not the exceptionally striking, horse breeder, Devlin Mathews.

...she's the woman of his desires.

Posing as commoner Devlin Mathews to escape a potentially fatal confrontation, Devlin is enthralled and infuriated by the audacious, duke-hunting dark haired vixen. Bedeviled at every opportunity, he finds dealing with the tiny she-devil exasperating as well as intriguing. Without revealing his true identify, the infamous rogue pledges to thwart Merry's plans to wed the man of her dream-never imagining the bewitching strategist would turn out to be the only woman he would ever dream of marrying.

Needing Gill
Bad Boys Book Eleven

He's a bad bad boy...a man with no heart.

Gil Allemand wants to be left alone, especially by the beautiful outcast who's invaded the vineyard where he meant to wallow in his grief. She has a ton of impudence and brazenness, a talent for trouble, and a child who brings back memories better left in the dark recesses of his mind. Yet Jenna's feisty spirit might just be heaven-sent to save a hard, inflexible man.

...she's a desperate young mother.

Jenna Bonnet's bad luck has taken a turn she never imagined. With twenty-five silver francs, a mare that can't walk up the hill to the chateau that is her five-year-old son's birthright, a son she is desperate to keep alive, she's come home to a village that despises her. However, this single-minded young widow with a shocking past has learned how to fight. She'll do anything to keep her child alive—even take on a man with no heart.

Just For Michael
Bad Boys Book Twelve

He is a bad, bad boy...
Michael Flannigan has burgeoning ideas the moment he meets the woman who has inherited Mayfair. Clare will fit into his big plans quite nicely. Mayfair Plantation is his heritage. Even before the Revolutionary war Flannigans owned this land. No woman is going take what is his. Realizing the only way he can possess the land that is his birthright is to marry the impulsive woman who waltzes into his life, he sets his sights on making her his, slowly seducing her until she unwittingly falls into his scheme.

...but she is determined

When Clare Carter-Brown returns to Mayfair Hall in Virginia after several years absence, she intends to claim her inheritance. Bypassing Leslie Hall, she moves into Mayfair without a chaperone intending to take over from the manager. Michael objects to her tactics. At every turn, he adeptly points out her failings. As the fires rage around them they find a love that burns more fiercely than either could ever imagine.

Foolish for Piper

The pickpocket...

Piper has spent her life surviving the streets of St. Giles Parish in London, a den of iniquity and crime. Masquerading as a boy she escapes the whorehouses the young girls are sent to as they come of age. The day she encounters Brett MacLachlan begins the same as every other one. When she picks his pocket, she has no idea her life is going to change irreversibly.

...and the mark

Handsome aristocrat Brett MacLachlan has come to London for his amusement only to find his world turned upside down by a thief and her dog. From the moment he spots her, Brett knows there is something intrinsically wrong. In his arms, Piper discovers passion and joy. Yet secrets of her past haunt her, and a scar will tell the true tale as well as her identity.

Taylor's Destiny

She traveled to another time and place to change destiny...

Enjoying a day of sailing, Taylor Maxwell never expected after a suffering a concussion she would wake up in another century. A resilient independent woman in the twenty-first century, the blond beauty is ill prepared for life in the 1800s. Her first sight of the naval captain who rescues her makes her heart stop, giving her hope for her future.

His life is transformed by a woman who appears from nowhere...

Born to a life of ease, Reid Stewart defies the dictates of those born to aristocracy and chooses a life of adventure in the navy and as a spy for the crown. When he discovers a nearly naked woman on the bow of small sailing ship, his heart warms. His love for Taylor and his need to protect her from a man who pursues her might cost him his life as well as hers.

Caitlin's Duke

She played a fiddle in an Irish pub...

Caitlin O'Shea Is the most beautiful woman Roc Leighton has ever seen. With her blue violet eyes and long black hair she captivates him. In turn he mesmerizes Caitlin. Caught in the power of his gaze as he watches her, she is wise enough to know he desires her but will never give his heart to her. Caitlin has vowed to never be any man's mistress.

And fell in love with an English Lord...

Roc knows the first time he watches her play the fiddle and dance around the pub, she will be his next mistress. Despite her protest, he will find a way to convince her that her place is with him. While Caitlin's determination to keep her vows, fate takes a cruel turn and she is forced to seek refuge with Roc.

Catching Meara
Book One in the McKenna Clan Series

Meara Thorton was a feisty, world-class computer hacker—cornered by the FBI and shockingly given the chance to be their newly acquired technical analyst. Brilliant and intuitive, yet aching with the loss of everyone she has cared about, her restless heart led her to discover a love she fought and a world she didn't know could possibly exist.

Sweet Sexy Sadie
Book Two in the McKenna Clan Series

From the first time Sadie's eyes met those of Brody McKenna in the hot Sierra Madre Mountains, theirs was a potent attraction—not gentle, slow, and easy, but hot, hard, and all-consuming. The daughter of a dysfunctional family, Sadie had dreams no man could wrench from her with hot sex and an all-consuming passion. She'd challenge this alpha male with all the strength she possessed. But her red hair, fiery temperament, and indomitable spirit obsessed Brody...and he knew he had to find a way to show her he was more than he appeared and convince her to make a life with him.

Sweet Misbehavin'
Book Three in the McKenna Clan Series

Cast adrift after fleeing the home of Jokul, the ice demon, Atantsi, a firestarter, grew to womanhood as she moved through time to keep the demon from finding her. Though stubborn and courageous, she was ill prepared to use powers she had not been taught. Her first sight of the intoxicating Carr McKenna left her breathless, and her second encounter gave her hope for a future she never thought she had.

A playboy, a second son and a shifter, a man who thought his life would be carefree, Carr McKenna was shocked to discover the woman he'd paid as an escort is a firestarter who is running for her life. He is the leader of all the McKennas around the world and that he has multiple powers. His passion for Margo and the need to defend her might cost him his life as well as hers.

Sweet Talkin' Sugar
Book Four in the McKenna Clan Series

Lyonesse McKenna, was dreaming, or was she? From the instant Lyn saw Deacon McClain across a black jack table in a crowed Las Vegas casino the unmistakable attraction sent Lyn's senses flying into overdrive. Her family of shapeshifters believed in soul mates. She'd always been skeptical yet she couldn't help but question the way her heart sped when he looked at her.

When Deacon appeared in Las Vegas he knew his first job was to save Lyn from a Sea Demon, but the next order of business was to convince her he would someday mean more to her than she'd ever expected. But her stubborn nature and unbendable spirit consumed Deacon...and he had to chase away all the demons real and imagined in order to win her heart.

Sweet Surrender
Book Five in the McKenna Clan Series

Ripped from her family at the top of Infinity Cliff, Kimi McKenna finds herself thrust somewhere into the future. Dark elements threaten to destroy the earth unless Kimi can work together with the white witch to stop the destruction. Confused by her mate's role in the conspiracy, she refuses to acknowledge the connection. But amidst raging fire and attacks on the people she is coming to hold dear, she allows Maska O'keefe into her heart.

Maska O'keefe has loved the beautiful shapeshifter for years. Unable to save her life years ago, he vows to watch over her as he is given a second chance to convince her that even though he is a witch and not a shifter, they are indeed soul mates. Kimi's divided loyalties between her family and the cause she is now a part of will determine their relationship. Only the part she plays as the messiah can bring this to a conclusion in the final battle.

Sweet Dreams
Book Six in the McKenna Clan Series

For Cas Doyle finding the shifter of her dreams was a matter of life or death. She walked into the Red Neck Bar and Grill in Cactus Junction with a hope and a prayer he would be there and she would recognize him. What she needed was for him to take her home and take her virginity. Cas never thought to be a one-night stand. She had no choice.

Guy McKenna knew eventually he'd find his soul mate. He didn't expect the reality to happen this night. When he saw her he knew. She was dressed provocatively, enticing him to an extreme he never felt before. What he didn't know was if he could convince his protective family that Casidhe Doyle was indeed his soul mate.

Dakota's Bride
The first book in the Lakota/Pinkerton Series

When Emma St. John received her brother's letter imploring her to escape her stepfather's vengeful scheme and to trust Dakota Barringer with her life, she was willing to chance it. But the handsome, brooding riverboat owner Emma found in Natchez a danger of another kind. For Emma soon found herself surrendering to an unrelenting desire.

Raised by the Sioux when his parents were killed, Dakota had been betrayed once before by a white woman. He wasn't about to trust another, especially one claiming that her stepfather, a powerful U.S. senator, had framed her as a murderess. But he couldn't let Emma's intoxicating effect on him. Now Dakota would risk his very life to protect the innocent beauty who had seduced him with her tender love.

My Angel
The second book in the Lakota/Pinkerton Series

A BEAUTY IN BUCKSKINS
When her father decided to send her to a finishing school back East, Angela Chamberlain refused to be confined to stuffy drawing rooms. Instead, the daring spitfire who could shoot like a man and ride like the wind longed for a life of adventure and romance—and she knew exactly who could give it to her. Devil Blackmoor was a hired gun with a dangerous reputation. But Angela was willing to go to the ends of the earth to capture the handsome devil's heart.

A DEVIL IN DISGUISE
He'd come to America looking for excitement, but Devil Blackmoor got more than he bargained for when he encountered a beautiful rebel who answered his kisses with a wild innocence that touched his very soul. Yet standing between them were more obstacles than either ever dreamed. For Devil had strapped on a gun for the wrong man. And that made Angela his enemy. Now he'll have to choose between his duty and the woman he loves more than life.

The Locket
The third book in the Lakota/Pinkerton Series

The year is 1894. Seeking revenge for crimes against his family, Misha Petrovich follows a path that leads straight to Ariel Cameron's boarding house in Mist Harbor, Oregon. A family heirloom in Ariel's possession leads Misha to believe she is guilty. The locket has been handed down to the oldest girl in the Petrovich family for generations. Ariel is innocent of wrong doing, but her father is not. Misha is torn by his feelings for Ariel and his need for restitution against her father. Knowing that the relationship between them is fragile, Misha does everything in his power to protect Ariel's father. His efforts are to no avail when her father is shot. Ariel comes to realize Misha's steadfast courage and determination to protect her and her father despite what has happened to his family. Ariel's love and devotion heals Misha's heart.

The Talisman
The fourth book in the Lakota/Pinkerton Series

Running from a marriage that lasted one night, Dr. Moriah McKeown discovers the land she has settled on is coveted by determined and lawless men. Yet the proud young woman who once vowed never to abandon her home has second thoughts when her adopted children are threatened. Her only recourse is to enlist the aid of a dark, dangerous gun for hire.

Haunted by the past and a betrayal he will never forgive, Ian Civanovich uses his fast gun and his reckless courage to forget the faithlessness of a woman in his past. He will trust no female—nor will he rest until the threat hovering over Moriah McKeown is put to rest.

Forever His
The fifth book in the Lakota/Pinkerton Series

Struggling to come to terms with the part she played in Jacob St.

John's death, Etta Barringer resigns from Pinkerton Agency and seeks peace and solace in a Rocky Mountain Cabin.

Jacob has vowed to discover the reason Etta has betrayed him, sold him out to his enemy and left him for dead.

Isolated in their cabin, they discover their love for each other and learn to trust. But the trust is shattered when Jacob learns she is married to his sworn enemy; the man who left him in the desert to die.

Allura's Secret
Twelve Dancing Princesses Book One

Allura McClellan is horrified by her father's decision to take out an ad in the Times awarding her to the man strong enough and smart enough to win her hand and uncover her secrets. She's an intelligent young woman who takes great delight in the freedom allotted to her by her father. She's well aware that marriage would effectively curtail the adventures she's shared with her sisters and cousins.

Hunter Gray is nothing like the other men who've arrived to vie for Allura's hand in marriage and everything that goes along with it. However, he is the first to refuse to concede defeat and pursue her despite her attempts to disguise her true appearance. It's her temperament that is of more concern to him than her looks. Hunter has worked all his life with the hope of someday owning his own land. Now that it looks like there's a very real possibility that everything he's ever wanted is within reach nothing is going to deter him – including Miss Allura's disagreeable disposition.

Amorica's Wager
Twelve Dancing Princesses Book Two

Amorica Hepburn was sent to London to find a husband. Finding a man was the last item on her agenda. With her two cousins, Amorica wagers she can dissuade her suitor before the others. Despite her efforts she discovers a chemistry that cannot be denied. Suddenly she is the arrogant man's wife, pledged to a marriage neither desire. But swept off to his ancestral home above the Dover cliffs and into his strong embrace, Amorica is soon possessed by a raging passion for the husband she had vowed to despise...

Damian Andrews couldn't afford to trust the emerald-eyed spitfire who happened upon his secret. Amorica's hatred of all men of his kind only inflames the war that rages between them. Still, he can not control the intense desire his stubborn bride inspires, or make her surrender to his will until he has conquered the headstrong beauty on the battlefield of love...

Ravyn's Marriage of Inconvenience
Twelve Dancing Princesses Book Three

A REGAL BEAUTY
When the duchess decides to wed her to a wastrel and a fop, Ravyn Grahm takes matters into her own hands and declares her engagement to another man. Instead of fessing up and telling her great aunt what she has done, she goes through with the pretense. Ariec Lakeland is the bastard son of an earl and has a dangerous reputation. But Ravyn is willing to do most anything to keep the duchess from discovering the lie.

A DEVIL-MAY-CARE SMUGGLER
He'd bought land in America, looking to put down roots and end his life of adventure, but Ariec Lakeland got more than he bargained for when he encountered a beautiful heiress who made a promise she didn't want to keep. But the promise could not be undone and standing between them were more obstacles than either ever dreamed. Ariec had made plans to spend the rest of his life in America and that was at odds with Ravyn's plan of living in England and running her father's estate. Now, he'll have to choose between his dreams and the woman he loves more than life.

Christel's Sunrise
Twelve Dancing Princesses Book Four

He Made Her An Offer...

Life has thrown Christel McClellan some experiences that could have devastated a less determined woman. Beautiful, self-assured and fiercely independent, she is trying to forget the loss of her stillborn child. But is the child alive?

She Couldn't Deny...

Life is carefree for Ryder MacLaren who loves to see what is on the other side of the sunrise. Laird of Clan MacLaren, he is wealthy, handsome and happily unencumbered...until stunning Christel McClellan enters his life. When he hears her story, he believes the child she thought dead has been sold to a wealthy buyer.

Storm's Passion
Twelve Dancing Princesses Book Five

SHE MADE A PROPOSAL...

Life strikes Storm Graham a shattering blow when she learns her father has bartered her to a man she detests. Storm is beautiful, self–assured and fiercely independent, and refuses to be a pawn in her father's schemes, yet she can find no way out of this bargain made in hell. Going on the offensive she asks the wealthiest man on the eastern coast of England to marry her, never believing she might fall in love.

HE TRIED TO REFUSE...

For Hadden Johnston life has provided everything he ever wanted, including a sanctuary for homeless children. He is wealthy, handsome and happily unencumbered...until stunning Storm Graham marches into his life and proposes a marriage of convenience. Yet this type of marriage to a woman who inflames his senses is far from acceptable. If he's going to be tied down, he will move heaven and earth to have this woman warming his bed.

Gotta Have Fayth
Twelve Dancing Princesses Book Six

A regal beauty with raven hair and piercing blue eyes, Fayth Graham is unwilling to parade herself in front of the wealthy Lords of England during the season. Seeking a means to dissuade any man wishing to wed her, she seeks a way to ruin herself for marriage. When she unexpectedly meets a man with sparkling gray eyes and an infectious grin, she decides this is the man who will keep her from agreeing to obey.

He returned from six months at sea, looking for a few nights of pleasure with a willing lass, but Jarret Kinsley got more than he bargained for when he met a beautiful debutant who responded to his kisses with a wild innocence that touched his heart. Yet the obstacles looming between them might rip them apart. Both had vowed never to marry, so when consequences of their dalliances got in the way, Jarret would have to choose between the life he's always desired and the woman he loves more than life.

Ella's Pleasure
Twelve Dancing Princesses Book Seven

A WHISPER OF PLEASURE

Ella Hepburn was an auburn haired debutant from the harsh Scottish coastline—a wild innocent to be seduced and tamed. A spirited beauty, she captivated Drake Montgomerie's jaded heart—while succumbing to the smoldering desire she felt for her unyielding suitor.

A WHISPER OF DANGER

In Drake Montgomerie's glittering world of money and privilege, young Ella discovered passion and desire could overcome everything she'd been taught to resist—entangling Drake, the heir apparent, in a lethal coil of aristocratic family intrigue. But grave peril would only nurse the sparks of a love that knew no limits and a magnificent ecstasy that would not be denied.

Eveleen's Seduction
Twelve Dancing Princesses Book Eight

A WHISPER OF SEDUCTION
A brutal attack on Eveleen Hepburn's cherished island off the Scottish coastline leaves her shattered and bewildered. Learning a man she once trusted can kill as easily as he can breathe even though the deed saves her life, creates questions that need answers. An innocent beauty, she enchants Logan Maxwell's cynical heart—giving in to the raging passion she feels for her mysterious suitor.

A WHISPER OF INTRIGUE
In Logan's Maxwell's world of espionage and privilege, young Eveleen discovers truths about herself she never expected, and a need for passion and love can overcome all her fears if she learns to accept certain truths. She finds herself entangled in a lethal battle for land that was once owned by French nobility, taken from them during the revolution and sold to Maxwell. But grave peril would unleash the flames of love that simmers, creating a magical union that cannot be refuted.

Tavia's Deception
Twelve Dancing Princesses Book Nine

WHISPERS OF DECEPTION
When her father decides to send her to London for her season, Tavia Hepburn resolves to see the world instead. The raven haired beauty decides to disguise herself as a lad and find employment on a ship bound for Barcelona as a cabin boy. But she never bargains on finding passion and love to a red haired sea captain who rescues her from certain death.

WHISPERS OF MURDER
For James Macmurra, the world is black and white until he meets a young debutante, who turns his world upside down. He's unable to deny Tavia's intoxicating effect on him. In a match tense with obstacles, unwillingness to divulge secrets, and unforeseen peril, irresistible desire

and passion grows into undeniable love. James would risk his life to shelter and protect the innocent debutante who seduces him with her sweet love.

Larena's Fascination
Twelve Dancing Princesses Book Ten

WHISPERS OF FASCINATION
Fiery, free spirited Larena Graham never wanted to marry a duke. She is thrilled to be in love with the fourth son of an aristocrat, Gavin Broon. But when it seems Gavin ignores her, she set her sights on politics and bettering human life. Unsuspecting intrigue and a plot against her, she continues her dangerous plans despite Gavin's wishes.

WHISPERS OF TRUST
Gavin has every intention of properly courting the beautiful Larena until he must leave the city in order to put his affairs in order. Returning to London, he finds the woman he means to make his own is embroiled in political protests that could lead to a prison ship. Larena must learn to trust the handsome Scotsman whose most pressing mission is to protect her and keep her from harm.

Tira's Education
Twelve Dancing Princesses Book Eleven

WHISPERS OF EDUCATION
Learning how to build ships is Tira Hepburn's only dream until she meets Jamie Lundin and her world is turned upside down. With her raven black hair and vivid green eyes, she tempts Jamie and pushes him to defy his vows. She never bargains on finding an irrevocable love and a passion to a man who cannot fulfill her dreams despite his burning desire for her.

WHISPERS OF A BARGAIN

Arrogant and self-assured Jamie is brought up short when Tira captures his heart. All his carefully made plans are put to the test when he decides to teach her the art of ship building if she will spend a week with him alone on his ship. He is unable to deny Tira's intoxicating effect on him. When Tira leaves him behind unwilling to live with him without the benefit of marriage, he races after her. Jamie will risk everything to shelter and protect the innocent debutante who seduces him with her sweet love.

Aidan's Love
Twelve Dancing Princesses Book Twelve

Whispers of Love
Aidan McLellan has loved since she first set eyes on him as a young girl. Spontaneous, wild and eager to grow up, Aidan haunts his waking thoughts day and night, insinuating herself into his life. With her fiery red hair and sparkling sapphire eyes, she seizes Blade's heart even while he tries to resist the innocent child until she becomes a woman.

Whispers of Courage
Blade has waited what seems a lifetime to claim the woman who captures his heart as a little girl. Claiming his inheritance before his younger brother takes what is rightfully his, Blade must convince Aidan of his sincerity after years of avoidance and wed her before his father dies so he can return home, securing his rightful place. Everything is put to the test when his life as well as Aidan's is threatened by the man who once called him brother.

Don't Hustle Letty
Good Girls Book One

She's a good girl...

As tempted as Scarlett was, she had too many secrets to let

someone enter her world—secrets that would send any reasonable man to the farthest ends of the earth. Bobby was far from reasonable and despite her desperate attempts to hold him at bay, he would not let her past destroy their future. With her escort service, Scarlett used men and their insatiable lust for women to capitalize on the means to survive and prosper. She vowed to never wed, to never put herself in the control of a man.

...nonetheless he has other ideas.

Lord Robert Munroe, with his newly acquired title of marquis goes to Scarlett's for training on how to comport himself. The marquis, better known as Bobby, knows how to pick a pocket as well as get into a bloke's home to steal them blind. What he doesn't know is how to be a gentleman. When he sets his sights on the prim Miss Scarlet, Letty, to his way of thinking, he decides she is the woman he wants to call his wife. He tempts all that she is with sweet words and tender coaxing until she is unable to refuse all he hopes to give her.

Only Caro's Baby
Good Girls Book Two

The Scheme

Genius botanist with theories of inherited traits, Caroline Kenworth desperately wants a baby. Finding a suitable father won't be easy. Caroline's super-intelligence makes her feel pushed aside, unwanted as a woman. As a bluestocking she is determined to spare her child the suffering that plagues her life. Which means she must find someone very special to father her child. A person very...well...ignorant.

The Target.

Duncan Murray, the Earl of Downsberry, well known for his lack of intelligence as well as his rakish ways with women, seems as if he is the flawless man to fulfill the role. His amazing good looks and Scottish brogue are misleading. Caro learns too late that this debonair earl is a lot smarter than she first thought—in addition he's not about to be used then abandoned by any woman who has schemed to steal his sperm.

The Detonation

A dazzling solitary woman whose desires to learn what it would be like to become a mother... A man who is in control of all he does never allowing anyone to usurp his role will settle for nothing less than surrender... Can lust coupled with physical attraction drive two strong-minded yet vulnerable people to a completely unforeseen love?

Only Caro's Baby
Good Girls Book Three

She's a good girl...

Born a bastard, Honey McRae is taunted and bullied by her half-brother most of her life. Branded with a tattoo of the Saber and the Rose by the men's association. she is desperate to be free and escapes the country estate where she was held prisoner. Resigned to a passionless life devoid of men, she fights the nightmares that haunt her. Despite her past fears, she accepts the fact she will never be able to give herself wholly to the man she loves. Until that man, bold and breathtaking, decides he will find a means to woo her into his arms.

Nonetheless...

Stolen at birth and sent to live in the bowels of London, Billy— once a pickpocket and thief–discovers he is actually the Duke of St. Aubries. He is determined to win the woman he fell in love with the first time he saw her, the lady with a tattoo on her breast, a woman who has been cruelly used. He disputes her notion that men are only capable of inflicting pain...instead he binds her to his heart with his gentle and patient loving.

Twelve Days to Love

When Archer Steele shows up at Calanthe Durand's failing plantation with an alligator over his shoulder, Cali thinks she's never seen a more handsome man. During the war she had to defend herself and her servants from both union and confederate soldiers. Independent and self-sufficient, she vows to never marry.

But Archer Steele has different ideas. The first time Archer sees Cali in town, he feels an instant attraction. He decides he will do everything and anything to convince the beautiful Miss Durand he is worthy of her love. During the weeks leading up to Christmas, he gives her twelve gifts in hopes she will fall in love with him. Yet they are faced with challenges they must overcome before Cali can commit to a marriage.

Door to Heaven

Jessica Lawrence is the stepdaughter of a woman born in the twentieth century transported back in time to the year 1868. An acclaimed suffragette, she raises Jessica to believe in the equality of women. Jess Law believes everything she was taught, and when the time is right she becomes a private investigator. Courageous and impetuous, Jess finds danger in her quest to save all women from white slavery. Her passionate mission results in a wedding to Roc Newman, a man she knows can steal her heart...

Roc can't trust the sapphire-eyed spitfire who invades his home in search of secret papers and knocks him flat with her karate moves. Jessica's refusal to obey his wishes serves to inflame the war between them. Still, he cannot control the intense desire his reluctant bride inspires, or make her surrender her independence, until he has conquered the headstrong beauty on the battlefield of love...

Rebel Heart

HER REBEL SPIRIT DEFIED HIS OUTSIDERS SOUL...She was velvet and silk, eyes the color of a summer storm and amber hair. Victoria DeMontville, because of a promise and a codicil to her father's will, was forced to marry one man to protect her from another. She hated Cameron Savage with a fierce passion. But to hold on to her genetic research and find a cure for the deadly Signe virus, she must pretend to love the enemy at her door, come with weapons of fire to melt her icy heart...

HIS OUTSIDERS TOUCH IGNITED RAGING PASSIONS... He wore a mask, disguised as the Phantom, a true legend come to life. Even as war and debate over new genetic research engulfed them all, he would find his greatest adversary in the beauty who'd branded him an outsider and barbarian, the woman he was born to possess, his soul mate.

Safari Moon

Solo St. John, a wildlife photographer, is preparing for a trip to Alaska. Suddenly, Solo finds women of all sorts invading his privacy, his home and his office, all cooing nonsense words and blatantly throwing themselves at him. Solo doesn't know why, and he has no idea how to rid himself of the persistent women. He finally decides to beg a favor of his best buddy Nyssa Harrington.

In love with Solo for the past ten years and knowing he doesn't return her feelings Nyssa doesn't want to talk to Solo. She knows if she accepts his phone call, she will not be able to resist the temptation to hope again.

Straight to Heaven

Running from demons, Alexandra McMurdie stumbles into Forbidden Ground where up is down and elements of nature are contested. Though a strong independent woman in the twenty-first century' she is unprepared for life in the 1800s. Her first site of the formidable James Lawrence makes her heart skip a beat, giving her cause to reconsider her desperate need to find a way home.

Born with a silver spoon, James' life was torn apart during the War Between the States. Moving west he vows to put the life he once knew in the past. When he discovers a half-frozen woman near Gold Hill, his heart begins to thaw. His love for Alexandra and his need to keep her from a man who has pursued her through time might cost him his life as well as hers.

A Valentine's Anthology

The Lending Library-a fantasy by Christie L. Kraemer
Faeries try to fit into the human world when the forest where they make their home is destroyed by a mysterious enemy.

Chasing Rainbows-a contemporary romance by Genene Valleau
An eccentric aunt, an inventive uncle, a mother who wears poodle skirts, and a brother who wears pearls provide a hilarious backdrop for the courtship of a young woman who yearns for a "normal" family.

The Gift-an historical romance by Christine Young
A man and a woman on opposite sides of the Civil War get a second chance at love after one final battle returns soldiers to their war-torn homes to rebuild their lives.

A St. Patrick's Day Tale
Christine Young, C. L. Kraemer, Genene Valleau

Tumble through time...
...to Ireland in 1817, when tensions are high between Protestants and Catholics and fae people guide the fate of villagers. A lovely Catholic lass stumbles upon the weakly ritual fisticuffing between Irish lads. She

falls into the lap of a handsome young Protestant. Family ties, grudges, and two conniving faeries threaten their budding love. But the faeries outsmart themselves when they hijack a time machine that has mysteriously appeared in their forest and are whisked to...

...Eugene, Oregon in the 20th century, amid a property feud between the local faeries and night elves. The conniving faeries from Olde Ireland try to stir up more mischief. However, a warrior gnome convinces the magic folk to control their own destiny, and forces the intruding faeries to take refuge in the time machine again, spinning their way toward...

...A modern day castle in western Oregon. An eccentric inventor is determined to reclaim his wayward time machine and save his beloved wife from her latest misadventure. If only they can travel safely past the black hole...

a May Day Anthology
Christine Young, C. L. Kraemer, Rosemary Indra, Genene Valleau

Highland Miracle — Christine Young
HURTLED THROUGH TIME, Sean Michael Sterling, landed in the midst of a May Day celebration he didn't understand, assuming the role of Laird Sterling.

ILLIGITAMATE CHILD OF NOBILITY, Reagan Douglas searches for a way out of her half brother's house.

Defying the Odds — C.L. Kraemer
The night elves on the hill aren't happy without their magic. They concoct a plan to punish those who were involved in the act that rendered them almost human. Meanwhile, Uther, the rogue night elf, has returned to woo the Librarian to be his eternal mate.

Love in Bloom — Rosemary Indra
When childhood friends reunite it takes two fairies and a matchmaking daughter to help them admit their true love for each other.

No More Poodle Skirts — Genie Gabriel

After drifting for years in the innocent age of the 1950s, a woman struggles to join today's world by finding a career and a new love, with some help from her zany family.

Once Upon a Christmas Moon
Christine Young, C. L. Kraemer, Genene Valleau

TWELVE DAYS TO LOVE

When Archer Steele shows up at Calanthe Durand's failing plantation with an alligator over his shoulder, Cali thinks she's never seen a more handsome man. During the war she had to defend herself and her servants from both union and confederate soldiers. Independent and self-sufficient, she vows to never marry. But Archer Steele has different ideas. The first time Archer sees Cali in town, he feels an instant attraction. He decides he will do everything and anything to convince the beautiful Miss Durand he is worthy of her love. During the weeks leading up to Christmas, he gives her twelve gifts in hopes she will fall in love with him.

BOOTS AND BLADES

An ancient evil from the old country has arrived in the high desert of Oregon. Gnome children are vanishing then re-appearing, showing various stages of traumatization. Tiamoon, warrior gnome, will put her skills to use alongside Killian, a handsome warrior, also in need of a cause.

CHRISTMAS PAWSIBILITIES

With their world destroyed and their space ship malfunctioning, the dogizens of Planet Canid have little choice but to crash land on Earth. They face tortuous experiments at the hands of the Geeks in Green...or they can trust an eccentric inventor and his zany family to deliver the Canine Queen's puppies and help them celebrate new lives.

VISIT OUR WEBSITE
FOR THE FULL INVENTORY
OF QUALITY BOOKS:
http://www.roguephoenixpress.com

Rogue Phoenix Press
Representing Excellence in Publishing
Quality trade paperbacks and downloads
in multiple formats,
in genres ranging from historical to contemporary romance,
mystery and science fiction.